C000278848

Winter in Volcano

By the same author

Outer Islands

Winter in Volcano

GARY KISSICK

HUTCHINSON
London

1 3 5 7 9 10 8 6 4 2

First published in 1999 by
Hutchinson

Random House (UK) Limited
20 Vauxhall Bridge Road, London SW1V 2SA

Random House Australia (Pty) Limited
20 Alfred Street, Milsons Point, Sydney,
New South Wales 2061, Australia

Random House New Zealand Limited
18 Poland Road, Glenfield,
Auckland 10, New Zealand

Random House South Africa (Pty) Ltd
Endulini, 5A Jubilee Road, Parktown 2193, South Africa

A CiP record for this book is available
from the British Library

Papers used by Random House UK Limited are natural,
recyclable products made from wood grown in sustainable
forests. The manufacturing processes conform to the
environmental regulations of the country of origin.

ISBN 0 09 1801389

Typeset in Ehrhardt by
MATS, Southend-on-Sea, Essex

Printed and bound in Great Britain by
Mackays of Chatham PLC, Chatham, Kent

To my grandmother, Ruth Alexander,
roll in her grave though she will.

Thanks to my readers, in (roughly) their order of appearance: Dana Czapanskiy, Ann Yoklavich, Mari Kubo, Tom Moore, Lynn Flanagan, Tom North, Tom Crain, Janet O'Bryant, Bernard Gautier, Cynthia Gracianette, Don Hymel, Maxine Feifer, Ray and Linda Aragon, Liisa Gellerstedt, Dana Shields, Aaron and Belinda Ashley, Jon Taylor, Wendy Roberts, Nick Cayou, Sharon Skibinski, and Paul Sidey.

Special thanks to Yuki and Dean.

a pact
with spirits

It is a pact I have made with spirits.
They will not reveal themselves.
When I turn to examine an echo,
I'll see no old Chinaman
forlorn in an overcoat
worn thin by moonlight.
When I sleep in the woods,
I'll hear no ancient songs, no women crying
where there are none. The desolate
babies in the graveyard
will be cats. The clack of bamboo
only that. Coat hangers
will not rattle in the closet,
the lock will not come undone,
nor will the rocking chair
rock of its own accord.

I, in return, will believe in them.

from *Outer Islands*, by Gary Kissick

'If we do not govern our passions, our passions will govern us.'

The editor of *Mother Goose's Melody* in a maxim
appended to 'This little pig went to market'

1

Sister Lucia Bretagno, Chairman of the Holy Mount Department of English and Head of the Adult Education Program, sat cleaning her gun as she explained to Cullen Richard Kinnell the impossibility of granting him tenure 'at this point in time'. It was a .38 Special with a frisky colt stamped just above the stock. She used a nylon brush dipped in Hoppe's #9 Nitro Powder Solvent to lovingly swab the bore in swift even strokes. Cullen, who had requested this meeting, was beginning to see her point. It was like one of those notorious points in time: sharp and nasty, never agreeable. Time was thick with them. At this point in time, enrollments were down. At this point in time, the future remained uncertain. At this point in time, as in all points in time, the college could ill afford a pay raise. And then there was, of course, the Yager affair. He wondered if she would mention it.

'And then, of course, there's the Yager affair,' she said. 'Not that you're responsible – I understand that – but it *has* caused a bit of a stir. If you had only told me, I might have . . .'

She failed to complete her sentence – had abandoned it, in fact, with haughty disdain. Now she began on the chambers. On campus she was noted for two questionable achievements: habitually shattering her ulna and/or radius by discharging firearms, and single-handedly swelling the ranks of the evening classes by enrolling cops bent on furthering themselves. One of these, Detective Yager of the Vice Squad, had furthered himself all the way to California with a young Chinese girl he'd met in Cullen's Romantic Literature class.

'I didn't *know*, Sister. It surprised me as much as it surprised you.'

'Of course. But I'm sure it surprised neither of us as much as it surprised his poor wife and children. What about them?'

She had stopped cleaning her gun to ask this question and to deliver one of her strange, fixed smiles with tilted head. For six years now she had been smiling at him cryptically like a painting that comes with the house.

He made a feeble gesture that was nothing more than a squiggle in air. He had a picture of the abandoned Yager family moving into his place.

She sighed, suddenly softer. 'Love certainly makes people do foolish things. To think of giving up one's whole career and family. I wonder if it's really . . .'

As part of the torture, she aborted this sentence as well. 'Yes, it really is,' he could confess. Or, just as readily, 'No, it really isn't.' Neither answer would earn him his sinecure.

'You gave them Incompletes,' she said pointedly.

'I've changed them to F's.'

Inadequate atonement. The Sister was now doing something with a toothbrush.

Six years. For six years now he had worn Sister Lucia like a hair shirt – had squirmed beneath her dictums, scratched at her requests, been collared by her jokes. *Six years*. For six years now her eyes had twinkled ruthlessly like polished maces. Six years, and she still remained for him an unfinished sentence. To begin with, why a nun? Where was her halo, the amber glow of her sanctity? Where was her ruddy Latinate warmth? What had she done, of late, to better the lot of the lepers and beggars of this world? More to the point, what had she done for the untenured beggar at hand, her fellow man – the only one in the English Department, in fact, unless one counted Father Plecko, whom clearly one shouldn't. But most importantly, most bafflingly, and certainly most disturbingly, what covenant had she made with the Almighty that required her to accompany policemen on their beats? For that was what she did, right down to the fine sordid details of sounding the siren and carrying a gun, the gun to which she now applied a squirt of Dri-Slide. It was unquestionably the gun that irked him, that sent her catapulting effortlessly over the head of even Father Plecko into the highest circle of his studied contempt. She was enamored of it, as she was enamored of cops. Now she was playing with the cylinder, spinning it like a ponderous wheel of fortune.

'Salt's the number one culprit. It's in the air.'

'Ah.' Bad hombre, salt. At first he imagined that salt had somehow corroded his chances of tenure, but he was quick to grasp that that was not it at all. What she meant, of course, was that salt was bad for guns, and that if he hoped to ingratiate himself he would convincingly bemoan this tragic fact, would yearn aloud for a land of greater justice where guns could freely breathe desalinated air. Or *was* that what she meant? What did she ever mean? Some folks unleash a muddy, panting mutt to paw your white trousers and ream your nose with its tongue, and when they say sweetly 'He likes you,' they really mean '*I* like you.' It isn't rudeness at all; it's intimacy, the sharing of a beloved pet. Was that it then? Did she want him to stroke and admire her pistol, view the world through its bore, appreciate the way it comfortably filled one's hand, perhaps ask to swab and brush it himself? Was she offering, by way of introduction to her true self, a brief look at the care and maintenance of a favored possession? Many hobbyists tendered their friendship in this way. Would you care to see my chopstick collection, my ceramic badgers, my newly acquired Moroccan anglesite? The warmest moment he had shared with his last chairman had come when the man had invited him to feel his samples of toilet paper gathered from all the major reading rooms of Europe.

He deliberated how best to show interest. He considered 'How many men have you killed?' 'How often have you had to use it?' and 'Do you use real bullets?'

'Do you use real bullets?'

She looked surprised, even wounded. 'Of course! But I don't gun people down in the streets, Cullen. It's just for target practice. Look at it rain!'

It had been raining all afternoon, not in drops or even dollops but in huge unbroken sheets dashing against the window like the petitions of all the world's untenured English instructors. It had, in fact, been raining persistently for days. He was fond of rain, approved its dampening of the city's daily newspapers, welcomed the chill that justified sweaters. To his way of thinking, even more romantic than palm-lined beaches were the island's long winter rains sweeping down the pali, battering wild white ginger, commandeering hillside streets for their relentless flow leeward. It being February, this would probably be the last of such rains till next winter.

'I'll have trouble driving home,' he said. 'Sierra Drive's like a river, and Wilhemina's worse.'

'A waterfall. Be careful. I'm sorry I can't offer you anything more definite. We *are* grateful to have you, but you have to bear in mind that it's a very small college. Perhaps we can talk again next term.'

'Yes. I understand. Thank you, Sister. Goodbye.'

'Thank *you*, sir. Goodbye and God Bless.'

Sister Lucia delivered her *thank you*'s with a disconcerting verbal jerk that yanked at the word *you*. She delivered each with all the clout of a bowler's post-delivery kick – the kind of voodoo where one boots oneself swiftly in the buttocks to topple one last, indecisive pin.

After such an exchange – an intimate exchange, actually, in which she had shared with him her gun – he felt that he should go farther away than simply next door to his office. He should go to a rain-soaked Hotel Street bar where old-timers talked story about *da kine*. He should go to a Korean bar with hostesses, actually, but he had never done that sort of thing and had been told that one could get taken for quite a bundle. Even, he supposed, if one didn't have quite a bundle. The *Atlantic* was still running that personal ad out of a box in Honokaa claiming that attractive Oriental girls were simply thirsting for male companionship. In Honokaa? He wondered what that was all about. It had been only a month since he had known the comforts of a woman, if one could call the final bouts with Alice comforting, but a month was about thirty or thirty-one days – a long time. Worse, he had no woman on whom to pin expectations.

On a Friday like this he wished to cuddle with a lover in his cottage, listen to Fleetwood Mac or Oregon, get moderately drunk or stoned, fall asleep to the sound of a fat rain and reawaken to its drippings after dusk. Then dine Cantonese, Hakka or Thai while the wet city streets reflected the lights of revolving restaurants or scintillating condominiums. Sex would be in there somewhere, perhaps before falling asleep – indolent, cashmere eurythmics, no frenzied checklist of erogenous demands. *Okay*, he confessed to his desk, *I'm lonely. With or without tenure*, the denial of which was merely a flesh wound. Other denials seemed suddenly more critical. Like abused pets, his emotional needs tended to spring upon him with a hungry, desperate violence. Talking with Sister Lucia was the last thing he had to do that week, and now that he had done it the night loomed as large and unpromising as a batch of freshman essays.

He gathered his books and a batch of freshman essays in his briefcase and left the office, one in a roomful of many. It was cold in the arcade. Through the arch before him he saw a plumeria tree throttled by the rain, its flowers hopelessly ravished. Every arch had its private puddle. As he walked he recalled almost fondly the troublesome couple conversing in this very loggia, beside this very soda machine, during their evening breaks. The warm nights had served as an invitation to heart-sized toads to gather outside the classroom. The scent of plumeria had wafted in from the garden, the two royal palms had no doubt swayed, the stars had twinkled coquettishly above the amorous city lights. It had been a lousy time to be teaching. The air had reeked of romance like a salesgirl in Perfumes, but he hadn't imagined that Detective Yager and Miss Chung would succumb so scandalously to its blandishments. The world had seemed safe and content last term, its inhabitants living in harmony. One wife, four kids, and an English teacher – that was a lot to leave behind.

As he turned the corner he descried a lone figure standing at the end of the otherwise empty loggia. It was a woman, the last between him and his weekend. Could it be – ? Yes, the long dress, the shawl, the sunglasses perched atop her head – these were distinctive trademarks. He had never seen her alone before. Even as he approached her she failed to notice him but appeared, instead, transfixed by the downpour. As he reached her side, however, he saw that she was more peeved than enchanted. She turned toward him with no apparent surprise.

'Hi,' he said.

'Hello.'

'Can I give you a lift somewhere?' His voice was too high.

'My car's parked off-campus. I'm just waiting for the rain to let up.'

'That could take a while. It's been raining for three days. My car's right here. Let me give you a ride to yours.'

She raised her eyebrows at the novelty of this suggestion.

'Okay.'

It was, he assured himself, all a matter of civility rather than flirtation.

Both of their umbrellas proved spineless contraptions unfit for combat. Hers was too pink and polite to withstand the slightest hectoring. His flapped irrelevantly, like an old crow, while he stood gallantly in the rain unlocking the passenger door of his Volkswagen. There was a trick to it, but he knew it. It was all in the depth and angle of insertion. By the time he reached the driver's side, she had already unlocked his door. This he considered a small intimacy. It was a major criterion by which he judged women. He had known first, second, even third dates who would sit primly and unperturbed like peahens while he struggled valiantly with the lock on the driver's side, to which there was an even greater trick. A rainstorm would not have fazed them.

'Thanks.'

His Volkswagen was a fastback, an experimental model, according to his mechanic, that had been promptly discontinued. It smelled delicious when wet. He would die, however, a quick and boisterous death should a roach appear to spoil everything. He had recently spotted a few. Life was tenacious in Hawaii; he had even known seeds to sprout in open ashtrays.

So, now for some conversation. Flummery had always been his weak suit. When it came to conversing with women, his witticisms, like colored chalk, were seldom as bright as expected. Could he tell her the role she had played in his sex life only two nights ago? Did she share his interest in photography? He had the latest *Nikon Annual* in his briefcase.

'I dreamed about you last night,' she said.

'Oh?'

'You were taking the class on a field trip. In Italy. We were going through catacombs or something. And you spoke very good Italian. In fact, that's all you spoke. Do you speak Italian?'

'No.'

'I didn't understand a word you were saying. You were very animated and you carried a golden pointer. You used it in a café to point out things on the menu, but the menu wasn't really a menu at all, it was a beautiful dead bird with printing under its wings. There was something about a museum, too. Have you ever been to Italy?'

'No.'

'That just goes to show what a bunch of crap dreams are.' She stared straight ahead as if Freud might be hitching on the curb.

'But this is fascinating. I bet you never would've told me this if we hadn't met today.'

'I bet you're right. My car's on Third, across Waialae.'

'Okay.'

'Think it will rain?'

He smiled. The rain had been for days something poured out of foundry buckets, a torrential, umbrella-mocking downpour only now subsiding to mere rainfall. He welcomed it and all that came with it: the incessant drumming on the roof of the car, the frantic tattoo of beleaguered wipers long overdue for replacement, the African tulips plummeting from the sky like crumpled birds of plumage, the sense that all of Oahu might be momentarily swept away in one grand, precipitate gesture. Without it, he might never have found his courage. Holy Mount was, after all, a small struggling college where enrollments fell as surely as raindrops.

'There's my car over there – the Vega.'

She opened her purse. It was now or never. *Never* held a certain appeal. *Now* was badly jangling his nerves. His thoughts were falling all over themselves like dancers on the Titanic.

'Listen' – his ship pitched to port and glassware reversed its slide. It was still not too late to change course – 'Would you like to go have a drink at the Kuhio?'

It was too late.

'Now, you mean?'

That was what he'd meant. Should he confess it? Later was another possibility – after the term had ended, after she'd graduated, after her first unhappy marriage.

'Yeah, now. It's a good day for it.'

His ship rolled starboard, groaning deep within. He would never live through this. Her car was perilously close, a gleaming white iceberg that threatened to puncture his dreams and well-being. It was a quiet street with no traffic, empty as the mid-Atlantic. All things considered, he felt he was doing wonderfully well. When had he ever done so well? Was he doing well? She still hadn't found her keys, nor had she raised her eyebrows at the novelty of the suggestion. She had simply frozen, peering into the abyss of her purse with the same composed indifference some women address to their cocktails. It was dark in there.

'Can I leave my car here?'

'Sure. There's no point in taking two.'

'Can I use that towel?'

'You don't want to use that towel. That's just a rag I keep for the beach. It's full of sand.'

'That's all right.'

'It's filthy, in fact.'

'It'll do.'

2

They sat in the dark Kuhio, sharing a bottle of Kirin, while rain swept shapeless figures across the window behind the cash register, figures that often appeared momentarily, framed in the bar's open doorway, as real people clasping things to their bosoms and bravely leaning into the wet air as if it were mere adversity. Beneath the establishment's shabby gray awning, schoolchildren in bright vinyl raincoats joyously awaited buses, swinging their satchels and colliding with passersby. A few senior citizens stood among them with umbrellas, statues among pigeons. That's what Cullen liked about the Kuhio: one was never cut off from the street. Rain fell, traffic hissed, children squealed.

Beyond a curtain of dusty umbrella plants, three men drank studiously at the bar, brown Japanese men who seemed, like drying seaweed, to be shrinking quietly into oblivion. Otherwise, the place was empty, abandoned to that commercial twilight between lunch hour and dinner.

'I like this one,' she said, turning toward him the *Nikon Annual* he had brought along on rain-inspired impulse. It was a bold flash photo of Nuba wrestlers bathing in ashes. They looked like creatures never before seen, let alone photographed – cave-dwellers drenched in sudden light. At first he thought he was viewing a black and white negative, but there was color: three brown calabashes. From one of these a Nuba poured ashes over three wrestlers huddled in the remains of an extinguished fire. A dozen others stood about, some holding branches. All had stippled, seemingly peened, shaved heads. They wore necklaces, loincloths, and on their arms, leather amulets. As images, their gray, sooty bodies leapt from darkness – ghostly, gangly, ferocious.

'That's impressive all right. Looks like the Holy Mount Trojans before a big game.'

'Honestly, Doctor Kinnell.'

She was already chastising him. He liked that. All his girlfriends had chastised him. He liked to imagine himself as the sort of swashbuckling, unrestrained personality who stood in need of constant admonition.

He was not, however, a doctor. Students simply assumed that he was something other than Mister, and he'd left the assumption uncorrected for so many years now that Mister seemed too mundane even to him.

'Just call me Cullen.'

'Okay,' she said, but did not. 'How does it feel to have two superstars in your class?'

'You and who else?'

'I mean *Dunk It Plunkett* and *Dhabuuuul the Cooool.*'

He laughed. 'Is that really what they call themselves, or are those your nicknames?'

'That's what *everybody* calls them. Don't you read the papers?'

'Not Sports. I'm sort of a snob that way. And I'll tell you why. When I was a kid I was a Brooklyn Dodgers fan. All us kids were.'

'Was that a baseball team?'

For Cullen, the room shook, and a shallow hairline crack bisecting the table fissured to chasm. This wasn't going to work out at all. What did they teach them in school these days? But what the heck, he could barely remember the Dodgers himself, so why should her ignorance surprise him? He had to consider the age difference. And the gender difference. And the geographic. It was all wonderfully refreshing, actually, like a brisk slap of Aqua Velva.

'Yes, it was a baseball team, a very famous one, and all us kids were fanatics. We had Dodgers' caps and Dodgers' pennants and Dodgers' trading cards that smelled like bubblegum. I'd be a rich man today if I'd kept all my trading cards. I hoarded Campanella. That's Roy Campanella. He was a catcher. Anyway, we idolized the Dodgers. And I mean idolized. Our fathers used to take us to the games a lot. And then, one fateful day, our dreams were shattered.'

'How so?'

'The bastards moved. Just upped and left town. Left us stranded with our useless baseball caps and pennants and our gloves with Jackie Robinson's signature. Moved to sunny California. I could never forgive them for that. It was devastating. To our knowledge, no team had ever just packed up and moved before. We didn't think it could be done. We thought they were all hometown boys who would rather die than besmirch the honor of Brooklyn. Furillo, Hodges, Snider – bunch of crummy traitors if you ask me. They sold out the town that loved them for big bucks and artichoke hearts. They went Hollywood. They turned their backs on a bunch of innocent little kids who would've died for them. And Brooklyn has never had a baseball team since. And frankly, I don't blame it.'

'Sounds like you took it pretty hard.'

'We all did. Who wouldn't? That was the end of my childhood. I haven't rooted for any team since. I guess you could say I'm wary of making an emotional commitment.'

'I see.'

Did she really see – see that he'd trotted out the Dodgers so often he felt like the Ebbets Field organist? He rated this a weak, uninspired start. For one thing, he'd suggested his age, not to mention his alien cultural background. Why mention Brooklyn when he'd been so happy to forget it? He wondered how old she thought he was.

She refilled their glasses, a surprise. He would never have envisioned her as a girl who poured. Kirin came in large bottles, but the Kuhio served very small glasses in which to drink it. It was therefore necessary to pour frequently. He supposed that to be the Japanese influence. It was nice, actually; it kept one's hands busy and created a sort of social bonding. Now he had to think of something else to say. Christ, he was nervous. She wore her absinthe-tinted sunglasses cocked in her hair and they seemed to be staring at him.

But there wasn't any doubt about which photograph was his favorite. He turned decisively to the double-page spread in the middle.

'I like this one,' he said. It was a photograph of ohia trees silhouetted before a tattered curtain of molten lava. 'Ever been there?'

'Ever been where?'

'Volcano National Park. That's where this was taken. On the Big Island.'

'I've never been off Oahu.'

'You're kidding.'

'Nope.' Her *nope*'s, he had discovered in class, were always proud, puckery *nope*'s ending in a provocative labial. 'Have you been there?'

'To Volcano? Once. For a day. There were no eruptions though.' He caught her eyes. 'Nothing like this.'

'It was erupting last year, wasn't it?'

'It erupts off and on. I've always wanted to see it in action.'

'Me, too. Every time they show it on TV, I feel like catching the next plane to Hilo. My mother thinks I'm crazy.'

He envisioned whisking her off to the Big Island as Detective Yager had whisked Miss Chung off to California, and with much the same intent. Such a fantasy was not outside the realm of possibility. It would, he reminded himself, be called the Kinnell Affair.

'This is the reason I got this book. For this one photograph.'

'Why not?'

How the conversation had moved from there to her remarkable divulgence would forever escape his recollection. Perhaps it had been prompted by a discussion of what sort of evil spirits one might ward off with ashes, for that had been the purpose of the Nuba's gray bath: protection from evil. Or maybe he'd simply remarked that the Nuba looked like ghosts. Or perhaps in speaking of volcanoes he'd spoken of Pele, always a sure transition to the supernatural. All he knew was that suddenly there he was, a confidant, and there she was, confiding.

'It's invisible. Sometimes I feel like I'm sleeping and I have to wake up, but other times I am awake, I can stare right at the ceiling while it's happening.'

'It holds you down?'

'Yes!' She emphasized this with a sudden smile, as if to mock his incredulity.

'For how long?'

'Oh, I guess a couple minutes. Then it fades away. But sometimes longer.'

He smiled – not to disparage her story, but only because she had. He had meant to convey how lovely he found it that they were having this intimate chat, that together they had rescued this day from the great bovine herding of days into the unmemorable past. But what if she viewed his smile as merely a messy discharge of excess male enthusiasm, the slobber of the sort of overexuberant mutt she must encounter daily? He stopped smiling.

She, however, did not. Hers was a smile he would have found attractive on any woman, let alone one whose dark eyes engaged him like some Fitzgerald *femme fatale*. For that was what he'd always considered her: a privileged beauty as self-absorbed as a sponge. And all because she'd never failed to be seductively overdressed for class, wearing dresses while the other girls wore slacks or jeans or swaths of what seemed to be old circus tents. Today she wore a black shawl over a black dress strewn with roses. Her scintillations emanated from two rings, modest hooped earrings, and a delicate amethyst pendant. And as always, she wore those thick high heels that tighten the calves, underscoring each with a shadowy, erotic bruise. They were much in vogue among the downtown office girls. Like brass hoops elongating a feminine neck, such shoes held a certain tribal appeal related, somehow, to their utter impracticality. They reminded him of photographs he'd discovered as a youth in magazines hidden beneath his father's underwear. In the one he best remembered, a woman in red heels and black nylons was stooping over, bare rump hoisted high into the camera, and with the agility of a camel expecting to be mounted, had turned her head to beckon dumbly. This and other variations on the theme of the wobbly pedestal had raised his first erection in memory. But at the same time, they had filled him with a vertiginous sadness, as if he were the one on stilts who might at any moment topple. It was a sadness that a woman should so readily degrade herself, and the sadness of confused desires. He supposed this potent mixture of guilt and arousal made him a Catholic, one who still grew dizzy in the presence of sexual women. He was dizzy now. He'd felt almost seasick in the car.

Carelessly mixed in there with his father's underwear was yet another sadness – that his father, like the Dodgers, had simply run out on him, in his case by one day clutching his briefcase firmly to his chest and dying. He'd been cleaning the drawers of his father's belongings at his mother's request. An odd request, now that he thought of it.

'How old were you when this first happened?' he asked.

'I think I must have been fourteen. But it didn't happen as often then. One time I thought I heard a voice, too, but I might have been dreaming.' Her eyes flicked away to a rain-drenched student in track shoes who, with a meaningful glance in her direction, had just splashed into a nearby booth. He supposed there would be a lot of that sort of thing.

'What kind of voice?'

'A man's voice.' She looked him straight in the eye, more solemn than before, but still far from dramatic.

'What did he say?'

'You don't want to know.'

'No, tell me.'

'It was something vulgar.'

'Oh.'

'But like I said, maybe I imagined it. I really don't know anymore.'

The tales women told. Alice had once told him, with no shame whatsoever, of having been ravished as a girl by a 'spirit', an invisible presence that had brought her to orgasm while she sat reading in a rocking chair. Reading *what*, he'd wanted to know! But then, Alice had had a long affair with the supernatural; this girl, at least, seemed willing to credit an equally powerful and invisible force: imagination.

Her name was Felicia, a name he liked. He wondered, as he sipped his beer, what ancestral dance had produced such impish raccoon eyes – eyes she was fond of hiding behind oversized sunglasses that only served to emphasize her nose, a perfect miniature, though now her glasses sat in her hair. And what, he wondered, might be the genealogy of that wickedly sullen mouth? He had been embarrassed more than once that afternoon to realize how dangerously long he'd lingered on it. It would occasionally burst from speech into an unexpected smile, a scarlet torch ginger blossoming before his eyes, and then he'd discover her own eyes seemingly taunting him. But then those eyes always seemed to taunt somehow; even in class they suggested she knew conjugations he'd never imagined, had discovered the illicit joys of willfully dangling a modifier – as certain women, with legs crossed, will dangle a spiked-heel shoe.

'I heard an ominous voice today, too.'

'You did?'

'Yes. The voice of Sister Lucia telling me that I could not possibly be granted tenure *at this point in time*, what with the earth wobbling on its axis and poets on their arses.' He felt certain that that pun, like the name of Roy Campanella, had gone sailing into the abyss woefully unappreciated. Nevertheless, it smelled as sweet as plumeria. 'What made it ominous was that she was cleaning her gun at the time.'

'The old bat. And I bet she gave you one of those demented, cockeyed smiles that look like you could load it with ammunition.'

'Right!' He was suddenly alerted to the girl's mental possibilities. He caught himself slouching and straightened up. 'I don't get it. She's always blowing her nose up – *Her nose*! I'm getting as bad as Father Plecko. Let's try again. She's always blowing her *bones* up with that stupid gun, it's not earning her any gold stars in Heaven, she's constantly complaining about the damage she does to her arm, but she keeps on firing it. What's the point?'

'Some people just love to suffer.'

'Okay, I can see that. But there are lots of ways to be masochistic. Why the gun and this obsession with policemen?'

'She's their mascot. They're crazy about her. Haven't you seen them flocking to her office like it was Lourdes or something? It's an honor to have Sister Lucia ride in your patrol car. They rub her head for good luck.'

There was, he had to admit, considerable truth in this. Whatever joy Sister Lucia derived from serving as chaplain to the cops, for that was her official role, was balanced by their joy in having her so serve. They did love her. They did flock to her office. How many times had he sat within its walls discussing, say, the verbal inadequacies of Plunkett and Dhabul, only to have a cop poke his head in the door to be greeted with 'Oh hello, Officer Ramos. Come right in,' her eyes lighting up like the JESUS SAVES sign in Palolo? They were more welcomed than he was, but what they'd come for, exactly, he never knew.

'I guess you're right. She's their good luck charm. But still, why the gun? Why not a rosary or a Bible?'

'They don't pack the same firepower. I don't know. Frankly, I think she just wants to be one of the guys. Her father was a cop, you know.'

'That's right. I remember hearing that once. She pays a hell of a price though. She's always griping about bone chips.'

'Tell me about it. I had her last term, remember? I felt like I was minoring in anatomy. But that's the price she pays for being an interesting person. She's getting her picture in the paper, she was on TV once—'

'I guess it helps her recruit more students for the night classes. Chat them up on the firing range.'

'Hey, let me tell you something. Those boys in blue don't need much chatting up. They're falling all over themselves just to be part of the campus scene and meet us sexy young coeds. What they mean by night classes isn't the same thing Sister Lucia has in mind. Look at that guy in the Vice Squad who ran off with Cheryl Chung. I took a night class last term and I swear every cop in there tried to put the make on me. All three of them! And every last one of them was married.'

The depravity of this made Cullen's blood boil.

'And let me tell you something else. They can be very persistent. They're hornier than the John Philip Sousa Marching Band, if you now what I mean.'

'More persistent than Plunkett and Dhabul?'

On campus, Plunkett and Dhabul hovered over her like gunships pursuing an elusive butterfly, flirting mercilessly with a searing barrage of innuendoes meant to singe her wings and render her helpless. She handled it well, flitting evasively and countering with well-timed bon mots, but these direct hits merely sent her pursuers into explosions of laughter. They seemed to like nothing better. Dhabul addressed her as 'Felicia *Dah*ling', or 'Felicia Delicia', and more than once this term Cullen had been unable to commence teaching until Dhabul had completed his tormented soliloquy d'amour. Now it was Cullen's turn to try his luck.

Rather than answer his question, she rolled her eyes at the waitress, who had appeared with a pupu platter.

'I couldn't eat a thing,' she appealed to Cullen.

'That's okay,' he said, not wishing to discourage this new plump and apparently Vietnamese waitress. 'I can.'

The waitress seemed pleased by this solution. Pupus were, after all, the reason one chose the Kuhio. Never ordered, simply delivered, they arrived at one's table steaming with good fortune, fragrant as an unexpected bouquet. They had their own social hierarchy which more or less determined their order of appearance. At the bottom rung were pupus without papers, such as the dockyard mélange of fried cabbage, bean sprouts and generic meat that Cullen now ate with gusto. At the top were pupus without portfolio, established names such as the rich Teriyakis and the Sashimis bedded on shredded daikon. Not everyone had to eat his way to the top, however; men who put their money on the table with the unspoken promise of leaving it there were often spared the preliminaries and feted immediately with the best. When it was over, one paid with a generous tip.

He now realized that while eating, dwelling on those damned horny policemen, he had lost track of the conversation. She was nevertheless maintaining it with all the happy animation of alphabet soup coming to a boil. She was turning talkative, surely a good sign. He had passed many of her conversations in the college's arcade – he the preoccupied teacher, she the laughing coed loquacious among friends. He liked voluble women – they had an inner heat that simply churned words to the surface. With them, one was never at a loss for conversation. Gossip, complaints, ideas, observations – all rose together like a magnificent net of whale bubbles for the sole purpose of trapping krill, the minutiae of life tasty only in numbers.

He gathered that she was now discussing an episode of *The Twilight Zone* in which a woman had undergone plastic surgery but to no avail, she still looked ugly, 'except she wasn't really ugly at all. Everyone else was ugly – all the doctors and nurses. She was gorgeous! It was just the planet she was living on. Tough break, yeah? It's all relative.'

He was quick to catch on, as when one discovers the TV on a different channel.

'You'd have a tough time on that planet,' he said.

She smirked and wiggled her eyes as if she was used to that sort of talk.

There would, he told himself, be no further acknowledgement of her beauty. Women of her caliber liked strong men, not men who melted into mush.

'I once had this student named Agatha who always wore outlandish hats to class.'

'Outlandish hats?'

'Yes.' He held his hands above his head and drew a disturbing picture of such a hat. 'Really outrageous concoctions.'

'So?'

So? '. . . Well, uh . . . nothing. I mean, maybe she was relative. No one else wore hats. It seemed a bit odd at the time. They were quite . . . well, *bizarre* hats. Veiled hats, feathered hats. Anachronistic hats. On another planet, a planet with a lot of milliners and haberdashers as well . . .' He was losing her, just as he'd lost all the others in her class, the subset of those whose portraits might legitimately grace the cover of any 'explosive' bestseller illuminating the complex world of power and romance, intrigue and lust. What had been a dazzlingly colorful conversation buoyant with possibility was now a flaccid hot-air balloon losing altitude at an alarming rate. '. . . maybe she would have fit right in.'

'I see.'

With thumb and index finger she smoothed the bridge of her nose, then stretching taut the flesh above her cheekbone, removed with her pinky a bit of troublesome mascara from her eyelash. As she did so she gave a kind of watery, vacant optical yawn, and, when she was through, fluttered both lashes rapidly.

He had never before seen her naked eyes so close. She had golden-brown irises warmed by their own flames, but the key to their effect, he saw clearly now, was her brilliant whites. They were coconut white. They were puka shell white. They were the white asterisks of sunlight reflected by a turquoise sea. It was not simply that they looked clean and well cared for – we all do what we can – but it was rather that they looked new and pristine, as fresh as this morning's gardenias. His own whites, he knew, had been chipped from old bathtub enamel. There was only one way to account for the freshness of hers. She was young.

He ordered another Kirin, disturbed to have discovered this obvious flaw, a flaw she had so cleverly disguised as an asset. Only a young girl could dry her hair with a salty, smelly towel one wouldn't use on a dog and emerge like Venus from a half-shell floating on the sea. Not only young, but too young, too ravishing. Far too young for him to have committed the indiscretion of asking her out for a drink. In the turbulent wake of the Yager affair? In the choppily churned waters trailing that iniquitous California-bound liner? What on earth had he been thinking? And was she not, indeed, much as he'd always envisioned: just a bit ornamental, like the umbrella in a Mai Tai? Just a bit aloof, like a portrait in the Louvre? It was her disarming smile that had undermined his perceptions. It made her seem too mortal, too accessible, when in fact she was utterly beyond reach. She had the nerve to smile at him now. He wondered what it could possibly mean. In his experience, gorgeous women seldom smiled without purpose. They all wore starched, solemn expressions, as if beauty were maintained solely by rigor. And they were certainly never voluble, nor even friendly. He was thinking of the color-coordinated monuments to perfection that had always glided by him as disinterestedly as tropical fish in an aquarium – the haughty Oriental beauties with cheekbones carved from coral, the Liberty House girls demure as pearls.

Very well then. If she could be young, he could be old. Certainly old enough to remember that Brooklyn had once had a baseball team. Perhaps even old enough to summon the distant past, which for his students had been tainted by the same fuzzy mold and hint of ordure that made foreign cheeses so suspect. Neither processed nor sliced, history had spread like a runny Brie, devouring not so much ancestors as those unfortunates deprived of modernity. In class he had seen even recent decades swallowed whole by that blank, bloated epoch Plunkett and Dhabul called 'Way Back When'. A ravenous blob, it crept closer each day, nibbling even now at the Sixties.

He began with the radical suggestion that even on this planet, beauty had a history of relativity.

'Consider, for example, the decline of fair skin and the rise of the suntan. Now what woman before the twentieth century ever basted herself with coconut oil and lay near-naked under the sun for the questionable end of turning brown? It just wasn't done. She would have been locked up for indecency. Or insanity. Poets wanted maidens "not broun ne dun of hewe, / But whyt as snowe y-fallen newe."'

'Shakespeare?'

'Chaucer. But Middle English poetry's swarming with maidens white as morning milk, white as any swan, white as the blossom on the briar. In those days, they liked 'em white. If you had dark skin, forget it. You came from peasant stock.'

Reminded, by a careful look, that *she* had somewhat dark skin, the result, no doubt, of the very basting and baking he'd been describing – and, it might appear, deriding – he hastily clarified his position.

'Don't get me wrong, I like a healthy tan myself. Those white-skinned girls from Nebraska look anemic to me. But that's just my point – I'm a product of my time. We all are. In the Middle Ages I would have seen things differently. All I'm saying is that the suntan's something new in beauty. It came on the scene with the expanding leisure class and suddenly it no longer meant that you worked in the fields; now it meant you had time to lie on the beach all day. It was a class thing, pure and simple.'

'Okay. I see what you're getting at.'

'And what,' he asked, raising a finger and venturing into old scholar turf, 'what about those Venuses of Titian and Giorgione, all those recumbent plump lumps positioned with block and tackle?' Had he actually said any of this or had he invented it later? 'What about those ample nudes of Rubens, Rembrandt's *Bathsheba*, Renoir's *Seated Nude*,' – he hoped she knew none of these – 'weren't they all, by today's standards, more like potatoes than pears? Had they never heard of portion control? When had the fickle male abandoned them, opting for svelte over porcine?'

With impeccable timing, the waitress arrived with a platter of sweet and sour pork.

'She's found my weakness,' said Felicia, cracking open a pair of chopsticks with a deft snap that left both sticks equal. This was unexpectedly reassuring. A woman who ate seemed human. At the same time, however, it left him with nothing to say. Classic folds of fat dissolved with his memory of what, exactly, he had been getting at and how it would make her love him.

A yellow bus pulled up outside the doorway, sloshing brown water out of the gutter. The black umbrellas of the elderly folded like bats' wings; kids' raincoats glistened; bodies inched optimistically forward, up, towards the back; doors closed pneumatically behind them. When the bus had departed, the rain suddenly intensified, falling now like chopsticks, both wooden and lacquered, clattering off awning, sidewalk, and street, and filling the doorway with new refugees. It was the sort of outburst that would have been accompanied by thunder and lightning on the mainland.

'Tell me more,' she said.

He noticed that his beer was remarkably golden.

'About what?'

She raised her eyes to the ceiling to consider the possibilities, then looked at him, then opened the *Nikon Annual* at random to an arctic scene.

'About polar bears.'

'Polar bears?'

'Polar bears.'

He hadn't meant to throw open the topic of discussion quite so widely. There were, after all, some subjects on which he was not qualified to lecture. But thanks to *National Geographic* and a special friendship with his college biology professor, he was a walking repository of all sorts of odd facts about animals. He knew, for example, that certain vultures stone ostrich eggs. He knew that what aroused a male mosquito was the hum of a female's wings, though a tuning fork tuned to B held equal allure. He even seemed to recall something about polar bears, though he'd be damned if he saw one in the picture before him.

'Did you know that all polar bears are left-handed and that when they eat a walrus they turn it inside out?'

'What do you mean, left-handed?'

'Left-pawed. Whenever they kill something, or when they defend themselves, they always favor the left paw.'

'Fascinating. Elephants.'

'Pardon?'

'Elephants.'

'Well, they really do have fabulous memories – elephants' graveyards and all that. But you know that already. Hmm. Wait a minute. I've got something here.' He buried his face in his hands and in the rush of ensuing darkness realized he was giddy with drink. It proved a surprisingly congenial darkness once it slowed from a whirlpool to a plush velvety swirl into which one might comfortably sink like a large beast doomed to extinction. What had he come in here for? There was, he knew, an old Irish saying. He wondered what it was.

What *had* he come in here for? If there was one thing he hated to lose, it was his memory. He was about to attempt a backtrack, a difficult and not necessarily fruitful maneuver requiring an accurate reverse recollection of one's thoughts – a recollection which, if within his powers, would have negated any need for backtracking in the first place – when something like an inner Bantu whispered 'elephants'. Elephants. Yes, he had a file here somewhere. The human brain's remarkable capacity to store countless oodles of irrelevant data in a gelatinous mass of – Wait, here was something, something from the past: the *Physiologus* had claimed that these admirable beasts had been blessed with reverse genitalia to preserve their modesty during intercourse. Did he know her well enough to broach such a delicate subject? He could already hear her testimony at the inquisition: *And then he wanted to talk about . . . about . . . about . . . he wanted to talk about . . . how certain animals will . . . will adopt certain positions to . . . to . . . to . . . to copulate.* And then she would break down weeping and he would be tied to a stake and a pile of student essays would be ignited at his feet.

The *Physiologus* had also claimed that elephants slept standing against a tree because they had no joints and could never rise again if they – Voila! He emerged refreshed to announce triumphantly that—

'Only elephants have four knees.'

She looked at him as at armor that had raised its own beaver.

'You still here? What does that mean, only elephants have four knees? What about horses, camels, llamas?'

'Apparently not. Their legs bend different ways. Think of a horse's rear legs. Do they have knees?'

'I'm amazed. You're an absolute wealth of information.'

'Did you know that white elephants aren't white at all, just pink-eyed?'

'I thought they were albinos.'

'And do you know where the expression *white elephant* comes from, as in *White Elephant Sale*?'

'Macy's?'

'In Siam, white elephants were held sacred, and whoever owned one had to treat it like royalty, whether he wanted to or not. So if you wanted to play a dirty trick on somebody, you gave him a white elephant. He couldn't simply dispose of it, could he? He had to feed it, wash it, clean up its crap, and in general treat it like a king. So today a white elephant is something you'd just as soon get rid of.'

'But it's too valuable to just throw away.'

'Exactly. Can I interest you in some etymologies? That's my specialty.'

'I know!'

But of course. She was, after all, his student. Was he forgetting that? He rid the world of one more beer and his mind of lingering doubts. It really didn't matter anymore. He had bubbles of his own to blow, giant krill to ensnare. So much of life escaped daily notice. It was true that he could not fold fitted sheets, plan a marketing campaign, or rise above the poverty line, but he had, nevertheless, select areas of expertise. He began with bits likely to interest a Catholic. Did she know, for example, that a *cretin* was once a *Christian* and that *Calvary* meant *skull*? That *maudlin* derived from Mary Magdalene, who was invariably portrayed as weeping? That 'Hip hip hooray' was originally 'Hep hep Hu-raj', the battle cry of the Crusaders? *Hu-raj* was a Slavic expression roughly equivalent to 'To Paradise, you infidel worm', and *hep*—

'No kidding. I bet you can't name three words that come from Portuguese.'

'Hmm. Let's see. *Mango*, *flamingo*, and . . . *dodo*.'

Unfortunately, his inadvertently pregnant pause had made this sound like a 'Portagee' joke. And she was Portuguese.

She tested him now with the tines of her eyes.

'I'll have to take your word for that. But okay.'

She poured more beer while he informed her that *tawdry* had derived from *Saint Audrey's laces*: women's scarves, apparently none too decorous, sold at Saint Audrey's Fair in Norwich. *Prestigious* had once meant *deceitful*, while *silly* had once meant *happy*. A *ukulele* was a jumping flea. He explained that to *overlook* was once to cast the evil eye; that *dandelion* came from *dent de lion* and was still *Löwenzahn* (lion's tooth) in German; that *Sahara* was simply the Arabic plural of *desert*; that though we had borrowed few words from the Chinese, one should not overlook *kowtow*, *typhoon*, *gung-ho* and *kumquat*; that to Hindi we owe *cummerbund*, *pajama*, *seersucker* and *thug*, the latter having killed for Kali; and that though we tend to downplay our linguistic debt to Malay, to run *amuck* is really to run *amoq*, that is, in a murderous frenzy, as Malays do when so moved.

She had doubts or delights to express for each of these revelations. When he next raised his glass, she pronounced it all 'quite fascinating' and pointed out that a little beer did wonders for his personality, not that she had ever considered him the dull academic type. She did, however, have to be going soon. 'My mother will be worried, what with the rain and all.'

But two children running gaily through puddles outside the doorway, and her sudden sneeze – a mere delicate whiffet – reminded him of yet another sodden hatch that remained to be battened. He did not want her to go home thinking that Ring-around-the-Rosie was an innocent nursery rhyme when in fact it referred to plague buboes: rose-colored lesions encircled by black. The true chorus was 'Achoo, Achoo, all fall down', sneezing being one of the plague's first symptoms. And that, of course, was the source of 'God Bless You.'

'That's sweet. My mother believes that if you sneeze once, somebody's speaking ill of you. Twice means they're saying nice things. Three times means somebody loves you. And four times, you're catching a cold.'

'Then somebody must be speaking ill of you.'

'I know. If my mother was here, she'd try to make me sneeze again.'

'How does she do that?'

'She goes kootchie-kootchie-koo under my nose. It's not very effective.'

Soon, he realized, she would again be sitting before him in class, her pale lacquered fingernails floating on the black of her shawl like fallen petals. What on earth was he saying? Soon she'd be sitting before him in class, lovely among the purblind . . . Soon she'd be sitting before him in class thinking something about him, something nice or something brutally sharp and nasty like a wedge of green cheese. He felt, somehow, that it might yet be something nice. He had drunk a little too much beer and had sailed off on something of a tangent, true, but conversations were like that and at no point had he embarrassed himself by praising her unduly or professing undying love. He had almost maintained a teacher-student relationship. It had really been something like a spontaneous tutorial in etymology. A recording of their conversation would reveal no indiscretion, though he would, of course, be willing to pay handsomely for its destruction. Not that he had ever been in a position to pay *handsomely* for anything. He wouldn't want Sister Lucia to hear such a recording, nor, for that matter, Father Plecko. But that was not the point. The point had been in the vicinity only a second ago and like the revolving Budweiser sign over the bar, was bound to come round again. The point, but this was not the same point – it was, nevertheless, *a* point, a sharp bitch of a sliver not readily dismissed – the point was that he had sinned by merely being with the girl. Oysters can *mate*, for Christ's sake, sitting further apart than this. That was it. An impropriety had been committed. Now his untenured goose was cooked – fucked, plucked, skewered, and charbroiled in a windowless cell of Hades reserved for such ganders.

Who had witnessed their departure, he wondered, as he drove her back to Third Avenue in ongoing rain. The car had a damp, earthy smell – the smell of freshly turned soil or of the heavy black clods thrown on the casket when they bury one alive without extreme unction.

So, now she had seen the human side of Cullen Kinnell, English Instructor. The slightly inebriated Irish side. The rusty undercarriage, so to speak. The side one could blackmail. She hadn't lowered her sunglasses to shut him out. Surely that was a good sign. She was no longer talking, but that could mean anything. Perhaps she was thinking, as he, of what a wonderful afternoon it had been. Perhaps she was envisioning a happy transformation.

While Cullen stopped for a light on Waialae, he spied a roach to the left of the clutch pedal, waving its antennae toward the same shapely legs that had alerted his own sensory apparatus. This would be Misfortune. He had one foot on the clutch and one on the brake. He'd have to balance swiftness with discretion. He didn't want her to see him stomping at things on the floorboard like a Spanish dancer – things visible or otherwise. The light turned green, the roach turned left, he reached second, the roach hit fourth – vanishing, mercifully, into the car's labyrinthian recesses. She'd noticed nothing.

He pulled alongside her Vega.

'It's been an interesting afternoon,' she said, searching her purse for her keys.

Interesting fell short of the adjectival glory he'd hoped for. The Twenty-first Ecumenical Council had no doubt been interesting, and so, probably, was the history of trepanning.

'Very interesting,' she amended, as if making some small concession. 'I learned a lot.' She underscored this with a mysterious smile.

'It was fun. We should do this again sometime.'

'Thanks, I enjoyed it,' she said, hugging her purse and bookbag to her chest before stepping into the rain. 'Have a nice weekend.'

'Felicia,' he said in her absence. And again driving up Harding heading home. And once more ascending Sierra, where the rain indeed descended in torrents.

Drenched by the short walk from his car to his door, he sat half-naked with a towel draped over his shoulders and considered this new and promising development, the remote yet enticing possibility that fortune might mistakenly smile upon him as Felicia had smiled so often. *Felicia.* Say it once, and there's music playing. Say it twice and . . . In truth, he had always been somewhat afraid of her, had always pondered her legs discreetly – as she wrote her quizzes, as she walked from class before him, as she glided through the cool stone arcade like the vision she was. She was different, proud. Something other than heels carried her through corridors of students as if with a different density, buoyant yet magnetic, the focus of attention in the opening crowd scene of a film. She was special. It was clear that she required no more virtues than a soap-opera murderess. Men would fall regardless, moving the plot along.

3

In the bright days that followed, Felicia proved the perfect model of discretion. So much so, in fact, that Cullen himself began to wonder if anything had transpired between them. Perhaps they had simply had a student-teacher conference, or a chance encounter in the rain.

She smiled. She always had. She crossed her legs – a simple, legal, even decorous act that seemed, to Cullen, provocative. As if solar-powered, she flipped up her shades when thinking. She continued to occupy two desks, one for herself and one for her books and purse. It didn't matter; it was a small two o'clock class. Most students preferred morning classes so they could float upon the sunny blank rafts of free afternoons. At the front of the room, 300-pound Roland Plumley offset a frail skinny vine named Laura Katsui. At the back of the room, Plunkett and Dhabul swayed like vorticellae. The class had a strange, sweet languor encouraged by ginger and oleander lounging at the open windows. The windows faced *mauka*, toward the mountains. Beyond their greenery rose the four terraced tennis courts, whose use was Cullen's one treasured perquisite, and above the courts spread the college's tax-free treasure, the residential real estate of St Louis Heights.

He found himself glancing outside to avoid entanglement with her eyes, sultry eyes that seemed to flirt with life itself, not the teacher. There was always the possibility that he had muffed it. Perhaps he had drunk too much, rambled too long, disgraced himself too gracelessly. And what on earth made him think her available – a single shared afternoon? A goose barnacle was more likely to be unattached. Didn't he know that one never found such women sporting freely in the sea, that one had to pry them away from the hulks of old lovers? Yet she seemed to sport freely enough on campus. He'd noticed no boyfriend, no tattoo, no slave bracelet. She'd never mentioned someone special. But that, of course, proved – like student essays – absolutely nothing. He knew so little about the girl.

Days passed, adumbrating spring. The wili wili protested. The last jacaranda leaves fell into the streets while lavender broke through the branches. One morning, in Foster Garden, near the Kamakura Buddha, the bombax popped open like sudden pink heart attacks. Early poinciana shot into bloom; orchid trees simply unfolded. On every limb, primavera flaunted bangles of gold. In Manoa, the first shower trees opened coral pink umbrellas. If it rained at all, it cleared by afternoon.

He noticed then that he had contracted a long-remissive gastric disorder: a queasiness, an aspiring emptiness, as when one prepares to do the reckless and irrevocable. Run off the Makapuu Cliffs with a hang glider. Go over Akaka Falls in a barrel. He recognized it, in fact, as a kind of falling, an old ecstatic torment he hadn't experienced since college. All night he clutched his pillows to his chest, but they proved flaccid lovers by morning.

One day he searched the phonebook for Mattos, her surname, and found Mattoses running from one page to the next. 'Prolific buggers, the Portagees,' his friend Earl had once said at a Chinese wedding. But she had mentioned that she lived on 17th Avenue, in that quiet neighborhood shaded by ancient swamp mahogany, considered Kaimuki but bordering Kahala. This narrowed the possibilities to one: Sebastian Mattos, 432 17th Av . . . 734–7762. He circled this indelibly with the same red laundry marker he used to correct graffiti in the toilet stalls, and dog-eared the page. He perused it religiously, a fragment of Hebrew unearthed in an Essene cave. He recited it, seeking its revelation. And though it was a treasure too precious to use, its mere existence comforted him. Should falling enrollments land on the college tomorrow, pummeling it into rubble, he would still know where to find her. The city was that well organized. Should the semester end without a profession of love, with neither a bang nor a whimper, his world would not end as well. He'd still have this promise: 734–7762. The first digit was seven. The second digit was three and the third digit four. Three plus four equals seven. The fourth and fifth digits were seven also, making four sevens. Four was the medial number between the last two digits, six and two. Four sevens equaled twenty-eight – two eight. Eight was the sum of the last two digits, and two was the final digit. Its cabalism was easy.

4

The ball came whizzing over the net with something on it, some sort of warbling English that caused it to take a strange lurching bounce just beyond reach of Cullen's lunging backhand.

'Fifteen-love,' announced Earl. 'Ogilvie takes an early lead.'

Cullen wiped his hands on his shorts and moved to a position just before the left side of the baseline.

'Service,' said Earl.

This crisply clipped the outside corner. He gave it a two-handed backhand, aiming to drop it just over the net on the far right side. It dropped, instead, in mid-court with embarrassing civility. It was rudely returned.

'Thirty-love,' crowed Earl. 'Ogilvie takes a commanding lead and seems headed for certain victory. Kinnell seems befuddled by the heat.'

Cullen smiled bravely. It *was* hot. The sun patted Earl's back in a complimentary sort of way, but it was bullying poor Cullen, pouring soup over his head, pounding his chest, depolarizing his sunglasses. He once again wiped his hands on his shorts.

'Service.'

This clipped the net and jumped wide.

'The louder they come, the harder they fall,' he gibed hopefully.

The second serve slid over slowly, safely in bounds. He firmly returned it to the opposite baseline and danced back. Aroused by his soles, a heat-seeking missile hurtled toward his feet. He leapt to the left and picked it up on the bounce with a deft, automatic scoop born of desperation. The ball wambled peaceably back across the net, where Earl's racquet repulsed it – one bounce, two – and now it was rolling once more toward Cullen's burning feet.

'Forty-love,' declared Earl. 'And that just about puts this game on ice. This is it, folks. It looks like Ogilvie will finish with a humiliating skunk. Talk about rubbing salt in the wound. This is it – game, set, match – this is the big bazoola, the grand banana. All those years of blood, sweat and tears now boil down to this one serve. Let's watch tennis history in the making, shall we? Service!'

Earl took a spring-loaded windup, tossed the ball high above him, addressed it with a scream, and flicked it tenderly just over the net. It was a dirty dog-dropping. Cullen came charging with all he could muster – it had already bounced, and not high – and with what seemed one of the most spectacular extensions in tennis history – perhaps what Earl had been referring to – he flipped the damn thing back again. And with good placement, too, one of the fringe benefits of having no time to formulate strategy. Now it was Earl's turn to scramble while Cullen recovered position. The ball fell close to the net, on the far side, and bounced apathetically.

Earl's return was propitious. The ball sailed back slowly, a short lob without top spin, back spin, wobble or ill intent. It seemed, for the first time, flirtatious. It offered itself. *Slam me*, it urged like a slut. *Take me here, now*. Cullen cocked taut as a crossbow, rose to address it in its descent – a candid descent without deceit or guile – and unleashed upon it all the pent-up frustrations of those who haven't had a good slam in weeks. It slashed across the net with authority, with lightning speed – beyond Earl's control, beyond Cullen's, and well beyond the baseline, where it took one curt bounce and smashed into the fence, rattling it.

'You lose,' said Earl. 'Kuhio time.'

Thus began another lonely weekend, for it was Friday afternoon.

A visit to the Kuhio was a post-tennis ritual, and this was the first tennis of spring. When Cullen had suggested the Kuhio to Felicia, it had been more out of habit than inspiration. But now he felt reluctant to resume the tradition, irrationally afraid he might disturb events set perfectly in motion, or that Earl might somehow defile a perfect memory. Nonetheless, as the buying loser, he could hardly demur.

They arrived exuding the virility of sweaty jocks, a duo that might have won in doubles. Nothing had changed since Cullen's last visit. There were a few more customers, the weather in the doorway had improved, and that was all. The bar seemed to prop up the same drinkers as before; the Budweiser sign continued its lonely vigil. From the booth where they sat he could see the booth where he and Felicia had sat. It was empty now. He would have it remain so forever, eternally sacrosanct, an altar of rain-engendered love. Instead of a flame, an eternal bottle of Kikkoman Shoyu. Instead of incense, a glass of disposable chopsticks.

They drank Primo, not Kirin. He recognized their waitress as the same cheerily pudgy girl who had served Felicia and him on the day of unrivaled rain. He sat patiently while Earl tediously reviewed the afternoon's highlights.

'I'd say that long rally in the fifth game was the turning point. I delivered three perfectly executed lobs that made you look rather foolish. You seemed to choke up after that. The coup de grâce, of course, was my slam. I'd say—'

Cullen waited until Earl had said it all, then waited further until he had cracked open his chopsticks and begun his assault on the hot dog chop suey. He'd brought Felicia with him, carrying her close to his breast like a secret scrolled missive – perhaps what had hindered his backhand through two grueling sets – and now he was eager to announce her. Hoping life might just once imitate the novels he'd been reading, he strove for a British effect with his first line.

'I've met the most extraordinary girl.'

'Good-looking girl?'

'That's what I said.'

'Japanese?' Earl, who had a soft spot – and a hard one – for Japanese women, suspected an infringement. He'd taught English in Kobe.

'Portuguese, actually.'

'Pocho! Consorting with undertakers' daughters are we? Or did you spy her coming out of the confessional with an unusually long penance? No, no, don't tell me, she's in your Remedial English class.'

This seemed an inauspicious beginning. Awaiting reverence, Cullen turned his attention to the Budweiser sign. It was not so much a sign as an illuminated representation of one of the thematic circles of Purgatory. A simple, carbonated panorama rotated clockwise: waterfall, canoe, campfire; waterfall, canoe, campfire; waterfall, canoe . . .

'Well, have you inserted the proper drill bit? Plumbed her depths?'

'Don't be crass, Earl.' Earl was often crass. He had a handsome jaw with a hint of irrepressible beard – the very thing women liked, felt Cullen – and this mandibular coarseness seemed to promote in him crassness.

'Oh, I see. *Sumimasen*.' He raised his chopsticks in a placating gesture. 'I beg your most honorable pardon. It's love then?'

'Let's call it *lust with honor*.'

'Let's introduce her to your best friend, shall we?'

Cullen had to smile. He'd only claimed to have *met* an extraordinary girl, not to have captured one. In matters of lust, he knew men to be pirates.

'I think that'd be premature.'

'But so much in life is. Birth. Burial. Ejaculation. I guess not in that order. Have you given her a name yet? Does she speak English or *da kine*?'

'Speaks English – quite well, actually. Writes it, too. Learned it from her English teacher.'

'Ahh, *so deska*. I should have known. I did know. In every class there's a little ass. One of the fringe benefits of an underpaid profession. So what's this virgin's name?'

Reluctant to hear it sullied by lips sucking noodles, Cullen hesitated to release this information, but finally confided, almost in a whisper, 'Felicia.'

Earl drew in the last of a wriggler, considered the name as if it were wine, exhaled and proclaimed – 'Lovely.' It was one of his disarming traits to suddenly introduce Sincerity into a conversation. She appeared from nowhere, like a visiting great aunt, and while present was necessarily accorded respect. She was incontinent, however, and seldom lingered.

'Did I tell you about Noriko?' asked Earl.

It was three pupu platters later when Cullen unscrolled his missive further.

'Felicia, the girl I was telling you about, told me about a very odd experience she's been having.'

'Hmm.'

'She claims she wakes up some nights, or tries to wake up, but something holds her down, she's paralyzed.'

'*Kanashibari*.'

'Did you say something?'

'*Kanashibari*. Bound by metal. Hand and foot. At least, that's what the Japanese call it. You can't budge. Something heavy presses you down. You're not asleep and you're not awake.'

'This is common then? They have a name for it?'

'Seems to be. Of course, not all things named are common, Cullen.' He hit his chest with his fist, a gastronomic gesture. 'Take multiple orgasm, for example. Or Uranium 235.'

'Wait. Who told you this? How did you learn the word?'

'Noriko, but she thought she was being haunted.'

'She experienced it?'

'Apparently, when she was younger.'

'Haunted by whom?'

'I don't know. I don't think she knows. Our relationship is primarily sexual, you know. We don't delve too much into the macabre.'

'I wasn't aware you made a distinction.'

'Oh! *Auwe*. I'm hurt, Cullen. I truly am. I'm eating this last shrimp without regret. I *was* going to treat you to *my* ghost story, since you seem to be so interested in the spirit world all of a sudden. I was working up to it. It took place, interestingly enough, in a hotel room.'

Cullen was suspicious. He'd known Earl for more than a year now, and together they had talked much story, yet he'd never known of a ghost story. 'I'm sorry. Let's hear it.'

'Mmm. Where's our waitress? This story is true, interestingly enough. It happened in Waikiki, long before I met you. I was working for the DOE on the Big Island and I had to come over here for a two-week training program. It was my first real job. I had a per diem of something like $20 a day and I thought it was wonderful. So I rented a room in one of those tiny hotels near the Ala Wai. The Something Lani. I got it damn cheap, too, when I told the manager I was from the Big Island. He was from the Big

Island too. Chinese Hawaiian guy. Said he'd heard of my dad. It was one of those places where the whole family sits around the TV in the lobby watching *Kikaider Man. Biru o motto kudasai.*' This to the waitress, who seemed to understand his empty bottle better than his Japanese.

'I think she's Vietnamese.'

'And deservedly so. Are you ready? Have I built up the suspense sufficiently? The first night I was out late with some of the local riff-raff. I got back to my room around one. Nothing happened. Nothing. I fell asleep. I got my chicken skin on the second night. Midnight, to be precise.'

'Oh my God,' groaned Cullen. 'Midnight.'

Earl slammed his hand on the table, which caused some stool-swiveling at the bar. 'You don't know the bounds of human decency, Cullen. Truly you don't. Your tennis game's collapsing, you don't get along with nuns and priests – who, by the way, are God's representatives on earth – you've got a haunted girlfriend, yet you continue to insult those who can offer you guidance. Sometimes I just don't understand you. You don't listen to people. This is a true story; try to appreciate it. This happened to *me*.' He paused to let the full weight of this sink in, a piano in quicksand.

'Now you know I'm not normally the superstitious type, don't you? I subscribe to *The New Yorker*, for Christ's sake. But I grew up on these islands and I can tell you that there are some things here that simply defy explanation.'

'I'm listening to one.'

'Keep your balls in bounds, Cullen. It was midnight. Okay, maybe not *exactly* midnight, but pretty damn close. Midnight's a real time like any other. Why not? So I was reading Agatha Christie in bed. *They Do It With Leeches* or *Fellatio Is Fatal*. One of those. I was coming to the good part, too. I had the bedside lamp on, and that gave me just enough light to see what I saw. First came the creaking. There's nothing creepier than creaking, Cullen. That's one spooky sound effect. I looked up to see the closet door swinging open. This was not alarming in itself, but it was the first time I noticed there was another door *inside* the closet. Suddenly the coat hangers started rattling violently like in a strong wind. That's when I got the tingly-tingles. Ever get those, little mites crawling up and down your spine? Then the rattling stopped. Nothing. Silence. Just my heart pounding. And then I heard a very distinct metallic sound. Not from the closet but from the front door. When I looked up I saw the chainlock swinging, pendulum-like. Edgar-Allan-Poe-like. I know I locked it. I *know*. And even if I didn't, why was it swinging? Got the picture? That lamp stayed on all night.'

'What did you do?'

'I didn't do anything at first, but the next night I was treated to an encore. Same time, same place, same everything. Only this time I looked quick enough to see the lock come undone.'

'Did you check out?'

'The room was *very* cheap, Cullen. Something like five bucks a night. I was actually making a profit off my per diem. Imagine that. No, I didn't check out. Not right away. But I did get rid of those damn coathangers. Some hotels attach them to the rod, yeah? I won't stay at a hotel like that. Why would I want to steal a bunch of crummy coathangers? And I did tell the manager about it first thing in the morning. Described it in vivid detail. He didn't say anything, just hobbled out of the office. I didn't know what was going on. Then he came back carrying something in his hand, which he handed to me. It was a yellowed newspaper clipping that had been laminated. It was from the *Star Bulletin* and it was dated July 12, 1968. Know what it said?'

'What?'

'It said, "Murdered Lovers Haunt Hotel Room?" They had to put a question mark, yeah? It seems my room had been the scene of a double murder, something the manager had failed to mention. A minor oversight. This guy's wife had been cheating on him and he finally caught her doing the dirty deed, *in flagrante delicto*. In between the sheets. Knifed the man before he could say "Now don't do anything rash". He got away but later died. She ran into the closet to try the door to the next room. But nothing doing. So she came out of the closet, so to speak, and made a lunge for the front door. Much like one of your lunges on the court this afternoon, I'd imagine. That's where she got hers. *Coitus interruptus*. A terrible thing.

'I stayed in that hotel a few more days, but staying out till one every morning was starting to take its toll. So I checked out. I later got a little certificate in the mail. I'll show it to you sometime. That manager had a real sense of humor.'

'What does it say?'

'It says I'm a goddamn hero with nerves of steel. You'll see what it says. But I'll tell you one thing. Ghosts are real. As real as you or me. And that's the truth, so help me God.'

'But you didn't see any ghost.'

'For which I'm grateful. But they bring a musty chill into the room. They must sleep in old refrigerators or something. You can tell when they're there.'

'When you're scared you get chills.'

'But you don't get musty. Eh? Okay, forget the chill. Next time I'll bring a goddamn thermometer. How do you account for the door, the coat hangers, the chainlock, the newspaper article? Figments of my imagination? Pure coincidence?'

'Beats me.'

'You're right about that. That's twice today. You should press charges.'

It was the poor credibility of Earl, not of ghosts, that had provoked Cullen's skepticism. But it was a lazy, precariously perched sort of skepticism, the kind that came from nothing more substantial than having never seen a ghost himself. Not that he'd be keen to encounter firsthand evidence to dislodge his doubts. He'd certainly heard a great many ghost stories in Hawaii – like dead ancestors, everybody had some. He tried never to scoff too loudly – he prided himself on having an open mind – but he *had* rather hoped for a small patch of peaceful oblivion when he died, something with flowers he'd never see, smell, or think about. Still, in a world as improbable as this, nothing bizarre was impossible.

5

Take, for example, Father Plecko. He had enormous splayed hands that gamboled like unleashed setters when he sat, dashing and whirling, leaping with sudden joy or anxiety, knocking and toppling, until they had forgotten completely what, if anything, they had set out to fetch, and instead circled each other restlessly, sniffing and snuffling in flux. His face, red and easily flummoxed, was screwed in place by a black cigar. Cullen always addressed the cigar, which glowed with talents of its own. It could nod in affirmation or wag in negation, and it could ponder difficult questions by doing both at once. It could even snap Father Plecko out of his distractions by dropping live sparks in the man's lap, a trick Cullen had witnessed more than once. It could not, however, express the great enthusiasm the old priest felt for his annual college-sponsored jaunts abroad. For that he maintained, though sorrily, a grinning mouthful of crown, amalgam, cohesive gold, and tooth. Although his nose, long inured to fetid combustibles, hung as stern and implacable as the head of a rhino in a smokers' lounge, his eyes, underscored by dark pouches, were the tender eyes of a harmless leaf-eating marsupial. These, too, could twinkle at the prospect of a junket. Old age had tonsured the poor man's head, giving him a monkish look, and Cullen had long ago determined that what lay below the bald spot was essentially a head cold.

Yet on this spring morning Cullen had been summoned to Plecko's office with great urgency. Father Plecko was 'over' Cullen in some indeterminate way. He could claim seniority, of course, by virtue of his antiquity, but he held no official title of which Cullen had been apprised. It all came down to the difference in door plaques. Cullen's read 'Cullen Kinnell / English', while Father Plecko's read 'Father Plecko, Ph.D. / English'. Consequently, it was understood that the English Department consisted of Sister Lucia, Father Plecko, and Cullen, in that order. Cullen did the trench work, harrowing the clods into loam, transforming fallow brains into fertile minds soon to be seeded by the good Father and Sister. Occasionally, but not often, he would be rewarded with an upper-level literature class of his own. Sometimes he taught night classes, especially in the long dry summers when it became a matter of economic necessity. But Sister Lucia taught night classes too, and even Freshman Composition, with egalitarian gusto. Only Father Plecko evaded such duty. How remained a mystery. Now the bottom echelon of the English Department sat before the middle.

'Yes, well . . .' Father Plecko lit his Grenadier, instantaneously afflicting the air with that distinctive dead-horse smell of a long and bitter Russian campaign. Cullen had once had an unfortunate incident with a Grenadier and had been wary ever since.

'May I?' he asked, removing from his pocket an English briar he'd purchased only the week before as part of a plan to combat the foul odors drifting from Plecko's office. He'd been practicing at home, though without real zeal.

Without raising his head, Father Plecko fixed him with soupy, disobliging eyes.

'Yes, of course.' He straightened some papers, moved closer an ashtray. His hands drummed the borders of the desk blotter then flew to a noisy mid-air collision, grappling with each other until one broke away to pluck his cigar from his mouth. 'Now my friend Coach Thornwell has informed me . . . About these three basketball players in your writing classes. I had their names here somewhere.'

'Tall black boys?'

The hands scooped up the sheaf of papers and began a test of its physical properties.

'Yes, I'm sure those are the ones.' A cloud of concern suddenly crossed his face. 'All three of them are black?'

'If we're talking about the same students. There's one in the morning class and two in the afternoon. They look like they could be basketball players. They talk about basketball a lot.'

'Now that could have racial overtones, don't you think – all of them being black?'

Cullen, having prepared the delicate seedbed of his pipe with a mixture called Light Brigade, now lit it with studied sloth. He loved the snotty advantages a pipe afforded. He believed a well-practiced pipe man could outmaneuver a cigar man any day of the week. It gave one such time to think!

'Having an all-black basketball team in a school with no blacks, you mean?'

'No, no. Honestly, what a thing to say, Cullen. It's not an all-black basketball team, and we have students of many, many races in attendance here. What I mean is . . . Coach Thornwell says you told these three students that they were flucking – flunking! – this um . . . term.' He flucked the ash of his cigar, narrowly missing the ashtray, which had moved. 'Did you tell that to any other students?'

'No.'

'So that's exactly what I mean. It could appear – this just popped into my head now – but it could appear that you're discriminating.'

Like a locomotive pulling a troop train, Cullen's pipe was starting out slowly, but with the promise of ample power.

'Well I suppose I am discriminating in a sense, Father. I'm discriminating between those who plagiarized their papers and those who did not. You see, one of these students submitted an editorial on gun control that I had just read the week before in the *Star Bulletin*, and the other two submitted virtually identical papers on the uncertainties of a preemptive nuclear attack. Bear in mind that they play on the same team. For basketball players their actions seem remarkably uncoordinated.'

'Which is evidence, I maintain, that they didn't understand the seriousness of their actions. They didn't really understand that they were doing something wrong. If they had, they surely wouldn't have done anything so foolish. But we all make mistakes, Cullen.'

His hands momentarily still, Father Plecko leaned back to take a long, satisfying draft of toxic gases.

'What are you suggesting, Father?'

'What I'm suggesting is that, as you know, all our athletes must maintain a C average on their midterm reports. Without it, they can't play. We have our academic standards to uphold. Now these three students . . . Where did I put that? Here it is.' (The right hand found it, the left hand snatched it away.) 'Webb, Plunkett, and Dhabul. I could have sworn Webb was white. Anyhow, these three students are very good basketball players. I'm sure you're aware of that. Coach Thornwell says that Plunkett and Dhabul are headline makers. He says we're very lucky to have them. They traveled all the way from New Jersey to play for us. Coach Thornwell feels that with these three players in the line-up we actually stand a chance of beating *Louis*ville. Could you imagine that, little Holy Mount beating Louisville? David smiting Goliath. Do you know how something like that could spark the public invagination? Imagination! And then, of course, there's the uh . . . tournament. The tournament. *The* tournament, I might add. To put it simply, there's the matter of the school's honor to uphold.'

Palming and traveling at the same time, Father Plecko had shamelessly dribbled around him.

'Hmm . . . Well, it was the school's honor that I was thinking about, Father. They've plagiarized their papers.'

'Yes, yes, perhaps they have. But their papers won't be televised nationwide, will they? You're a fine young man with moral principles, and I know you feel you're doing the right thing, but instead of helping the school by flunking these students, you might actually be hurting it. Have you thought of that? I'm just trying to look at the big picture here. After all, having a high-ranked basketball team attracts students from all over the country, and not just basketball players either. Students like to be associated with a winner. More students means higher enrollments. Higher enrollments mean better health for the college, more money to channel into academic programs, more money for teachers perhaps. Higher enrollments would mean we could keep our faculty fully employed. More books for the library. Better classroom facilities. Maybe even get those Shakespeare videos you've been asking about. Et cetera. This college could become a university. Think of that.'

Flushed with exertion, Father Plecko called on his cigar for sustenance. By now the air had grown fuliginous with the sour-sweet clash of Grenadiers and Light Brigade. His right hand was either clasping, or trapped under, the head of his stapler.

More students means higher enrollments. Cullen had never thought of it that way. Higher enrollments were the opposite of falling enrollments. With higher enrollments he could keep his job, perhaps even achieve tenure. He could marry and raise a family. He could buy life insurance. He'd study money market funds. In a way, his personal success depended upon the success of the Holy Mount Trojans. Like wax earplugs, he could soften. Their cause was his cause. It was a just cause. It was the college's cause.

'What are you asking me to do?'

'Just give them another chance. Don't be so severe. You know, these are underprivileged kids who never had a fair shot at life. They probably don't even know what *plagiarism* means.'

'Or *preemptive*.'

'Then they need to learn. That's what they're here for. Just give them a reprieve.'

'When I asked Webb and Dhabul why they'd submitted the same paper, they said they'd worked on it together.'

'Athletes are used to teamwork.' Father Plecko's left hand extricated the right. 'Just give them one more chance.'

'Well, unfortunately, Father, that raises another issue. One more chance won't help. I just don't think they're college material. I agree that they deserve an education, but not quite on the college level. They write like children.'

He punctuated this point with a barrage of Light Brigade. He'd paid a heavy price bringing his pipe to a boil – the damn thing bit like a horse and was so hot he could barely hold it – but he felt he was winning the smoke battle and doing quite well in the verbal as well.

'Then you'd be closing the door on their only chance of making something of themselves, wouldn't you. How can they make it to the pros if they can't play in college? And how can they play in college if you give them F's on their midterm reports?'

'By simply maintaining a C average. Isn't that what you said?

Their fate's still pretty much in their own hands. A C average shouldn't be that difficult to maintain. A few A's and B's should offset that F quite nicely. And now that they've been thrown out of my class, they'll have that much more time to devote to their other classes.'

Father Plecko's hands stopped dead in their romp.

'What do you mean, *thrown out*?'

'Well, not thrown out exactly. That was a poor choice of words. They can still come to class, of course. But they don't because they've already earned an F for the term. I warned them on the first day of class that that would be the penalty for plagiarism. I'd lose all my authority if I changed that now.'

Plecko's Grenadier stiffened. He leaned forward.

'You've given them F's for the *term*? And they don't come to class anymore?'

'That's right.'

'Then how will they learn anything?'

'They'll learn lesson number one. Don't cheat. Next term they can learn lesson number two.'

'Which is?'

In the all too brief time that had elapsed since mentioning it, Cullen had been wondering the same thing himself. Driving recklessly down court in the heat of the exchange, two on one, his mind had promised to pass him lesson number two for a slam dunk at the basket. Now his mind was nowhere to be seen. He concealed this hopefully momentary abandonment by stoking his pipe, creating the impression that he was savoring what he was about to say rather than mindlessly ripping it off the wall of his high school locker room.

'Lesson number two is "A quitter never wins and a winner never quits." True sportsmen should understand that.'

Now he wondered if he wasn't simply bitter because he had not made the basketball team in high school. Nor the baseball team. Nor even tried out for football. All through high school he had born the stigma of the valedictorian, the crewcut kid who got straight A's but couldn't play ball. He felt as if he had somehow expressed this shameful fact to Father Plecko, whose left hand was now conspiring with the right. He had somehow overextended himself. Roy Campanella had never gone to college. The Dodgers collectively would have struggled to describe their winter vacation. He suffered the guilt of the self-righteous and the nausea of the novice smoker. Confused alarms of struggle and flight seemed to sound in the roiling clouds above him.

'That's very well put,' said Father Plecko. "A quitter never wins and a winner never quits." But that's just it, isn't it? You're *forcing* them to quit by giving them F's for the term. They have nothing left to fight for. You've taken away their incentive. Why not just give them F's on their papers, explain to them where they went wrong, and give them a chance to rewrite them? Encourage them to write about something they know, like basketball. And maybe give them C's on their midterm reports. You can always flunk them at the end of the semester if that's what they truly deserve. All we're talking about here is a little Christian chattery – ch-ch-chast – ch-ch-charity!'

Cullen caught an acrid breath of Grenadier. Plecko's hands were staring at him now, one crouched on either side of the desk blotter, knuckles raised. He had visions of himself at the gymnasium inquiring into the whereabouts of Webb, Plunkett and Dhabul. Perhaps he'd be directed to the locker room, where the three of them, fresh from the shower, would surround him like naked Nuba warriors.

'I really feel it's a bit late to call them back, Father. They've missed a whole week. We're already on the next paper. If you want me to falsify their midterm reports, however—'

'Falsify? Dear no. No, no, no. I'm not asking you to falsify anything. No. You just do what your conscience dictates. I can see we have a very messy situation here.' Puffing on his cigar, Father Plecko sat back to better ponder the carnage.

Cullen rose into a cloud of smoke while his stomach remained seated. He felt as if he'd lost both a game and a battle. 'Well, if that will be all then, I've got a bit of work to do.'

'Yes, certainly. Thank you for coming to discuss this with me.'

'I'm glad I did.'

'Yes, well . . . goodbye.'

'Goodbye.'

He returned to his office in a dour mood, smoked but not cured.

He placed his pipe in his desk drawer, among the paper clips and rubber bands. His hands stank. His breath stunk. His tongue had lost the will to loll. He slumped into his chair, propped his feet on the desk, and loosened his necktie, a garish red silk he'd picked up for 50¢ at Mama Rice's Thrift Shop, where he'd bought a great many fancy ties that other men simply couldn't abide. He owned eighteen such ties. This particular one, when he'd first brought it home, had been covered with the word *sly* – SLYSLYSLY from top to bottom – but since he'd discovered the label tucked in the back, it had been covered with the initials of Yves St Laurent, a rare find indeed.

Almost twelve. He had an hour to kill until his next class. He considered going to the school cafeteria, where he might encounter Felicia, but he had no appetite and he'd told Father Plecko he had work to do. He opened his second righthand drawer, riffled through some papers, and, finding what he was looking for, settled back to read 'Cars' by Duncan Q. Plunkett. It was the first paper Duncan had written in his class, and he'd made a copy.

Cars

Automobiles to most young people are more than just something in which you get from one place to another. Kids today see cars as an institution. For a young man a car is his bread and butter for going out with a nice looking young ladies. These days in alot of cities around the country, a young man is measured by weather he has a car or not and if its' a decent one. On the otherhand alot of women get attention by driving a very nice sports car Most of them by choice drive red two seater sports cars, which is a symbol of how hot to trot she is. With men the role in most cases is to have a 'lean mean fighting machine', in which to be sporting around, which shows how tuff he is. Like in the house and buggy days of the past, the stronger the horse and buggy was the more money a person has. For example a young man who has a Rolls Royce is assumed to be rather wealthy on the otherhand a man who has a Volkswagon is looked upon as bearly making ends meet. And throughout the years have been used to rate how rich people is and probably will

> continue to do so for years to come. I guess its a system which has its checks and balances just like alot of other but for the most part it is a system which in most cases is telling how much money a person has. Yes money isn't everything but it sure is nice to have!

He propped his feet on his desk and stared at his shoelaces. He was feeling guilty about Jesse Webb. Plunkett and Dhabul were arrogant, loud-mouthed bastards, but Webb was a doe-eyed, soft-spoken kid who seemed aware of his shortcomings and determined to overcome them. He'd shown some character early on, and Cullen just couldn't understand how he'd allowed himself to be drawn into plagiarism. No doubt Dhabul had had something to do with it, but even Dhabul wasn't dumb enough to furnish Jesse with the same filched paper he himself intended to submit. When Cullen had called both of them into his office and confronted them with the evidence, Jesse had looked like a child caught with a stolen melon, but for one brief moment, before concocting that cockamamie story about having worked together, Dhabul had looked stupified, as if in the final seconds of a game, as he stood wide open before the basket, someone had passed him that melon instead of a basketball. He'd looked even more stupified when he discovered he'd been called for a foul, ejected from the game, and suspended for the season. Shortly thereafter, en route to the men's room, Cullen had heard him berating Jesse in the arcade.

He felt no remorse about flunking Plunkett and Dhabul; it was cleaner and simpler than coaxing them along all term to a level they'd never achieve. But he felt bad about Jesse, the only one of the three who seemed to recognize his dismissal for the disgrace it was. Most teachers would have simply slapped the offender's wrist and sent him away to do the work over again. And when it came back poor instead of dishonest, they would have rewarded the paper with a C. No point in hurting anyone's feelings. Sister Lucia had passed all three with C's. The sad truth was that giving poor grades to poor students was emotionally draining. One had to confront the hostility, the importuning, the pleas for extra help that would never really suffice. The point was not to educate or even evaluate; the point was to pass them on. Someone further down the line would stop them before the goal. Or let them pass.

He felt bad about Jesse not because he'd flunked him – that was probably inevitable – but rather because Jesse had shown some genuine desire to learn, was the kind of kid who whacked himself on the head because there was so much to learn, so much he kept forgetting. The tragedy was that Cullen could have tutored him daily, successfully, without bringing him to the college level. The education Jesse deserved, and needed, was elementary. Society had failed the boy, not Cullen. The fact that he'd given him an F didn't make him a goddamn racist. Everyone was so goddamn sensitive these days.

Someone knocked. He reluctantly removed his feet from the desk, but he'd be damned if he'd tighten his tie. This would be either the Holy Mount Trojans or a student in need of a topic.

'Come in.'

In walked Felicia, a first.

'Anything you say will be held against me,' he wished to warn her, for what he called his office was actually a plywood cubicle whose walls stopped short of the ceiling. And on the other side of the back wall sat Father Plecko, humming poignantly to his hands and cigar. Cullen might have been in a confessional, tabulating impure thoughts. God knows he'd had some lately. But it was too late to say or do anything – they had already exchanged their *hello*'s and he'd already offered her a seat.

'Why is it so smoky in here?' She waved a hand before her face.

He gestured with his head toward Father Plecko's office.

'I don't know.'

'Smells like a pet turtle. I had a turtle named Abner once. Cute little bugger. Can I ask you a question?'

'Sure.'

'My explanatory paper is going to be on handwriting analysis.'

'Sounds like an interesting topic.'

The crinkum-crankum of her own handwriting – full of liquid squiggles, as when honey drips from spoon to jar – had intrigued him all term.

'It's fascinating. But before I go any further I'd like to gather some data to see if I can corroborate some of the theories. So I was wondering if you'd be willing to participate in a little experiment.'

Cullen could think of any number of little experiments in which he'd be willing to participate.

'Sure. I'd be happy to.'

'Good. Wanta do it now?'

Staring deeply into her eyes, he silently transmitted the following message: *I would like to do it now, tomorrow, the day after; on Kamehameha Day, Lei Day, and Samoan Flag Day; on the World Day of Poetry and Childhood; on Slavic Script and Bulgarian Culture Day; twice on World Gratitude Day; in conjunction with equinoxes both vernal and autumnal; in celebration of solstices estival and hibernal; on the road and before all home games; on Referee Appreciation Day and Super Bowl Sunday; while Santa loads lots of toys and goodies on his sleigh, while the Groundhog roots for his shadow, while Chinese dragons dance in the New Year; on Tree Planting Day, Bean Throwing Night, and the Night of the Living Dead; before, during, and after monthly tsunami alerts; on holidays, holy days, workdays, weekdays, wet days, dry days, Wednesdays, Fridays, birthdays, Thursdays, many days, any day – It without end. Amen.*

'Sure. Why not? As long as I get to class on time.'

'It won't take long. Okay, I'm going to show you four shapes, and I want you to say which one you like best, second best, and so on. Don't think about it. Respond instinctively. Got it?'

'You want me to tell you which shape I like best, second best, et cetera. Are you going to show me all four shapes at once?'

'Right. Okay, ready?'

'Ready.'

She placed before him a sheet of paper on which she had drawn a circle, a square, a triangle, and a squiggle. He imagined each tattooed on his bicep, then quickly ranked them in order of preference: squiggle, triangle, circle, square.

'Very good,' she said. 'Now I'd like you to fill out a short questionnaire. For each question just check *yes*, *no*, or *uncertain*. If you need some time, you can give it back to me later.'

He surveyed the questionnaire. There were questions such as 'Do you enjoy the company of others?' 'Are you slow to become emotionally involved with another person?' 'Do you tire easily?' et cetera.

'I'll do it now. You can read *The History of the English Language* if you want, or anything else there that catches your fancy.'

'Okay.'

To his surprise, she did indeed choose *The History of the English Language*. Meanwhile, he addressed himself to the questionnaire. Yes, he did enjoy the company of others. No, he was not slow to become emotionally involved. If the truth be told, he did tire easily – witness his performance on the tennis court. He checked *no*. 'When making a decision, do you tend to rely upon the opinion of others?' Having just resisted the pressures of Father Plecko, he felt *no* to be a fair answer, but then again, weren't many of his opinions influenced by the informed opinions of essayists, scholars, experts in their field? He checked *uncertain*. At the bottom was a list of adjectives such as *moral*, *amoral*, *frugal*, *shy*, *witty*, *sarcastic*, etc. He decided to give quick responses. Yes, he was Moral. No, he was not Amoral. He was of necessity Frugal. Yes, he supposed he was Shy at heart, but he also felt he'd done a remarkable job of hiding this fact and that therefore he was not actually Shy. In fact, with a few drinks, he could sometimes be downright aggressive. He checked *uncertain*. Yes, he was Witty, wit was knowledge, but was he also Sarcastic? Sarcastic came from the Greek *sarkazein*, to tear flesh like dogs. He wasn't like that. Earl was. But had he not been sarcastic toward Father Plecko? He checked *uncertain*. Vain? It depended. Earl had once said, while surveying all the near-naked bodies on the beach, 'Most people are physically deformed in one way or another, don't you think? I'm not quite perfect myself, but when you look around . . .' And then he'd screwed up his face with cheery disdain to suggest what one saw. As if to illustrate his point, two bowlegged gents with trunks to their knees had waddled out of the water and past them – happy, to judge by their laughter, but not the sort to cast in bronze. And when he looked around him, Cullen saw much the same – the drab, the blank, the freckled, the frizzled, the pale, the blotched, the gangly, the squat – the great huddled masses of ordinary unblessed human beings. How he loved them for their vulnerability, just like him, and how he longed to rise above them, his own placement on the physical scale fluctuating dramatically from mirror to mirror as his nose changed length and his hair alternated unpredictably between styled and wild. At this very moment a Norman Rockwellian cowlick could be mocking him with all the treachery of an open fly. This tendency to alter rapidly like unstable matter had saved him, he felt, from vanity. But didn't he at the same time consider himself just a bit better than most? Jesus, he was taking this whole thing much too seriously. He checked *no* for Vain and, by way of atonement, *yes* for Proud. That had a much more positive connotation than Stubborn, for which he checked *no*. Intelligent? Well, *yes*. Self-confident? No, but he couldn't tell that to Felicia. He checked *yes* with aplomb. Decisive? *Shit*, he thought, this was harder than he'd imagined.

When he finished the survey she thanked him and asked to borrow *The History of the English Language*. 'It's very interesting.'

'Sure.' That would commit her to returning it, ensuring another meeting. Affairs, he'd noticed, often began with small borrowings. Conversely, at the ends of affairs, there were always things to return. (Alice had returned a Cat Stevens record and all his Japanese novels.) She had the most incredible lips – tart, bite-sized fruit ripened to perfect rondure.

'Bye,' she said as she walked out the door. It was a breathy, seemingly reluctant *bye* that cleared the air of the last wisps of smoke.

Damn, thought Cullen in the nicest sense of the word.

6

Don't take East Manoa. Veer left at the fork – really you're just going straight on Manoa – and that will take you to the cemetery. You'll see a Chinese gate. Turn left and pull into the first driveway. You'll see my Toyota. We're right across from the gate.

A bold moon hung over the cemetery as if tethered to one of the unkempt tombstones spiking a rolling landscape. Steep mountains sealed the valley beyond. He pulled in beside the Toyota and surveyed the moonlit graves in his mirror, suddenly appreciating Claire and Ernest's description of their new home as 'Neo-Gothic'.

He grabbed his wine, stepped into the moonlight, and rang the doorbell.

Claire answered.

'Cullen! Come in, come in. We haven't seen you for so long. You're looking good. Nice shirt. I hope you didn't have any trouble finding us.'

'This must be the fourth Chinese gate I've stopped at,' he said, slipping off his shoes.

'Ahhh. Look at it in the moonlight! Let me get Ern.'

He quickly pulled his pipe from his pocket. 'That's okay, I'll just use an ashtray like everyone else.'

Claire, who was local Japanese, had a lovely way of skewing her eyes to skewer his puns. She skewed them now. In her black jumpsuit, she looked to Cullen like a Ninja mechanic, an image reinforced by her swift, silent tiptoeing as she set off to fetch her husband.

Cullen took a few steps into the living room to survey all that depressed him about successful friends: the teakwood paneling, the lava fireplace, the liquor cabinet, the stereo system with reel-to-reel, the well-stocked record rack, the wine rack, the magazine rack, the rack of Japanese swords, the plush carpets one could sleep or make love on, the koa coffee table, the seemingly chamois couch and chairs, the wall of good books and well-stocked display shelves – genuinely weathered Japanese fishing balls, mounted scallops and volutes, blowfish, geodes and agates from Brazil, alabaster chess set from Volterra – and above the couch, Ukiyo-E framed in lacquerware. Eclectic, yet warm, and to Cullen's eye, opulent. The only thing casually placed in the room was a photograph on one shelf of a sign declaring in Chinese and English:

NOTICE
FIRE-CRACKERS
PERMITTED BY POLICE DEPT.

8 A.M. to 5 P.M. ONLY

MANOA CHINESE CEMETERY ASSOCIATION

He deposited his bottle of wine by the liquor cabinet, then looked in the hallway mirror to see what Claire had liked about his shirt. It was a purple and green aloha shirt bearing a print of exotic flowers. It did look nice, didn't it? It seemed to say he was a bachelor with a hairy chest who didn't give a damn.

He returned to the living room and sank into the couch. Claire and Ernest disappeared from his life for months at a time, then reappeared like satellites. He was their bachelor, they were his couple. Ernest was a lawyer with Fleet & Nomura, and Claire was both a legal secretary and a student of law. One of the ironies of teaching, he had discovered, was that as an impoverished professional he often rubbed elbows with his betters.

Tamping his tobacco lovingly into the bowl of his pipe, he felt suddenly heartsick and alone. He had brought his missive with him – not Felicia but the mere possibility of Felicia – and he was eager to unroll it, though not so soon as to subject it to the same easy dismissal as his puns. He struck a match carefully over the coffee table, lest some errant spark ignite the carpet, and lighting his pipe, deposited that match in the empty onyx ashtray, wondering as he did so if it was intended for actual use. Claire and Ernest didn't smoke. After one puff, a puff reminiscent of his duel with Plecko, he decided it best if he not smoke either, and so he deposited his pipe in the ashtray as well, allowing its fire to die a natural death. Their old house had seemed less intimidating.

Ernest entered the room in a purple and green aloha shirt and looked at Cullen as a parrot fish might eye a parrot.

'Good God, Cullen, where did you get that shirt? My mother has a muumuu just like it.'

'Help! I'm being attacked by an angry mauve.'

'Nnnh,' snorted Ernest. 'You could damage a chameleon for life with that thing.'

'I don't know. I like it. It shows my chest well.'

'It does do that,' said Claire, appearing at Ernest's side. 'You look like you've been swimming a lot.'

'Mostly tennis.'

'Well, Claire put me up to wearing this. I normally have better taste. What can I get you?'

'Gin and tonic?'

'My pleasure.'

Like Claire, Ernest was tall and slender. But while his wife accented her height with straight black hair longer than Felicia's, Ernest crowned his with a premature bald spot, which shone now as he bent over his ice bucket.

Claire stood there smiling.

'Well, how do you like it?'

'Fantastic. You guys are really moving up in the world. Do I get a tour?'

'After drinks.'

But after drinks they had dinner.

'This is delicious, Claire. What's it called?'

'Honey Pork Oriental.'

'Mmm. Sounds like a Hotel Street stripper.'

'You said that last time!'

'We had this last time?'

'No, we had Pigs in a Blanket,' said Ernest.

'We had Steamed Buns Bangkok,' corrected Claire.

'With Dicey Ginger Chicken and Stir-aroused Vegetables,' added Ernest.

'With Custard Tarts,' said Claire, suddenly giggling at her own joke and covering her mouth with cupped hands.

Cullen raised a wine glass containing his contribution to the meal, a French border wine that had offered little resistance. 'To culinary erotica.'

'Here – here.'

Claire hummed and smiled.

'Tell Cullen about your trial yesterday, honey,' said Ernest.

'Did you do something wrong?'

'No. And I'd much rather hear about your trial.'

'My trial?'

'Yes, your upcoming trial before Judge Kushimoto for – how many was it now? – *four* parking offenses.'

'You know about that?'

'It's all a matter of public record,' said Ernest. 'I'm sure it'll be in all the papers.'

'Well, four's not bad. I've handled a lot more than four.'

'Oh have you now? I'm sure we could learn from your courtroom experience.'

'Sure. My secret is the cop never shows up. He's too busy giving out traffic tickets. Once I had a prosecutor ask me with a straight face if it wasn't true that if Officer Honcho *were* in the courtroom, which he was not, he would say that he had found me in violation of such and such an ordinance. I mean come on . . . What am I supposed to do, wire my own electric chair? I turned to the judge, who can sometimes be a decent guy, and I said, "Your Honor, is that a serious question? How on earth can I know what somebody who isn't even here would or wouldn't say?" He threw that one out real fast. This whole thing's a racket just to make money for the city by denying law-abiding citizens the due process of law.'

'And how does it do that?' asked Ernest.

'By threatening people. If you don't pay within seven days, we'll double the fine. And if you insist on a fair trial with a jury of your peers, we'll give you a trial with a hanging judge who's got his own private parking place. And if you lose that, we'll really fine your ass.'

'You talk about your Steamed Buns Bangkok,' said Ernest. 'I think we're gonna see some Fried Ass Cullen real soon. Kushimoto's tough. And he doesn't like guys that say "Not guilty". That seems to offend him personally.'

'Shit,' said Cullen. 'Why don't you defend me?'

'Are you guilty?' asked Claire.

'Well, technically, yes, but that's not the point.'

'It never is,' she smiled.

'Okay, I'm not guilty. How can you be guilty when you need to park for two hours and the meter's only good for one? Are you supposed to float out of a dentist's chair, stoned on nitrous oxide, to feed a goddamn machine? How can you be guilty when the meter only takes quarters and all you've got is Indian Head nickels?'

'You think they should accept all coins, do you?' asked Ernest. 'Regardless of race or denomination?'

'Yes. And they should give change for bills, they should accept IOU's . . . You ever pay for sixty minutes and only get fifty-five? It's not fair.'

'Care for some Grand Marnier?' asked Ernest after dinner, after he and Claire had successfully embedded the still impassioned Cullen in the living room couch.

'Yes, please. Might as well get completely blottoed.'

'I didn't know you smoked,' said Ernest, noticing the pipe.

'Self-defense,' said Cullen, who proceeded to recount his confrontation with Father Plecko over the fate of Holy Mount's basketball team.

'What are you going to do?' asked Claire.

'Nothing. Give them the F's they deserve. Aid and abet the enemy. I don't see how Plunkett can even play the game; he's as crosseyed as a planarian.'

'That's what makes him great!' exclaimed Ernest. 'Nobody can cover him. They never know which eye to believe! He's a phenomenon. They don't call him Dunk It Plunkett for nothing, you know. The truly amazing thing about Plunkett is he's everywhere. He's all over the court, always popping up where you'd least expect him. So he's a great defensive player too. And he's only a freshman. That's the beauty of it. Half the team's freshmen. Think of what this team will be like in a few years. And you'll be able to brag that you knew them personally. Do you have Plunkett's autograph?'

'Better than that. I have an essay on the symbolism of cars that should be a real collector's item. Did you know that fast cars mean you're hot to trot and slow cars mean you're a loser? Did you know that, Claire? So who am I to stand between him and the big time, right? Why can't they just chuck their so-called academic standards? They don't believe in them anyhow. Why do we have to go through this farce? Why not a basketball league for college-age illiterates? That would simplify everything. Why do they have to make a liar out of me?'

'I don't think they're really their standards,' said Ernest. 'That C average requirement is probably a rule of the conference. Colleges aren't supposed to hire mercenaries and dress them up as students.'

'But that's exactly what they do, isn't it?'

'Have you ever considered getting out of teaching?' asked Claire.

Cullen saw his chance. He sipped his liqueur to savor the burning sweetness of the moment.

'I might have to. I'm falling for one of my students.'

'Ahh,' said Ernest. 'And what grade will she earn this term? And how?'

'She seems destined for a B. An A might create too much scandal.'

'I wouldn't go out with a teacher who gave me a B,' offered Claire.

'You're thinking graduate school, Dear. Cullen likes to let the fruit writhe on the vine before he plucks it.'

'When do we get to meet her? You should bring her over some night.'

'I'd like to. Maybe when this term's over and the moon is full over the graveyard. She has something of a spooky experience to relate, though my friend Earl is the one with a *real* ghost story.'

Something deadened in Claire's eyes.

'Ah,' said Ernest, 'that's a somewhat sensitive subject around here. You see, we've had a bit of an encounter' – he shifted in his chair – 'with our friends . . . from the other side.'

'Two friends,' added Claire.

'Yes, they seem to come with the house. I guess that's why we could afford it. We should have known with the cemetery and all. You're looking rather skeptical.'

'No, not skeptical. It's just that everyone seems to have a ghost story these days. But you're the last people I would've expected . . .'

'Yes, we were the last people we would've expected, too. Claire saw them first. I came home late from work one night and she was nearly hysterical. Said she had to shoo an old man from under the mango tree.'

'Maybe it was just an old man. Some of these old-timers will take a leak wherever the grass grows green. Just the other day I saw an old gent pissing on Keeaumoku, next to La Mancha's!'

'That's what Ern said. You don't say that anymore, do you, Dear?'

'No, not anymore.'

'What does that mean?'

Claire stared at Ernest, ready to oversee his explanation.

'Well, I've never believed in ghosts. When Claire told me about this old man under the mango tree, I discounted it, you know, much as you did. We had just moved in, everything was still in a state of chaos, she was all alone at night. I figured she was just a little bit on edge. And, in fact, neither of us has ever seen that man again.'

'What did he do when you shooed him away?'

'He walked over to the graveyard,' said Claire. 'There's an old paved road that goes right down the middle. He just kept walking until he was out of sight. It was hard to see, but it looked to me like he just faded away. The spooky thing is that he definitely looked Chinese. He was wearing an old brown hat and overcoat and seemed like he was from another century. It was eerie.'

'Like I said, she was nearly hysterical when I got home.'

'I wanted to move out.'

'Then she claimed to see this old, old woman in a white nightgown.'

'She was Chinese, too.'

'She said she saw her twice. Once was when we were watching a movie on TV. That's in the other room. We had all the lights out and Claire just got up to go to the bathroom.'

'She was walking down the hall, going away from me. She just disappeared when she reached the end.'

'Claire came back crying. Made me escort her to the bathroom. I was really beginning to worry about her. I didn't know what to do.'

'He wanted me to quit law school.'

'Temporarily. I thought she was overworking herself. And then came the night of the flying *maneki neko*.'

'The flying *maneki neko*?'

'Fortune-inviting cat,' explained Claire. 'You know, you see them in all the Japanese shops. They have one paw raised and they're smiling. We had one in the old house, a white porcelain one.'

'Oh yeah. All right. I know what you mean. Porcelain cats.'

'Right,' said Ernest. 'Well ours went flying through the window in Claire's room.'

'I was studying in there. I just came out to the kitchen for a cup of tea, and when I came back, there she was! That was the first time I saw her face. She looked ancient. She was just standing there in front of the window looking around the room. When she looked at me, I grabbed the first thing I could find and threw it at her. It happened to be the *maneki neko*. It was a stupid thing to do. Mom gave it to me when I graduated from Punahou. It went right through her.'

'And through a hundred twenty bucks worth of window,' added Ernest.

'And the ghost?'

'She vanished.'

'More Grand Marnier?'

'Just a little, please.'

There was a dramatic pause as drinks were poured.

'And then,' said Ernest, 'one dark and stormy night, as I lay sound asleep dreaming of torts, a rough tugging at my shoulder awakened me. "Whaaat?" I asked. Claire just said, "Look at the foot of the bed." I looked. And there she was, just as Claire had described her, a wrinkled Chinese lady clad in a thin white nightgown. She looked at us rather suspiciously, I thought, as if we were strangers in *her* house rather than she in ours. She was absolutely luminous. She looked like a projection on mist. The first and last thing she did was to vanish. She just disappeared under the bed, like a genie returning to a bottle.'

'What did you do?'

'Well, I just lay there for a long time, a little stunned. It's quite a shock to have a lifelong belief overturned in a matter of seconds. She was real. I saw her with my own eyes. I guess that's the difference. Until you see one with your own eyes, you never really believe. After that, it's a probatum.'

'She was terribly wrinkled. Wasn't she, Ern?'

'Yes.'

'You'd be wrinkled too if you had to sleep under the bed,' said Cullen.

'Well, when I finally collected my wits, and my guts, I turned on the sidelight. Then I knelt by the bed and peeked reluctantly underneath.'

'And?'

'And I saw just what I'd hoped to see. Nothing but dustballs. Claire said, "Now do you believe me?" I said, "Honey, I've got some good news and some bad news. The good news is – you're not crazy. The bad news is – we just bought ourselves a haunted house."'

'This house doesn't look old enough to be haunted.'

'No, it doesn't, does it? It's only about five years old.'

'And you guys still live here?'

'Well, it's funny. When it happens you say, "That's it. I'm gone." But when the sun comes up and the birds start chirping and a few days go by without incident, you think, "Hell, this is my home, not theirs. I like it here. I'm mortgaged up to my okole here. I'm *paying* for this piece of property, dammit. I've got a right to stay." And when you think about it, ghosts are really powerless. They can't do anything except scare the living bejesus out of you.

They can't even say "Boo!" I've never heard of anyone being injured by a ghost, have you? They may be a private nuisance, but they never do anything actionable. Except maybe trespass. Still, you can't very well get a mandatory injunction against them. You might as well just live and let . . . well, whatever.'

'That's Ern's attitude. My attitude is that if it happens one more time, I'm leaving.'

'That's my attitude, too. I'm leaving. But first I want a tour of this haunted mansion. This is going to be a lot more interesting than I thought. Maybe we should do it by candlelight.'

'No way. I've seen those movies,' said Claire. 'Something blows out the candles and you grab each other's hands. And then when the lights come on, you're all alone.'

Cullen returned home that evening wary of the dark. Fortunately, his was a small cottage apartment easily exorcised by a few flipped switches. It had no murderous history that he knew of, no horrid secret to drive him to prayer. Coat hangers had never rattled in the closet, and if the thin walls had harbored a corpse, the termites would have disinterred it long ago. But then, just as Claire had predicted, when the lights came on, he was all alone.

He carried a rattan chair out to the lanai and sat between the three papaya trees and the royal poinciana, whose silver bark glistened with moonlight. A few mosquitoes circled overhead while a gecko clucked contentedly inside the living room. It was considered lucky to have a resident gecko, if for no other reason than that it devoured insects. Before him sloped the well-disciplined back lawn of his landlord, Mr. Ching, whose capacious old house rose above the cottage. The backyard was free of the large water jars that cluttered the front (to deter, somehow, defecating dogs). Hibiscus and bougainvillaea hid the fence marking the property line. Lights shone in only a few houses on the opposite ridge. He lit his pipe and thought about Felicia.

He supposed he had believed her story from the first – believed, that is, that she'd experienced what she claimed to – but he saw it now in a new light, not as a story he chose to believe, but rather as a story whose veracity required no endorsement from him whatsoever. He'd been carrying it around like a novel anecdote, a bit of otherwordly lore with which to season a conversation. Telling it had not committed him to a belief in ghosts any more than telling a dirty joke commits one to a belief in traveling salesmen and farmers' daughters. She herself hadn't used the word *ghost.* And she had told her story with such heartening nonchalance, how was one to succumb to its horrors? Without thinking less of her, he'd imagined an internal, neurological cause, as when one experiences *déjà vu.* In short, he had believed in a scientific explanation. Earl had tried to tell him that the supernatural was real, but belief in Earl was every bit as difficult as belief in ghosts. Claire and Ernest, however, were something else entirely. If Claire and Ernest claimed to have seen a ghost, then a ghost was what they had seen. Who was he to doubt? In ancient Hawaii, he'd been told, the world had been full of distraught ghosts who had failed to reach the netherworld for lack of a proper burial. Perhaps a dead man, dutifully anointed and wrapped in tapa, had been thrown down a bottomless puka only to land on a ledge and be recovered by an enemy. Perhaps a young man too avidly in pursuit of boar had lost his footing on a cliffside trail and plummeted to an unremarked death. Perhaps a swimmer had simply disappeared. Such ghosts had but one hope: to find their own passage from this world to the next. A certain breadfruit tree in Kalihi, for example, was said to have afforded an opportunity. Ghosts sat in its branches hoping one might break, casting them into the underworld. It must have been an odd sight at midnight, he thought, treed ghosts comparing misfortunes, bouncing dispiritedly on unperturbed limbs, praying for arboreal rot and gale-force winds. Now ghosts were disturbing his friends in hotel rooms, in their new homes, in their very dreams. The breadfruit tree had been cut down to accommodate a housing project.

He swatted a mosquito on his cheek and had the satisfaction of finding its crushed, bloodied body in his palm. To Cullen, the dead stayed dead. Any corpse, even this paltry one, testified to that. It was brutally self-evident. That's what dead was, the opposite of alive. Yet his friends claimed otherwise.

That night, trapped in a febrile half-sleep in which he had become a rowboat banging against a dock, he had to force himself to awaken, arise, turn on the light and rearrange the bedding, in order to disentangle himself from the nauseous rise and fall on black, oily water. There were no people in that dream, which was not so much a dream as an incipient fever, but in the morning, Felicia appeared to lead him through a garden. They passed under tree ferns and ohia. The dawn trembled with fine-grained light. Two large bubbles floated before them – circular rainbows inverting tree, fern, and flower – their colors oil on air, their passage processional. Riotous sprays of orchids lined the pathway, as did calmer white and yellow ginger. Monstera hung from the trees. The shimmering stillness was palpable, the holy air surrounding a minaret of plumeria.

With her back to him, she bent over a flower. He heard the glass stem crack. She turned around, head bent shyly, and between the thumb and forefinger of her right hand held a tiny white efflorescence no larger than a pin. This she presented to Cullen, who could distinguish each petal in its lacy cluster, even the yellow stamen, and with her breath pollen drifted to his chest.

He awoke refreshed and atypically energetic, delighted to be a participant in life's daily miracle. He had always sought to achieve a certain glimmering quality of light in his bedroom, as if it were a room by the sea – specifically, a room he had dreamt once, awash in cool green patches of reflected light – and today the breeze turned the poinciana leaves in just such a way that that light was present. He recognized it as outer island light.

Once in the kitchen, however, which did in fact present a view through power lines of the far sea beyond Kahala, he was sobered by the realization that Felicia was not the sort to pick flowers or bow her head shyly. And he was equally disturbed by a further realization: that as long as she remained his student, blatant flirtation remained imprudent. He counted off the weeks until semester's end – nine – and wondered if his luck would hold, if such a girl could possibly remain unclaimed for such an eternity. He then wondered what peculiar solipsism had led to his persistent assumption that she *was* unclaimed. This led to idle speculation about any number of things. When he found himself still sitting at the breakfast bar long after breakfast, aimlessly balancing silverware on the lip of his teacup, he felt embarrassed.

It was Saturday, another blank on his calendar. He supposed he'd go swimming – that is, lounge in the sun and bathe in the sea – at Queen's Surf or Ala Moana. At Queen's Surf there would be tawny girls melting like caramels and a jetty for diving into incoming swells. Blacks would congregate beneath the giant banyan to beat African drums; pigeons would flutter and strut in the sand. At Ala Moana there would be the same female deliquescence and a reef-broken sea as placid and green as a halved avocado. The conflicting music of passing cars would wax and wane in the background. At either beach, the heat would rise through his towel and he'd lie there, halfheartedly reading a book, sandwiched between sand and sun. He'd ogle the girls and feel strangely impotent, like a fire-eater at a fire.

A flipped coin chose Queen's Surf. What mattered was that he be among people and that he not shout aloud the annoying bits of Shakespeare now popping rudely to mind like muffins from a toaster, lines such as 'O, that you were yourself!' and 'My glass shall not persuade me I am old.' Not teaching Shakespeare that term, he was surprised to be so molested.

7

He submitted midterm grades to Sister Lucia on Monday and returned to his car after work on Tuesday to find the left front tire flat. It was only six months old. And still under warranty, if he recalled correctly.

Though the arcades held few students, he felt they were watching him, waiting for him to embarrass himself by opening the trunk instead of the hood, a novel reversal of the way in which he had first embarrassed himself when still a new VW owner – by pulling into a service station and opening the hood instead of the trunk, only to discover a corpse inside, a bald spare whose pressure he dutifully checked in lieu of the oil or battery. This time he opened the hood like a man of experience and pulled out his spare tire and jack, inadvertently dispersing a small symposium of roaches. As he assembled the jack, he reviewed the difference between clockwise and counter. His biggest fear was that the pneumatically tightened lug nuts would not yield to his mere mortal exertions and that he would be made to spend the rest of the afternoon in ludicrous herculean poses. But to his delight, they did yield. Imaginary snickers subsided. This was a man who could change a tire. He twirled the iron on each lug nut. He removed the flat and threw it into the trunk – the hood – with disdain. He mounted the spare. He spun the iron with the flair of a majorette. He lowered the jack, clackety-clack, clackety-clack. The shock absorber groaned like a rusty walrus and the car slumped forward. The spare was flaccid.

When adding air to your tires, always check your spare as well. How many times had Rex Adobe reminded him of that? Still, it should hold until he reached a gas station.

He heard ominous footsteps behind him. They were coming straight toward him and would soon reach the base of his spine. He grabbed the tire iron.

'Do you have a flat?'

He turned to confront Sister Lucia.

'Oh. Hello, Sister. Yes, I have a flat. Strangely enough, it's a new tire.'

'Do you have a spare?'

'That is the spare. I've already changed it.'

'Oh. I hope you can get home on that.'

'I'll manage. By the way, Sister, I've been meaning to ask you. Did Father Plecko talk to you about some basketball players I flunked for plagiarism?'

'Oh yes. I should say so. He's talked my ear off about it. But frankly, that's between you and Father Plecko. I don't know anything about basketball. Besides, you already turned grades in, didn't you? I'm sure I submitted them to the office this morning.'

'The midterm reports. Yes. I was just wondering if Father Plecko was speaking for himself or the college.'

'He's a good friend of Coach Thornwell. I think they may have played basketball together. I'm sure he was just trying to do him a favor. But no, not for the college. Father Plecko has a mind of his own.'

That's because no one else wants it, he wished to say smugly. 'I see.' A police car pulled up behind his.

'Here's my ride. I have to be going. I hope you make it home okay.'

'I might have to jettison some freshmen papers to lighten the load, but I think I'll make it.'

'God speed. Bye bye.'

'Bye bye, Sister.' He turned and winced. He hated saying *Bye bye*, which he ranked with *kootchie koo*. He gave a final twist to each lug nut, imagining Plecko's tonsured head as a hexagon, and asked himself if it had really been wise to make that final wisecrack about freshmen papers? *Witty*? *Sarcastic*? It hadn't seemed to bother her, but one never really knew what stirred beneath the surface of that seemingly calm exterior.

From the gas station he drove straight to Rex Adobe's Tire

Center, a large sun-drenched garage in mid-Kakaako whose trademark was a mechanical caveman chiseling away at a stone not quite round. During the drive he reviewed the teachings of Rex Adobe, the gospel of tire care and the parables of tire neglect. He could say in good conscience that he had maintained proper pressure and had had no brushes with the curb. The flaccid spare was a dark spot, to be sure, but he had made it right again and would err no more. Surely Rex would honor his warranty.

The man's sincere face loomed before him, the tempered face of a Calvinist, admonishing recklessness, denouncing frivolity, but always with fatherly concern. Though the unemployment rate for actors in Honolulu approached 60 percent, Rex had always appeared personally in his TV commercials – a tall, gaunt, angular man speaking with hoarse gravity of tread, balance and proper alignment as if they were matters of moral concern. He spoke of retreads as of rebirth, but saw true redemption in steel-belted radials.

A tire had once exploded in his face, pitting it with craters, and he had ever since worn the haggard look of a brutally battered planet. He was far too tragic for television. The studio lights cast harsh shadows that settled coldly in the hollows beneath his eyes.

Life, for Rex, was earnest. Sales were earnest too. No one could turn from those haunting eyes to buy a tire of dubious tread from some fly-by-night preacher in plaids. Rex was a rock, the touchstone of integrity. Any man so sadly pocked who would suffer the indignities of television to simply announce the latest statistics on tire wear and remind viewers to always check their spares – such a man was saintly.

Cullen was given a plastic number and told to wait in the lounge while they examined his tire. The lounge was simply one part of the garage that had been partitioned with plywood and furnished with vinyl chairs and a couch, on which sat a Japanese businessman reading the *Advertiser*.

The lounge doubled as a museum of sorts. Before the couch sat a coffee table bearing, beneath layers of yellowing surfboard resin, this sign: 'This represents half of the foreign objects taken from tires.' Preserved in the tabletop were nails, screws, brads, knives, spoons, wrenches, and screwdrivers, but surprisingly no glass, forks, or fountainpens. On the lounge walls hung examples of every other object of interest ever removed from a tire. The handwritten labels read: *Stabilizer link pin*, *Truck tailgate hitch chain*, *Needle nose pliers*, *Nail clippers*, *House key*, *Unusually large nail penetration*, *Wood penetration*, *Muffler tailpipe clamp*, *Bolt*, *Bit of chainlink fence*, etc. At one end of the wall hung two tires, each a dramatic example of tire penetration. Into one a garden rake had sunk its long red nails, puncturing the very heart of a radial. Around the other a reinforcing bar had wrapped itself in a deadly embrace. According to the captions, both had been picked up on the highway. He wondered idly if anything exotic would be removed from his tire. He didn't think so. He wanted to ask the businessman what misfortune he hid behind his paper, but tact restrained him.

Then came a wall of tires that had gained notoriety in other ways. First and foremost was the famous tire that had *Exploded in Manager's face*. This was followed by *Siamese tires*, *Defective tire casing separation*, *Spare tire blew out in trunk of car*, *Tire blowout at splice section*, *Impact break*, *Sidewall damage – careless parking*, *Tube melted in tire run flat*, and *Radial tire run flat at high speed*. The last two were particularly gruesome exhibits. It was not a pretty museum, nor was it meant to be.

Cullen thought he detected a subtle logic in the display's arrangement, that what had begun as a display of fate's wicked instruments – merciless objects one might encounter on any of life's highways through no fault of one's own – had ended with the implication that owners, too, must sometimes accept responsibility for a tire's demise. He asked himself if he might be such an owner.

'Number 43.'

That was him. To his surprise, Rex Adobe himself greeted him at the counter, a gnarled, grim, wild-looking man, as tragic in person as on TV, addressing him now with wooden solemnity like one of the trees in *Snow White*.

'I'm afraid we can't honor the warranty on this tire, Sir. You see, this tire appears to have been slashed.'

'I'll be damned.'

'See right here? See that? Looks like somebody jabbed a

pocketknife in there. I'm afraid that's the kind of world we live in today. Not much aloha left anymore. We can patch this up good as new though. And I'll give you a ten percent discount because you bought it here.'

Cullen searched the sad eyes of Rex Adobe. They were honest eyes hardened by experience, by tires that blow up in one's face. He wondered if Rex had ever been foolishly in love, perhaps with a groundskeeper's daughter who was always leaving her rake on the highway.

'Okay,' said Cullen. 'Let's do that then.'

'Will do. And there's one other thing, Sir.'

'Yes?'

Rex leaned closer, as if to whisper. This would be confidential, between the two of them.

'Did you know that you have roaches in your car?'

'No. Really?'

'Honest to God. One of the boys found them in your trunk when he went to fetch your tire.'

'I'll be damned.'

'What you want to do is get yourself a couple of them fumigation bombs. Put one in the trunk and one in the passenger compartment and let 'em rip. Do it overnight. Then six weeks later, when the eggs start to hatch, do it again. That's what we do when we get 'em in the dogs' kennel. Works like a charm.'

'Okay. I'll try that. Thanks for the advice.'

'My pleasure. I see by your bumperstickers that you're a Trojan. Work at Holy Mount, do ya?

'Uh, yes. That's right.'

'Great basketball team you've got this year, especially that new kid, Plunkett. I used to play myself. Anyhow, keep up the good work. I'm a big supporter.'

Cullen drew a mental picture of a big supporter and smiled.

'Well, I don't have that much to do with the team myself. Not the athletic side, that is. I serve as sort of a liaison between the boys and their teachers. I make sure that none of the teachers get out of hand and that no one gets flunked just because he cheats or skips classes. You know, that sort of thing. I'm what they call an academic advisor.'

'Oh. I see,' said Rex Adobe.

What bumperstickers? He had always maintained a virginal bumper free of call letters, endorsements, propaganda, jokes, sexual inanities – everything except the annual safety-inspection sticker required by Oahu county. He stormed into the parking lot to discover that same bumper now besmirched by a dozen or more enthusiastic Trojan decals that seemed to leer at him like drunken Boosters. Such treachery had certainly been witty and sarcastic on somebody's part.

That night, as he lay almost asleep, something fell softly on to his eyelid. He brushed it away automatically, thinking, after the fact, that it must have been a moth. Small and delicate, it alighted once more, this time before his ear. He reached for it, crushing it gently. He felt its pulp and the dust of its wings upon his temple. He brushed it away again. He opened his eyes.

Surprise! A bright unearthly light was streaming through the window on to his chest. Why? Only the other day, while waiting in the checkout line at Safeway's, he had read in the *Weekly Planet* of alien abductors who hovered overhead, froze their victims in a beam of bright light, and by some mysterious process far beyond human understanding, transported them to their spacecraft for scientific analysis. They probed with lasers, sometimes removed organs for further study, sometimes returned them, and later deposited their unconscious subjects in a remote dumping ground or Greyhound bus terminal, where the baffled humans would later awaken uncertain of what had transpired but with an uneasy feeling that their kidneys had been reversed or their heart had been mounted sideways like a Mazda engine. Only later, sometimes years later, would the dreadful memories come rushing in, along with reporters from the *Weekly Planet*. That there were no Greyhound bus stations in Hawaii did not preclude the possibility that this spotlight on his heart served as a prelude to an abduction by aliens or, worse, something similar to the cattle mutilations sweeping western America. Still, there had to be a more plausible explanation. And there was.

He drew back the curtain above his head to discover a spectral moon in the upper branches of the poinciana. How long had it been sitting there like that, just watching? He closed his eyes. He reopened them.

Not quite round, perched high in a tree, the moon reminded him of the chiseled wheel atop Rex Adobe's mechanical sign and the Flintstone-like caveman eternally perfecting it. His thoughts soon turned to real cavemen, stocky creatures stalking woolly rhinos and mammoths and competing with bears for abodes. It was important to remember, he felt, that Palaeolithic man had never called himself Neanderthal or Cro Magnon, which were simply place names, nor was he likely to have employed Greek or Russian to label his shaggy nightmares. The reality of that human past, even the names of things, had been lost forever in the dark of the real Dark Ages. Whole eons of drudgery and endeavor lay woefully unappreciated. Hunger, fear, and cold could not be found in bones. When he spoke to his students of this, they looked at him with polite disbelief as when he assured them that Homer had been a great poet. *So*?

He turned his pillow and closed his eyes, but a small cluster of nomadic hunters continued flaking flints before a dismal fire. The agricultural revolution was a picture of an ox and a plow. Did he have that right, or would the ox have come later? That would have been about – what? – 10,000 years ago in Mesopotamia? Not so long. He liked the name Mesopotamia; it had wallowed, since high school, comfortably in his memory like some large river-dwelling mammal. *Mesopotamia* was fertile and black. *Iraq*, however, was a brittle shard of baked earth.

He was off. Contemplation of Rex Adobe's chiseled wheel led to a short thankful prayer for machines. Those driven by wind, water and muscle gave way to those driven by steam. Screws, ratchets, rivets and couplings; cranks and rods, levers and gears; pins, axles and shafts; pulleys, belts and chains; toothed wheels and flywheels, bearings and blocks; valves, springs and pistons – all rattled about in his brainpan like so many loose but essential parts. Soon he was cataloguing all the machines he used routinely without any understanding of how they actually worked. The radio, for example, which drew sound from silent air. The television, which drew images as well. The telephone, which could transmit his voice to New York instantaneously, beaming it to outer space and back. The automobile. The washing machine. The simple osterizer. It took all his strength to conjure a 747 rolling down the runway to become airborne, buoyed not by magic but by laws of nature. There was no point in even considering the complexities of the computer, the cyclotron, the X-ray machine.

And those were just technological mysteries, understood by some men if not by him. Nature was worse. Ninety percent of all known species were now extinct. Why? What miraculous force kept primavera begetting primavera, papaya papaya? Deoxyribonucleic acid? What drove that? How did a seed convert soil and water to a single green leaf? What compels elvers to swim to Europe but eels to return to the Sargasso Sea? What draws the tiny hummingbird from Maine to Yucatan or the Arctic tern from pole to pole? And in the matter of murdering nestmates, how *does* the baby cuckoo know? How does any creature know its essential role?

And alongside wonder is there not also horror – in, say, the ingestion of a lizard by a snake, or the dispatch of a hapless gazelle by a cheetah? Hunting dogs take down an antelope and devour it live. A crocodile snaps at a wildebeest and drags it under. Nature, red in tooth and claw. Tennyson had that right.

These thoughts were taking a wrong turn. He looked out the window past the budding poinciana. There was a flag on that moon, and footprints, so we must understand it. What was the latest theory, a big splash? Without the moon, some said, poised just so like a gymnast, the earth would be misaligned and thus too hot or cold. True?

He looked beyond to the heavens. If one felt of consequence in the world, which he didn't, there were always astronomical facts to underscore one's insignificance – the multitude of stars one found in any square inch of night sky, the incomprehensible distances, the queer laws of both time and space. A quasar had been newly discovered fifteen billion light years from earth. Didn't that mean, then, that we were peering fifteen billion years into the past, perhaps to the dawn of creation? If in those fifteen billion years that quasar had grown to galaxy, and if, in that galaxy, one planet circling one star had spawned not merely life but also a race of intelligent beings much like our own – a race that lived in caves and cities, that walked barefoot and flew, that beat hollow logs and beamed messages to space, that bathed in holy rivers and sundered atoms, that believed in ghosts and radio astronomy – and if that race turned its telescopes toward us, what would it see there, fifteen billion light years away – a blossoming quasar, the dawn of creation? Stupid question. There'd be no us to turn toward. It would certainly see no Earth, the light of our solar system being much too young to have reached even halfway there. Our mere existence is an idea rushing through space, struggling to announce itself.

If he could not imagine time and space coming at some point to an end, yet could not imagine time and space coming at *no* point to an end, didn't he inhabit an unimaginable world?

With one inadequacy leading so willingly to another, he soon realized it was just going to be one of those nights. There was nothing he could do to stop its swirling. There were simply too many things he failed to comprehend, too many commonplace mysteries. His complacency, never tightly knit, was unraveling.

He made trips to the bathroom and refrigerator. One feeds the body, the body extracts what it needs and excretes the rest. That was easy enough to understand. If only he did.

Soon there were teleological questions to consider, such as why humans began their lives as beautiful, vibrant creatures and ended as ugly, dessicated ones when it would obviously have been more encouraging the other way around.

And for dessert, religious questions. How could the God who plotted the universe be the same God as that of the Bible? How could the Old Testament be bound with the New? How could a saint enjoy the slightest breeze in Heaven while others roasted in Hell? At what stage of evolution did the soul appear? These last two were easy: No Hell. No Heaven. No soul. Only the unfathomable.

He heard the abrupt tick of some tiny winged creature in the lampshade. That seemed as much a soul as he.

This drove him back to the refrigerator for a beer. He sat in bed drinking from a cold green bottle. He heard the reassuring suspirations of the night's myriad insects. Things seemed in place. He liked this land where one could sleep with open windows, awash in celestial light and perfumed breezes. A yellow poinciana in the neighbors' garden smelled faintly of apricot. He liked the unspoken assurance that here he would never freeze, nor go hungry while indolent mangoes plopped sweetly from trees. Had he made a rhyme? He should write it down, because someday he was going to be a poet. If he could express only half of what rushed through his mind . . .

A knife lay on the bedside table, its blade gleaming in darkness. Funny, he hadn't left a knife there. He reached for it, cautiously, and touched not steel but moonlight. Lunacy?

The luminous culprit still sat in high branches, untouched by all he'd imagined because of it, but his luminous watch read 3.10 a.m. Like an air mattress, his sleep had been hopelessly deflated. He could no longer deny that something – something more acute than a stabilizer link pin – had punctured his well-being with an unusually deep penetration.

8

As for his embarrassment and anxiety, both failed to abate in the following weeks. He had better luck with the roaches. Following Rex Adobe's advice, he had fumigated his car with two bombs meant to render uninhabitable 1500 cubic feet of air space each. They died on their backs, like cartoon bugs.

The spring semester drew toward its inevitable close. The golden shower trees opened like Japanese fans. The first crimson flirtations appeared on his royal poinciana. Mealy bugs attacked his coleus. He was found guilty of four parking violations and fined $25 each. Louisville squeaked by Holy Mount, with Plunkett and Dhabul very much in the game despite their academic disgrace. And one day, in the last week of the term, in the last stall of the men's room, he found a shocking announcement of what some anonymous graffitiist would like to do to Felicia Mattos. It was, alas, exactly what he would like to do, but that some scum should so crudely express the same desire appalled him. He had only his trusty red laundry marker, useful for corrections, but not dark enough to expunge this obscenity forever. Burning with indignation, he drove directly to True Value Hardware and returned with a can of spray paint. When the crudity reappeared the next day, he promptly re-blackened it. When it appeared yet again, he blackened it again. The next day there was a new message: *Dr Kinnell, your dead.*

Finish the thought, thought Cullen. What had the mysterious graffitiist meant to say? *Dr Kinnell, your dead will be resurrected on Thursday?*

Dr Kinnell, your dead are taking up too much room in my solarium. Would you please be so kind as to make arrangements to remove them as soon as possible?

Or perhaps it had been something less polite.

Dr Kinnell, your dead stink.

Or *Dr Kinnell, your dead are rotting, while my dead show no sign of corruption whatsoever.*

Well, he'd never know, but the vulgarities that cojoined *fuck* and *Felicia* came to an end. He thought Duncan Plunkett, who would soon receive his official F in English, might have something to do with all this, so it was Plunkett he chose to hate.

But mostly his thoughts were turned to love. The day of the final exam found him strangely giddy, like a housewife whose knowledge of film stars has carried her to the point where she must stake her newly acquired self-defrosting refrigerator to win a living room set, a motorboat, and a trip for two to Hawaii. It was his intention to call Felicia after submitting final grades and risk all for whatever lay behind door number three. He had already started casting anticipatory glances toward the telephone. But the unexpected happened, as was its wont. Less than an hour after submitting her exam and walking out of the classroom and perhaps his life as well, she appeared cheerily in his office to present him with an analysis of his handwriting based on comments he'd written on her paper on handwriting analysis, which had contained, he'd noticed, no mention whatsoever of the little questionnaire to which he had been so happily subjected. He could barely contain his delight as she placed her findings before him.

'The angle of the slant means you let your emotions rule your reason.' She chided him darkly with those eyes whose black rings seemed to encircle him, the eyes of a secretary whose indiscreet remarks have driven a prominent congressman from office.

'Yes.'

'And the spaces mean you're very analytical.'

'Isn't that a contradiction?'

'In you, yes. These f's and g's without loops I can't quite figure out. Maybe they mean you're forceful.'

He liked that – he tried to maintain a guise of forcefulness in his classes – but if he were forceful he would've had a riposte to Sister Lucia's pronouncement that very morning that she'd be unable to provide him with any courses for the summer. Enrollments were down.

'Maybe they indicate a strong sex drive.' He had no sooner uttered this inanity than he felt like slapping himself hard on the forehead, preferably with a pickaxe.

Dark eyes chastised him. 'Not necessarily. Your downward strokes would linger more in the lower zone. Your strokes would also cut through letters in the next line, but you actually avoid letters in the next line. See how you space your words to avoid all the tails?'

Why did he do that? He supposed because it was neater. Neatness counts, he had always told his students. As for the unlooped f's and g's, he remembered having consciously adopted them a few years earlier when loops had come to seem as awkward as shoelaces tied too long or loose. At the time, it had seemed to represent a thirst for purity of form.

Purity of form: the outline of her breasts as she leaned over his desk, her blouse opening like the delicate petals of a nocturnal flower destined to close at dawn. He supposed he should offer her a seat. He did. She accepted. He offered her a macademia nut cluster from a box he kept in his desk. She accepted that, as well. He wondered how many other offers he might make without her declination. He wondered how many other offers he might make without losing his job, for the walls of his office still stopped short of the ceiling. He listened closely for signs of life on the other sides of the screens as he practiced a sort of flow-of-consciousness chatter with Felicia in the interest of detaining her further. Plecko was clearly not at home, for when not fouling the air with cigar smoke he had the errant hum of an electric football game, yet neither scent nor sound now betrayed his presence. Cullen listened hard in the direction of Sister Lucia's larger and more prestigious cell to his left, for she was usually his only company at this hour. He heard no papers shuffling, no bone chips rattling, none of the metallic clicks and whirrs that accompanied the careful grooming of her Colt .38, but in matters of eavesdropping he knew her to have the patience of a Russian submarine, and he imagined her nevertheless on the other side of that thin partition submerged in breathless anticipation of his coming indiscretion. If she *were* there, however, his unfortunate reference to his sex drive – with its suggestion of something technologically carnal, and his admission that he had one – not to mention all that loose talk about lower zones and lingering strokes, would have raised his cross already. And so he pursued his madness.

He began with the realization that Felicia had just said something about the letter K. He stared attentively into her eyes, hoping to discern just what. But she simply fell silent and gazed at him with twinkling, still amiable orbs.

'It's funny you should mention that about the letter K because . . . well, it's so damned asymmetrical, isn't it? It's not a letter one dwells on. Most calligraphers disdain it, in fact. And . . . uh . . . apart from symbolizing potassium, a rather common element really, it doesn't serve much of a meaningful . . .' A cue card in his speech center thudded heavily to the floor, face down.

'Do you remember that questionnaire I asked you to fill out a long time ago?'

'Yes.'

'There's pretty good correlation. You were a squiggle, triangle, circle, square kind of person. That's what shows up in your handwriting, especially the triangular letter forms. Here's what the book says about your choice.'

She handed him *How To Really Know Yourself Through Handwriting* by Shirl Soloman. Following the symbols squiggle, triangle, circle, square was his graphological horoscope.

> You are truly a dynamic individual, possessing all the qualities for success and leadership. You have a mind that is never at rest, but is operating in high gear all the time, generating new thoughts and images. You explore vague possibilities, bringing them into focus with keen comprehension and then proceeding to produce solid ideas.
>
> You enjoy challenges; in fact, they are a source of stimulation and pleasure. You search for a variety of areas to discharge your mental energies which are continually building up as they are being released. Receptive to new ideas, you are still too sharp-minded to become a pawn for any way-out philosophies or movements which you believe do not conform to an intelligent order.
>
> You are far from the ideal companion or mate, for you have

> spent little time developing socially, and are intolerant of the weakness of others. Because you are so highly individualistic, you rarely encounter satisfying company. The price you pay for your dynamics is loneliness.
>
> You are least motivated by the desire for security. With all your serious thinking, you would like to be able to relax with people, be playful, and enjoy more simple pleasures.

'Gee. My handwriting says all that, huh?'

'Like I said, there's pretty strong correlation.'

'Except for that part about not being the ideal companion. That probably didn't pan out, huh?'

She smiled.

'No, of course not.'

And so, though he half-wondered if these flirtations weren't simply a game student plays with teacher, he made an attempt at uttering – casually, as his heart misfired, with only slight modification – the line he had polished silently all day, scarcely imagining fate would so soon afford him the opportunity to deliver it. The snail fires its love darts, sometimes fatal.

'Listen, since it is in my character to explore vague possibilities,' *bringing them into focus with keen comprehension and then succeeding to produce solid ideas*, 'how about letting me take you out to dinner this weekend?'

It came out rather well – unbroken, unstuttered, unforgivable if overheard by a single ear pressed patiently to plywood. The silence deepened in adjoining cubicles. A snake had slithered into the compound. Vital organs switched to standby. Now he could feel the cholesterol accreting indifferently in his arteries, sense a wobbly tofu where his heart had been, review the numerous character flaws that had made him something less than aggressive – having spent so little time developing socially – in his haphazard pursuit of women.

'Really, Dr Kinnell, you must be kidding! My boyfriend would kill me! And you must be, what, at least thirty-five?' she might have said, in which case the flesh would have simply slid off his body in one giant unloved wrinkle to resemble one of those vacant walrus skins he had once told her about, but what she actually replied was simply, 'That would be nice.'

That would be nice. *That would be nice*. Yet somehow he ended up naked, shielding his genitalia with a banana leaf, begging her as dynamically as possible to please open the door.

9

Advancing behind a banana leaf and shielding his derriere with same, he asked himself how he had come to such a state, he who had so recently been fully clothed, honor and dignity intact. To begin with, there were incontrovertible facts: that somewhere between her acceptance of his invitation and the actual arrival of this miraculous evening, she had called to ask if he wouldn't prefer to go instead to her girlfriend Melanie's house for a dinner party, not her first house but her second – this house, before which he now stood like Adam flushed from Eden – a country house on the sea, near Hauula; that he had accepted, flattered by the thought that she would not be ashamed to show him to her friends; that she had driven to his house (to avoid showing him to her parents?) and that Melanie had picked them up there in what, to Cullen's untrained eye, was more or less a Lincoln Continental. Melanie had worn a large floppy hat and matching body, and had been accompanied by a local boy named Kimo.

The interior of the car had smelled wonderful, like a saddlery, or tannery, or Old World library, and he'd remarked to Felicia that he'd like to be buried in such a car, a possibility not at all remote given the large floppy way Melanie was handling the curves on the coastal highway, reaching at the same time for the joint in circulation, and always turning her head to do so. 'Puna buds,' said Kimo as he passed it, inhaling his words proudly and holding them in.

'Ah, Auslese Pakalolo,' had replied Cullen, to no one's amusement or understanding. Now, in retrospect, it made no sense even to him; it was one of those tropical nerve impulses that swim through the brain like fluorescent yet illusory fish. But it also seemed to have been jointly understood by those in attendance that while Cullen, being an English Instructor, would occasionally utter the incomprehensible, such behavior was not to be viewed with alarm.

Shortly after Chinaman's Hat he had begun uttering, without preface or explanation – and he saw this now as telling – his rendition of the classic student composition of the 70s.

'Marijuana, hashish, grass, pot, reefer, dope and marijuana are a few names given to preparations that are prepared from a herbaceous weed called *Cannibal saliva.* When growing in a hot climate, like one's backyard, cannibal secretes a resinous resin as a defense against the hotness of the climate. In which it grows. It is this resinous material, tetrahydracannibal, better known as THC, that contains the pleasant affects associated with the smoking of the plant. The usual techniques for smoking marijuana is . . .'

He had applied some of these singular techniques and had discovered that they did indeed lead to 'pleasant affects', as well as to effects not easily classified. Two inner voices seemed to compete for his attention. One spoke to him as always – cajoling, reassuring, caustic, funny, frightened, calm – while a second ranted unintelligibly in the corner, occasionally uttering a whole cryptic sentence that circled in the echoes of the first like a cawing crow. It was stronger dope than what Alice had smoked, yet smoother than Light Brigade. He wondered how Melanie could drive at all when it was all he could do to keep from projecting himself astrally out of the roof. At times he would look to his right and see nothing but inky sea far below and the occasional rock jauntily catapulted into the abyss. It was a paved highway, but he heard at every curve the disparaging crunch of loose gravel and felt somewhere in the void of his ribcage the disheartening thump of each rock and rut. Sometimes the narrow verge would reappear at a proper distance and he would resume breathing, but then it would rush toward the car like a mongrel and throw itself under the tires. None of this, however, had successfully impinged upon his pleasure. Life had simply grown precious and transcendental.

Felicia had sat on the side of the car that would be the last to slide over the cliff. She seemed quite relaxed there, happy to be with him. She described to Melanie and Kimo what a lark his

English class had been. She quoted verbatim a line from Roland Plumley that he himself had almost forgotten: 'To many women, their bodies are very important to them.'

'I hear they never go anywhere without them,' quipped Cullen. 'Like hermit crabs and shells.'

She'd told stories about the lecherous cops in the evening classes, which had launched Cullen's random recitation of great lines from adult education – e.g., 'One of the hardest things to teach the toddler as well as the small kitten is where to dispose of their bowels' – and had led to his singing, out loud and unabashedly, Kinky Friedman's 'Homo Erectus', a song about an upstanding university student who finds himself staunchly in love with a lady professor of anthropology.

Yes, in retrospect, the signs had all been posted: Caution – Dangerous Verve, No Passing Joints, Fasten Your Clothes. The amazing thing was that they had lived – he, Felicia, Melanie and Kimo – strangers united by fate. It was not the dope but the irrepressible joy of survival that had made him so reckless upon arrival. The sun had just set. Though it was Melanie's house, or rather that of her absent parents, the soirée was already in progress when they pulled into the driveway. He had been introduced to several guests, young people who seemed accustomed to having beachfront homes to themselves. They all sat in lawnchairs on the lawn. Drinks had been served, palm trees rustled like crepe paper props for a prom, and at the edge of the lawn lay the ocean.

'This bud's for you,' said Felicia, passing him a roach on a clip. 'Wanna go skinnydipping?'

This momentarily concussed him. He found himself staring at a coconut while his neurons pulsed furiously to consider the linguistic possibilities.

Wanda goes knee dipping?

Improperly stressed.

Wanna go skin a chicken?

Unlikely.

Won ton goatskin bao bing?

No. What he had heard, he was almost certain, was *Wanna go skinnydipping*?

It had been no more than forty minutes ago that he had replied

'Yes, I do' – seeing the invitation as a sort of dare, not to mention opportunity – yet it had already taken on the air of improbable memory, more dream than reality. She had disrobed right in front of him, within twenty feet of the other guests. It was already dark, the last light blotted out by the Koolaus, and the night air seemed to oscillate like frenzied gnats as his eyes pulsed between seeing what they saw and what they imagined. He followed her back and buttocks into the sea. He discovered that he was holding his trousers and that only his undershorts stood between him and Eden. The other guests were polite about it, conversing without interruption, tactfully ignoring them. He dropped his trousers, stepped out of his shorts and into the ocean, felt not sand but pebbles at his feet, and swam to her side as soon as the water reached his thighs.

'Hi.'

He smiled. The pali loomed close here, a sheer verdant cliff rising four hundred feet or more. Black clouds shot over it like ink from a squid. They stood in a small sandy pocket surrounded by coral. There were, he realized, mammals well adapted to life in the sea, and even people for whom swimming and drowning were antonyms, but Cullen was a terra firma kind of guy who, when in water, liked to confirm every minute or so that one could walk out of it. Fortunately, Felicia showed no inclination to venture further into that black incognito of ocean and reef that lay beyond her naked shoulders.

She took his hands. Swells buoyed them, lifted them sometimes off their feet and deposited them gently elsewhere. The water drew their weightless bodies together and apart in an aquatic poussette that mated sole and calf, knee and thigh. It was better than dancing naked in a mare on the moon. Well it would be, wouldn't it, since here they could breathe, not explode, etc. And though erotic, though Cullen danced with a third leg that could find no footing, it was a strangely innocent dance, the immense black canvas of the sea placing nudes in their proper perspective.

'I'll take you to my favorite cove someday.'

'Where's that?' he asked.

'Near Sandy. You'll see.'

He hadn't kissed her because, he realized now, he'd been too shy.

Too soon it had started to shower. The guests had fled like kudu. But why a shower should faze people both wet and naked remains one of the human mysteries. The ocean seemed colder, wetter, suddenly inhospitable. When they stepped out of it on to the lawn, they discovered that someone, in a fit of thoughtfulness, had taken their clothes inside. A single beachtowel hung on the clothesline. Felicia grabbed it and ran to the house.

At first he'd feared a conspiracy, a student-plotted humiliation in which the entire basketball team would leap from the bushes with Polaroids. But, with the exception of Felicia, none of the guests were Trojans; they were Melanie's friends from the beach and university. Furthermore, he had seen Felicia's breasts, had discovered that they were upturned, like the green bananas on the plant he'd soon denude; had discovered that they floated symmetrically, nipple-high, dark buoys in a dark sea. He had therefore already reaped more benefits than a conspiracy could possibly negate. He was drunk, one with swaying palms and undulant sea. He was stoned, one with the Precambrian and a good-natured God. He was being rained upon. Not maliciously, perhaps, but nevertheless wetly, rain having a cumulative effect. He was suddenly chilled – by the innumerable ways he could now be embarrassed and ridiculed. He wrestled the banana plant for two of its leaves.

He had come as far as the door. This should answer once and for all, he thought, the question of shyness. He could hear Santana, steel drums and marimbas. Holding both leaves to his chest, he cautiously turned the doorknob.

Locked.

He took a deep breath of salt air. The outside light, fortunately, was off. But it could be turned on. Then he knocked. In all his imaginings regarding his first date with Felicia, the picture of him naked had arisen only in conjunction with Felicia naked. In such reveries, both nudes were recumbent and often entangled. Dress and/or remove Felicia and one still had a recumbent Cullen – golden candlelight, perhaps, warming his sated flesh. Naked and erect, yes, he had so imagined himself, but he had meant something more noble – more Ionic, Corinthian, or Doric. Naked and erect, standing in a gentle yet nevertheless damp drizzle, clutching at foliage like some primitive food-gathering pithecanthropoid – no, the image had never materialized.

At the same time, however, he was stunned to discover that he was not quivering with gelatinous trepidation. He felt a certain dark-rum bravado coupled with a doper's perception of the world as a colloidal suspension of inconstant bits of matter in a strangely veridical dream. It was the perfect mix – this alchemy of uppers and downers, speed and sloth – to provide the right edge for night patrol. The modern combat soldier, equipped with infrared, he saw through the door the heat of moving bodies. One approached, a magenta flambé growing larger. It was too late now; there'd be no turning back. He stiffened his pluck. But as the door opened an amber crack, he was suddenly filled with nothing more assertive than a soft, billowy longing for his clothes. He imagined them spinning in slow motion in the dryer, as warm and freshly scented as lovers gamboling among wildflowers.

'Yes?'

'Felicia?'

She opened the door as wide as her face. It was adorable. He was smitten. She spied his banana leaves and laughed.

'Come on in out of the rain.'

And that was all there was to it. She could have salted him with ridicule and watched him squirm like a slug, but she hadn't. She could have made him beg. But instead, she'd shown mercy. She was a goddess of light. She opened the door to his triumphal entry, laughter and cheers from her and a roomful of strangers. 'Oye Como Va,' sang Santana. It seemed sympathetic enough, not at all the prelude to human sacrifice he'd envisioned as one possibility. The Incas had drugged their victims with beer before burying them alive. But he was greeted as one who had worn an imaginative costume to a party where no one else had. And what made it more bearable was the fact that the room was lit by the glow of a single blowfish rather than the battery of floodlights he'd envisioned as a second possibility. Furthermore, the party had distributed itself equitably throughout the house, leaving only a small contingent of guests – hardly enough for a good stoning – in this first room furthest from the sea. Why, he wondered, as he inched toward the bathroom under Felicia's guidance, was she not attached to one of those finely sculpted lads in the kitchen, where they might have been filming a beer commercial.

Banana leaves are large, cold testes small. Backing into the bathroom, the salty wooden sort littered with seashells and starfish, he'd suffered no breach of etiquette.

'I'll bring your clothes,' she said, closing the door behind her.

He propped his banana leaves proudly beside the toilet and turned on the shower. All was going remarkably well. He lathered up a body that was at least trim if not muscular. It was nothing to be ashamed of; he'd seen worse in natural history museums. He liked, especially, his legs, streaked now with suds and tanned from afternoons of losing tennis. In a New York winter, their pallor would have humbled him. This was better. When Felicia reappeared, bearing his clothes, he felt as if he'd passed through some rite of initiation. The cult of the Portuguese coed.

'Don't be long. Dinner's almost ready.'

'Okay.'

This seemed intimate already, almost marital. She hadn't even knocked. As the door closed behind her, leaving him alone in a strange shower stall by the sea, he felt a new Cullen Kinnell emerging like Triton from unsuspected depths. Confidence, he reminded himself, was what women admired most in a man. And each new lover provided a fresh opportunity to fake it.

Upon his belated entry into the dining room, where all the guests had noisily seated themselves around an immensely long table, Melanie slipped a Foster's into his hand. He accepted it as a well-deserved accolade. His new lover smiled from halfway down the table, where she had saved him a seat.

'Have a nice shower?'

'Yes, thank you. Just the thing.'

'Suck 'em up.'

She was referring to the spread of sashimi, teriyaki, mock huli huli chicken, sweet and sour pork, Chinese vegetables, steaming rice, freshly sliced pineapple, tropical fruit salad, and shredded carrots with raisins. Ravenous, he said hardly a word throughout dinner except to express appreciation.

The other guests remained indescribably young, some local but most haole, a blur of brown-haired girls in airy dresses and blond boys in sun-bleached aloha shirts. His own shirt had a penguin on it, a totem which carried some significance for his mother, who had sent him a penguin necktie as well.

After a dessert of lilikoi chiffon pie, the ubiquitous joint was circulated at a time when sobriety was within Cullen's reach. He succumbed, again, to temptation. Later he found himself in the kitchen with Felicia and a tanned, muscular boy named Steve. Like a spider, Steve had descended some invisible filament from above, for Cullen had neither noticed him at dinner nor witnessed his entrance, yet there he suddenly was, *deus ex machina*, conversing familiarly with Felicia while speaking volumes with his disgustingly azure eyes. Something about Steve's demeanor disturbed Cullen. Perhaps it was the way Steve ignored him as if he were merely one of the appliances, a life-sized device for holding a beer. Was it inconceivable to the lad that the not quite geriatric gent before him, a member of the Penguin Club, had that very evening waddled into the sea nude to sport and cavort with the very girl now smiling so impenetrably at him (being polite or receptive, amused or seductive – Cullen couldn't really tell)? It also disturbed him that Steve *knew* Felicia, or seemed to. How long? How well? *Oh hell*, thought Cullen.

'Yeah,' said Felicia. This was something she'd been saying with alarming regularity. In fact, it was all she'd been saying, all that seemed necessary to keep young Steve careening onward with his paradiddling jabber. It was a measure of Cullen's condition that he had no idea what Steve was talking about. Of what wocky did this jabber consist? He tuned in.

'. . . fantastic. I can't describe it. It's like being inside . . . I don't know, I can't describe it, there's nothing else like it. It's so glassy and green, you know? You just have to experience it.'

'Do you work in a greenhouse?' asked Cullen.

'Wot?'

'Do you work in a greenhouse?'

'No, I work in the Sheraton Waikiki. Why?'

Felicia was looking at Cullen oddly.

'Oh, nothing. I was just in a greenhouse the other day and I thought maybe I saw you there. Working.'

'No, man, I wasn't in no greenhouse.'

'Sorry. Didn't mean to interrupt.'

Steve resumed, but with the rhythm of his dribble broken by this unexpected sweatslick. Still, Cullen couldn't read Felicia's response to this fumbling drive down court, and he doubted that Steve could either. He assumed her smile to be as perfunctory as that on neatly balled socks, but he had to admit that he didn't actually know much about the girl, only that he wanted her and that while he continued to want her she would perhaps come slowly into focus, a police drawing whose features grow increasingly more accurate. The friends she kept, the dope she smoked, the way she waded into a dark sea nude – all were contributing to the picture. But whatever the picture, his final wish would be to apprehend her, frisk her, hold her without bail and press charges. Of that much he was certain. He had a lot of mental energies continuously building up that needed to be discharged.

And so, in pursuit of love, to prove he was neither jealous nor possessive, he slipped quietly out of the kitchen to the lanai. All the other guests had drifted into small isobars in and around the house. The rain had ceased. The lanai had the wild salt smell of the windward side, of crabs scuttling, kelp rotting. Clusters of green sea grapes grew on either side. Sitting on the sea wall, he surveyed the raw sea chopping at the black rocks before him. There was no beach. The moon, rising to his right, was a large golden sliver between clouds and horizon. Warm moon, constant sea, leaning palms – this was the romance of the tropics.

He wondered what might be transpiring in the kitchen. It seemed important that Felicia come to him, be drawn to him like a leaf to the vortex of a whirlpool, which was how he could now best envision himself. Though he gazed at the moon toasting the clouds, he had only one thought, one desire: that when she next appeared, it should be at his side. It was a matter of principle. He had resolved not to turn around; he would simply sit on the sea wall and stare at the great Pacific, trusting animal magnetism to do the rest. Life, he knew, was unpredictable. At this very moment liver flukes from the sashimi might be burrowing cozily into his vital organ, settling down for a long night's rest before undertaking the arduous task of destroying it. Or Steve's tongue might be insinuating its way into the mouth of the woman who had given him an erection in this very sea now gilded with moonlight, this sea of shimmering fish scales and beckoning depths. The indifference of the sea was profound. It was exactly what one expected of a large body of water. White ribbons of surf materialized and vanished.

It would be tragic to have come this far, to have shed his clothes for love, to have braved the sea and rain and the social unknown, only to lose her on account of some stoned vagary. Great dope ideas, he mused tentatively, wondering if this was one of them, were like colorful stones that lose the very luster that has led one to retrieve them. But as he tried to focus on the stream in which he imagined such stones, he found himself instead on the bottom of the sea peering at an undulating bouquet of meat-red tube-worms. This came from reading too much *National Geographic*. Unbidden images were always popping into his mind, though in *National Geographic* the worms had looked more like worms and less like wanton penises.

Perhaps he was being too passive. He could return to the kitchen on the pretext of getting a beer. If he threw this beer away, that is. Or drank it.

He heard approaching footsteps. A dress rustled quite near.

'Isn't it nice out here? Melanie and I come out here a lot.'

'It's beautiful.'

She sat down beside him, neither illusion nor accident, and gazed upon the same gilded sea. She smelled of gardenia. A bass guitar began to throb within the house. The windows shivered.

It was about 2.30 when Melanie returned them both to his cottage. There they sat in Felicia's Vega darting their tongues into each other's mouths with a passion surpassing even that of anteaters violating the tender heart of a nest. This went on for a long time until she said it mustn't any longer, she really had to be going.

'Okay,' he said in that breathy whisper with which lovers inflate the simplest word. He kissed her goodbye. 'Thanks for a lovely evening.'

'I'll call you.'

She would call him.

He watched her glide down the hill, past the night-blooming cereus, then returned to his cottage to sing a few songs recklessly before the mirror.

10

Yet in subsequent conversations with Felicia – summer conversations now, conversations that should have led somewhere – he felt his every honest word betray him, weaken him, dangle before her laughter. Her kisses were like her eyes: round, warm, capricious. She'd come to his house in the afternoons and leave unseduced. She seemed content to gossip about family and friends, return his kisses, gossip some more. She'd often drop by with Melanie while enroute elsewhere. Mammoth even in her muumuu, Melanie would flump on to his punai and stay there. He liked her; she seemed to travel through life with the aimless languor of unclaimed luggage. She admired his jazz collection, so he'd entertain the two of them with gin and tonics, music and idle conversation.

It was during these afternoon visits that he discovered Felicia's inordinate fondness for crackseed. Often she'd sit nibbling something like Yick Lung's Salty Plum until nothing remained in the cellophane but round brown raindrops splattered on a dirty windshield. The sticky stuff made him uneasy. It was like having a child in the house. Alice had always eaten wholesome, fibrous snacks of stoneground doormats.

It was not unusual on such afternoons for Melanie to fish deep into her handbag and hook a hefty joint. She never seemed to know if there was one in there or not, so it was always a pleasant surprise when, after trolling the depths, she reeled in her admirable trophy. Cullen called her a Hemingway of handbags. Soon after, she and Felicia would depart in the Lincoln Continental he now knew to be a Cordoba, leaving him beached on his own stony island. And that felt too much like loneliness, a desert island circled by sun and surf. He realized he was slowly reverting to character, losing whatever bravado he'd banked early on.

So Felicia came and went, visited his embrace and withdrew, in a performance that made little distinction between coyness and mockery. It was now more than embarrassment that he suffered; it was self-incrimination. After weeks of wrestling with elusive emotions, he wished to grasp something tangible and strangle it.

Then one bright June afternoon she arrived unannounced to ask if he'd like to go swimming – she had a special place. She seemed to operate on the assumption that she could interrupt him at any time of day and he would drop whatever he was doing – in this case, the dishes – to entertain her.

They took her Vega.

Cullen thought he knew the southeastern coastline pretty well, that short nameless stretch, neither windward nor leeward, running from Hanauma to Makapuu. Running it through his mind, he began with the turn above Hanauma where, on good days, one first sees Molokai across a treacherous channel. Kalanianaole winds through desolate heaps of black lava – Koko Head above, muscled waves bashing a broken coastline below – and soon reaches the first turnoff, a lookout perched above Halona Blowhole. The waves churn against a broad lava shelf and a whistling waterspout shoots intermittently from the blowhole. Then the road descends to Sandy, a surfer's beach despite its onshore wave breaks. It then speeds through desert while gradually veering from the ocean, though as it climbs it affords a more expansive view. Lava outcroppings mark the shoreline. Panini cacti crowd the highway all the way to Makapuu Lookout, from which he had once seen a giant redwood wash like a corpse into the rugged bay below.

He thought he knew the coastline well, but Felicia changed his map of it. She parked the car in the desert.

'Here?'

'Here.'

They crossed the wasteland, towels and sodas in hand. By the time they reached the coast, the sodas were warm. A modest breeze blew off the ocean.

The coastline was, as it had appeared from the highway, a coastline of lava. What had not been visible was a shallow pocket-cove lined with white sand. Miniature swells swept diamonds of sunlight across turquoise water. It was an exposed place, naked beneath a blue sky, but from the road it had been invisible.

'I told you I'd bring you here someday.'

'This is great. Is it always so deserted?'

'Any time I've been here. This is where the tradewinds divide.'

He wanted to ask with whom she had been here, but thought better of it. He had a whole battery of such questions that could not be broached until they were lovers.

She stepped out of her sandals and unbuttoned her blouse. He sat to remove his sneakers and socks. The mere sight of her lacy black bra aroused him. Why should a white bra be utilitarian and wholesome, while a black bra promised illicit pleasure? It made no sense. She disrobed with a casual grace he admired, slipping off dress and panties simultaneously as if they were mere lingerie. The bra was last to go. She drew both arms behind her, unfastened its clasp, and allowed it to fall from her shoulders. Two slender bands of white marked the shape of her absent bikini. He hadn't seen her naked since their first date. She was in the water before he finished unbuttoning his shirt. He slipped off his trunks. It was embarrassing to enter the water with an erection – women always knew what men were thinking – but there was nothing for it. Earl had once told him (and why should this occur to him now?) that in Japan there were hardy souls who toughened their penises by dousing them with cold water and pounding them with stones. He'd have to try that someday. He swam to her side. *Déjà vu.*

'Look! There's Molokai.'

'Yup. It's always there. You can usually see it from here.'

That was another thing he liked about the islands: one saw further. One followed a slowly shrinking ship to the horizon, a crisp line where blue meets blue, not an oppressive muddle of earth and cloud. One tracked the moon in a pristine sky. The day began with a sunrise, and ended with a sunset. These were visible events, not rumors.

They swam – did the backstroke, the sidestroke, the breast-stroke, moved underwater like porpoises or, in Cullen's case, an old sea turtle – and the sunlight swam over their swimming bodies, cool white light divorced from all heat. Once, as they swam in slow motion toward the mouth of the cove, an indescribably striped fish with large head and bright yellow lips appeared from nowhere, stopped, swam off.

'That was a Humuhumunukunukuapua'a!' cried Felicia when they rose for air. 'I could swear it.'

'Here? You think so? Let's look it up when we get back. I've got a book on fish.'

'You've got a book on everything.'

She pulled the sodas into the water to cool them. He swam behind her and fondled her breasts. She leaned her head next to his and floated.

It was amazing. Those fleeing Honolulu come to this, the easternmost point of the island, and the road tells them nothing is here and turns them gently back again like children. But the road deceives; here lies an undiscovered cove for lovers.

He kept a sharp eye for intruders. A gang of vacationing Hell's Angels could spoil everything. Twice fishermen rounded the distant point and passed without incident. The cove belonged to Cullen and Felicia, a single treeless piece of paradise the rich had overlooked. A new lover, a new world.

'Do you like it?' she asked, wrapping her arms around his neck.

'I love it.' He wanted to elaborate upon what else he loved, but restrained himself. Instead, he kissed her and swept her weightless body off its feet. They fondled each other into a passion, until she said, meaningfully, 'Let's go back to your place.'

There they salaciously showered. Without her make-up, she looked like a girl. She kissed him on the chest and gave his cock a friendly squeeze, his poor cock that had been pulsing all day like a wind sock in a hurricane. It was more pleasure than man was meant to bear, but he bore it, the hot shower working almost as well as a cold one. He soaped up her buttocks, then gently massaged her pubic hair. In old Japan (Earl had once told him), women were bought that way, by feeling their pubic hair while they themselves stood blindfolded before potential owners. To achieve a desirable softness, their hair had been ground with pumice, for in that strange country stones that harden men soften women. Felicia's hair felt downy. He kissed her, water pouring over them like a wet dream. He led her from the shower to the bedroom, where they dried each other perfunctorily and clutched in a damp embrace. They did the backstroke, the sidestroke, the breaststroke. 'Fuck me,' she said dreamily, which shocked him so much that he did. Her ear tasted of salt, and as he kissed her he was weightless once more in their cove.

When their passions subsided, they lay together in his purple sheets, she singing a Linda Ronstadt song while staring at the ceiling. Like a breeze through a forest, he had passed through her.

'Love Has No Pride,' he said.

She turned the pillow. 'Know what I like about this place?'

'What?'

'It has a very masculine smell.'

'It does?'

'Mmm. I noticed it the first time I stepped in the door. You can tell a man lives here.'

'You can?'

'Absolutely. It was like walking into a lion's den.'

'Lions are both sexes.'

'A male lion's den.'

So, thought Cullen, score one for Alice, who had first alerted him to this remarkable aptitude of women to smell what men cannot. He hadn't quite believed her. She'd claimed, cupping a small milky pool in her hand, that it smelled like chestnut flowers. He'd never smelled chestnut flowers and wondered if that scent, too, existed only for women. They could smell it, the male ambergris, as surely as a salmon smells her river in the sea. The pillows must have been impregnated with it. It was tantalizing to think of his cottage as a giant chestnut flower luring women with seductive exudations, though he envisioned instead a wild, slippery-throated Arum lily with an inner chamber of sticky sweet sap.

He produced his book on tropical fish and turned to Humuhumunukunukuapua'a. And there was their fish, as improbable as its name, yellow-lipped with a blue mustache, all head and belly, with three tourmaline stripes running vertically past its eye, and a single dash of red below its gill. A triggerfish, so called for its ability to raise its first dorsal fin and lock it into place with its *trigger*, or sliding dorsal spine, wedging itself in its nest. *Humuhumu*: to fit pieces together. *Nukunukuapua'a*: nose like a pig. Felicia was delighted, as if its sighting had been auspicious.

'We should go to Hanauma Bay,' she said.

'What's at Hanauma Bay?'

'The best snorkeling on the island.'

They swam often at their cove, while summer days passed as aimlessly as the wisps of clouds dispersed between horizons. At other times, she'd come to his house, sit in his rattan chair, cross her legs, raise her long dress above her knees, and flash her naughty arrogant eyes in what seemed as much a challenge as an invitation. This was usually in the late afternoon – a time, apparently, when her mother trusted her, and a time when he should have been returning from job interviews. In the city, men and women were working, laboring toward future goals and for the betterment of mankind. But not at Cullen's. He found his downward strokes lingering more and more in the lower zone.

Not wishing to appear too Pavlovian, he responded warily to her coyness, feigning coyness himself, feigning a shared awareness of what they were up to. He was, however, in the habit of wearing jogging shorts about the house and could but ill conceal his enthusiasm. The mere hum of her wings aroused him.

At first it was awkward to seduce her as she sat enthroned. He could approach her from behind, kissing her ear and unbuttoning her blouse, or he could kneel at her feet and slide his hand under her dress. In either case she'd continue chattering, even as he stroked her, about her mother's suspicions and newly imposed curfews, about her father's obsession with the care and maintenance of his Ford Fairlane, about the sexual misadventures of Melanie, who had badly sunburned herself in pursuit of a surfer, about her plans to seek employment and get her own apartment, about the recurring sensation of being held down in her sleep. At times she'd slap his hands and scold him, accusing him of taking no interest in what she was saying. Or she'd simply say, 'Down, Rover.' But he soon learned the unnatural art of forcefulness, discovered her protestations to be mere sham.

Whereas most women spurred desire with breathy *yes*'s, Felicia, he discovered, employed coquettish *no*'s.

He learned to take her as she wanted, with a breathless violence that slapped her against bed, wall or floor until she abandoned her chatter for hoarse honest cries, writhing shamelessly in that swamp of scratches, moans and kisses. It was her only surrender. *Rape*, he recalled, shared the same root as *rapture*. When she succumbed to her pleasure, when she cried out for it, she was, for a while, truly his – a convulsive she-devil he had to mount and break for the privilege of such brief possession.

But when it was over, it was over, and time to do something else. Usually she played – singing, tickling, pinching, punching, asking, while she pushed him from bed, how many steaks in a cow. Sometimes she'd make him up – she'd had some experience in high school theater – and he'd become whatever suited her fancy: a cat, a vampire, a clown.

None of this was quite what he'd expected. Though admittedly not the most experienced of men, he *had* bedded women who had surrendered completely, their eyes a watery gray, a silent entreaty – the eyes of prisoners hoping for the best. And when they'd talked, they'd told everything. They'd nestled in his arms and confessed. He'd thought all women were like that, hopeless romantics at heart. Felicia, however, felt no compunction to utter the passionate idiocies he longed to hear, asked no baited questions, failed to cast her eyes longingly into immeasurable distances.

To Cullen, who played along for lack of an alternative, her playfulness was a violation of something sacrosanct – the calm after the storm, the tranquil drift through another body, the aftermath when two souls lay perfectly entwined while the sounds of breeze-blown leaves, passing traffic, and a single distant hammer bind the world together. He was ready to fall through secret dream passages as opposed to on the floor. He was eager to indulge his melancholia, his memories, and the strange jumble of icons representing his life to date. Felicia, on the other hand, believed that what properly followed sex was a pajama party. For her, mattress served as trampoline.

'Me hungry,' she growled one typical afternoon. 'Opu rumble.

Plenty pilikia. Number Ten on Richter Scale.'

'There's nothing. Really. Look for yourself. It's a wasteland. Ice and mayonnaise as far as the eye can see.'

'It's a Frigidaire.'

'It's empty.'

Barking, she went for his neck, bit him, tickled him, jabbed him once in the ribs for good measure. A bumper car bearing the license POST-COITAL DEPRESSION whalloped him on his blind side.

'This is like making love to the Three Stooges,' he cried.

'Learn to love it.'

Once, when they climaxed, the hilltop tsunami alert screamed into action and all the neighboring dogs set to howling in unison.

'The earth moved,' said Felicia.

Or shook with laughter, thought Cullen.

Paradoxically, he was happy. Precariously happy, like one who has almost mastered the art of tightrope walking, but happy nonetheless. He supposed he could play her game, follow her lead. He liked, after all, what was in her eyes: naughtiness, a glittering licentious pool of it. His other lovers had been staid by comparison. He couldn't keep his hands off her. Eventually, given the limits of human endeavor, both would settle down. Then she'd torture him in other ways.

Hardly a day passed, for example, in which she failed to lodge some complaint against the latest male to make a distasteful pass: the 'kanaka' who'd grabbed at her ass on Bethel Street; her haole dentist, who, finding nothing wrong with her teeth, had jokingly offered to drill elsewhere; the black who'd approached her at the beach, reaching out once to slide his orange palm along her leg. He seethed as she detailed each incident and wondered sometimes if she didn't embellish these tales to torment him. But he supposed them to be true, having frequently witnessed her predictable effect on his sadly predictable gender. Felicia's passage could not go unnoticed. Life was suddenly dangerous in a way it had never been with Alice or, for that matter, any other woman.

Once, while he escorted her from house to car, they had been peppered by the obscenities of the local garbagemen. A victim of his own poor timing, he was shocked to hear the words 'sweet pussy', the very words he had been confiding to her ear in sexual delirium less than an hour before. According to Mr Ching, who had considered filing a complaint with the city for damaged garbage cans, the largest of these beasts had amused himself in Oahu Prison by tearing quarters in half. His smiling face, on which Cullen chose not to linger, now shone as dark and oily as kukui. These were the kind of men who would turn a broomstick into an instrument of torture, the kind of men who had never known a mother's love, the kind of men from which men like Cullen had to protect girls like Felicia.

'Assholes,' he thought vehemently.

And still came the raucous taunts and wolf calls as they deftly dumped garbage and tossed away cans with disdain. He was feeling especially vulnerable with a Charlie Chaplin mustache beneath his nose, a magic-marker creation Felicia had penned impulsively as a final amusement. It was not the first time he'd succumbed to her make-up artistry, but it was the first time he'd allowed her to lure him into public, not that he'd felt at great risk before his own abode. Both were a wee bit stoned. 'Pebbled,' as Felicia called it. They ran the garbage gauntlet silently and indignantly, saving their epithets for the car, where Cullen sat in the passenger seat until the garbage departed.

'Men are animals, you know that?'

This was one of her common themes. She seemed to scorn males in general, depicting them as leering buffoons who either shout their obscenities from passing cars or whisper them over dinner.

'Yes.' He felt a sudden longing for his pipe, but it was in the cottage. 'I should've overturned the truck.'

'You couldn't do anything. I'm used to it.'

She was right, of course, but that was just it: he couldn't do anything. He wondered if he should carry a gun, like Sister Lucia. With a gun, and a little practice, he could mutilate his own quarters. With a gun, one could shoot strangers or graze impertinent friends. A gun was something he'd actually suggest to Felicia in his worst moments of impotent anguish – a lovable Undercoverette with which to discourage flirtation. It was not outrageous to suggest that an attractive woman who brought out the worst in men should carry some form of protection. He envisioned her wheeling on Bethel Street to shoot the ass-grabber dead, threatening to drill her dentist full of holes if he didn't rinse his filthy mouth with Clorox, reaching into her beach bag and with platinum-plated authority and six-chambered persuasiveness telling the orange-palmed black to be sure to *fuck off*. Guns put people neatly in their places, some of which bore tombstones. What they lacked in neatness, they made up for in finality.

Yes, she should carry a gun and so should he and together they should shoot any flirtatious males too dumb to see that she belonged to him and only him and that he'd go crazy if that should ever change.

11

Felicia arrived early, with her sunglasses nested in her hair, a black shawl draped over her shoulders, and a large bowl in her hands.

'Here,' she said, looking beyond him. 'When will your friends be here?'

'Soon. Thanks. It looks great.'

'I made avocado. That's okay, yeah?'

'Yeah, sure. I'm making moussaka.'

'Smells good.'

She didn't follow him past the breakfast bar into the kitchen. Instead, she rearranged a picture of herself that sat on the shelf and, as was her custom, drifted from room to room in search of changes, secrets, significant clues to Cullen, as if his life changed with the daily mail. He, meanwhile, felt as transparent as an elver. Soon she'd grow bored and dump him.

While sprinkling cinnamon, he heard unexpected music, flute notes rising miraculously, like lunar moths, nameless at first but soon familiar. This was a new development. Normally she would have first requested permission, then chosen Fleetwood Mac or Linda Ronstadt.

'Jeremy Steig? Jazz? What am I to make of this?'

'I'm just trying to get into it, that's all. Don't jack your hopes up.'

'How 'bout a Pina Colada?'

'I was wondering when you were going to offer me a drink.'

She sat on the lanai to read the *Star Bulletin*, while hibiscus shadows lengthened across the sloping lawn. The royal poinciana above her had come into full bloom, an annual scarlet upheaval, and Java finches, natty in gray, conversed among its branches.

They quarreled a lot, he'd noted over the years.

'Jeeez,' she said. 'Did you read about this guy who sexually molested a six-month-old baby?'

'I don't want to hear it.'

'What do you mean, you don't want to hear it? You don't have any choice. This is reality.'

'That's why I don't want to hear it.'

'What kind of pervert would do a thing like that?'

'I don't know. I don't understand. When I think about it, my mind goes blank.'

'Guys like this should be disemboweled.'

If one sought happiness, it was not to be found in the newspaper. Before she could extract any more grim reality, the doorbell rang. It was Earl. At his side stood a frail Japanese schoolgirl he introduced as Laura.

'A little gift,' she said, presenting Cullen with an assortment of cheeses.

'Thank you. That's very kind of you.'

For once, thought Cullen, he had outdone Earl in women. Laura was cute but pale and undernourished. Her sleeveless dress revealed thin arms the color of mochi. She lacked the feline sensuality of the arch Felicia, whose tan was growing daily darker.

'And this must be the lovely Felicia,' said Earl.

She didn't deny it.

'Cullen's told me all about you. It seems you've ruined his tennis game. The boy's completely infarcted. Can't move anymore. He wanders the back line reciting sonnets, for Christ's sake.'

'Cullen's sweet.'

'So is molasses.'

'Now that we've got all the social niceties out of the way, why don't you sit down and let me get you something to drink. I've got rum, gin, pineapple juice, coke, tonic water, all the makings of a Pina Colada, Mai Tai, Daiquiri, Cuba Libre, Gin and Tonic . . .'

'Nothing for me, thanks,' said Laura.

This was too Japanese for Cullen. Empty-handed guests seemed subversive.

'Not even a little pineapple juice?'

'Oh . . . Okay. That would be nice, thank you.'

'I'll take whatever you're having,' said Earl.

Ernest and Claire arrived shortly thereafter.

'It's mango season,' she said, offering him not one pie but two. 'Our tree's loaded with them.'

'Thanks. But why two?'

'One for tonight, one for later. I'm telling you, we have beaucoup mangoes.'

'There was a two-for-one sale at the Yum Yum Tree,' said Ernest.

'Nooo,' said Claire, elbowing him gently.

'Naw, I'm just kidding,' said Ernest. 'You know how mango trees are. They can't do enough for you. They just don't know when to quit.' He smiled at those he hadn't met.

Cullen drew them into the living room and made all the necessary introductions.

'Is that a Pina Colada you're drinking?' Ernest asked Felicia.

'Yes.'

'Ohhh,' he intoned, casting a dreamy glance at Cullen.

'I'll make you one. Claire?'

'I'd love one. But easy on the rum, please.'

She followed him into the kitchen.

'I'm afraid this pie didn't turn out very good.'

'Looks fine to me. What's wrong with it?'

'I don't know. I haven't tasted it yet. I think it's lacking something esthetically.'

Despite two years of law school, she still sometimes sounded the traditional Japanese note of apology. He noticed it at times on the telephone, the kind of bowing intonation that conveyed a proud humility. Bring her a present and she'd suffer a week debating the proper reciprocation.

'Well, yeah, now that you mention it, I see what you mean.' He held one pie at eye-level and turned it slowly. 'Round. I mean really, Claire, what an unimaginative shape for a pie. And this crust, it's so flaky. Can't you do anything to control it?'

'Okay,' she said.

Deprived of an apology, she looked about for something to compliment. 'Your plants sure are flourishing. Do you talk to them?'

'No. Just cast meaningful glances.'

He caught Felicia casting a meaningful glance from her seat. Not that he knew the meaning. It might have been that he was alone in the kitchen with Claire, it might have been that he had left her to fend for herself, or it might have been neither or both. At any rate, disaster struck soon after that.

All the guests had seated themselves about the tiny living room and the conversation had taken on the promising crackling of kindling, a good sign when one has assembled a roomful of strangers. But an invisible mudslide passed swiftly through the house when he served Laura's cheese platter and Earl, having helped himself, innocently lodged a kitchen knife in a ball of Gouda.

'Don't do that,' said Felicia darkly.

'Don't do what?'

'Don't stick a knife like that.'

'Like what?'

'Like that.'

'Why not?'

'Because it brings bad luck, okay?' And with that she'd reached over and removed the offending knife herself.

It was as quiet as a second wedding.

Cullen disliked the open contempt in Earl's eyes, but he had to share their amazement. He had never quite imagined this of Felicia. Bad luck? She might have more credibly claimed that it violated the tenets of the Council of Trent. He tried to think of something clever to say that would clear the room of debris, but words failed him. It was Claire who finally said, 'My grandmother believes something like that, too. She says you should never stick your chopsticks in your rice.'

'A sentiment I've long shared,' said Cullen.

'Why does she say that?' asked Earl.

'It invites ghosts into the house.'

'*So deska*. Do they like rice?'

'And cheese,' offered Ernest.

Felicia was wearing a fixed, wire-thin smile that could have sliced cheddar.

'Actually,' said Cullen, 'Mary Pukui says they live on moths.'

'Live on?' questioned Ernest.

'Well, sure. Ghosts live on, don't they?'

'The willowy ones might eat moths,' said Earl, 'but the chain-rattlers eat geckoes.'

'How about the ones that rattle coat hangers?'

'Oh, he told me that story!' exclaimed Laura, suddenly animated.

'Cigarette butts and used prophylactics,' sneered Earl. And since he had not told his tale to the others, it was necessary to do so during dinner, which was served on the darkening lanai. Felicia, still visibly perturbed, subjected him to a rigorous cross-examination. She wanted names and dates and seemed upset that he was able to provide them. Naturally Ernest and Claire followed suit with a description of their own encounters, a description that now seemed as perfectly polished as their geodes.

'Any recent developments?' asked Cullen.

'Spooky feelings,' said Claire.

'Short-lived light bulbs,' added Ernest.

'Glowing lights in the cemetery.'

'Cold drafts.'

'Have you considered having the house blessed?' asked Felicia of Claire.

'Then it might be repossessed,' said Ernest, eliciting an affectionate frown from his wife and a communal groan from the others.

'Who would do it?' asked Claire. 'A Chinese priest?'

'I guess so.'

'I'm ready to try anything. What do you think, Ern?'

'I think we should drive them out with firecrackers. Violence is the only thing these ghosts understand.'

'Laura has a good ghost story,' said Earl.

'I do?'

'The story about your brother.'

'At the heiau, you mean?'

'Yeah.'

'Do I have to?'

'Yes.'

She tucked her eyeballs into the upper left corner of their

sockets and looked at Claire. It was the kind of look one local girl might exchange with another. It said 'Aren't haole men the most exasperating creatures?' But she no longer seemed *hasukashi* – shy as an ingrown toenail. Cullen had pegged her all wrong.

'So, this is a secondhand story, yeah? My brother told it to me. You've got to understand that my brother has never told a lie in his life. And he's not the kind to talk story. Anyway, he's a photographer on the Big Island. That's where I'm from – Waimea. One day he had an assignment to shoot a heiau for a record jacket. The heiau was way down in Kalapana. He wanted to shoot it at dawn, so he decided to just spend the night there. He said he got down there "round midnight".'

'Make it one o'clock,' said Earl. 'Cullen has an irrational prejudice against ghost stories set at midnight.'

'Okay. One o'clock. But it was really midnight. Anyway, there was a stone ruin there and he sat down in the corner of it. He said the walls were only a few feet high and it had four entrances, one on each side. It was a kukui moon, full and bright. He was looking at the grass in the middle of the ruin, not doing anything really, but every once in a while he thought he saw a shadow moving across the grass, like something was flying over it. A moonshadow, yeah? He looked up to see if he could see anything. And a couple minutes later he did see something. He said it was just a form, sort of egg-shaped but not really any shape at all. He said these forms kept flying into the ruin. After a while he got this very strong vibe that he wasn't really welcomed there, so he crawled over to the door and walked out. Once he was outside, he couldn't see anything. He sat in his car for a while and tried to sleep, but then he decided to go back in.'

'Why?'

'He wanted to see if he could capture anything on film. You'd have to know my brother. Anyway, he walked back to the same entrance, but when he tried to walk through it, something stopped him. He said it was like a force field. He tried the other entrances, but it was always the same. He was locked out. So he spent the rest of the night in his car. And all night long he kept having the same dream over and over. He was in exactly the same place, inside his car. Then he heard the sound of laughter coming toward the heiau, not just one person but a lot. He didn't see anybody though. But when it got close, the laughter stopped and he saw a dog. He said it walked in a straight line behind the car. But when it got directly behind, it started running toward him, and when it reached him it wasn't a dog anymore but a Hawaiian warrior. The warrior looked at him, then started to reach through the window, but that's when Dwight, my brother, always woke up. He said he had that same dream four times that night. In the morning it was okay, he could go back inside the heiau. That's the end of the story. Pau.'

'Whew! Did he get his pictures?'

'Of the heiau, yeah. Not of the ghosts.'

'That laughing that he heard – isn't that supposed to be the first sign of the headless army?' asked Ernest.

'That's what I told him! That shook him up a little. You look at the headless army, you die.'

'And wasn't there supposed to be some Hawaiian god that could take the shape of a dog? I know one of them was a wild boar.'

'I don't know. It wouldn't surprise me any.'

'Your brother's a gutsy guy,' said Cullen. 'I wouldn't stick around to have that dream four times.'

'Oh yeah. He always has been. But you hear a lot of stories like that on the Big Island.'

From that point on, all further conversation, no matter how desultory, was subsumed under the general heading of Big Island. All but Felicia had been there.

Laura spoke, with some coaxing, of her family's roots on the island, of how her great-grandmother had been a picture bride whose husband, when she arrived, was already dying of dysentery. From that point on, she'd been known on the coffee plantation as 'the picture widow'. She eventually married the dead man's brother and gave him four children, one of whom became a fisherman and Laura's grandfather. His only son fought in World War Two in the famous 442nd. He fought his way up the boot of Italy, fought in the Vosges to rescue the 'lost battalion', won medals, survived disasters, and returned whole to Hilo to marry his high-school sweetheart. Four months later he disappeared at sea. His wife had some good news she wanted to share with him as soon as he returned from that fishing trip. They were going to have a baby.

'And here I am,' said Laura. 'A quirk of fate.'

'But I thought you had an older brother.'

'Not older, younger. He's my half-brother. Earl knows him.'

'I knew him a long time ago. He used to help us cut calves at the ranch.'

'You have a ranch on the Big Island?' asked Claire.

'Used to. We had a ranch in Kohala.'

'What do you mean cut calves?' asked Ernest.

'Castrate 'em. Cut 'em off at the pass.'

'No kidding. How do you do that?'

'Well, it's a three-man job. One man locks the front legs, another spreads the rear legs, and the third man cuts off the unnecessary appendage, as my dad used to call it. And do they thank you for it? Nooo.'

'I wouldn't want to be the poor bastard that cuts,' said Ernest.

'You wouldn't want to be the poor bastard that spreads 'em either. They shit green all over you and kick like it ain't fun.'

'And which poor bastard were you?'

'A little of each. I bled 'em and I spread 'em.'

'Can I eat my dinner?' asked Claire.

'Really.'

'I always thought I detected a faint odor of cow manure.'

'Cullen, you'd be a real man today if you'd had some mountain oysters as a young 'un. That's why Dwight wasn't afraid of no heiau. Balls build hormones.'

'You ate them?' asked Claire.

'With a dash of Worcestershire.'

'That's a lot of bull,' said Laura straightfaced, and Cullen and Ernest cracked up.

'What *did* you do with the trimmings?' asked Ernest.

'Well, we didn't perform a memorial service or anything.'

'And why do you have to castrate them?'

'Because a bull's an expensive proposition. You can't afford to keep a whole bunch of bulls, and it would just ruin your herd if you did. Nowadays you don't even need a bull; you can collect semen from someone else's bull and inseminate artificially. I think that's gonna catch on.'

'Excuse my ignorance, here. I'm just a city boy. But exactly how do you collect semen from a bull?'

'Oh, first you arouse him, and then you apply an electric shock to his testicles.'

'Um, how do you arouse him?'

'Well, you don't show him filthy pictures or anything. You use your hand. You show him a good time.'

'I'm eating,' insisted Claire.

'Disgusting,' said Cullen.

'Every job has its perks.'

'Are these your best memories of the Big Island?'

'No, not the best. Just the most vivid. My best memory . . . well, *gau gee* – maybe fishing off Kona with my old man and catching a 150-pound swordfish when I was sixteen. He was so proud of that fish he had it stuffed and mounted. No, that's not my best memory. My best memory was the day my mother tried to skewer him on it during one of their domestic quarrels. Just grabbed it off the wall and started chasing after him like it was loaded or something.'

No one knew if this was true or not, though Cullen, who'd heard it before, suspected it might be. He was keeping silent about his own memories of the Big Island since all had resulted from a four-day excursion with Alice. He recalled driving the Puna Coast road in the rain, both stoned as balloonfish. He remembered a state cabin in Volcano dwarfed by tree ferns. Kilauea had not been erupting, so they'd merely stood on its rim and peered into its smoldering desolation. At the Kona Hotel in Holualoa, the rooms could only be locked from within. From theirs they had witnessed, for the first and last time, the famous green flash at sunset, a viridescent mirage so brief they'd later questioned whether they'd seen it at all. In the morning, the proprietors had sent them off with a bulging bag of avocados that took two hands to carry. *Avocado*, come to think of it, derived from the Nahuatl word for testicle. Felicia had brought mountain oyster salad!

'What I remember best is the volcano,' said Claire. 'That's what sets the Big Island apart from all the others. It was steaming a lot, but we didn't see any action. But still, it's a fantastic feeling just to know you're standing on top of a live volcano. I can't believe they built a whole town up there. Don't they worry?'

'Volcano's safe,' said Laura. 'It's that crazy Royal Gardens that keeps getting wiped out by lava. What a place to build a housing development, yeah?'

'My folks used to own a cabin in Volcano,' said Earl. 'They never seemed to worry. It's a slow, laid-back sort of volcano. It runs on Hawaiian Time. It usually gives plenty warning when it's gonna blow. The pressure builds, the ground swells . . . It's like a Sumo wrestler eating his tenth bowl of chankonabe. You know what's coming.'

'Besides,' said Laura, changing the tone, 'Volcano has to be one of the most beautiful places on earth. And for sure one of the most mysterious.'

'Why mysterious?'

'Hard to explain. The fog, the rain forest, the way the tree ferns grow higher than the houses . . . But mostly Pele and the other Hawaiian spirits. You can still feel them over there. Do you remember the last eruption?'

'Sure.'

'That was spooky. I was spending the night in Volcano with my girlfriend Kumi. She works in Volcano House. Anyway, about two in the morning we were awakened by tremors. We got out of bed to see if anything was going on outside. And then we saw this tremendous white light flash across the sky. And soon after that, Halemaumau erupted. Nobody knows what caused that flash. We weren't the only ones who saw it. Some people at the observatory said it might have been a meteor, but I've never seen a meteor like that. It was low. It lit up the whole bedroom. Kumi thinks it was Pele. She's supposed to travel like that, you know, in a fireball.'

'I guess everybody has their own superstitions,' said Felicia. Coming from one long silent, this pronouncement struck like a snakebite. Laura tried to measure its venom.

'Yes, I guess they do.'

'Let's have dessert,' suggested Cullen cheerfully, rising to the occasion in order to escape it. 'Claire brought some rather unesthetic mango pie, but if we cover it with ice cream nobody will notice. And there's coffee if anyone wants it.'

Claire joined him in the kitchen to administer her pie.

'Felicia's very lovely.'

'Thanks. That's about the best one could say for her this evening.'

'She feels on display. She thinks we're here to judge her. I understand it.'

'I guess.'

'Can we heat this up a little?'

'Sure.'

Putting the pie in the oven, he recalled that Claire had sighted her first ghost beneath her mango tree. Yet another example of how their food reflected their conversation. She crossed her arms and stood on one leg, dangling one high-heeled shoe behind her, in a pose that struck him as more secretarial than judicial. She looked lovely in lavender. Her glance meant something, but he had no idea what. Was it something about Felicia? Might it be that a girl like that was all wrong for a guy like him?

'Is Felicia Portuguese?'

'Yeah. Why?'

'Nothing. I was just wondering. I thought I remembered you saying something to that effect. I'm surprised how young she is.'

'You think?'

'Mmm.'

'Too young?'

'No. I'm not saying that. Don't get defensive. And I'm sure she's a very nice girl and all. It's just that I keep thinking that what you need is someone who's not only beautiful, but also as well read and cultured as you are . . . someone – and please don't take this wrong – but someone on the same intellectual plateau.'

'You're already taken.'

She said it all with her eyes: *I'm flattered, you're joking, don't do that.*

'I think what I like about her,' he said, 'apart from the obvious interactive bits' – he made a vague gesture with his hands as if carding wool – 'is her vitality. Which, I must admit, is not particularly in evidence this evening. But usually she's a psychic battery charger.'

'Then that's good.'

'*I* think so.'

'By the way, how did you fare in your trial?'

'Oh, I lost. About a hundred dollars. The cop showed up.'

'I know.'

'The neat thing, though, is that just before my trial there was a deaf and dumb trial.'

'Meaning?'

'Meaning the defendant was deaf and dumb and so was his witness. So the whole trial had to be conducted in sign language.'

'That must have taken a while.'

'Oh yeah. The prosecutor was totally futless. In the end, he asked the judge to dismiss the charges, which he did, even though the witness was lying through her fingernails, so Kushimoto wasn't as heartless as you said. Unfortunately, I was the next one up. I guess he couldn't be merciful twice in a row. The sequel to this story, however, is the defendant and the witness just got married. I saw their picture in this week's *Star Bulletin*. He's a Samoan the size of Diamond Head and she's this little haole lady you could hide under a tea cozy.'

'See? Who's to say who's right for whom? But imagine their marital arguments.'

'You say that as if arguments are inevitable. Do you and Ernest argue?'

'Sure. Two different cultures? You bet we argue. Arguments in sign language, though – that would be different. You could just leave the room and you wouldn't even hear him yelling.'

'Ernest yells at you?' Ernest heard this and strode slowly toward the kitchen.

'Sure. And I yell at Ernest. That's what an argument is.'

'I can't picture you yelling at anyone.'

'Yeah. I know.'

'Of course, you yelled at that ghost, didn't you.'

'Yeah,' she smiled. 'I yelled at the ghost.'

'Someday, Cullen,' said Ernest, 'on a wild and crazy whim, you'll put in your shopping cart a pint of Amaretto Almond Frozen Yoghurt – or maybe it will be a bag of Oreo cookies that you used to eat as a kid and you're thinking, "Gee, I wonder if they still taste the same." Someday you'll put this impulsive selection into your cart and saunter leisurely down the aisle, checking out new products and old, imagining what joys each might afford, perhaps accepting the mental challenge of determining which is cheaper, 6.5 ounces for 57¢ or 12 for $1.04, when WHAMMO! – out of nowhere comes this strange wild-eyed woman who reaches into your cart, grabs your Oreos – or Amaretto Almond Yoghurt, whichever the case may be – and says, arrogantly, and loud enough for all to hear, "Put this back." Just like that: "Put this back."

'*Who is this woman*? you'll ask yourself. *Who is this woman? Who is she to stand between me and my Oreos? Just who the hell does she think she is? I want my Oreos. I want my childhood memories. I want my Amaretto Almond. I want a new taste sensation. I don't need anyone's permission. I'm thirty-two years old!*

'Ah, but don't bother calling the cops. They can't help you. Don't appeal to the manager. He doesn't want to get involved. Don't reach for another pack of Oreos. You'll only cause a scene. Don't stamp your feet or break down weeping. It will all be to no avail. Because that woman, Cullen, that woman who has snatched away your taste sensation, that woman will be your lawful wedded wife. There's no point fighting it. There's no point offering resistance. There's no point pulling from your pocket a wad of dough thick enough to choke a tax collector. That's moot. It's irrelevant. Immaterial.

'What I'm trying to tell you, Cullen, as your friend and counsel, is that in marriage there's no such thing as defeasance. Once you're married, you've waived your constitutional rights. The law can't help you. You've entered a lawless land where only the strong survive. Did you see *Midnight Express*? And the only baksheesh that can buy back your freedom is a chunk of moola as big as your house and car called alimony.

'I just wanted to share this with you in case you had any thought of giving up your sacred bachelorhood.'

'Thanks, Ern. I'll keep that in mind'

'Ernest is just overreacting to one little incident at Foodland,' said Claire. 'Don't pay any attention to him.'

Mango and nutmeg, cinnamon and ginger – the scent of Claire's pie soon asserted itself. They ate dessert on the lanai, the stars burning coolly above them. The night was fully upon them now, though not so darkly that one could not distinguish Diamond Head, the one blot darker than the sea. This was not the classic silhouette but the rear view exposing the crater. A romantic landscape upon his arrival, Diamond Head had since become for Cullen something more domestic, the scene of rock concerts and the home of the National Guard. He saw it now as a stage prop, or an old ruin none would dare demolish. It had never, of course, contained a single diamond.

The evening ended with a short walk uphill to the park, where all reclined on the grass to view the city lights, those of Saint Louis sweeping off the mountain to Lower Manoa and Waikiki. They pulsed like harbor lights, or floating candles, such was their affinity for the sea. High-rises rose like boxed constellations, and a moving ribbon of red and white clearly marked the freeway. Honolulu had become a modern metropolis, a twenty-four-hour city. At any time of the day or night, one could stand on a hilltop and trace its features, pointing to places that had mattered, the scene of a first or last encounter, the setting for a friendship or tryst. And in the sky, just over the coast or in some far corner, one could usually sight a plane, which had flown or would fly a great distance. He could not imagine himself ever boarding such a plane to begin life anew somewhere else.

His guests seemed calmed by the shimmering wings of their city. There were no more disparaging words, and all later departed in peace.

'So, I guess they didn't like me,' said Felicia.

'Why do you say that?'

'I'm too immature for them.'

'Nonsense. These things take time. Claire told me in the kitchen that she thought you were very nice.'

'I've got to go soon.'

So, his friends didn't care for his lover; his lover felt threatened by his friends. Something like that. It would all sort itself out in the long run. Love conquers all. Felicia departed shortly thereafter, promising to return the next evening, a welcome reassurance. And that was the last day in Cullen's life that he lived in total ignorance of the dead man who featured in hers.

12

It was the very next evening when he unearthed Uncle Ricardo. They lay in bed, already sated. A crack of dull light from his bathroom fell through her hair, illuminating strands of auburn, russet, blonde. It was as he brushed that autumnal hair from her eyes that something occurred to him.

'Have you ever known anyone who died?'

Her eyes fixed him warily.

'I mean . . . before you started having the feeling of something holding you down . . . in the middle of the night, the invisible . . . Do you remember anyone dying? A neighbor, or relative?'

'Yes.'

'Who?'

'Uncle Ricardo. He died when I was four years old.' She smiled, remembering something.

'What?'

'He always used to call me his little booger. I thought that was just the nicest thing in the whole world.'

'Booger?'

'Yeah. Booger. Like in your nose.' She smiled broadly, not lifting her head from the pillow. 'He always treated me like a princess. Maybe because I was the youngest. Or maybe because I was the cutest.' She laughed. 'He always brought me sticky black licorice, which Mom hated, and he used to put me on his knees and play Charley Went To Boston.'

'I remember that!

Charley went to Boston
To get a loaf of bread,

And when Charley got there,
Charley fell *dead*!'

He recalled plummeting giddily through his father's knees whenever the rhyme had reached its unvarying, but sometimes delayed, conclusion.

'Right. I was crazy about Uncle Ricardo.'

'How did he die?'

'Very strange. He was married to Aunt Maria, Mom's sister. And one day he just left her and ran off to South America to be a sailor. This was long before I was born. And then, about ten years later, one day out of the blue he calls up Aunt Maria and says he wants to come home to die. Can you imagine? "I'm dying. I want to come home." And she took him back! I can see why though: he was really handsome – tanned and muscular – a real Latin lover type.' This she embellished with a suggestive cocking of her eyebrows. It was one of her seductive traits, this sudden dramatic posturing as if dancing the tango. 'When he came back he had two tattoos: one of a sea serpent and one of a heart with a woman's name inside. One on each bicep.' She flexed a muscle. 'Our whole family liked him, even though he ran away from Aunt Maria and used to slap her around a bit after he came back to Honolulu. He was always insanely jealous. There was a rumor that he'd shot a woman in Argentina for being unfaithful to him. Or that he'd done something awful with a knife. Who knows? He even cussed out Aunt Maria for taking other lovers while he was away. Can you believe that? It was really stupid. Even so, the whole family usually sided with him in an argument.'

'Maybe they just felt sorry for him because they knew he was dying.'

'Ahh! But here comes the good part. He wasn't sick! Nobody ever told him he was gonna die, it was his own idea! It was just something he felt. After he'd been back for about six months he realized he wasn't dead, so he went to the doctor for a physical and the doctor told him he was perfectly healthy. He asked the doctor to check his heart and the doctor said his heart was fine.'

'Maybe he checked the wrong one. Okay, okay. So how did he die?'

She seemed to be studying the ceiling.

'He died of a heart attack in our living room two weeks later.'

'In your living room! Were you there?'

'I was sleeping. All I remember is my parents taking me to the funeral and holding me over the coffin to kiss the corpse.'

'Is that a Portagee tradition?'

'That's a Port*uguese* tradition. Yeah.'

He groaned in disgust. And noted the wild scent with which she had filled the bed. Her scent was tropical, the warm, steamy fragrance that rises from a rain forest floor.

He could hear the barely audible sounds of the Chings' television, the rhythms of dialogue and laughter that bore no resemblance whatsoever to the commerce of life as he knew it. The Chings, though wealthier, were not living life as fully as he. He pulled her closer.

'This corpse-kissing stuff turns me on.'

'It's just like kissing a tombstone. You don't feel anything.'

'Did you cry?'

'Sure I cried. I loved him.'

'And you remember all this?'

'What I don't remember I know. Uncle Ricardo was a legend.'

It offended him that she should have such feeling for a man who had beaten and abandoned his wife, returning only to repeat the offense, but the story that had come out of the near dark seemed to provide a vital clue. He touched the back of his hand to her cheek, and leaning over, kissed her lightly. Every way in which he touched her now was an act of restraint. He felt foolish for loving such a girl.

Cheap red wine, the scent of extinguished candles, empty yellow-lit buses parked in a row on Koko Head, the chubby Vietnamese waitress at the Kuhio (tipped well and smiling roundly), huge white cereus blooming at midnight, the city lights, sudden rains – these and a thousand other things sought reflection in her eyes, an assurance that they were being shared romantically. But her eyes darted this way and that, waterskaters across a pond – playful, laughing, mocking – or, if still, still as now, merely distant, remembering a private past.

She returned his kiss perfunctorily and continued the story he thought she'd already finished. She told it slowly now.

'About two weeks after the funeral . . . my folks were just sitting around in the living room reading the newspaper, and my sister was doing homework or something . . . it had just gotten dark and I went into my bedroom. I was too small to reach the lightswitch by myself, so my father had set up a little stool for me to stand on. I was just about to step on the stool when someone lifted me on to it instead. It was a strange feeling, because I knew it couldn't be my parents. Imagine you're standing in a room all alone and suddenly you feel two big hands lifting you into the air. My little heart skipped a beat. I turned around, and who should I see but Uncle Ricardo. He was stooping over me, holding out his arms and making smooching sounds. He was smiling real happy like, and he said, "Come here, little booger, give Uncle Ricardo a big kiss! Come here." He looked as real as you do right now.

'I ran into the living room screaming. My mother says I was so blue I could hardly breathe. I was so frightened, Cullen. I already kissed him once after he died and I wasn't gonna do it again. It was like he was calling me to the land of the dead, like he wanted me to join him. I was terrified. For a week I had to sleep in Dana's room with a light on.'

'What did you tell your parents?'

'I told them I saw Uncle Ricardo. They believed me. They heard him, too, but they couldn't understand what he was saying. Besides, two weeks later Dana had a conversation with him when she woke up and saw him sitting at the foot of her bed. She's much braver about these things than I am.'

'What did they talk about?'

'Nothing special. He just asked her about school and stuff like that. Said he missed smoking. Said he was lonely.'

'Missed smoking. Why didn't you mention this last night? You had the best ghost story of all.'

'In front of that asshole? Are you kidding?'

'In front of what asshole?'

'Your so-called friend. Mr Castration!'

'Earl?'

'That guy doesn't even like you.'

'What makes you think that?'

'He was putting you down all night.'

'He's just sarcastic, that's all. He doesn't mean anything by it. The rest of us would have liked to have heard your story. You hardly said a word the whole evening.'

'I didn't feel like it. It's personal. Those guys were all talking about complete strangers. Uncle Ricardo wasn't a stranger. He was family. It's different.'

'Was that the last time anyone saw him, that time he talked to your sister?'

'Yes. Mother had the house blessed after that. She also had it fumigated.'

Fumigated! He suddenly recalled that he had never set off the second wave of bombs as Rex Adobe had advised.

13

He met her mother soon after the start of fall term, after rehearsing with Felicia a number of necessary lies that would restore his youthfulness and erase his record of summer unemployment.

'Mom, this is Cullen. Cullen, this is Mom.'

'Hello, Mrs Mattos. Nice to meet you.'

'Oh, hello.' She held one hand to her cross. 'You're Cullen?'

'Yes,' he said guiltily.

She was a soft, squat woman with a face of old snow. Deep in her visage glowed her eyes, sad Catholic grottoes that seemed to burn candles for the dead.

'Cullen teaches English at Holy Mount, Mom.'

'Oh? What do you teach?'

'English.'

'Oh. Where are you from?'

'New York.'

'You have family there?'

'My mother lives there.'

'Your father?'

'He's deceased.'

'Oh, I'm sorry. In New York?'

He supposed his father to be deceased not only in New York but in all other forty-seven contiguous states as well, equally void in Alaska and Hawaii, not to mention *muerto* in Puerto Rico.

'Yes. He died there and he's buried there, if that's what you mean.'

She nodded, her mouth still hanging open in ill-suppressed astonishment. Something about him perplexed her, though she looked like a woman who'd been fuddled before. Was it his age?

His financial status? Or could she, through merely a glance, divine his soul?

'Would you like a Coke, Cullen?' asked Felicia.

He hesitated, uncertain which answer would rescue him and which would leave him stranded with her mother.

'No, thanks.'

Dressed, like beef, in burgundy, Mrs Mattos stood guard before a tragically green couch, the picture window behind her framed by raised blinds and heavy spinach-colored drapes smothering bouquets of broccoli in their folds. Yellowing doilies lay on equally green armchairs, a TV tuned soundlessly to a game show sat on a dark mahogany altar, and at the far end of the room stood a walnut dining room ensemble backed by a wall of cumbersome credenzas. So this was the house Felicia had grown up in. It was large – from the Fifties, he guessed – and admitted much light, which more or less offset the funereal furnishings. He wondered where Uncle Ricardo had had his heart attack.

'I'm going to show Cullen the backyard, Mom.'

'Okay. It's such a mess right now.'

'We'll be right back.'

He followed her past the credenzas to the kitchen. Here Felicia had made her mark. Penned directly on the door jamb next to the wall phone was a disorderly list of names and numbers. His own was there, and southeast of that was 'Steve 737 2223'.

She led him to the back door.

'I don't think she likes me.'

'That's just her way. Dogs sniff strangers, my mother—'

'Wait a minute. Don't move. There's a—'

'Oh, hi Dad. Dad, this is Cullen, the English teacher? Cullen, this is Dad.'

'Hi, Cullen! Glad to meet ya.'

'Hi, Mr Mattos. Glad to meet you.'

'Felicia's told me a lot about you.'

'Oh?' *Like what*?

'Like mangoes?'

'Love 'em.'

'Like 'em in bread?'

'Absolutely. In bread, pie, smoothies, on cereal, *au naturel*, as an aftershave. I love 'em.'

'Heh heh. Well what we've got here, as you can see, is a lot of mangoes.' He raised his eyes to the flourishing tree above them. 'I was just picking some. Some people are allergic, that's why I asked. We had a neighbor once who broke out something terrible whenever this tree was in flower. Just breathing the air. He looked like he was stung by jellyfish.'

'That was Mr Kwok,' explained Felicia. 'He owned a clock store. Kwok's Clocks.'

'That's right. Mr Kwok. Tick Tock Kwok. He wanted me to chop this tree down. But I told him this tree was here when Kaimuki was still an ostrich farm. He didn't believe any of that. Anyhow, I'll pick you a bag to take home. We've got more than we know what to do with. And I'll get the Missus to make you one of her special mango breads.'

'Thanks. Sounds great.'

Felicia beamed, proud of her old man, who poked a long-handled picker into one of the tree's upper branches, positioned the blade around a mango stem, pulled the cord and caught the fruit in the sack rigged for that purpose. He worked in khaki pants and sleeveless undershirt bulging at the waist. He had reached the age of no pretensions. He retrieved the mango – firm, with a blush of red on one side.

'Isn't that a beauty?'

Accustomed to picking his mangoes out of the street and washing the ants from their ruptures, Cullen agreed that it was indeed a beauty. He could see now that Mr Mattos was not the wealthy plumbing contractor he'd first imagined but merely, as Felicia herself had put it, 'a pipefitter who manages to make both ends meet'. She'd described him as a man forever puttering between garage and backyard. Repairing things. Growing things. Improving things. And he proved a man of his word. Cullen left that evening with a bag of firm, ripe, sweet sappy mangoes, and two days later Felicia appeared with the promised bread.

'You really hit it off with Dad.'

'I did? How 'bout Mom?' *Whose relation to you, by the way, stands as a clear refutation of Darwin's claim that the evolutionary process is a gradual one.*

'She respects you for being a professor but distrusts you for being an untenured one.'

'That's fair.'

'She doesn't like you, Cullen. By the way, if I'm going to be a passenger in your car, Mom would like you to hang this on the mirror.'

'What is it?'

'A St Christopher medal, like the one in my Vega.'

'He doesn't have tenure either, you know.'

'What does that mean?'

'He lost his canonization. He's not a saint anymore. The Pope said he was away from home too much.'

'Just hang it on the mirror.'

'Sure. I used to get these free from my brother. He ran a wrecking service.'

'You don't have a brother.'

He felt something like sawdust at the back of his throat, a dry, raw itching sensation. It brought tears to his eyes as he tried to speak.

'What's wrong? You *don't* have a brother, do you?'

'No,' he laughed, eyes ludicrously wet. 'I think I'm getting a sore throat.'

'How about one of your mango daiquiris?'

'Sure.' He went into the kitchen and promptly washed the blender.

She plopped her purse authoritatively on the breakfast bar and wandered over to inspect his desk.

'Whereat with blade, with bloody, blameful blade,
He bravely broached his boiling bloody breast.'

She was reading aloud from his typewriter.

'What the hell is that?'

'Shakespeare. *Midsummer Night's Dream*.' He *was* teaching Shakespeare this term, one of three preparations and easily the most painful given the double barriers that English and the sixteenth century presented to his students.

'That's bloody blimey awful.'

'What?' He was skinning mangoes under a running faucet.

'That's awful!'

'It was meant to be. He's making fun of high-flown rhetoric.'

'And the letter B?'

'Excessive use of, yes.'

She continued to poke about his desk, but could find nothing else suspicious.

He added a couple of jiggers of rum and some ice to the orange pulp in the blender, then pressed 3. He had purchased a three-speed blender after comparison shopping had revealed that BLEND, CHOP, GRATE, GRIND, MIX, STIR, PUREE, WHIP, FRAPPÉ, LIQUEFY and all the other forms of intimidation appeared in different orders in different brands. They were purely arbitrary! His had only numbers: 1, 2 & 3. He could imagine them to be anything he wanted. CHURN, CHEW, & CRENELLATE. MOLEST, CASTRATE, & DISEMBOWEL. A LITTLE, MORE, & A LOT.

When he returned to the living room, Felicia was once again enthroned in her favorite armchair.

'Here you go.'

'Thanks.'

He sat in the matching chair. It was six in the afternoon, bright and warm, and through the open glass doors that led to the backyard he could see two mejiros flitting flirtatiously in the papaya trees.

Felicia was depressed. Her sunglasses sat despondently atop her head. She withdrew a yellow joint from her purse, rolled the way women roll joints, pregnant as a guppy.

'If I smoke that, I won't get any work done tonight.'

'I'm not going to let you get any work done tonight.'

'But I've got to. I've got to get this stuff reproduced tomorrow.'

'Can I hear that Weather Report album?'

He put *Mysterious Traveller* on the turntable. 'I thought you didn't like this.'

'I said I was ambivalent.'

He smiled and sipped his daiquiri. *Ambivalent*, he felt certain, was a word she'd adopted in his class. She filled the air with pungent blue smoke. It was the earthy aroma that seduced him, the promise of mystic revelations. A weed was, after all, of the earth, and the earth was a mysterious body. They were smoking the spirit of a place: of Puna, Kona, or Maui. They were parting five-fingered leaves to glimpse sacred rituals.

Her white cotton peasant skirt was ankle-length, her legs cockily crossed as always. She passed him the joint as if it were growing burdensome. She had a way of lowering her eyelids to suggest to just what extent her consciousness had been altered. The smoke now carried music, deliciously eerie notes that led one down dark stairs and corridors, slowly accreting dollops of bass dripping from a high cave ceiling. He supposed he could let things slide, slip into the evening as into a tar pit.

'I had that sensation again last night.'

'Being held down?'

'. . . Yes.'

'How long did it last?'

'The usual. A couple minutes. That's a long time. Especially when you never really know if it's going to end.'

'Can you describe it to me?'

'I already have, haven't I?' With eyes closed, she took a long drag. 'I'm asleep, but then I feel . . . I have a sudden need to wake up. Urgently. But I can't. Someone's holding me down.'

'Some*one*?'

'I don't know. I think maybe so. It feels like someone's on top of me, pinning me down. Last night I could open my eyes but couldn't move. I felt drugged. I panicked. It's like being buried alive. It finally passed away, but what if some night it doesn't? I'm afraid something awful's going to happen.'

'Did I ever tell you that the Japanese have a name for it?'

'The Japanese? . . . No, you didn't. What is it?'

'I forget. But it's the same as you described it. It means bound hand and foot.'

'Hmm. How do you know?'

'Earl told me. Did you tell your parents?'

'I told Mom.'

'What did she say?'

'What could she say? She doesn't know what to do any more than I do. She thinks maybe we should have the house blessed again.'

'It seems like once should suffice.'

'Mmm.'

'Maybe if you moved out of the house.'

'I was thinking about that. I'm putting in some job applications. Melanie and I might get a place together.'

'What kind of job?'

'Salesgirl, waitress, stripper, that sort of thing. Or maybe financial analyst. Something part-time.'

He focused on the mejiros and said, 'Why don't you move in here?'

She drew her hands to the nape of her neck and with a snap of her head threw her luxuriant hair forward, over her face. From behind this veil she announced gruffly, 'I'm gonna live in a cave and let my hair grow over my eyes.'

That was Felicia. She had a knack for making him feel clumsy, one step off the beat, a foolish romantic who knew the waltz but not the tango. If he was flippant, she scolded him for not taking her seriously. If he was serious, she clowned.

'Please don't get a job.'

'Why not? Do you want any more of this?'

'No, thanks. Because it will interfere with your schoolwork, for one thing, and we won't be able to see as much of each other, for another.'

'Then you'll have more time to prepare for your classes. You're always kicking me out of here anyhow.'

'I never kick you out of here. You're always running home to your mother.'

'You said you had to work tonight.'

Her lower lip pouted, while her eyes cast a mock accusation, flashing once again the promise of misbehavior. The ease with which she gave him an erection embarrassed him. As usual, he was wearing shorts.

'My mother would hang herself with her rosary if she knew the naughty things you do to me. I turned crimson in Foodland the other night when she picked up a can of Redi-Whip. I thought I'd been talking in my sleep. What if she peeked into your bedroom window and saw me licking that throbbing bambucha of yours? She might, you know. She's very suspicious of you. She calls you "that old man". What if she saw the things you do with that cute little—'

He began by kneeling to remove her heels.

'Show me something mauve in size five.'

He raised her right foot to love each toe one by one. *This little piggy went to market. This little piggy stayed home. This little piggy ate roast beef. This little piggy had none.*

He kissed her sole, where he smelled damp leather, and slid his hand to her thigh. *Sweet, sweet, sweet – all the way home.*

'You're lucky she doesn't know where you live, Cullen. She's always asking. What if she drove up here with an exorcist and heard you panting like a wild boar? Or what if my daddy did? He keeps a shotgun, you know. Of course, it's—'

He'd recently read in *National Geographic* that when squirrelfish courted, their grunts could easily be heard above water. This failed to surprise him. Courtship was ludicrous. Just the week before, while sunbathing at Queen's Surf, he and Earl had observed a white pigeon on the beach pursuing the opposite gender – any or all of it. Puffing up his chest feathers seemed to propel him forward in a preposterous, mincing strut that repeatedly crossed the path of one female pigeon or another, all of whom found him boorish. Spastic jerks of his head and sweetly gargled coos did nothing to further his cause.

'Males are always making fools of themselves,' Earl had remarked coolly, and Cullen had to agree that this one was trying too hard.

Now, kneeling on a yak mat, his cock foolishly turgid – and deprived, like both pigeon and squirrelfish, of something soft and loving against which to squirm – he spread her legs indecorously and kissed his way to her undies, lacy, gossamer things he could breathe through or brush aside with his tongue.

'This is uncomfortable,' she complained.

It was darker in the bedroom, though the curtained windows glowed glacial blue. Deprived of sighs, he had come to relish her passionate vulgarities. 'Does my cunt feel good?' 'Do you like fucking me?' Clearly rhetorical questions. Fucking her was what he was doing when she suddenly withdrew her tongue from his ear and bit hard.

'Goddamn it! Cut it out!'

'Make me.'

The praying mantis, not normally given to open displays of affection, will lovingly devour her mate after sex. But sometimes, when mounted, she'll gaze in his multiple eyes and, unable to suppress any longer her rasping joy, will give him a playful love bite, nipping him neatly in two. While the impulsive wench eats the superfluous half, the other goes right on screwing.

He flipped her over, propped her rudely on her knees, and reentered from behind, stiffening his legs in a rigid brace. If she turned to bite him, he'd defend himself. She was still wearing her skirt and open blouse. While such dishabille held appeal, he wished to feel his chest upon her back. He tugged blouse from waistband, unhooked her bra, and threw the blouse over her head, intending to leave it there as a cruel restraint. She wriggled out of it with ease, even expertise. The bra fell to the bed beneath her belly. Leaning back, he drew her with him. He abused her breasts, squeezing rather than fondling. She liked it. She liked everything he thought she might not. She responded with moans of pure delight. He wrapped her hair around his hand and drew back her head that he, too, might kiss and bite an ear, whispering vulgarities from a repertoire he found disturbingly small and unpracticed. With the other hand he gave her pleasure without quarter.

He pushed her forward to continue this perpetration of petty crimes. Her sobs, her urgent gasps when she finally succumbed to bliss in one long shuddering trill – these were his greatest joys. He had discovered after much unnecessarily timid exploration that he could twist her into whatever contortion suited his fancy, subject her to whatever discomfort, with the result that his little debasements only served to arouse her more. Or at least they prompted no protest. This gave him some sense of control, and so, in the interest of prolonging his one victory, he had made a fine art of what seemed sexual domination, driving her repeatedly to orgasm, until that art, in the end, bore little resemblance to love and was better described, it was true, as fucking.

When she again lay still, he held a palm to each thigh. A mucilaginous sweat bound them together. He could come now merely wriggling, a sweet overflow rather than a gush, but he chose to turn her over, pull her to the edge of the bed, claim her again, and carry her thus skewered into the kitchen, where he propped her as a punishment on the narrow formica counter, fouled with mango juice and crumbs, between the stove and the refrigerator.

'Do you like my lipstick? It's new.'

'What's it called?'

'Raspberry Honey.'

'Let me taste.'

She laced her fingers behind his neck and kissed him. He almost lost himself in that kiss. She leaned back, her legs splayed straight, and rocked once again what she called her Li Hing Mui, that object of all men's desire.

He came between stove and refrigerator.

Cullen considered their sex epic, something the world could learn from.

Her half-tanned breasts glistened with sweat. They were small firm breasts that filled his hands perfectly. Throwing her wet hair over her shoulder with a quick flick of head and hand, she gave him one of those haughty Byzantine looks of which she had a limitless store. Its principal features were white needles of light in eyes ringed by black, and the slight parting of dark brandied lips.

He carried her into the bedroom and lay beside her. He knew she wouldn't stay long. Their first bout of love had been the longest they'd spent in bed together, except when watching TV. Felicia was fond of TV; she liked to insult the main characters. But usually, after sex, she'd raise a leg and evaluate it, finding it either fat or sexy, depending upon her mood. It was always a signal that she'd soon rise to shower, after which, if the verdict had been sexy, she'd strike a few provocative poses with a towel in a kind of pin-up parody, and then be dressed and gone, home to her parents and the house she'd grown up in.

'Oh,' she asked, 'did you hear about that guy in San Francisco who was killed by a vending machine?'

'Did he push the wrong button?'

'Nope. He was rocking it because it wouldn't give him his candy bar. It fell right on top of him and crushed him to death.'

'There's a word for that when you get robbed by a vending machine.'

'What's that?'

'*Slottery*. If the vending machine's on a highway, it's *highway slottery*.'

She groaned appreciatively. 'And whatdya call it when you get *murdered* by a vending machine?'

'*Homicidal slottery*.'

'I guess there's a million ways to go. I heard some guy was killed by the frozen crap falling out of an airplane toilet.'

'What an ignominious death.' Cullen stared skyward to contemplate the irony.

'It's hot,' she said, addressing the ceiling and blowing her hair off her forehead.

The windows were open right above the bed, which had no headboard, but no breeze stirred the cheap blue curtains. He propped himself on one elbow to admire her. She cocked a knee. Then she pushed her breasts together and examined them with a scowl.

'My nipples are too small.'

'Nonsense. Your nipples are just right.'

Alice, a skinny girl, had had pointy, earthy nipples that pushed against her tie-dye halter like bean sprouts about to erupt.

'I think my right breast is a little more in demand.'

'What?'

'My right breast. It's a little more developed . . . than my left.'

'Good God. I thought you said it was more in demand!' He fell back to the pillow laughing.

'It's the one *you* suck more.'

'The one *I* suck more? Are there others, then, with different feeding habits?'

'Other what?'

'Other men.'

She now raised the fateful leg. 'What do you think?'

'I'm asking you.'

'About my leg, stupid. How does it look?'

'Nice.'

'I think it's a wee bit chubby.'

And then she was off to the shower. Soon he heard the patter of water against the vinyl curtain she'd been nagging him to clean.

The combination of dope and dusk now threatened him. He imagined the sailboats returning to their slips, the shoppers to their homes, the tourists to their hotels. He pictured the light subsiding among koa and kukui in the Koolaus. He imagined the lights of the city shimmering into a purple darkness as if only a mirage. But as he lay becalmed, eyes closed in a postcoital stupor, something brushed his forehead, its touch barely discernible. For a long moment he suspended his thoughts, anticipant. Then it passed again, returning, gentle as a kiss. It seemed the touch of love itself, tranquil yet profound. But it was only the bedroom curtain stirred at last by a passing breeze.

14

This nausea must be love he told himself later that evening as he lay alone in darkness, the world swimming around him like a shark. But it was, in fact, intestinal flu. It prodded him into the bathroom, where he knelt before the toilet making rash promises to an unseen deity. He was trembling with a bad chill. The oily bilge of his fever sloshed uncomfortably within him. It could subside miraculously, by definition unlikely, or he could pump it out by inducing in himself just a bit more nausea. Either would be preferable to its simply remaining there, sloshing. He'd gone sailing once with Claire and Ernest off Diamond Head and had returned to the wobbly dock feeling very much like this, gyrostabilizer awry, kneeling that time before the filthy toilet of the Texaco station in the marina. He blamed his present state on Felicia's pot, which had thrown a coarse gauze over the day's events, had made of the dusk a dark whisper, and had left him lonely, parched, numb in his extremities, and now deathly ill. It had been treated with paraquat. He'd been poisoned. He gripped both sides of the toilet bowl and closed his eyes to watch his own innards rising like the spinning front-page news in old-time movies. VOMIT! PROFESSOR PUKES AFTER SEX WITH STUDENT! Vomit it was – heave upon heave, contraction after contraction. Each internal avulsion prompted a half-gagged cry that rose feebly from the back of his throat until it was drowned in vomit – acrid, bilious, pea-green vomit speckled with orange mango. It had been a mistake to open his eyes. Another wave of convulsions swept through him, stealing his breath, leaving him gasping for air while still drooling. And yet another. He vomited until there was nothing left to vomit but thin trickles of acid wrenched from his very gut. His stomach ached as if pummeled. *The human condition*, he thought caustically. When it was over, nothing could quite purge the smell from his nose. Only then did he realize he had had no supper, that it might have been better if he had. He poured himself a glass of juice at the breakfast bar, missed his mother, his childhood, the sturdy books with talking animals and friendly policemen, and crawled into a bed still wet with sexual secretions.

'Oh dear,' said Sister Lucia. 'It does sound like the flu. Dreadful. How long do you think you'll be out?'

'It's hard to say, Sister. These things usually hit me pretty hard. Maybe the rest of the week.'

'I see . . . Well let's do this then. Do your students have any papers due this week?'

'The Shakespeare class has a paper due Friday, and come to think of it, so does the Lit class.'

'Nothing in the Freshman class?'

He sensed in her intonation the suggestion that there should be something in the Freshman class, something as big and brutish as a bear that would dance on his chest all weekend while refusing to learn new tricks.

'No, I have a batch to return to them. Their next one's not due until next week.'

'I see. Then here's what we'll do. I'll cancel your classes today, but I'll tell them to turn in their papers on Friday, that if you won't be there to collect them, I will. Call me Friday morning and let me know how you're feeling. If you still don't feel well, I'll leave the papers on your desk. That way you might be able to get to them over the weekend if you're feeling better. These flus usually don't last more than a few days. Who knows, you might just have one of those twenty-four-hour bugs. Don't let yourself get dehydrated. Drink lots of fluids. And if I don't hear from you tomorrow morning, I'll just assume that you're not coming in and I'll cancel for you.'

'Okay. That's very kind of you. I appreciate it. Thank you, Sister.'

'Thank *you*, sir. And how is that Shakespeare class going, by the way?'

'It's going quite well,' he lied, while something vile and liquid dropped rudely into his bowels with the aplomb of a hostage-taker. This new stage of his disease had started that morning, at dawn. Now it was issuing demands. 'We've just finished *Othello*.'

'Ah yes. The torments of love. Do you suppose it's all it's cracked up to be?'

'Well . . .' He might as well be decisive about this. 'Yes! Actually, I think it's a very good play. A bit wordy in parts, but—'

'I know it's a very good play, Cullen. I meant love. Do you suppose love is all it's cracked up to be?'

Love? Cullen, whose torments were, for the first time in months, not those of love, suddenly realized that in her peculiarly cryptic way she was trying to tell him something, something important. There was a message here, he felt sure of it; he had only to pay attention.

'Well, what do you mean exactly? Are we talking about Christian love or . . . ?' Carnal love was the only alternative that came to mind. There was, he knew, at least one other kind as well – they had studied all this in catechism – but he'd be damned if he could remember what it was. It was a long telephone cord. Perhaps it would reach to the bathroom.

'No, no, just plain old love. You know, the kind that makes people do foolish things. I'm sorry, I really shouldn't be troubling you while you're ill. I'll let you go now. I do hope you feel better soon. Goodbye and God Bless.'

'Thank you, Sister. Goodbye.'

He hobbled purposefully to the toilet, where he brought the hostage crisis to a quick and violent conclusion. 'Now that was bizarre,' he said aloud. 'You know, the kind that makes people do foolish things.' That's not very subtle, is it? Even Iago could do better than that. She knows! The old witch knows everything. It's all over but the gouging. And what else would I drink but fluids?'

Felicia appeared in the late afternoon.

'Sister Lucia told me you canceled classes today. You've got the flu?'

'Sister Lucia told you?'

'Yeah. I was looking for you at your office.'

'She knows. She knows everything.'

'Are you referring to our torrid affair?'

'Yes. She probably already has a name for it. The Kinnell Affair.'

'Why not the Mattos Affair?'

'Affairs are named after defectors. That's me.'

'I don't think she knows anything. She was very kind to me.'

'Don't be deceived. That woman's poisonous in all parts. That was indiscreet of you, going to my office like that.'

'I don't see why we have to run around like spies. We're not doing anything illegal.'

'Are you kidding? These are the people that gave the world the thumbscrew and the rack! We stand as much chance as the Albigensian Heresy.'

'Whatever that is. Don't be so paranoid.'

'Felicia, I had a very strange conversation with that woman today. She wanted to talk about love, the kind that makes people do foolish things. Do you think there just might be a message there? "The kind of love that makes people do foolish things." Who could she possibly be referring to? And then she said, "I really shouldn't be troubling you while you're ill." You know what that means, don't you? That means she plans to trouble me when I'm not ill. Then the axe will fall on my cooked goose while my back's against the wall.'

'I think your goose is overcooked, Dear. You're feverish. You should be in bed. Look, I brought you some Sautéed Beef Ear and Dim Sum.'

'Put it in the toilet. Eliminate the middle man.'

'That's not very nice. Here, look. I got Char Siu and Baked Curry Turnover. And here's the Beef Ear. Whoops! That looks like Shrimp Gau Gee. There must've been a mix-up. But you love Shrimp Gau Gee, right?'

'Right. That was sweet of you. Totally impractical, but sweet. I'm sorry. I really can't eat a thing right now.'

'You look terrible.'

'I know. I know. I hope you don't get it. Sit down.'

'No, I can't. I wouldn't want to look terrible. Besides, I've got to get home for dinner. I just came from a job interview.'

'You're really serious about that?'

'Sure.'

'Where did you interview?'

'A new place called Marvin's Grotto.'

'Marvin's Grotto?' A piece of middle-income property in a Polynesian board game?

'Yeah. It's sort of a jazz club across from the zoo. I really gotta run. Get better, my little *pondus.* Bye, bye.'

'Bye bye,' he winced.

Across from the zoo. The first place he'd lived upon arrival in Honolulu had been a house shared with two graduate students. It had been across from the zoo, separated only by the rose garden and Leahi Street. Cat growls tunneled through the night, sharp growls from the gut that filled a hollow in his ribs as he lay awake in the dark. Unidentified creatures filled the air with melancholy moans, wattled warbles, ardent declarations of love. Cries of peacocks and the percolations of doves anticipated the dawn, a dawn so gentle, so palpable, so freshly blown from the nearby Pacific, that he himself felt buoyant with light, rising while still in bed. Warm waves of animal smells wafted through the roses – fur and hides, manure and damp straw. He could see zebras from his bedroom window. Gibbons hooted by day while flocks of pigeons and doves swirled contentedly above the monkeypods. Once a peacock had roosted on the neighbors' roof until the zookeepers came to retrieve it, not with a net but with bare hands, scooping it up lovingly as if it were an errant child.

Baked curry turnover and gau gee. He stayed sick for three days, nicely fulfilling the Sister's prediction. Each was sunny and hot. Each passed languidly like a pristine ocean liner on which he had meant to book passage. Each was a day without Felicia.

Ripe orange streaks appeared on the papayas beyond his lanai.

She called on Wednesday, though, to say that the manager of Marvin's Grotto had seemed to like her, and on Thursday to report that Duncan Plunkett had invited her to a luau.

'A luau! What did you say?'

'I said I'd think about it.'

'Why not just *no*?'

'There's no need to be rude.'

'Didn't you tell him you had a boyfriend?'

'I thought I was supposed to be discreet about that.'

'You don't have to mention my name.'

'Okay, I'll try that. Can I just tell him it's an older man who once flunked him for plagiarism?'

'Just tell him it's someone more mature and that he can go dunk his balls in an osterizer.'

'Cullen!'

15

And on the third day he arose again – to turn on the TV and watch the late-night movie, a Western in which unkempt men spat their words and their tobacco and failed to resolve their conflicts peaceably. He declared himself well.

The next morning, a Saturday, he drove to his office to surreptitiously pick up the papers. When he opened the door, the overhead lights were off and the entire honeycomb of cubicles was reassuringly silent. The silence of Sister Lucia's cubicle titillated more than that of others. Might she be slumped over a desk blotter, half-cleaned gun in hand? He scolded himself. That was just the sort of perverse venial thought that made him a horrid person.

The papers lay on his desk as threatened. He felt already a mounting hostility toward the inanities he knew them to contain. There was a Junior/Senior batch that would explain why Othello had – in student parlance – offed, snuffed, or done away with Desdemona, Desdimona, Disdemona or Desmona; and there was a Sophomore batch, mercifully thinner, that would express, under duress, an opinion.

He raked these papers into his briefcase and entered the mailroom, where he found in his puka his raison d'être totaling $425.02, an outdated invitation to a Friday afternoon reception for a visiting missionary, and the following announcement:

SPEND CHRISTMAS IN THE HOLY LAND!

Travel 2,000 years in only 14 days
with the Bible as your guide,
under the spiritual direction of

FATHER WILLIAM W. PLECKO
Veteran International Traveler
Professor of English, Holy Mount College

and

FATHER BLAINE H. PLANTAIN
Pastor, Holy Rosary Parish

$2399 round trip from Honolulu, Dec. 14–28

Holy Scripture springs to life before your very eyes as you walk the way of the Cross. Your faith takes deeper meaning as you pray where stood the Stable in Bethlehem or kneel in the Garden of Gethsemane. You will gaze out over the Jordan Valley from atop Mount Jericho, visit Nazareth, Cana, the Mount of Beatitudes and many other fascinating sites of significance to all Christians. Plus,

PAPAL AUDIENCE

On your way you'll stop for a pilgrim's audience with the Holy Father and a thorough tour of the Vatican and Rome.

There was more, but he could enjoy the rest at home. Gee, he thought, 2,000 years in only fourteen days. One wouldn't want to undertake a journey like that without the guidance of a veteran international traveler, one who knows which time-warps provide the best service and which to avoid at all costs. Of course a true veteran would inevitably bear the scars, would be a bit warped himself. Cullen would have to ask VIT Plecko about his experiences. He wondered what the Pope was *really* like under all that conservative glitter.

He checked his desk drawers to see if Felicia had left any candies, riddles, or incriminating love notes (she hadn't), offed the lights, and locked the door. Rounding the corner, he thought – as he often thought – of that fortuitous first encounter. He looked at the spot where she had stood on that sodden February day. It was now streaked with sunlight. Marlon Brando, an old resentment deepening his eyes and turning down the corners of his mouth, glared at him from one of the campus bulletin boards. He liked Brando; he was a no-nonsense kind of guy. It was *Appaloosa*, 7.00 and 9.00 that evening, at the University. He resolved to phone Felicia as soon as he got home.

Caught in a traffic jam on Waialae, where the right lane was closed to facilitate the work of men not working, he had little choice but to creep along in single file, inhaling exhaust fumes and sweltering in the midday heat. The pallor in his rearview mirror surprised him. So did St Christopher beneath it. Had he really been stripped of sainthood?

Among the several teenagers in the back of the stationwagon before him sat a Japanese girl with long black hair and wide, innocent eyes. Cullen found her lovely to look at. She looked as Claire might have looked as a girl. She leaned against a dark youth with strong Hawaiian features who paid no attention to the animated conversation of her and her friends. Instead he stared unflinchingly at the driver behind him as if Cullen were a creature on display, a helpless chuckwalla writhing under glass. His grin drew a sinister insult across his face. Had Cullen been gazing too openly upon his woman? How was he to fend off such eyes? To avoid them was cowardly, to engage them futile, so he did a little of both, pretending to fiddle with his radio or to have some interest in the Toyota showroom across the street, but returning unavoidably to the car before him, as a driver must now and then, only to find the eyes still upon him, staring him down. Why?

Readjusting himself so that the girl sat wedged between his legs, her back upon his chest, the boy licked his lips salaciously and cast another taunting smile in Cullen's direction, a broad smile baring healthy white teeth. Cullen returned the smile halfheartedly, something shared among men, while a prickly rage mounted within. Then, wrapping his arms around the girl, who had been oblivious of the confrontation, the boy kissed her with wide wet lips upon her neck, and then in her ear, where he whispered something. She turned toward Cullen and broke into a small laugh. The boy laughed too, teeth gleaming like polished rice. What was so funny? Cullen tried to avert his eyes but met the boy's mocking smile again and again as the traffic inched along, heat waves rising through the fumes. At the first opportunity, he turned left into Palolo, flush again with fever. He had to recross Waialae twice to finally climb Sierra to his home.

That unsettling incident somehow magnified his disappointment later that afternoon when, without explanation, Felicia declined his invitation to the movie.

'I got a job,' she said.

'Really? Where?'

'Marvin's Grotto.'

'Doing what?'

'Cocktail waitress.'

'Wearing what?'

'Nothing too skimpy.'

'But skimpy nonetheless.'

'Tastefully skimpy. My nipples will be covered, and most of my ass. I'll have to even up my tan a bit. Maybe I'll go to our cove, or that nude beach on Diamond Head. And no more hickeys. It's in my contract.'

Like gasoline poured under a doorway, there it was again, a thin sheet under the skin, liquid and combustible.

'Do you work tonight?'

'Nope. Start next Thursday.'

'Then let's go out tonight.'

'Nope. I'm too tired, honey. I just wanna stay home and go to bed early.'

'Well shit. When am I going to see you again?'

'I doan know.'

'How 'bout the beach tomorrow?'

'Can't. I promised Melanie I'd go shopping.'

'Tomorrow night then.'

'Homework.'

'I'll help you.'

'No, you won't.'

'Okay. All right. I'll come to the club on Thursday.'

'That's a no-no! I'll lose my job. The boss doesn't like *boyfriends* hanging around.'

'Well screw the boss.'

'Now I know you don't mean that. Look, I've got to go. Mom's expecting a call from Aunt Maria. Goodbye, my little *pondus*. I'm glad you're feeling better.'

'I was feeling better. Now I feel worse.'

'Goodbye. I gotta go.'

'Goodbye, love.'

But it wasn't good enough for Cullen. Why did he have a bad feeling about this? He felt a queasiness that had nothing to do with his flu. Now she was marking with quicklime the boundaries of a private domain open to any man but him. The thought of his girl being 'managed' by another man was distasteful. Working as a cocktail waitress in a jazz club, working for a man, always among men – flirted with, wooed, propositioned – she'd slowly slip away. *Jazz.* Consider the vulgar origin of the word. No man in his right mind would allow it. She didn't like jazz anyway. All she knew about it she'd learned from him. And it was dangerous down by the zoo; he'd had his car broken into once.

'What should I do?' he asked himself after dinner. 'Grade papers?' This was the weekend, a critical time for a bachelor, and she was punishing him for having taken her for granted. But he'd been sick. How was he to know when he'd recover. He poured himself a ginger ale and sprawled on the back lawn, lonely among the hibiscus. He lived near the juncture of two ridges. The backyard sloped downward and then, beyond the fence, the land dropped precipitously, forming a gorge thick with kiawe, cassava, lantana and Christmasberry. The shadow of the Chings' house had crept as far as the fence. The houses on the opposite ridge basked in molten amber, had moments of pure, unadulterated glory in which each appeared to blossom. Then the light passed from their windows, the night came slowly on, and silently, like a negligée, a cool breeze slid off the mountain.

Later that evening he lay fully clothed on the punai, reading the *Atlantic* to the accompanying patter of a light rain, when something fell on the page before him and slid silently to his chest. There it scurried, a gentle, harmless thing. He crushed it with two fingers, relishing the ease with which he did so. Another, he then realized, was crawling in his hair. He plucked it out and dispatched it. A glance at the overhead lamp revealed four or five more in orbit. That was the trouble with termites. They'd fly into one's hair as if by invitation. They'd circle a light bulb until they dropped, wings singed. Little Icaruses, they were always plummeting helplessly from the skies, shedding impractical wings, wallowing about supine, their vulnerable bodies inviting termination. He had no idea why they did it.

A few more dropped on or about him, and one he crushed behind his ear. All the lights in the cottage, he now noticed, had attracted their devotees. But only when he glanced toward the lanai did he realize he was under siege. The sound he'd mistaken so happily for rain had in fact been termites swarming on the screen. Two plump geckoes clinging effortlessly to the mesh dined to their heart's content.

So, it was mating season – an annual event, like Chinese New Year, of which he was never properly informed. He extinguished all lights, checked all screens, and after a few minutes slipped quietly out to the street, where he found Mr Ching and his teenage son Warren observing the same phenomenon. The golden aura surrounding each streetlight was thick with a pale winged fury. He longed to share this with Felicia, as lovers in New York must long to share snowfalls. He imagined they themselves could mate, grinding hapless termites between their passions.

Mr Ching addressed him. 'You know the funny kine pink streetlights they have in Kahala?'

'Yeah.'

'They say that's why they have *da kine*, 'cause they don't attract termites.'

'No kidding. Well I'll be damned.'

'Yeah. I wish I could afford to live in Kahala, ha ha. I just fumigated this house three years ago.'

'Isn't it awfully late for this?'

'It's only 9.30.'

'No, I mean late in the season.'

'I don't know. I guess the termites don't think so.'

He drove to Thrifty Drugs for insect spray and rum. By two he was drunk and driving – down her street. A sportscar driven by a young man passed him in the opposite direction, but there was no telling where it had come from. Had he come sooner he might have found it parked in her driveway with two shadowy figures embracing within. Instead, he found only a dull yellow light filling her bedroom window like a single brushstroke. So much for her claim that she was going to bed early. The rest of the house was dark. He stopped the car but caught no glimpse of her. All her neighbors were asleep. She'd told him stories about the bachelor next door – how, after she'd undressed and turned off the light, she'd suddenly hear his 'Goodnight, Felicia' from the darkened window facing hers.

Wherever she'd been, he concluded, she'd returned home late. Still, it wasn't much to go on. He'd driven from Maunalani Heights to see nothing more than a light in the window. He made a U-turn at the next intersection to see it again. What might he have seen had he arrived earlier?

He headed home via Koko Head, past two Korean bars and a strip of dimly lit shops. At the second stop sign on Wilhemina Rise, he noticed that the lipstick tree in the yard on his left had come into bloom. The streetlight dusted it with chalky, ghostly light. The house behind it stood in shadow. It was a tree of mouths, alien spiked pods opening with silent voracity. Brown on the outside, flesh-toned within, they seemed to open before his very eyes. While the whole hill slept, this tree eerily awakened. And he was the only witness. Open mouths revealed pale tongues. Blooming. Plotting.

He drove on, the only car on the rise. Sierra Drive snaked up the climb gradually, but Wilhemina tackled it directly, rose straight up á la San Francisco, with stop signs at each intersection. A half-moon hung leering at the top of the hill.

Suspicion and jealousy were, like Felicia, new to Cullen. His other women had been quietly faithful lovers in whom he'd eventually lost interest. None had danced for him at the foot of the bed. None had turned heads or charged the air with anticipation by merely entering a room. He had needed them and they him. Then he had stopped needing them.

Time, he'd noticed, had a deleterious effect on romance. Sex with Alice had grown surreal – always stoned on her homegrown dope, which made everything turbid and dense – until one day he had lost the distinction between himself and a taxidermist working an elephant skin into a lifelike position. Not that she had been a large woman. If anything, she had been counter-culturally thin, wasting away on organic good health and, near the end, the master cleanser fast – a daily diet of water, lemon, maple syrup, cayenne, and enema. She'd gotten it out of a book she'd borrowed from the Whole Earth Bookstore, where she worked. It told her to roll on the floor from side to side to wash the large intestine. It told her to lift her legs over her head and touch her toes to the floor to spread water through the large bowel. It told her to stand on her head and contract her anal muscles for reasons not specified. He found this obsession with visceral cleanliness a peculiar terminus for a movement that had begun by boycotting baths. Puritanism wore many guises. If the sex were free, the tariff for other bodily needs increased dramatically. Hence tasty foods were tainted foods, and the devil lurked in soul-clogging additives. Meat was mortal, pastry venial. Once, pointing out to her the tarry resins coating the glass steamboat they'd used to smoke their dope, he'd suggested that a few months without marijuana would do more for her health than all the brown rice and wholegrain breads in the world. 'Dope cleanses my head,' she'd replied. 'It helps me unwind.'

It was just one step, of course, from master fast to master, and when she found herself a bona fide guru who could enlighten devotees with a swift whack to the head, that made it easy to say goodbye. He could cite her puritanism, her masochism, her perpetual role of follower; he could point out that her shampoos came in more flavors than her granola; he could tell her that she dressed like a Calcutta swap meet; he could claim her waterbed made him seasick; he could tell her anything but the truth – that he had simply lost interest in her wholesome, organic body, that his ejaculation had grown puny, had dwindled to nothing more than a green worm in a terrarium. Sex was not everything, but neither was love.

The sharp scent of hyacinths powdering the air came from a trellis of stephanotis. In conspiracy with the lipstick tree, a cluster had blossomed by his door that very evening. One was always assailed by smells in Hawaii. Plumeria were inescapable, forever unfurling their perfumed umbrellas like showgirls. Brunfelsia nearly accosted the unwary passerby. Driving down the makai end of 22nd Ave any day or night, he could always smell pikake, the jasmine in Chinese tea. Before, it had been simply a piquant surprise. Now, it never failed to remind him of Felicia. That was love, wasn't it, when someone entered one's thoughts unbidden? Termites still engulfed the streetlights. So as not to attract them, he had left the outside light unlit, and now he was struggling to insert his key in darkness.

As he opened the door, a man's moonlit face leapt at him from across the room, and a sudden pain shot through his chest like a well-thrown knife. He stood stunned in the doorway, one hand pressed to his sternum. Misfortune strikes without warning. He switched on the light to discover a motionless curtain where the face had been. The pain, however, was not as easily transformed. *Heart attack* was his first and only thought. He wasn't ready for it. He turned off the light and saw, with some relief, that even in moonlight the curtain was once again a curtain. He preferred this semi-darkness. He shuffled gingerly across the room and lowered himself into Felicia's chair, his arms trembling like an old man's. There he sat perfectly still, afraid the viper now coiled about his heart might sink its fangs even deeper.

How clearly he had seen a face in the curtain, had felt the dead weight of its stare. The curtain had hung lifelessly for years without alarming him. Had the face caused the heart attack? To be frightened to death by an illusion would be too shameful, too ironic. Yet no one would ever know.

He waited, frightened and cold. The slightest movement would be dangerous. The key was to not move at all, to outlast it. The pain still girdled his chest, breathing as he breathed, inhumanly patient. It would either slither off or kill him. It was killing him. In his worst imaginings, it killed him, squeezed out his life and passed on, there being so many others to kill. But it hadn't killed him yet; it had merely paralyzed him, this pain that was not so much pain as the implicit threat of pain. What it would actually do remained, he believed, largely a matter of luck. It was incomprehensible to him that he might actually die, and so young, serious misfortune having always been something that only afflicted others. He was too deeply tanned to die, too deeply in love. His cottage was just as he liked it. Drinking in the wake of his illness had been foolish, yes; he'd never do it again. All he needed was a reprieve. Here he sat, an untenured instructor of English literature and composition, one false heartbeat away from his obituary. He wondered what hack would write it and what grave grammatical error it would contain.

A sleeping python now, the pain rested, neither quickening nor subsiding, and yes, it was only yesterday that he had read of a father entering the nursery to discover a python devouring his baby daughter. Horrid things do happen, and this was but one of a catalogue of mundane disasters, a single entry in a quick-reference medical guide thick with afflictions, nothing at all like being swallowed headfirst by the family python while your stupid fucking father tugs helplessly at your dainty pink feet. Or could this be only heartburn? Perhaps a nasty angina. It seemed that inexplicable pains were always pricking and squeezing him like an unwanted lover, all mere mortal reminders. He wondered why he'd been ill in the first place. No one else had. It didn't seem to be one of those promiscuous illnesses 'going around'. He would not have minded so much had he been stricken more equitably by a communal disease, but to have succumbed to the flu alone . . .

The snake momentarily writhed and constricted. A real python could swallow a sharp-horned gazelle whole. What did it matter that he knew that? What did anything he'd learned or done matter? He could perish here in darkness, curled around his anguish on the floor, and a fly might walk across his face a day or two before Mr Ching peered in from the lanai to realize that essentially what he had here was a serious tenant-disposal problem. Life is cheap, and its loss a daily statistic. There were too many people in the world anyhow.

The moonlight glossing the papaya trees seemed painfully romantic. They might have been royal palms instead of skinny trunks each bearing a single clump of fruit beneath a tiny green umbrella. They were a miracle; he was a miracle. They rocked ever so slightly in the mountain breeze, a movement barely discernible. He felt like crying. Something had happened, had changed without warning, and he hadn't the vaguest idea what it was. Breathing deeply . . . sitting absolutely still and breathing deeply . . . that might help. He mustn't hyperventilate. The main thing was to not shiver, which would lead to shaking, which would spill the vital contents of his heart. His left arm was growing numb, turning to styrofoam as he sat. One of the symptoms of heart attack, if he recalled correctly – something he'd read in a women's magazine in a dentist's office. His father had died of a heart attack, and death is easily inherited. But surely he was too young for a coronary. If he lived, he should see a doctor. Diagnosis: petty espionage. Prognosis: chronic self-loathing. Last words if fatal: just sit still and breathe deeply. If he could simply give her up, cut out that sodden bit of his heart and discard it, that would be the end of that particular anguish. This possibility seemed to stretch before him like one of the abandoned city streets he had just crossed in his covert expedition. All things in the dark room sat mute, familiar, still contaminated by the stench of his illness. A shard of light pierced the dustcover of his turntable. A sluggish breeze carried the faint odor of insecticide. He liked it here in this room, on this island, on earth in the late twentieth century. He'd drawn one of life's better lots. He would make wiser use of his time and consider more seriously the possibility of Christ. It wasn't that he didn't want to believe; it was rather that in the grand cosmic scheme of things – in the universe so vast as to quench one's breath while mesmerizing with the spark and scintillation of dead light, in the world where every seed and sand crab twitches according to law, where continents drift and atoms collide, where whales change their song with each season and blind tube-worms sway at the bottom of the sea – in a world so deep and alien, so strong and incomprehensible, so miraculous and improbable, he felt he and his beliefs mattered less than the paltry termites.

He watched the moonlight cross the papayas. After a long wait, and for no apparent reason, the pain slithered off into the night.

16

> Funeral services have been held for Walter Whipple, a 26-year-old New Jersey man who gained more than 500 pounds after a 1975 accident. Whipple, 5-foot-7 and 750 pounds, died of a heart attack at Pennsylvania's Chester-Crozer Medical Center. He weighed 230 until the accident, in which a falling hay elevator tore open his left shoulder and crushed a bone between his left knee and hip. 'I just kept gaining and gaining ever since,' he said two weeks ago, when admitted to the medical center. Mystified doctors said he continued to gain in the hospital despite an 800-calories-a-day diet containing no salt, sugar or bread.

Cullen reread this clipping for what must have been the sixth or seventh time. He just couldn't get over it, the way bad luck could tap one on the shoulder with all the courtesy of a falling hay elevator. Something about Walter Whipple's bizarre demise had touched him, and not just because his own heart had suddenly proclaimed his mortality. He saw in the story of Walter Whipple some dim reflection of his own condition, though he'd be damned if he could express it. Perhaps he was simply indulging in self-pity, the same self-pity to which he considered Walter to have been thoroughly entitled.

This clipping was one of four to be found in a drawer by the phone. The others were well summarized by their headings:

'Liquor sales rise in Turkey', 'Bitten man reconsiders, leaves cage of snakes', and 'Dentist repossesses teeth'. In truth, liquor sales *were* rising in Turkey; a man *had* left a cage of poisonous snakes, while trying to break a record for cohabitation; and a dentist *had* repossessed a patient's partial plates when the poor man opened his mouth in expectation of a check-up.

Cullen suspected that a universal truth lay in these four snippets: All things change, usually for the worse. The same could be true of his heart.

He'd never collected clippings before meeting Felicia but had recently resorted to doing so only as a means of holding up his end of their daily phone conversations, for daily was, on the average, how often she called – a blithe fact that had contributed significantly to the affair's adolescent air. He appreciated her calls – a day without one unleashed, as now, his purgatorial demons – but sometimes, with his ear griddled by the receiver for an hour or more, and unnaturally deprived of the filler of simple gestures and facial expressions and even acceptable silences, he would reach for a thought and come up instead with a styrofoam nugget, a sure sign that his brainpan had been crammed to the parietals with such. Hence the clippings, which he consulted like Cliff Notes for a Harlequin Romance.

He also kept a list of interesting events and observations that might otherwise escape his recall. His list now had, and had had since his last day of teaching, only a single uncrossed entry: 'Leroy Wong's hard-on'. Leroy Wong's hard-on had sprouted in class one day in the middle of Leroy's oral presentation on Japanese haiku. Like the American flag on Iwo Jima, it was just suddenly there, undeniably and monumentally erect. Cullen had never before witnessed such enthusiasm for poetry. Pushing against poor Leroy's chinos with the determination of an armored division bent on a breakout, what the school graffitiists would surely term 'Wong's whanger' had filled the classroom with twitters, titters, and something like stifled clangor, and the hell of it was that oblivious Leroy had said something 'funny' and was so pleased with its reception that he suddenly brightened – as if struck by the happy recognition that his future lay in public speaking. This tidbit, yet another example of life's inconstancy, was so good that

Cullen had been saving it, a light fruity wine to uncork on that special occasion.

But it seemed less and less likely that such an occasion would arrive any time soon. This had been the first weekend in many that they hadn't seen each other. He hardly felt that his illness accounted for such an anomaly. He could call her, of course – he'd been reviewing his clippings with that dimly in mind – but it was clear that no good could come of it. For one thing, she'd asked him not to call as this would only serve to remind her mother of his existence. For another, she'd lied to him. Why? He sat by the phone, mentally reviewing the sequence of actions that, if initiated, could result in dinner. Halve an avocado. Open a can of tuna. Open a can of cranberry sauce. Place the tuna and cranberry sauce in the avocado. Open a soda.

He felt as heavy as Walter Whipple. That it was Sunday evening added more weight. Sunday evenings were traditionally morbid since each condemned him to prepare for Monday and the miseries queued beyond that. Sunday evenings were also a time reserved for grading papers collected on Friday, though in this case he had collected his weighty onus on Saturday. More pounds.

Then the phone rang, surprising him as much as if some other household object – a lamp or ashtray – had broken into song. She would be cheerful, he would be dour. Where was the promise in that? He scowled at the instrument, helpless to resist it. He had never ignored a ringing phone nor discarded an unopened letter. He was curious.

Then her voice was upon him, seducing and cajoling. It had the rolling viscosity of a lava flow – molten, warm, enveloping. It went well with her body and was therefore a source of frustration when divorced from it. She wanted to know how he was feeling.

'Like shit.'

'Oh, Poopsie. I thought you were feeling better.'

'I've suffered a relapse.'

'Are you teaching tomorrow?'

'Yeah.'

'You don't sound very happy to hear from me.'

'It's just Sunday night. I've got a shitload of papers to grade thanks to Sister Lucia. What did you do last night?'

'Well, let's see. I watched *Hawaii Five-O* with Mom. That was a mistake. It was about a radical UH professor who sold drugs to students and turned them into sex slaves. I hope you're not like that, Cullen. And then Melanie came over, and then I did a little homework. And then it was time for beddy-bye.'

'You had time for Melanie last night but not for me.'

'She just showed up.'

'Doesn't sound like a very exciting Saturday night.'

'So?'

The road from there descended sharply, Cullen hating each reckless innuendo that drove him toward certain disaster, but it seemed one way of overtaking the truth. It wasn't long before she was saying, 'What makes you so sure?' and he was blurting what he'd never meant to: 'Because I drove by your house last night. That's what makes me so sure!' It was one of those shrill, irrevocable confessions one regrets on utterance. He left it ambiguous as to what he had seen, bluffing his prosecution as he had for so long bluffed his seduction.

'You just happened to be driving by my house last night?'

'No.'

'And may I ask what you saw that upset you so?'

He sat there silently, twisting the cord around his fingers the way the python had embraced his heart, a potent mixture of shame and suspicion filling the recesses so recently vacated by fever. Finally, and feebly, he said, 'I saw that you hadn't gone to bed early like you said.'

'I start my job in a few days.'

'I don't want you to.'

'I have to. I already bought the outfit. I wish you could see it. I know it would turn you on.'

He hung up shortly thereafter. It seemed the only way to curtail the desperation rising in his voice. He'd given her every opportunity to explain her lie, but she hadn't. She'd only turned cruel. He knew he was handling this all wrong, but as Felicia had once pointed out, on the basis of his slant, he let his emotions rule his reason. The great secret he had meant to hide was that not very deep within lay a soft pulp sensitive to the slightest hurt.

Alice had uncovered it. She'd gently stripped his outer layers until his weakness lay exposed like a fuzzy-topped artichoke heart, and then she'd eagerly exposed her own weakness so that together they might soak like vegetables in the tenderizing marinade of tears and truth.

Celia, whom he'd dated all through graduate school, had uncovered it, too. Then she'd fallen more deeply in love. That was when Cullen first discovered that there is a sort of woman who loves nothing more in a man than a weakness, something to serve as a focal point for the envisaged reconstruction. Such a woman eyes a man as one might eye an old house and asks herself the eternal marital question: 'What changes would make him tolerable?'

But Felicia was like neither Alice nor Celia. She was, he suspected, the type for whom weakness was repulsive.

In any case, nothing was worse than exposure. In the cases of Alice and Celia, it had paradoxically hardened him. In the case of Felicia, it clearly had the opposite effect.

The next days passed slowly, like the white clouds in his fingernails – the result of a zinc deficiency, according to Alice – and in each he agonized over the possibility that she drew her strength from righteousness rather than indifference. He didn't see her at all in school, and he lacked the courage to cruise Third Avenue in search of her car. The winch in his stomach had tightened again – a daily occurrence – and in his hand he constantly found meaningless objects: an empty Kirin bottle reflecting the light of an overhead bulb, a twisted paper clip, an embossed book of matches from a restaurant he'd never patronized, a $5 bill bearing the handwritten inscription 'Happy Birthday, Jaimie, from Gram.'

His life had opened like some nickel toy, revealing its utter uselessness.

He cleared the bathroom of her trappings – Estée Lauder Automatic Cream Eye Shadow, Clinique Gentle Brown Eye Pencil, and Max Factor Fiber Formula Lash Maker and Newborn Peach Foundation – the minutiae with which she had worked her magic and staked her claim. He had thought to sweep them passionately off the counter and on to the floor, but found himself instead dropping them one by one into a plastic bag. He hung the bag in his closet. From his pillow he removed a long auburn hair.

She had a certain scent, Tahitian Gardenia, that had buried itself in his sheets, a lingering spirit. Occasionally he'd catch a hint of it tangled in a stronger musk. But what he caught eluded him.

When he envisioned her face, she smiled at him roundly, eyes flashing. He could envision her so well that she would sometimes walk right into the room, sit in her rattan chair, and engage him in conversation. Would it actually end like this then, each a ghost for the other, less a person and more a memory each day? Surely he was exaggerating.

Nevertheless, the weekend approached like an ice age. She still hadn't called by Friday. She wasn't going to call. She'd begun her job the night before and was no doubt working that night as well. After work she'd have a drink with the saxophonist or meet the other man in her life. Or perhaps she'd penned that in for Saturday. When he found himself actually scraping away the crud that had accumulated in the hole of his toothbrush, he raised his arms in despair and called Earl.

'What are you doing tonight?'

'I'm gonna catch a couple flicks with one of the guys I play volleyball with. Why? What's up?'

'Mind if I tag along?'

Earl's Datsun pulled up at 7.15.

'Sorry we're late. Wayne forgot his zoris, so we had to go back.'

Wayne, a handsome local boy dressed to disco, smiled broadly to indicate that this was one of Earl's feeble jokes.

'Howzit?'

'Hi.'

'You wanna indulge first?' Wayne was asking Earl.

'Sure, let's indulge first.'

They retired to Cullen's living room to indulge first. Cullen opened some beers, took all proffered hits, and searched through his records for something suitably black and depressing.

'Cullen's a music aficionado. He used to play marimba for Sergio Mendes.'

'No lie?'

'Have you ever known Earl to lie?'

'Hmm. Yeah . . .'

Wayne's dope, like a Korean bar girl, seemed to understand Cullen's blue funk. So did B. B. King.

'This is bad shit,' said Earl. 'What is this?'

'Maui Zowie.'

'Ah, the darling buds of Maui. This is' – he pursed his lips like a ventriloquist – 'very bad shit.'

'More where that came from.'

Cullen had no idea if this meant Maui, the Mob, or Wayne's shirt pocket, but this was an ambiguity soon clarified.

'You're no good,' sang B. B. 'You been mean to me, Baby. You been mistreatin' me.'

'I like this,' said Wayne.

'Yeah,' said Cullen. 'King of the Blues.'

'The thrill is gone, Baby. It's gone away for good.'

They were driving down Kapahulu toward Waikiki.

'Where are we going?'

'Ala Wai,' answered Wayne.

'Ala Wai?'

'Yeah.'

'What are we going to see?'

'I don't know exactly. Good stuff.'

It suddenly dawned on Cullen that he was experiencing a chest pain, one that throughout the drive had been slowly rolling toward him like a gutter ball. *Oh Christ. Oh Christ.*

Dear and loving God. Let's go easy here, okay? This is not a good time. Not a good time at all. Merciful Jesus? Okay? Damn but you are stupid, stupid, stupid, smoking dope so soon after . . . When are you going to learn that this stuff is no good for you? Grow up. This time you're going to the doctor for sure. We'll just live through this and next week we'll go to the doctor for a death certificate. Ha, ha. This was one of his mother's *ha ha*'s. She punctuated her letters with them to underscore feeble jokes and ironies. Wouldn't *she* be disappointed by his autopsy report, she who had raised him with Christian values. Once, at a children's matinee, he'd asked her how they'd filmed such a spectacle – scores of cavalrymen riddled with spears and arrows, already dead as they fell backwards off galloping horses. Did they just get people who wanted to die? 'Yes,' she'd replied, eating her popcorn, and for years he'd lived with that skewed vision of life and art. Now something barbed had pierced *his* chest. *Actually . . . actually, this is just a mild chest pain. That stuff has cauterized your lungs. It's the lungs, not the heart. It's as common as a cold. Remember that you have a tendency to exaggerate . . . Just calm down. Calm down. If you make a big deal out of it . . .*

'There it is,' said Wayne.

Pulling into a side street, they parked before nondescript apartment buildings dwarfed by overbearing condominiums. Apparently they were picking someone up. Contrary to his expectations, it felt good to get out and walk.

By the time they'd climbed to the third floor, his pain had subsided. *See, not a heart attack at all.* Wayne knocked on door 33. Earl looked at Cullen.

'Where's Felicia tonight?'

He hesitated, wondering if he should mention Marvin's Grotto.

'Out with her folks.'

The door opened.

'I brought a couple friends,' Wayne said.

'Wonderful. Come on in.'

Cullen followed Wayne and Earl. A fat old man in a white Filipino shirt seemed genuinely pleased to see them.

'Sit down, sit down.'

Wayne and Earl sat on the couch. Cullen chose an armchair. The furniture had clearly come with the apartment. On an end table next to Cullen stood a hula doll with green plastic skirt. Beside it stood a bronze replica of the Empire State Building. And beside that stood a family portrait of what he assumed to be the old man's daughter, son-in-law, and grandchildren, though there was no way of really knowing. They looked healthy and sturdy, like a family one could order from Sears.

'You'll find everything in here. Take a look. I'll be right back.'

He handed Wayne an index file. Paperbacks lay everywhere, their covers packed with action. Ceramic heads of pirates and W. C. Fields hung on the opposite wall, next to a tropical sunset. Bowling trophies crowded the top shelf of a walnut credenza.

Cullen smiled. 'What are we doing here?'

Earl placed a finger to his lips. 'Shhh.'

Wayne leaned over the coffee table to thumb through the index file. The Seven Lucky Gods stood like lovable dwarfs on the second shelf of the credenza, beside a plaster likeness of Snoopy in Lederhosen. A plastic schooner sailed toward the neck of its bottle. A brass clock read 8.20.

He felt better. What girdled his chest now was just the usual dope-affiliated discomfort.

'Find anything you like?'

'You said you had something with animals?'

'Oh yes. That was you. I think that's available. Lemme see. What was the number on that?' The old man put on his glasses and opened a cabinet on the far side of the room. 'Here we go.' He brought a film can to the coffee table.

'*Women's Lib* sounds good, too,' said Wayne.

'Oh sure,' said the man, stepping over Wayne to plop between him and Earl. He had a jolly face with rounded red nose. 'They're all good.' He removed a reel of film and mounted it on a machine sitting before him on the coffee table. Cullen, who could see only the back of this machine, determined that it was some sort of handcranked viewer.

'Just turn here slowly, like this. You'll get the knack of it.'

'Yeah. I remember.'

'Criminy, that's right.'

The old man lit a cigarette. Wayne commenced cranking and Earl moved to the edge of the couch. For silent minutes, Cullen watched the light of moving images flicker over their faces.

'Unreal,' said Earl.

'It looks like a silent movie,' said Wayne.

'It *is* a silent movie, Dumbo.'

'You know what I mean.'

'Lookie here, lookie here,' said the man, his fat cheeks fattening, his thick glasses twinkling with sparks of mirth. 'Did you know a pig has a corkscrew cock? Let me back it up just a little.' He took control of the crank.

'Goddamn. You could open bottles with that thing.'

'I never knew that,' said Earl. 'Nature in her infinite wisdom.

Come look at this, Cullen.'

He walked to Earl's side.

'See that?'

He saw, obliquely, what everyone else had seen: a close-up of pig penis. It appeared much as the man had described it, helical at the end, but it was impossible to determine how much of the corkscrew was penis and how much hair, for in this particular extremity of the swine the flesh tapered off into a sort of exaggerated spitcurl, a slovenly twist of gray in grainy eight millimeter chiaroscuro.

'Didn't know that, eh?' sang the man, cranking gleefully on. Cullen found the name he'd been trying to remember: Charles Laughton.

A woman's hand appeared at the base of the penis. Then a mouth drew its hair to a fine point, as an artist will when priming a brush.

'Back it up so Cullen can see it from the beginning.'

'That's okay,' said Cullen.

Nevertheless, the man obliged.

A woman in a loose print dress that stops short of her knees is carrying a bucket across a barnyard. A mottled pig enters stage left, trots eagerly toward her, and saddles her leg provocatively. She smiles, brushing her stringy hair from her forehead, and kicks the pig aside. Undaunted, the pig cheerfully mounts her leg again, hobbling along to keep stride. He has lecherous slit eyes.

'They call that pig Lambrusco. Quite a character. He's dancing the Bacon Fat today.'

The woman reaches the chicken yard. In one motion she empties the bucket of feed, and as she does so Lambrusco playfully sticks his snout up her dress. She slaps him and wriggles away.

She reaches the yard of the farmhouse, where a skinny mongrel is leashed to the fence. The dog seems shy and uneasy. She drags him along toward the house. Dragged even more cruelly by the faster pace of the fat man's cranking, the dog moved with the jerky, Chaplinesque motion of silent comedy.

'What's the dog's name?' asked Earl.

'I think they call him Detroit Red. He was a walk-on.'

Cullen was surprised to hear a door open elsewhere in the

apartment. Someone passed from one room to another and a door closed. When he returned his attention to the screen, he saw that the scene had shifted to a harshly lit interior.

'You boys crank this while I look for *Women's Lib*,' said the man. Earl, accepting the responsibility, moved over to make room for Cullen.

Now the woman – grainy, flickering, shopworn – reclines on floor cushions. The pig roots under her dress, as if for truffles, but is redirected elsewhere. It's the dog she wants. She drags him closer and reaches between his hind legs. The dog fears castration. She strokes him. Not easily reassured, he clings tenaciously to suspicions. And he does what actors are told never to do – looks straight into the camera. She pumps the stark, raw muscle. He seems to whimper. He has the sad, puzzled eyes of a Catholic, of one who long ago resigned himself to a staid life unburdened by sin. Now he seems painfully transfixed, a helpless novice trembling before the event.

The desultory camera zooms in, not on the dog but on the swinish corkscrew.

As if necessarily rising for breath, Cullen looked up. Strangely, inexplicably, as if drawn by the gaze of unseen eyes upon the back of his head, he looked over his shoulder. And there, above him, stood Jesus, smiling handsomely at Cullen while shamelessly exposing his sacred heart. When he returned to the screen, he saw what seemed a blind, slithering, lower life form – a larva wriggling toward transformation according to the irrevocable dictates of nature.

The restless camera zooms out. The pig shivers with heat as the woman's kiss carries him down a stream of ancestral memories.

'That woman does not love that pig,' said Cullen matter of factly, sending Earl and Wayne into fits of glottal laughter.

'Of course not,' wheezed Earl. 'He's a chauvinist pig.'

The dog again. A hand pumps him with the heartlessness of a beast subduing prey. He has a timid, virginal thirst for climax, yet looks to the camera for counsel.

She spreads her legs widely now, the left one in the air, her buttocks propped on a cushion, and with one hand tugs the spindly prick toward her vagina, a malignant blackness between bruised thighs. She has not abandoned the pig; she is adroitly juggling two lovers. She prods the mutt's rump with her heel. Although he has stiffened his hind legs with pathetic resolve, he follows his errant cock in short helpless hops. It is, arguably, a sort of rape. Entry triggers madness. He jerks uncontrollably and his eyes roll backwards as if to survey his beheading. He flails wildly, thrashing the cushions.

Lambrusco, finding this contagious, can sustain his good fortune no longer. The camera zooms in on gruel. Detroit Red succumbs as well. When finally released, he searches the room for his cue.

'Howdya like that?' asked the pornographer from across the room.

All three seemed to weigh their answer.

'It has a climax,' said Earl. 'Strong characterization.'

'How much is it?' asked Wayne.

'One night, ten dollars. Here's *Women's Lib*.'

A man, clothed only in an apron, mops the floor on his hands and knees. Two well-dressed women sit idly over tea, occasionally rising to whip him.

Cullen sank back into the couch, clothed in lost innocence. He felt strangely weightless, as if he might float from the room. He realized that the eyes of the velour Jesus had been directed toward the screen. Was that some sort of joke? And the unwelcomed erection he'd received – a bad joke as well?

An itchy, flea-bitten bunch, the cast of *Women's Lib* no sooner sat than they stood, no sooner stood than they knelt, no sooner knelt than they sat. The abrupt, hand-cranked pace of the film made it a pornographic *Modern Times*, with the actors as machines – pumping, coupling, inserting. Contrary to the promise of the title, the man seemed well serviced in traditional fashion, the whips having been discarded with the apron. It ended as it began, the mopping of the floor serving as a framing device. After the first film, and with the promise of yet another, it seemed a farcical interlude. He waited patiently while Wayne and Earl previewed others. It was he, after all, who had asked to tag along.

'Can you hold these for next Friday?' asked Wayne.

'Certainly,' replied the man, cheerful in his very bones. 'I'll need a 50 percent deposit.'

'Wayne's having a party,' explained Earl to Cullen.

'Yeah. You're invited.'

'Thanks.'

'No mention.'

He saw now that the box of index cards was labelled 'Recipes'.

Upon their departure, they opened the door to a black fist. Four tall dark shadows loomed in the doorway.

'Doctor Kinnell,' said the first one.

The population of Honolulu is approximately half a million, thought Cullen. That made the odds of encountering Duncan Plunkett approximately half a million to one. And yet . . .

'Sheee-it!' said the second shadow. 'We didn't know you were into hardcore stuff.'

'I'm not. My friends are the perverts. I'm a soft-porn kinda guy.'

A sort of wheezing horse laugh issued from the darkness.

'Hoo boy.'

'A man's gotta do what a man's gotta do. Right, Doctor Kinnell?'

'That's right, Duncan. Well, you boys have a good time. Hi, Jesse.'

'Hi, Doctor Kinnell.'

'We will, we will,' said Dhabul. 'I jes' hope you saved some fo' us.'

Dhabul's apocope was phony, something he did for effect.

'Absolutely,' said Cullen, trying to put the best face on it. 'There's more than enough to go around.' He was almost out the door.

'And Doctor Kinnell. Doctor Kinnell. I jes' wanta tell you one thing.' Duncan looked left and right with his crazy eyes and began to nod his head rhythmically, as if he might burst into song. 'I know. I know it's you, man. I know it's you who's been messin' with my graffiti. I know. No one else would do a crazy thing like that. And I do not appreciate it. I like my words the way I writ 'em. Got that?'

'Right on,' said Dhabul.

Cullen felt prickly, flush with both cowardice and anger.

'Hey, you've got the wrong guy. What graffiti? How would I know yours from anyone else's?'

'Because mine's *dis*-stinktive. That's how. I know it's you. And now *you* know that *I* know. Okay?'

'Goodnight.'

'Good luck next season, you guys,' said Earl, who had grasped the situation.

'We won't need no luck. We're gonna kick ass.'

'That's what I said.'

The sky was that inky maroon peculiar to the tropics, a lush, kinetic darkness. The lights of Ala Wai high-rises twinkled in the canal.

'What was that all about?' asked Wayne.

'Ex-students,' said Cullen.

'Looks like you taught them to take pride in their writing,' said Earl.

'They seem a little sore. They basketball players or what?'

'Jesus, Wayne. You are so out of it,' said Earl. 'That was Duncan Plunkett and Dhabul the Cool.'

'No shit!'

'Who were the other two?'

'Jesse Webb and I don't know who the other guy was.'

'No kidding. Some guy jumped from that,' said Wayne, pointing to a glassy condominium high above them. Cullen raised his eyes to consider what that would be like. He was ready to slink home, tail between his legs, to lick his wounds. Unfortunately, he'd have to trot along.

'Chopped up his wife with a kitchen knife, then just jumped.'

Cullen looked again.

'Yeah,' said Earl, 'women can drive a guy fucking crazy all right.'

They went to Zippy's Saimin Lanai for a late dinner, then spent the rest of the evening in nightspots where he soured their fun by not dancing. The girls were lovely as always, but . . . Everywhere they went he looked for Felicia. What if she were trying to call? No, she was working. He made the mistake of confiding in Earl.

'You're being an asshole, Cullen. You really are. You're letting that woman ruin your life.'

'What do you recommend?'

'If you want to tenderize an octopus, you've got to grab hold of one tentacle and slap it against a rock. It's the only way.'

Friendship was fine, it seemed, but lovesickness was an

embarrassment for all concerned. He ordered a Mai Tai and played with the paper umbrella. He recited her phone number and recalled the day he had found his own written on her door jamb. He had a wild idea, so wild that its mere consideration brought an ironic smile. He stared into his Mai Tai. *Maita'i. Good.*

The next night he sat at his desk, determined to work rather than call Felicia. He'd been a dedicated teacher, but 'toxic chalk syndrome' was turning him snide. He could no longer summon the strength to check the epidemic spread of sheer stupidity. Sweet Marsha Middleton's interpretation of the 'night-heron's screech' in Basho's haiku as resulting from a sudden stop had driven him over the edge. How could a student possibly confuse the meditation of a seventeenth century Buddhist monk with a *Roadrunner* cartoon? Felicia's generation had been pickling too long in a dangerous marinade. TV, drugs, additives, X-rays, radiation, pollution, the inhalation of hair spray and surfboard resin – all had snapped tired genetic chains and burned out vital synapses. Intelligence quotients had plummeted, the classics had grown arcane, man would need incalculable good fortune to recover his flag from the moon, and in another decade or two the miraculous electric toaster would stand beside the pyramids as further evidence of a visit by ancient astronauts.

The sound he'd mistaken for a roach was that of newly discarded paper unfolding in the wastebasket. He looked at what he had typed and underlined at the top of a clean sheet. *Dangling Modifier.* A short ladder hanging senselessly in the deep end of a drained pool. At other times he'd shake himself, realizing he'd lingered too long upon the single typewriter key dusty from disuse (¢) or the amoebic movement of water where ice melts in a glass. It was his custom when depressed to drink corrosive dark rum. He felt unworthy of the stuff, but drank it anyhow with false bravado. He was the one who had hung up on her, so if anyone called anyone . . . No, she had lied to him. It was better to focus on his wild idea. It had been nagging him all day. He recognized it for the petty demon it was, the little devil with a pitchfork, and yet . . . He searched his address book for a number he'd never dialed.

17

His eyes kept straying to the columns shouting diamonds – Diamond Appraisers, Diamond Buyers, Diamond Drilling, Diamond Setters, Diamonds Retail, Diamonds Wholesale – but he guided them firmly back to the business at hand.

Acme Detective Agency was right out. Acme, if he recalled correctly, was the manufacturer in *Roadrunner* cartoons of explosive devices, catapults and elaborate booby traps that always backfired.

Austin Mick, Private Investigator, sounded like a fictive dick in cocked fedora probing his teeth with a toothpick.

Chung Claymore S PhD ABFP Inc, licensed, bonded, insured, member ISSH, had overqualified. Besides, land mines were named Claymore.

DETEK Agency handled Insurance, Skip Tracing, Surveillance, Photography, Missing Persons, Records Location, Undercover Operations, Process Service, Electronic Debugging, Polygraph Examinations, Integrity Shopping, 24 hours. Though a Polygraph Examination was tempting, Integrity Shopping both puzzled and offended him.

Nothing appealed in E, F and G though most held PhDs.

Hawaiian Detective Agency, Lahaina Detective Agency, Rainbow Detective Agency – all blurred together like Waikiki neon in the rainy season.

Tropical Detective Agency sounded balmy.

It was thus that he arrived at the final entry: Warner Agency. It sounded solid enough. Simple, to the point, more respectable sans 'Detective'. Its ad read 'Thorough–Reliable–Affordable'.

This whole exercise served as something of a revelation to

Cullen, for whom such agencies were mythic, the stuff of Bogart movies and dime novels. He thought one or two vestigial dicks might hang out their shingles by the waterfront, wrinkled old things circumscribed by privacy laws, but he was surprised to find so many listed, all sounding young and upright, and some with PhDs. Had he accidentally stumbled upon a refuge for untenured instructors?

One thing seemed obvious: to take up so much space in the Yellow Pages they had to serve a real purpose in the real world. He wondered what gumshoes did exactly. He supposed they did what one wanted done. They spied. They snooped. They stooped to anything. He assured himself that this would be a one-time thing, like cheating on one's income tax to protect a windfall. It wouldn't be messy and he wouldn't carry it beyond the bounds of propriety. There was simply this nagging suspicion that must be confirmed or allayed. It was very much like asking the doctor for an X-ray.

'Warner Detective Agency,' answered a man's voice, thus disabusing him of the notion that he was perhaps dealing with something less seedy. He imagined a tall, straight-edged, gray-suited haole, a veteran of the service or of HPD. He imagined, in fact, Vice Squad Detective Yager.

'Hi. Listen, if I give you a phone number, can you give me a name and address to go with it?'

'Certainly.'

'How much would that cost?'

'Ten dollars. You can send me a check.'

'Okay. It's 737-2223.'

'737-2223. Give me your name and number and I'll get back to you in ten minutes.'

It was that simple. So for ten minutes he tidied up his apartment and his conscience, emptying wastebaskets and hosing down objections. What the detective was doing, he assumed, was looking up the number in a reverse directory. It probably took less than a minute. In a dilapidated corner of his mind, a mean-spirited voice was already suggesting other uses to which one might put a detective. He was ignoring it.

Ten minutes later the phone rang indiscreetly – louder, he felt, than usual.

'Hello.'

'Mr Kinnell?'

'Yes.'

'The name you want is Steven B. Tillman. That's T-I-L-L-M-A-N. The address is 504 Beretania.'

'Thank you. I'll put a check in the mail today.'

'Thank *you*, sir. It was a pleasure serving you.'

18

His Friday afternoon class passed unpleasantly. He had begun by returning a batch of justly graded fetiparous papers, and the air had grown quickly thorny. Like fishhook cactus, thought Cullen, loosening the noose of his tie. When he lectured, his words hung in the air as if skewered. His students had a mutinous slouch that distressed him. He counted the steps to the door.

He was happy to escape to his office, and happier still to escape to his fastback. The campus, once as compact as a root ball, had suddenly swollen to a vast labyrinth. He hadn't seen Felicia all week, not even momentarily – in the distance – before she vanished. It was amazing how easily one could torment the other. Two weeks was a seriously long time that threatened to grow longer.

He crossed Waialae and cruised all the quiet side streets shaded by African tulips and monkeypods. Pink filaments of monkeypod flowers floated on to the windshield. Failing to find her Vega, he headed for Beretania. 504, he was not surprised to discover, was not a house but a towering steel and concrete apartment complex. It had a name, too: Kamani Plaza. Its parking lot rose seven stories, an uncrenellated citadel blotting out the sun and casting a cold shadow across Beretania. Casual surveillance was out of the question. He'd have no choice but to drive through it, floor by floor.

Circling the block for courage, he ran a mental review of the possibilities. There seemed to be only two: either her car was there, or it was not. That was the beauty of it. If she wasn't cheating, she'd never know. If she was, his actions were justified.

If he encountered her in the parking lot, fresh from her

assignation, he imagined he'd simply drive off, out of her life and the appalling shadow of doubt she'd cast over his. Perhaps he'd throw her a kiss in the rearview mirror. What, after all, had *he* to be ashamed of?

But as he climbed the winding ramp he saw it differently. If he failed to find her Vega, it proved nothing; it was he who would never know. If he did find it, it was over. The price of certainty would be confirmed suspicions; the price of not losing her, uncertainty. It was a no-win situation. And, goddamnit to hell, what was that on the floorboard if not a roach?

He drove past every stall in the lot, all seven floors, expecting at each turn to uncover the incriminating evidence of a white Vega, license HN4223. After a weekend of surveillance, he began to recognize certain cars, even anticipate them as landmarks. All roads, it seemed, at all hours of the day and night, led to Kamani Plaza. One night, tossing in a fitful sleep, he confused his torso with the down ramp and heard again and again, like an alarming heartbeat, the squeal of his tires descending that concrete spiral. One day, he entered the lobby to discover that Tillman shared apartment 433 with someone named Magann. Meanwhile, the silence widened. Another week had passed without her phonecall, a week that distilled his thoughts to a single nagging question: did he owe her an apology or himself his pride?

In the evening, darkness descended upon him like a fine dust as he lay prematurely in bed, fully clothed. The telephone, a bloated toad, had become an object of repulsion. He imagined the cold eyes, chiseled smile, and burnished pectoral muscles of Felicia's new lover, a lover who did not necessarily live at Kamani Plaza. To complete the torture, he added a mustache and sailboat. Perhaps this very minute they were rendezvousing at the Yacht Harbor, sipping white wine as a prelude, while the stars drew the last light from the purpled sky and the mysterious sailor got an inspiration that made the boat list to starboard. By not calling, Cullen had made such a rendezvous easy. And who was Steve Tillman? Surely not the wiped-out surfer at Melanie's party. Old lover? New lover? A little of both? Why could Cullen not picture him as anything other than photogenic? He imagined them grappling in bed, their legs entwined like banyan roots – her clenched eyes, her torrent of naughty whispers, her hands beating his broad back . . . His fists hit the mattress! Though he struggled to uproot these thoughts as quickly as they sprouted, his imagination proved overly fertile. So fertile, in fact, that it had left him with an unsummoned erection, a kind of insult added to injury. He turned on the sidelight.

When he fished out his penis, it returned his stare, as if he were a voyeur discovered at the window. Nevertheless, he scrutinized carefully what he held in his hand. Mushroom. Mottled lettuce. Chicken skin. It was a sad appendage that had been fried in deep fat. *Cock* seemed a good name for such a vulgar contraption. Felicia used it frequently. He held it, without enthusiasm, as if it were stale Chinese eggroll. Earl had called him, mercilessly, a classic case of the pathetic worm squirming on the hook. But what else could a worm do on a hook? The hook was stronger than he was. He returned his penis to its lair and considered the telephone. Twice he picked up the receiver and dialed all but the last digit. The second time, he placed the receiver to his ear and listened to its barely audible static, abandoning himself to the sound as if to a mantra. The electronic breath of the machine was outer space: cold unreachable dots of light embedded in blackness.

The last digit was two. Almost nothing at all.

He hung up. He contemplated the possibility of dialing yet a third time. If he was so weak, why was he so bloody stubborn? His hand was still on the receiver when the telephone sounded its alarm, startling him to the point of almost knocking it from its cradle. Composing himself, he allowed it to ring once more. He lacked the courage to tarry longer. He cleared his throat.

'Hello?'

'Cullen, thank God you're home. Can you come over right away?' She was sobbing. 'There's a man in the house.'

'Who is this?'

'Oh God. This is Claire. Cullen?'

'What do you mean there's a man in the house? Where's Ernest?'

'He's in San Francisco. Can you come?'

'I'll be right over. I'll call the police.'

'No, please don't! Come by yourself. Come to the kitchen door.'

'Claire, I could be too late. The police could get there faster.

Have you seen this man?'

'Yes. He's standing right behind me. Please come quick. Please.'

'What does he want?'

'I don't *know*, Cullen.'

'I'll be right over. Stay on the phone. Pretend you're still talking.'

Now he cursed himself for not owning a gun. He grabbed an imposing kitchen knife, found his keys, hopped into the fastback, drove straight down Wilhemina slowing only at the stop signs, then took the last leg of Sierra to 11th Ave. and the freeway. Of all the calls he had ever received, this was easily the most bizarre. Why no police? Why him? Why the kitchen door? Why had the man allowed her to call? To heighten his sadistic pleasure? He supposed some lunatic client of her law firm had followed her home. He had a picture of the kind of man that would be. Quietly mad. Wild in the eyes. He'd have to be dealt with coolly and carefully, but most of all, confidently. Should he bring the knife along or not? How big was he? Was he armed? Of course he was armed; there were swords in the living room, knives in the kitchen. He recalled a giant meat cleaver. He sincerely hoped he was up to this.

He sped off the freeway at University and hit his first light at Dole. It was maddening to simply sit there, yielding to the carefree and unendangered. He realized that in some sense of the word, he loved Claire. That committed him to her defense with a passionate disregard for the consequences. But what if he was too late? He was horrified to imagine what he might find. He'd go mad with rage. He wouldn't know what to do.

He's standing right behind me. There had been no mistaking the terror in that voice. What was happening now, this very moment? Which room had she called from? Was there a phone in the kitchen? Should he burst in noisily or sneak in quietly?

The reckless drive to the back of the valley took ages. He kept braking and downshifting as two-dimensional human obstacles sprang from nowhere, each a cartoon cutout, a caricature of a jogger, a skateboarder, a boy on a bike. And then, on the last leg, climbing toward the cemetery, when he would have welcomed the sight of even a bicyclist, the feckless human race disappeared altogether, unwilling to get involved. He felt awful – queasy in his stomach, numb in his hands.

The Chinese gate rose among the graves. He pulled into the driveway and squealed to a stop behind Claire's Toyota. Perhaps that had been a mistake. He wished the cops were coming behind him. The house stood silent and dark. This was going to take all the courage he could summon. He grabbed the knife, which had fallen from the passenger seat to the floor. He had last used it to halve a papaya. Rounding the corner of the garage, he brushed past a clot of enormous monstera leaves. A thick wall of them pressed close to the walkway, exotic parasites. The kitchen light was on. And there stood Claire, staring at him through the window, her eyes brimming with tears. She stood before the sink in a black dress splashed with red. No one stood behind her.

'Oh, Cullen.'

She met him at the door by throwing her arms around him and sobbing into his chest. He held the knife in one hand and nervously patted her back with the other, all the while feeling foolish as he eyed the kitchen. Her hair had a dark, frantic smell.

'Okay. It's okay now. Where is he?'

She drew back, her hands first clutching his shirt front, then smoothing it with awkward, uncertain gestures as if to apologize for her tears. She failed to raise her eyes but stared, instead, into his chest. He had never seen her like this.

'Where is he, Claire?' he whispered.

She turned her head slowly. The kitchen was empty. She released him, embarrassed, and drew back a stray wisp of hair.

'He's not here anymore. He was standing over there.'

'Is he still in the house?'

'Oh, yes. I'm sure he is. I think we could both use a drink, don't you?'

'Claire, where is he? Who is he?'

'I don't know. He was standing right there. I was peeling the leaves off a head of lettuce, at the sink. It was a very crisp head of lettuce. See?' She pointed to a bowl in the sink. 'Every time I peeled off a leaf, I heard an echo behind me. After a while, I began to wonder about it. Why an echo? Then I turned around, like this, with the lettuce in my hand. And there he was, just standing there. An old Chinese man. The same one I saw before. He was wearing a long brown overcoat, very worn, threadbare, and a sort of shapeless brown hat. He had a large mole here' – she pointed to her right temple – 'and I could see the kitchen light reflected in his eyes.'

'Then what happened?'

'He started to raise his hands toward his head. I was afraid he might remove it. So I turned back to the sink and kept peeling the lettuce. Then I remembered the phone and called you.'

There was, indeed, a green wall phone next to the sink.

'You were afraid he might remove what?'

'His head. One hears of such things. He was a ghost, Cullen. I'm sure of it. There's no point looking anywhere in the house. This one's different from the old lady. He seemed so real. I could see the light in his eyes, just above the pupils.'

'And then?'

'I kept peeling lettuce. I didn't dare stop. Then you came.'

In the sink sat a stainless steel bowl of finely shredded lettuce. He stood over it, looking for a clue. He was still wearing the lei of her frightened embrace. He could still feel the weight of her upon his chest and smell the wild panic of her hair – a pungent, tart jab like that of stephanotis.

'Maybe I will take a drink.'

'Seven and seven okay?'

'Fine, thanks.' He noted now that the red in her dress was orchids. It was closer to magenta, the color of cattleyas. She was wearing nylons, but no shoes. He stood where the ghost had stood and admired her.

'You can put that knife down.' She smiled, suppressing a giggle, her cheeks still wet with tears. Strands of hair had fallen over her eyes. That never seemed to bother women.

He laid the knife on the counter.

'Well Jesus, Claire, you didn't say anything about a ghost. You said there was a *man* standing behind you. What the hell was I to think?'

'I know, I know. I'm sorry. I was very upset. He looked, for all intents and purposes, like a man. What would you have done if I had said *ghost*?'

He sucked in his lips to think about this.

'Let's go into the living room,' she said, handing him his drink.

'Thanks.'

She turned on the table lamp rather than the ceiling light. Even the lamp cast a warm, affluent glow, like a pearl in a gloved hand. They sat on the chamois couch, Claire tucking one leg beneath her, the perfect vision of womanly distress.

'I would have come anyway. Just as fast. Just as frightened. Maybe without the knife.'

'I came home late from work and went straight to the kitchen. I was just going to fix myself a salad. This one was so different from the woman. He seemed so real. As real as you or me. But somehow I just knew he was a ghost and not some crackpot intruder.'

As real as you or me. Where had he heard that before?

'I think it was the same man I saw under the mango tree when we first moved in. In fact, I'm almost sure of it.'

'But surely ghosts don't need to piss under mango trees. Or anywhere else, for that matter. I seriously doubt that they have any excretory functions whatsoever.'

'I never said he was . . . pissing. That was your interpretation.'

He appealed to his drink for a ruling on this. The ice cubes were semicircular.

'Objection sustained,' he conceded.

Claire giggled. It wasn't quite like this when Ernest was there. A certain propriety had always made her wifely. Now he could see, in the dishevelment of her hair, in the unabashed cock of her leg, something of the swooning geisha in the Ukiyo-E above her.

'What's Ernest doing in San Francisco?'

'An ACLU convention. He'll be back tomorrow. I guess that's why I was feeling brave.'

'What do you mean?'

'I've been staying at my mother's. I don't even eat here. I just thought I'd drop in and get things ready for tomorrow. Groceries, that sort of thing. We're selling this place, you know.'

'No. Really?'

'Yes.'

'Will you tell the next buyers about the ghosts?'

'That's an ethical question, Cullen.'

'I know.'

'We haven't decided yet. We've been discussing that. I think we should, but Ern says nobody told us. Nobody would buy a haunted house. It's bad enough living across from the cemetery.'

'Oh, I don't know. That cemetery has character. The next buyer wouldn't have to worry about high-rises. And it's quiet.'

'Not with all the firecrackers it isn't. Some days it sounds like all the Chong Wongs and Lin Lums in the world are casting out spirits. I guess that's why they all come running over here.

'Our neighbors are Chinese. A young couple. They told us that when they first moved in they used to hear children crying in the middle of the night. At first they thought it was cats, but then they decided it couldn't be. So one day Robin – that's her name – walked over to the graveyard to see who's buried there. She discovered about a dozen children's graves right across the street. They all died on the same day. I don't know why. Anyhow, the graves were all unkempt and overgrown. They're quite old. She and her husband cleaned them up, cut the grass, even brought flowers. That did the trick, she said. They still keep up the graves, and they haven't heard any more crying.'

'Is their house haunted, too?'

'If it is, they didn't mention it. And I didn't tell them anything about ours, either. This place is only five years old.'

She stared into the fireplace.

'I guess we're honor-bound to tell prospective buyers, yeah?'

'Like you say, it's an ethical question.'

'The problem is I'm usually moral. I'm not sure I like being that way. Do you know what the naughtiest thing I ever did was?'

'What?'

'When I was a little girl, another girl talked me into making a crank phone call one day when her parents were out. I would have never thought of it myself. So I called up the first victim and said, with trembling voice, "Excuse me, sir. We're taking a survey. Is your refrigerator running?"

'"Yes it is," he said very cheerfully. "Would you like me to go catch it?"

'"Yes, please," I said. "Thank you, sir." I decided then and there that I lacked the criminal gene.'

'Then why do you want to become a lawyer?'

She leaned closer to swat him on the arm.

'I'm not going to be that kind of lawyer. I'm going to champion the cause of the underdog. Do you have any moral failings, Cullen?'

'Moral failings. Moral failings. Well . . . there is one thing, I suppose.'

'What's that?'

'You see, my feet are two different sizes. One's 10 and the other's 9½.'

'That's not exactly a moral failing, Cullen. I think we could forgive that.'

'No, no, of course it's not. But when I go to a shoe store, I always ask to try on size 10. And then I say, real nonchalantly like, "Can I try 9½., please?" And then what do you think I do?'

'You don't.'

'I do. I walk around and around, trying out these new shoes – Are they me? Are they an accurate reflection of my character? Are they comfortable? – And then when no one's looking, I make the switch. I walk out with a size 10 left shoe and a size 9½ right shoe in a 9½ box. And you know I've never been caught. But there must come a time when some poor sod who wears size 10 wonders why the left shoe feels so damned tight.'

'So you're the one! I wish you hadn't told me this, Cullen. My father wears size 10, and every time he goes to a shoe store he curses the baka who slipped in a 9½.'

'You're kidding.'

'Of course. Want another?'

'You can top it up.'

'Come with me.'

He followed her into the kitchen. Ernest had always made his drinks at the liquor cabinet.

'I think I should check out the rest of the house, don't you?'

'It's not necessary. I'm not staying here tonight.'

He saw her heels beside the kitchen door, one standing, one on its side. They were black, strappy things that seemed poised for indiscretion. The air cracked with the sound of ice.

'I'm not looking forward to dying,' she said.

He moved to her side. 'It's not the best part of life.'

'You know what I felt when I saw that old man tonight? I felt like I had penetrated some kind of barrier, like an invisible wall had come down. I don't really think he disappeared. I think the wall just came back.'

'What kind of barrier are we talking about here? Spatial, you mean? Temporal?'

'Good question, Cullen. Yes, maybe temporal. It was like seeing into the past.'

'Did he say anything?'

'No. Thank God.'

'Did he look at you?'

'Oh yes! It was the strangest moment in my life. It wasn't a cruel look. It was rather sad. It terrified me. But I thought that if I just turned away, maybe things would be okay. Then I remembered the phone and called you.'

'I don't know, Claire. If it works one way, it seems like it should work the other way as well. How come we never see any ghosts in the future? How come they always come dragging their chains out of the past?'

'I don't know. Maybe because the future isn't here yet. There's no one there to look back at us. Someday, *we'll* be the ghosts of the future. Maybe there is no future. The way things are going today. Sometimes it seems like this is the last sane place on earth.'

'That's all too abstruse for me.'

'Me too. I only know what I saw and what I felt.'

Back in the living room, seated once again beneath the Ukiyo-E, he studied the light in his ice and said, 'Can I ask you a personal question?'

Her eyes widened. 'As long as it's not personal.'

'Touché. I was just wondering why you called *me*.'

'That's not a personal question. I called you because you're the closest friend we have. Danny Lee lives all the way in Hawaii Kai. Jeff Holt's with Ern in San Francisco. You came. I knew you would. I knew I could count on you. Thanks.' She briefly touched her hand to his. 'I hope I didn't inconvenience you. You didn't have a date with your girlfriend or anything, did you?'

'No, not with anything. Nor with my girlfriend. We're on the outs. We haven't spoken to each other in weeks.'

She sipped her drink. 'That's terrible. What happened?'

'I don't know. I got sick, she got a job, things started sliding downhill. I don't know what happened. I guess she just lost interest.'

'That seems unlikely.' She drew her hair behind her ear, revealing a gold earring in the shape of a Chinese character.

To properly ponder the question, Cullen would need his pipe. He had run off without it. What if there had not actually been an old man in an overcoat? What if all these years he had misunderstood? What if she had called him here to . . . ? The question dissolved in its own unlikelihood.

'What does your earring mean?'

'Happiness.'

When he'd been racing to her rescue, envisioning the worst, he'd been surprised by a sudden burning surge of tears. All along East Manoa, he'd cried for Claire, for Claire in mortal danger. One of the dearest. One of the kindest. It alarmed him, this sudden onslaught of emotion. One arranges one's feelings neatly, like neckties, taking pride in their sincerity. It was dangerous to be so blind to their true colors, to have them riot when least expected.

'I cried for you, driving over here. I broke into tears. I was so afraid that I'd get here too late, that I wouldn't be able to save you. I thought you were in mortal danger.'

She put down her drink, took his hand, cocked her head, and smiled sadly, her eyes brimming with emotion.

'Thank you,' she said. 'I was afraid, too. Thank you for saving me.'

'That's an exaggeration.'

'Not such.' She lowered her eyes.

There was no doubt now about what his passions were urging. He was connected to her by cool, delicate fingers. His pulse was filling the room; surely she could feel it. It had taken certain courage to rush to her defense, armed with only a kitchen knife, but it would take even greater courage to lean toward her lips.

Ernest was in San Francisco.

Her cheek was the palest pink. He could envision her blush, her shock and indignation. What had she done to encourage such behavior? The whole friendship would collapse like day-old hibiscus, leaving an unpleasant stain. The favor would become a crime, the heroism a violation. And he'd become the strange man in the house.

But what if Claire – Claire who had always acknowledged his puns with compassion and understanding, not to mention lovely optical arabesques – what if Claire, receiving his kiss, hesitated – merely hesitated – allowed his lips to linger, and then, tender as always – one of the dearest, one of the kindest – responded to that kiss, acknowledged it with passion and understanding? What if, through wet lashes and ravaged mascara, her eyes fixed his, mirrored their desires, said, in effect, I have always loved you too? What if she fell beneath him like a geisha, her face a pale flame in darkness? What if she fingered the buttons of his shirt with a woman's delicate reservations? What if he smelled, in the darkness of her hair, the hothouse breath of those orchids, those extravagant unfoldings? And she would cry, of course, for the betrayal and the years, would sob in erratic bursts as she kissed him, as that black dress, even now above her knees, slid with silken dereliction to her thigh, and he found there her clarity, her opalescence, and knew, for the first time, Claire.

'I'd better get going,' she said, rising from the couch. 'My mother will be worried.'

And soon he was driving home alone, more shaken than ever.

19

'Hello?' The wary voice of one who has entered the country illegally was, as always, her mother's.

'Hi, Mrs Mattos. Is Felicia there, please?'

The dense silence that greeted this question was a good sign: it meant that Mrs Mattos, deflated by the discovery that the caller was not her sister, had shambled off dejectedly to fetch Felicia – assuming, apparently, that the caller could deduce as much without being so informed. That allayed one fear: that she wouldn't be home but would instead be serving cocktails in some sleazy jazz club near the zoo. *Cocktails.* It sounded as vulgar as *jazz.*

'Hi.' She sounded more sleepy than defiant. That allayed a second fear.

'Hi . . . How are you?'

'Oh, as well as can be expected. And you?'

'About the same . . . You would've never called me, would you?'

'I was going to call tomorrow,' she conceded with unmistakable languor.

'I called to apologize for being . . . so suspicious.'

But he knew it was not suspicion but pride that had subsided, that now he lacked even a banana leaf with which to conceal his nakedness.

'You know what your problem is?'

'What?'

'You think I don't love you. But I do.'

He caught his breath. He could not have been more flabbergasted had she stepped directly from the receiver and washed his feet with her hair. What a fool he had been. Suddenly he saw her as Portuguese, standing in her mother's kitchen, phone numbers penned on the door jamb, a woman poured from her race like wine from a bottle – dark, robust, a vessel of light. He didn't know what to say.

'Would you like to know *why* my lights were on that night you were spying on me?'

'If you want to tell me.'

'Because they were on *all* night.'

'Why's that?'

She sighed . . . that sigh that always seemed to labor such a great distance. And he imagined that she brushed her hair from her eyes as she did so.

'Because I felt that thing again, holding me down. Only this time it was really awful, like being in deep water and trying to rise for breath. It's worse than before. It was like someone sitting on top of me, trying to get inside me – like hands holding me down. Not just a weight, but hands! I keep remembering *Rosemary's Baby*.'

Once again, he felt the old, angry fever rising. It was no different than his hatred of Steve, or the garbagemen, or any of the lewd strangers in her life. But this hatred was for Uncle Ricardo. To cool himself, he opted for a quote from Chatterton.

'The death-owl loud doth sing/ To the night-mares as they go.'

'*What*?'

'A bit of medieval poetry written by an eighteenth century writer.'

'So?' She hadn't caught the anachronism, and now he was once again, so soon, on the wrong footing.

'So in the olden days, nightmares were supposed to be female spirits, goblins that sat on people's chests while they slept, almost suffocating them. That's where bad dreams come from. Only in your case the spirit seems to be male.'

'Oh, Jesus. Don't say that. I feel haunted. I don't need poetry right now. This thing is serious. I used to be able to handle it, but now I'm not so sure. I don't know what to do. I've even started praying.'

'It seems to me that you have to move out of the house.'

'Yeah, I think so too. I started work a couple weeks ago.'

'Oh? How is it?'

'Not bad. The tips are pretty good.'

'How's the music?'

'I like it. There's a house band playing now called Advent, but every once in a while they plan to bring in mainland groups. Chuckie, the manager, is a big jazz buff.'

And so it went, a sort of banal crisscross fagoting that slowly stitched them together again. They arranged to visit their cove on Sunday. He told her nothing about Claire and the Chinese ghost; he saw no point in feeding her imagination. It seemed that there were now two ghosts he had to believe in, not counting Earl's and the one in Claire and Ernest's bedroom. He couldn't say he was pleased by this turn of events.

But he was certainly pleased by the outcome of his call. She'd been easy on him. It no longer seemed he'd surrendered without honor. Together they'd reached an understanding: they loved each other – forever or a long time, whichever came first, as Felicia had once said in bed. And had liked it so much she'd written it down – in eyeliner, on his lecture notes.

20

They'd parked, as always, on the dusty shoulder of the highway and had crossed the wasteland on foot, hot cinders burning through their soles. Felicia had brought along a bag of Ah Pan, and Cullen cold cans of Guava Nectar. He anticipated fondling her aquatically, weightlessly, nesting his cock between her legs and carrying her about like an inflatable Dutch Wife. He had pretty much concluded that underwater raptures were ridiculous, that the Pacific invited undulant foreplay and nothing more, but he held no objection to that – he was in the mood for buoyant, bobbling tantalization. Perhaps Felicia had been right when she'd accused him of having a book on everything, for he had a book on aquatic sex which he'd consulted only the night before. It was called *The Kama Sutra* and it was of two minds on the subject. Suvarnanabha said that many amusing positions could be practiced in this way provided one kept one's head above water, while Vatsyayana said it leads to hell. Not very helpful, actually.

This time he'd brought his Pentax. He was going to capture his swimming nymph on film. The water would tease the light as she teased him, liquefying her image. She would dance and he'd compose. She'd float, he'd hover.

And then there would also be portraits of a motionless woman mirrored by the sea, studies that transformed her nakedness to nudity. Wet hair would curl on her cheek, fall to her breasts, float on the surface of her second image. Half would be real and half reflection, Felicia a pair of open wings. Or half would be true and half refraction; he'd have to wait and see. These shots he'd shoot in black and white and develop himself. Then he'd have the satisfaction of watching her materialize miraculously on a blank sheet in a dark room, her image rising like a water sprite from the depths of a shallow pool. Myriad Lilliputian sunboats that had tacked in unison whenever a breeze shook the water would be fixed forever as stars. And soon he'd fix her image and hang it on the wall, where he could gaze in her eyes whenever, studying at leisure the mystery that eluded him. Felicia was back, the sky was blue, the sea a tray of diamonds.

But nearing the cove, both sensed something amiss. A kind of staff had been planted near the water's edge, and something, perhaps a flag, rippled around it, making a territorial claim that silenced them. As they drew closer, the flag squirmed, a living creature. They stopped ten feet short of the cove, where a diver's spear had been planted shaft-first in lava. Impaled upon it was a large moray. The spear passed once through its body, behind the porelike gills. Its elongated mouth scissored the air slowly, rhythmically, yet emitted no scream, no rasp, no sound whatsoever. The gills, too, opened and closed as if still underwater. The eyes stared at nothing and revealed nothing, not even when a convulsion surged through the body like a wave.

'Somebody must be scuba diving,' he said.

'We shouldn't have come on the weekend. This spoils everything. Let's get out of here.'

'Okay.' But he approached the eel. 'Just let me get a few pictures first.'

'What for?'

'It's interesting.'

'It's repulsive. It gives me the creeps.'

'I'll say. But you have to feel sorry for it, too, no? How would you like being impaled?'

'Look at those beady eyes.'

Beads were all they were, black pellets ringed in brown. Perhaps they made it a creature too vile for pity. Or perhaps it was the precise rows of fiercely honed teeth set like sawblades, ruthless as the barbs ripping the animal's throat. With its mouth closed, an eel looked old and toothless. But an open-mouthed eel was a different story. He leaned closer, studying it now through the lens. From a certain angle, one couldn't see the spear. A living moray in a vacuous blue made a disturbing picture. He shot once and then again. But while he composed another, closer shot, one that confronted the viewer with his nightmare, the eel lurched suddenly toward him. He leapt back instinctively, the danger magnified by the lens. The eel couldn't possibly harm him. Skewered by spasms, it had wound itself even tighter around the source of its agony. As his fear trickled back down his throat, Cullen felt himself once again suffused with a curious pity – curious because its object was a thing so repugnant. As horrid as it was, all teeth and malignant eye, the eel did not deserve to suffer. Its tormentors – masked, black-skinned assassins cloaked by the calm of the sea – possessed a weird humor to have left it like this, baking in thin, parched air. Torturing it was such a human thing to do.

'*Cul*len . . .'

'Just a minute.'

He took one more picture and capped his camera. He could see now that the cove made a perfect stepping-stone to the deep; a scuba diver following it out to sea would suddenly have a whole new world open beneath his belly. It would be like swimming over the edge of a cliff. And in the depths below the shallows where he and his lover had swum had lurked this beast.

'Come on, Cullen. Let's go before they come back.'

'Okay.'

They left the eel to its grisly pantomime and returned to the car.

'Let's go to Hanauma,' she said.

'Okay.'

Ten minutes later they pulled into the parking lot high above the oyster-shaped bay.

'Good,' she said. 'It's not too crowded for a Sunday.'

Together they trekked down the steep, burning road to the beach and not far from the snack shop staked a small claim with their towels. He lay on his back and closed his eyes.

'Let's go snorkeling,' she said.

'No gear.'

'They rent it here. It's not expensive.'

'To tell you the truth, I've never been snorkeling.'

'All the more reason to go now. Come on.' She tugged on his arm.

'All right,' he said in one long exhalation, 'I'll give it a try. But please be patient with me.'

When they were waist deep he noticed shoals of silver fish darting about their legs.

'What are those?'

'Mullets. Put your flippers on.'

He did as told and she showed him how to use the mask and snorkel.

'Just float on the surface and keep your face in the water. Then your snorkel will always be above the surface. Just relax and breathe normally.'

'What if I take in water?'

'Just blow it out. Like this. Phooo!'

'Where are we going?'

'We'll just swim over the reefs. There's plenty to see there. Just follow me.'

She donned her mask and swam off, her flippers alternating in long graceful strokes like a walrus's. He followed as best he could. Once prone, he felt the push and tug of the ocean, drawing him out, sweeping him in. Water filled his mask almost immediately and he stood to adjust it. Felicia was swimming on ahead. He made a second attempt to join her. She turned to see how he was faring. He found it hard to take a breath while submersed, to place all his trust in the snorkel. A wave pushed him shoreward and he floundered, breathing water. He stood up again, coughing.

'Here,' said Felicia. 'You've got the angle wrong. Keep it like this and you won't take in any water.'

'I keep wanting to come up for air.'

'I've noticed that when we're making love.' She smiled. 'Come on, we're almost there.'

The reef ran close to the shoreline. One could swim directly above it and touch it with one's hands. He went under for a third try. This time he was more willing to let the door close slowly behind him. The new world he'd entered was silent and ethereal. A school of large oval fish – each black with a burst of orange near the tail – swam just before him, seemingly unperturbed by his presence. They had friendly, bovine eyes and striking white accents that ran the length of their body. At the time, none of the fish had names. He'd learn later that these were Achilles Tangs. He set off to follow them and soon found yellow tangs swimming harmoniously among them, the whole school a single reflex that could dart like the glance of an eye. He was over a deep recess alive with motion. Sergeant Majors swam everywhere, small silver dishes with black stripes and yellow sides. Felicia tapped him on the shoulder and pointed to his right. There swam a sliver of indescribable beauty. A foot long, it erupted with color, the orange head melding into a red body striped with irregular chocks of blue and green, the whole outlined in electric blue. It swam with a serious eye. Cullen followed it, stunned by its extravagance. He was snorkeling with ease now, unselfconsciously, drawn by nature's most fanciful creations. Nothing in the world of psychedelia, he'd decided, could surpass the frivolous palette of the sea.

When the fish moved on, he and Felicia surfaced.

'What was that?'

'Either a Christmas Wrasse or an Ornate Wrasse. I get the two confused.'

'This is wonderful. Why didn't you bring me here before?'

'Don't know. Oh look! A trumpetfish.'

He followed her back underwater to see a long yellow spindle gliding slowly below. It had a snout like a spoonbill and a tail like a black shaving brush. *Yellow Submarine* thought Cullen. Felicia pointed silently to a small brown puffer with white spots and sad blue eyes. A pink-tailed durgon swam by engrossed in thought – bulky dark fuselage, a boxer's lips, cerulean fins etched in black. They swam from one such delight to another, or such delights swam to them. Cullen had known that such fish existed – he had his books – but he had never known that they existed in such abundance and proximity, accessible even to him.

Shoals of golden butterflyfish surrounded them – the raccoons with banded eyes, the teardrops branded by single black tears, the lauwiliwilis neatly speckled in brown, the longnose butterflies with bristles for spines and straws for snouts. Moorish idols trailed long white streamers. Gray-white surgeonfish abounded, each with an orange brushstroke behind the eye. A large brown grouper dotted with turquoise swam indifferently between them. A green and indigo parrotfish grazed on coral. An azure unicorn headed for the deep, its horn protruding just before the eye. And lest the expedition be anything less than perfect, they saw at the end their fish, the improbable humuhumunukunukuapua'a with its paint-by-numbers body marked by double yellow arrows.

They must have swum for a couple of hours before going ashore for a burger. Afterwards they sunbathed. The sun toasted them to the point of discomfort and the sea cooled them again as they swam in innocuous green waves. They anointed themselves with coconut oil only to cleanse themselves in saltwater. They did the sidestroke and the backstroke, then lay side by side while a patient wind cleared the sky of loitering clouds. This was paradise. The sea was the ultimate jacuzzi, the sun the ultimate masseuse. His nose and shoulders turned agreement-error red, while she tanned as evenly as if turned on a rotisserie. They were together again. They stayed until ironwood shadows reached the fringes of their towels and Felicia announced that if they wanted to make love they'd better hurry because her mother expected her home for dinner. That made twice in one day that she'd said 'make love'.

On his unmade bed, she opened her legs and reached up to him. He'd thought he might first muzzle her darkness, but she soon drew him up by his hair. The trough between her breasts smelled of coconut. Her oiled legs were sandy. He made no attempt to contort her; she was already murmuring and so was he. He licked the afternoon's salt from her ear. 'It's been a long time,' he whispered. 'I can't control it.'

'Then don't control it.'

Pleasure craft, they rose and fell in swells.

'I love you.'

When their sea had calmed, they lay on the beach of the bed. With his ear to the sheet, he could hear the mattress springs twitching like tiny sandcrabs. Then, for the first time that day, he heard the Java finches in the poinciana and felt his shoulders burning with pain.

'Did you miss me?' she asked.

'Something terrible. I couldn't sleep nights.'

'Serves you right,' she said, slapping him hard on the shoulder, then cooling the pain with a kiss.

They showered, he soaping her breasts, she soaping his cock until it was once again topgallant. Life was simple.

That day enlarged him. Afterwards, he seemed to carry with him the new world to which she had introduced him. It was a special sort of grace. So that if he sat, say, in a café, his newly enlarged spirit sat with him, or rather swam about him, so that he was now always accompanied by an aura of yellow tangs, by a blue and green parrotfish, by an elegant wrasse gliding silently from one level to another, and the turquoise sunlight would accompany him as well, an undulating shoal of rays gliding weightlessly through space. As a result, his world seemed more abundant, more colorful, both dignified and jubilant. He had made a connection to a parallel universe where silence and extravagance reigned.

He still felt this way Friday evening as they dined at Doong Kong Lau, a restaurant 'certificated to be hygiened'. They'd agreed to order nothing on the menu that wasn't misspelled. They bypassed 'Chick in Grave' and 'Fish Lips with Four Kind Meats' to feast instead on 'Foul Delight' and 'Sauted Beef Book Trips with Sealions'. When the management made an unauthorized substitution of scallions for sealions, Cullen refused to make a scene as Felicia fervidly urged.

They drove early to Cinerama Theater, where he purchased tickets for *Seven Beauties*, then slipped into that nameless crackseed shop advertising BREAKFAST–LUNCH–SUNDRIES–SEEDS FOR ALL OCCASIONS. The shop was simply a niche in the block – a mouse-hole with no door to shut out King Street traffic – but crackseed was everywhere: in display cases, on wire racks, on crude wooden shelves that rose almost to the ceiling. As in a biological supply house, each variety either hung naked in a cellophane bag or squatted obscenely in a large glass jar. He surveyed the possibilities alongside Felicia, glad to have no voice in her decision. While attracted to Soft Wet Salty See Mui, he could ill deny the equal allure of Sweet Sour Salty Apricot. But he was not so egocentric as to be unaware that one with a different upbringing might favor simply Wet See Mui or Salty Apricot or Sour See Mui or Sweet Apricot. But wouldn't one then wonder what joys had been missed by shunning Sweet Salty Apricot, and how would that compare with Seedless Olive

Cake or Dried Mango with Rock Salt? It was not a task for the uninitiated.

Felicia had once explained to him that all crackseed was plum unless otherwise specified, that Kum Chow and Football and Bulldog merely referred to modes of preservation, though she couldn't elaborate on what those modes might be. When her hand slid past Hot Soft Legs and Tasty Red Legs en route to Sweet Li Hing Mui, Cullen felt lust for cuttlefish.

'Are you sure? Not Wong Pee or Baby Seed?'

'Don't knock what you don't understand, Dear.'

The little Chinese girl he paid wore an impressive set of braces that broadened her smile. In the world of crackseed, thought Cullen with poetic license, she would be Short Sweet Metallic Lychee. She rang up his purchase on an old wooden cash register whose Moorish archway price tags ranged from 1¢ to $1. 30¢ and 5c sprang to attention.

They sat at the three-stooled soda fountain and ordered milkshakes from the cheery Chinese girl who had come around to serve them once again. He felt comforted, somehow, by her flat-chestedness.

'Once,' said Felicia, 'I was sitting in here and I heard one old lady say to another, "You nevah ride bus? Someday you try go ride, yeah?"'

He smiled. 'It's never too late for a big adventure, huh?'

As they sat there, among the Sweetheart Drinking Straws and beneath faded scenics of Europe and the Mainland, he invented crackseed names while Felicia updated him on events he had missed in her life. Soft Dumpy Pumpkin for Mrs Mattos. Tender Salty Bulldog for her husband. Soft Wet Cherry for their daughter, though she called her soft wet cherry Li Hing Mui. For himself, he happily chose Hot Tumescent Passion Fruit.

He had now reached the stage where he could invite Felicia to join in. She loved the idea and immediately offered Sweet Balding Peach Seed for Father Plecko. He explained that she'd missed the whole point.

'The idea is to capture a person's essence. Sweet Balding Peach Seed doesn't capture Father Plecko's essence. Sweet Balding Peach Seed sounds lovable. You could hug Sweet Balding Peach

Seed. Something like Purulent Wet Cigar Butt is the sort of label one would affix to a jar of Father Pleckos. Get the idea?

'I happen to find Father Plecko very lovable. The man has charisma.'

He rolled his eyes in exasperation and offered a further example, one he was quite pleased with: Sweet Dour Bamboo Slivers for Sister Lucia.

'Here's one for your friend Earl,' she said. 'Mushy Pink Guava with Wormholes.'

'Great. That's perfect. Now you're catching on.'

This made Melanie fair game. His mind ran first to Cuttlefish, then ardently endeavored to work in Muu Muu, but soon settled smugly on Flatulent Stoned Red Balloonfish.

'Flatulent! Where do you get *flatulent*?'

'Okay. How 'bout *flagellant*?'

'That's worse,' she said, crinkling her nose but offering no alternative. Instead she launched into a synopsis and critical analysis of Melanie's latest misbegotten love affair. As a result, she failed to witness the small miracle of love or its facsimile unfolding before the manapua on the opposite side of the shop. It was not entirely her fault – a massive column dominating the shop like a banyan tree in a terrarium blocked her view – but if she had only once pivoted on her stool to follow his oscillating eyes she would have seen that an interesting couple had just arrived conspicuously by taxi, though he supposed their arrival by any other means would have been conspicuous as well. The girl was tall and blonde, fashionably attired in black evening dress and shawl, her nylons the color of rainclouds massing over the Pali, and in her hand she clutched a clutch bearing the costly gold initials of its designer. Unlike her escort, she cast a reflection in the soda fountain mirror; Cullen could see her there between stalks of red ginger.

The man at her side was dapper and black. His suit had the crisp snappy lines of a newly purchased road map. He wore a matching gray cap and carried a cane, and as he bought the lady the delicacies she desired (the ubiquitous Chinese girl reappearing to serve him), Cullen was struck by his happy self-possession. It didn't seem to disturb him at all that he was only three feet tall. Confidence shone in his broad black face, and his chest swelled beneath his bow tie like a parcel of laundry too tightly wrapped. The woman was his, and rightfully so. And if he lost her, he could surely find another. That he walked through life with pride, not apology, was for Cullen something of an epiphany. Of the two, who was the smaller man?

To Felicia Cullen transmitted code with his eyebrows and great torrents of unbound electrons with his eyeballs, but she merely thought his behavior playful if not downright odd, and when she said 'Cut it out', he had to. As midget and blonde stepped out to the tune of 'Keep the change', Felicia was saying something about the attraction of opposites, as illustrated in an oversized way by friend Melanie and whatever native surfer was now sharing her dope.

'And what about us?' he asked. 'Wouldn't you say we're opposites?'

'In what way?'

'Well . . . I'm older than you.'

'We can't all be born simultaneously.'

'Good point. I like jazz and you like Linda Ronstadt.'

'You must like Linda Ronstadt, too. You've got her records. I like some jazz. I'm liking it more these days. It's just that some of that stuff you like puts me to sleep.'

'I like foreign films more than you do.'

'I like movies.'

'Exactly. Those are differences.'

'*Viva la différence*,' she replied, cocking her eyebrows into a sort of accent circumflex and crossing her perfect legs.

'*Vive*,' he said.

In the theater, he wondered if the blonde also ate crackseed as Felicia now ate hers, squeezing each sticky seed to the surface like a bloodclot, plucking it out with long lacquered nails, inserting it into puckered red mouth and sucking the slime salaciously off her fingers. The blonde and her escort had appeared like a vision, an effect highlighted by Felicia's failure to see them at all. The black midget might have frozen time à la Hollywood to say to him directly, 'Be cool, man. Be confident. Walk tall. You're a lucky guy.' And then he would have tipped his cap, tapped his cane like cane-tapping rain, and, with his partner, vanished.

He had a wild idea, so wild that its mere consideration brought an ironic smile. This idea would solve once and for all the riddle of her affections. He'd propose. If she accepted, wonderful – they'd live in Hawaii Kai, raise two lovely children, and continue to keep as pets those slobbering but lovable bloodhounds, Fellatio and Cunnilingus. The money would come from unexpected sources, and the passion, like inflation, would never subside. It was not that improbable.

If she didn't accept, well, then he would know the truth sooner rather than later. The question was whether he could bear to know it. What if—

'*Stop*!' he ordered himself decisively. '*You're forgetting already what the visionary black man told you.*'

21

'*Tract*, dummy,' wrote Cullen gleefully, not in red but in anonymous black. This completed his annotation of the couplet 'Now I'm back for another crack/ at releiving my intestinal track.' The spelling rule '*i* before *e*, except after *c*' had been his doing as well, followed by 'This always works,/ except for jerks.' That it didn't always work failed to perturb him. That he was being puerile only heightened his pleasure. In the privacy of a john, one answered to no one. No one, that is, except the Lone Grader.

He wondered who had authored and correctly spelled 'Virginity is like a balloon – it only takes one prick', a refreshing change from the hackneyed verse of the flatulent brokenhearted. He'd never know. Well, that was it for the day. The personal references to Felicia had ceased, minimizing his editorial duties. He pocketed his marker, opened the door, and headed happily for the sink.

'Wo! Jes the man I wanta see. Jes the man!'

What Cullen said in reply wasn't quite a word. He proceeded to wash his hands.

'Cuz you know how you whopped that F on us last term for *Plaaay*gerism. Whooo, that hurt my mama. I ain't denying the basic, you know, configuration of the whole thing. The halls of academe and all that. What's right is right, true as rain, can't deny it, can't defy it. But we was thinking we really assimilated a lot from your class – you know, through the mental processes and all that – a lot of whatchoo was puttin' down, when you weren't puttin' *us* down, and a lesson *was* learned, *was* learned. It's engraved right here in my – what's it, frontal lobe? So we was thinkin—'

'*Were.*'

'What?'

'*Were*. You *were* thinking.'

'Right. We *were* thinking. But we *was* thinking too. Anyhow, we know you're a busy man, a man with a plan, you got books to read, you got . . . you know, toilet stalls to correct . . . Did you? Did you? Lemme see. Yup, you did. That's your work, sure as shinola. That's your trademark. Well, I can dig it. But there's jes one little thing, one little thing, and that's that, you know, there's this terrible injustice, and uh we just got to max this factor, go with the flow, move with the groove, and uh, let bygones be bygones.'

Jesus, is he on drugs or what? Compared to Duncan, who was bobbing, weaving, dribbling, and otherwise gesticulating wildly with his hands, Cullen felt like a geological marker. He turned to Duncan's silent but grinning teammate.

'What's he trying to say, Dhabul?'

'He tryin' to say we don't need no Fs on our transcripts, dat's what he tryin' to say.'

'Right on! Right on! This is my main man. This is a man after my own mind. That's exacto what I'm tryin' to say. That's my message to you this evening. They gotta go.'

'Why?'

'Why? Cuz the last time we saw you, you was in a, shall we say, *compromising* position?'

'Yeah, you was bendin' over real low.'

'Sweet chariot. Lordy, you was. When I saw you in that den of iniquity I jes sorta – well I don't wanta say I lost any respect or nothing, cuz I know you're a man of principle with a capital P, but I don't need no capital F, and neither does Dhabul here. It looked bad, Mr K. I mean I know that pornographer was probably your sick cousin or something, but you smell nachos, you think bean dip. Know what I mean? Go hand in hand. I don't think the world's gonna understand. I mean this is a Catholic college, Catholic college full of knowledge, and—'

'And you just thought you might try a little extortion, did you?'

'Wo, hey. Now we're getting into a legal domain here. You know, this is *mea culpa pepper* kinda stuff. Too hot, that's too hot. I don't know nothing bout no extortion. Let's jes keep this on a grass roots level here.'

'How about *blackmail*? Does that word appeal to you?'

'Blackmail . . . Yeah, blackmail. I like that. It's got a ring to it. You like that, Dhabul?'

'It's cool.'

'Well, for what it's worth, I was just accompanying my friends on that evening to which you refer.'

'Ohh, sure. We know that. Friend in need, friend indeed. We were companying our friends too.'

'Yes, you were. And that's probably the sort of thing you'd like to keep under your hat. After all, like you say, Catholic college . . .'

'Hey man, we're basketball *soop*erstars. We're an infusion of raw talent. *Soop*erstars are *sposed* to be oversexed. But English professors? Don't look good. Don't look good. You don't want that on your extracurricular vitum.'

'Look, it's been nice talking to you and I hope you say the magic word, but I've got a class to prepare. If you'll excuse me . . .'

Duncan looked at Dhabul as if Cullen had said something bumptious.

'Excuuuse me. You're a hard man, Mr K. I admire you. Really I do. You admire him, Dhabul?'

'Yeah. Sure. I admire him.'

'We admire you. We're one big mutual admiration society here. But – and I say this with no disrespect, Sir. We recognize that you're a Doctorate of Philosophy and all that – but I think, basically speaking, we gotcha by the, you know . . . balls.'

Both of Duncan's wayward eyes seemed firmly fixed on Cullen's. A long, jiveless silence permeated the men's room. Then Cullen walked out, into the sunlight dappled by the shadows of a monkeypod, through the nearly empty arcade, back to his tragic office. His testicles *were* feeling a trifle constrained. He adjusted his underwear and propped his feet on his desk to think, perhaps to combust spontaneously and disappear forever. He'd never been blackmailed before. He'd never had anything anyone wanted. The very idea was preposterous, really.

Buck up, he told himself. *Things could be worse.*

How?

Oh yes. Yes, of course. Yes, that would be worse. The merest hint, the slightest inkling, the barest breath, the most nugatory suggestion of . . .

Even now he was thinking too loudly of Felicia. His was a small office whose plywood walls failed to extend to the ceiling. His position was vulnerable, his status tenureless, his balls, indeed, gotchable.

22

Time passed. Plunkett and Dhabul did not. Cullen was not sure why he'd taken such a firm stand. With one word to the obliging Father Plecko, he could have easily become an equal opportunity instructor. Father Plecko would have talked with Rosemary Wood, who ran the Records Office, and soon a generous dispensation would have erased all disgrace from the record. Of course, in fairness, Cullen would have felt obliged to pass Jesse, as well, who had been present at the mortification and therefore would have qualified as a beneficiary even without joining ranks with the blackmailers. That was the operative word – *blackmail.* Not, as many imagined, a reference to dark threats sent by post, but a descendant of the Middle English *blakmal*, a tribute paid reluctantly to the brigands of Scotland and Northumbria. He'd be damned if he'd pay it. Let Plunkett and Dhabul do their worst; the ball was in their possession and they could dunk it where they damn well pleased.

In another matter, however, Cullen's resolve had failed him. He still hadn't popped the ludicrous question.

In December, the wind high on Wilhemina dramatically shuffled a few fallen leaves, but the winter rains failed to materialize. The days were as usual: warm and bright. The poinsettias bloomed along Pali Highway. The winds sweeping Tantalus stirred Christmas daisies, towering white sprays crowding Round Top from above Puu Ualakaa all the way to the summit. One afternoon, when Felicia could not be found, he cut several stalks for a living room display. At night he fell asleep to the ghostly sound of poinciana pods rattling outside the window.

Christmas Eve was lonely, a difficult time of the year. He

phoned his mother and talked for forty minutes. He let her know he'd been dating this certain girl, though his expurgated description of the girl and their relationship failed to suggest even remotely the tumult in his blood. 'That's nice,' she said. The girl under discussion spent the evening with her family, but appeared the next afternoon with her sister, home for the holidays from San Francisco State. Dana was a skinny intellectual majoring in French – not shy, but not vibrant either – a quiet periwinkle to Felicia's primavera. She'd brought Cullen a bright poinsettia wrapped in golden foil, or at least she'd been the one to carry it into the house. Felicia was wearing the malachite earrings and necklace he had given her, and perhaps the spray cologne as well, but not, he assumed, the provocative teddy she'd promised to open in private.

'Thank you,' she said, fingering the necklace. 'I love it. But you haven't opened *your* presents.'

It seemed odd to open them in front of Dana – or perhaps it seemed odd to have Dana there at all as it suppressed his natural instinct to reach for Felicia, to embrace her, to remove an article of her clothing or stroke her breasts or kiss her ear. Instead, he tore the wrapping from his gifts to reveal, in the order of their appearance, macademia nut clusters, a handsome teal blue bathing suit with matching shirt, and a necktie so tame his own ties would mug it.

'I thought you needed something tasteful.' Felicia turned to Dana. 'We call Cullen's neckties the ties that blind.'

'Really?'

'*Who* calls them that?' asked Cullen.

'All your students.'

Dana seemed mildly embarrassed by this discussion.

'She's not my student now,' said Cullen.

'She knows that,' said Felicia. 'Oh, and there's this.'

'Another present? You've got me so much already. Hmm, feels like a book.'

'That's because it is.'

And it was.

'*Hawaiian Fish*. Now this is really special.'

'That looks nice,' said Dana. 'Where'd you get it?'

'Whole Earth Bookstore.'

He thumbed through it. Butterflies, wrasses, parrot fish, triggers and tangs – they were all there, in living color.

'Felicia turned me on to snorkeling,' he said. 'I really like this. I'll treasure it. Thank you, love.'

He refrained from kissing her, as he surely would have had they been alone.

'I thought you might like it.'

They stayed for eggnog; then they were gone. Felicia had family; Cullen didn't.

It wasn't until New Year's Eve, after her sister had departed, that she was once again properly his. An hour before midnight, they parked on a lonely, wooded curve near the locked gate of Puu Ualakaa, high above the city.

'Are you sure this is safe?' she asked.

'Come on.'

He wasn't, of course, at all sure that it was safe. A carload of Primoed, pakaloloed, pugnacious parolees might arrive at any minute without dates of their own, or be sitting impatiently on his delicate fenders when he and she returned, but the park itself should be safe because it was locked and because no one else was in it, as evidenced by the lack of another car. They slipped through a break in the fence, crashed through ferns, then hand-in-hand ascended a tree-darkened road. The darkness intensified the piquancy of ginger, the tartness of lemon-scented eucalyptus. At a hairpin turn to the left, the smells receded and the black tunnel of trees opened to a corridor. The road was wide enough to accommodate the coaches that ferried tourists to the top of the hill by day, but it was still impossible to suppress that irrational fear of something unknown lurking in the dark. At the same time, there was the delicious frisson of the forbidden. After a second turn, to the right, the road ran straight to the open summit. City maps called it Round Top, but Felicia translated its Hawaiian as Rolling Sweet Potato Hill. At the viewpoint the trees thinned, the moon and stars leaned closer, and a panorama of constellations shimmered below, processional red and white marking the city's major arteries. The sound of the city was that of a large conch held to the ear, or of an amphitheater filling with concertgoers, punctuated, on this occasion, by a few premature bangs that were nothing more than the tympanic raptures of a restive percussionist awaiting the symphony proper. The view was what one held in open arms: lights sweeping from Manoa to the sea, from Waikiki all the way to the airport. Pulsing red, a single jet made its silent descent over Diamond Head.

He removed a blanket from his rucksack and spread it on the grassy slope. Most lovers parked on Round Top Drive, overlooking Manoa and the university, but this view was more expansive. The fact that the park was padlocked at night, uninviting from the darkened road, made it a private place where he and she could couple beneath the stars and above the teeming masses, masses whose impassioned lives were now nothing more than cool scintillations of white and golden light.

And couple they did. As Felicia would later put it, he rolled her sweet potatoes and she rolled his. And none too soon, either, for when they lost control so did the city, a city that had sedated its pets, postponed its births, and in the past year had stockpiled enough high-grade explosives to concuss forgotten ancestors. At precisely midnight, Honolulu exploded, shook with the din of urban combat, crackled with sudden phosphoric outbursts as if a bandolier of TNT had been strung from Kahala to Kalihi. Such synchronism was rare: when he popped his own little cracker, a million others went boom. No city on earth intimidated the future with such emphatic, insistent, outrageous, clangorous clamor. Firecrackers were sown like seed, sprinkled like shoyu, tossed like confetti, from yards and cars, from rooftops and high-rises, on to things adjacent, nearby, or below. It was chaos peppered by madness. It was a boot in the butt of the old and a ring in the ear of the new. It was a frantic xylophonist, a manic jackhammerist, a tin roof in a hailstorm. Even their high and lofty perch was besieged by raucous clatter. Each new year seemed to thunder louder than the last. When it was over, a sulfurous cloud rose from Makiki, and the city hummed just a little, like a piano that had fallen downstairs. And they were the only ones who had witnessed it all from the heights of Rolling Sweet Potato Hill.

From his rucksack, Cullen produced two pedestal glasses and a bottle of Piesporter, which he opened with aplomb.

'To the New Year,' he said.

'To the New Year.'

They were both naked from the waist down when they saw the sweep of headlights pass above them and heard the car pull into the parking lot. For Felicia it was simply a matter of pulling on her panties, but for Cullen there were trousers as well. He carried those and his shoes in one hand, Felicia grabbed the blanket, he the wine, she the glasses, he his rucksack, and together they scurried downhill for the shelter of shadowy shrubs. They stopped when they reached the chainlink fence.

Cullen was scared. He heard doors open but none close. He envisioned a gang. How the hell did they get past the gate? He'd put the two of them in a vulnerable position and now he was going to pay for his flippant disregard of the law and common sense. The two of them were huddled in darkness like refugees.

A brilliant searchlight mounted the crest of the hill, hung momentarily motionless like a predator inhaling, then fixed them in its glare. So much for evasion. It walked closer, slowly. Cullen could see the smoke of fireworks rising in its beam.

'What are you kids doin' here?'

Two pairs of boots, black silhouettes. Cops! *Jesus*, thought Cullen, *that's better than rapists any day of the week.*

'We were just enjoying the view.'

'And a lot more besides, it would appear.' The speaker was a chubby man with a moustache. In fact, unless Cullen was sorely mistaken, the speaker was Freddy Aragon of his American Literature class two or three terms ago.

'I guess.'

'What are your names?' said the second, leaner officer, a young Polynesian version of the handsome Detective Yager – alert eyes, high cheekbones, a swarthy Hawaiian complexion. He reminded Cullen of someone on TV, but Cullen didn't even wish to think about that at present.

'Cullen Kinnell.'

'Christ!' said Freddy. 'Dr Kinnell! It is you. I thought it was you, but you always seemed like such a responsible law-abiding type. You know you're not supposed to be up here, doncha?'

'Yup.'

'That your car near the gate?' asked the other officer.

'Yes, sir.'

'Put on your trousers, Dr Kinnell. Please,' said Freddy.

'Okay.'

'And *your* name?' asked the younger cop.

'Felicia Mattos.'

'Mattos,' said Freddy. 'Your father run a funeral home?'

'That's my uncle.'

'Small world, isn't it? Did you know I was in Dr Kinnell's English class? What was that called, anyhow? We read lots of books.'

'I think it was American Literature,' said Cullen.

'That was it. Hemingway, Fitzgerald. Wow, that Hemingway was some writer, huh? You ever read Hemingway, Sonny?'

'I'm going to. Soon as we finish this collar.'

'Right. Book 'em, Danno. That's Sonny. Sonny, this guy was Yager's teacher. Yager met that girl in your class, right, Dr Kinnell?'

'Right. I didn't give them a personal introduction or anything, but they somehow found each other.'

Sonny suddenly smiled. It was like watching a rock break into a grin. And the person he was smiling at was Felicia.

'Address and phone number?' he asked, pen and pad at the ready.

'Aww, cut the crap, Sonny. This guy thinks he's God's gift to women.'

Cullen made a noncommital twitch.

'So I guess we're done here?' said Sonny.

'Sure. We're pau. We just have to give these felons a ride to the bottom of the hill. I hope we didn't interrupt anything,' said the humane Freddy Aragon, smiling.

Cullen grimaced.

'Jesus,' she said in the car, 'that was close. If they'd taken us down to the police station and called my parents . . .'

'Or if this gets back to Sister Lucia . . .'

'Thank God you didn't flunk that chubby guy or they would've left us handcuffed naked to a tree.'

'Scared the shit out of me when I saw that flashlight. I thought it was an alien spaceship collecting specimens or something.'

He drove her home through streets choked with shredded red, his fears and embarrassment subsiding. He felt good again, lucky, dreamy, in love even with the streetlamps and the darkness between them. Trusting love was his resolution.

January was an orange month. The huapala bloomed along Sierra and the tiger's claw opened in Kahala. Then the rains came and with them a new semester. He had a chest pain on his birthday. The doctor held a stethoscope to his neck and listened, just listened.

'I want you to see a specialist,' she said. 'I do detect a slight abnormality.'

'A slight abnormality?'

The specialist held a stethoscope to his neck and listened, just listened. *He's been listening too long, thought Cullen.* Then Cullen listened – to the ominous silence of the specialist listening.

'Turn your head toward the wall,' said the specialist.

Cullen turned his whole life. The specialist listened, this time to his chest. Then he returned to his neck. Cullen waited, for good news or bad. Had it been a good life? It seemed incomplete somehow.

'Let's get an X-ray,' said the specialist.

The radiologist had cold hands. She covered with lead the parts worth saving. The X-rays passed silently through him. They were magic. He sat to wait.

'Here we are,' said the specialist. He showed him a picture of a few shadowy organs carelessly huddled in someone's thorax.

'Not a very good likeness,' said Cullen blackly.

'*Au contraire*. It's the real you.'

'How's the real me doing?'

'Tell me, do you ever experience numbness in your arms or legs, or even in your fingers?'

'No, not really. My fingers, maybe, when I'm typing.'

'How long does that last?'

'Not long.'

'Ever just go dead? Ever find that you couldn't stand on your legs or couldn't raise your arms?'

'No.'

'And this pain in your chest, how would you describe it?'

'Oh, how does one describe pain? It's not piercing. It's more like an ache.'

'Hmm. Let's listen just one more time. No need to undress.'

He's actually enjoying this, thought Cullen, as the specialist listened again to confirm his diagnosis.

'I hear it, what Doctor Nakata heard. I can see why she was concerned; it does sound like an abnormality. But I doubt that it's your heart. I think you're just built differently. See this line here? That's your esophagus. It's got a rather tight fit there. I think what we're hearing is just a bit of esophageal friction. I wouldn't worry about it. Your heart seems fine.'

'Thank you, Doctor.'

He went home to try his hand at poetry, and then perhaps a memoir, but when Felicia arrived he postponed it.

'It smells in here,' she said.

'You think so?'

'Don't you?'

'I thought I noticed something, but I wasn't sure.'

'Something died in here.'

'Not me.'

He told her about his visit to the doctor.

'You didn't tell me you were having chest pains.'

'No, I didn't.'

'Why not?'

'No particular reason. They were an off and on thing. Why don't we celebrate my continuing existence with some Toffee Pie at the Yum Yum Tree?'

'Can't. Gotta work tonight. I just dropped in to tell you the news.'

'What news?'

'Take a look.'

She handed him the *Advertiser* folded to EX-HPD OFFICER CHARGED WITH DRUG DEALING. He read aloud.

John W. Yager, until two years ago second-in-command in the Honolulu Police Department Vice Squad, has been arrested in Los Angeles for suspicion of smuggling nearly two tons of Hawaiian-grown marijuana recently confiscated by a newly formed joint federal task force. Yager is further suspected of playing a major role in a trans-Pacific drug ring responsible for smuggling perhaps as much as 25 tons of marijuana last year.

He read on in silence.

'I can't believe this. He was one of my best students.'

'I bet he still reads a good book now and then.'

'Incredible. Absolutely amazing.'

After Felicia had left he sat down with a soda to consider the implications of this staggering turn of events. He wished to share this with Sister Lucia, to point out that Detective Yager had been punished after all, and for crimes far greater than any he may have hatched as a result of his exposure to romantic literature. Surely the Yager Affair was now behind him. But then he reconsidered. Detective Yager had, after all, been one of the students she'd lured to night classes, her biggest catch. Sins of this magnitude were a blot on the record of the entire Adult Education Program. She would see it as a betrayal, not a vindication. It was best not to gloat. Besides, she'd surely learn from other sources.

Felicia had been right about the smell. It was stronger the next day. Something had died near the bathroom. Rats, he'd heard, crawled to dark holes to die. He tried to locate the source, but without success. Someday a putrid green spot would appear on the wall and devour it. Should he tell Mr Ching?

He tried burning incense to combat it and opened the windows whenever possible. At times it was barely noticeable. Then one day Felicia arrived in a huff.

'You won't believe what just happened to me.'

He put down the paper he was grading.

'What?'

'I don't believe it.'

'Okay, I *won't* believe it and you *don't* believe it. What is it?'

'You know where I usually park my car on Third?'

'Yeah.'

'Well I was walking back to my car after class when some guy drives up in a Mercedes and asks if I know how to get to Hotel Street. I told him he was about a million miles away, but if he followed Waialae to Beretania, that would put him in the general vicinity. "How do I get from Waialae to Beretania?" he wanted to know. So I told him. All the time, this guy's smiling like a Jehovah's Nitwit or something. Then he wanted to know how to get from Beretania to Hotel Street. I told him I really wasn't sure, I just knew you had to turn left into Chinatown. And then you know what he said?'

'What?'

'He said, "You sure have nice juicy tits, you know that?" And then it hit me.'

'Then what hit you?'

'Then it hit me that the guy was jacking off. All the time he was asking me stupid questions he was jacking off! What a jerk I was.'

'Did you get the license number?'

'Sure. What am I gonna do, report him to the Pervert Squad?'

'How did he know you had nice tits?'

'I let him squeeze them. What kind of a stupid question is that?'

'He must have seen something.'

'He saw this, okay? The same thing everyone sees. Is this so revealing?'

'A little bit.'

'Are you blaming this on me? Do you think what happened is my fault?'

'I think maybe you shouldn't walk over to a strange man's car just because he wags his little finger.'

'He wasn't wagging his little finger, he was wagging his whole damn whanger! Is that my fault, Stee— I mean Cullen.'

It was the way her face sank as she went into a skid on those long e's.

'Steve?'

'Steve is the name of the bartender at work, all right? It was just a slip of the tongue. I'm ordering drinks in my sleep these days.'

'It's also the name of Steve Tillman.'

This pushed a button he'd never pushed before. This definitely pushed a button. He'd discovered a hidden door in the library, the room was revolving, and now there was no turning back.

'So?'

'So you tell me. Are you getting the two of us confused?'

She stared angrily.

'Who told you about Steve Tillman?'

'A little birdie.'

'No, really. I'd like to know.'

'And I wouldn't like you to know.'

'You can think what you want to think. I've got to get home for dinner. I need something from the bathroom.'

He assumed she meant something in the line of cosmetics, something that would help her look seductive while serving cocktails to big tippers. Or did she mean she was clearing out?

'Help yourself. Why don't you eat here? Then we can discuss this.'

'There's nothing to discuss. I work tonight. Mom's expecting me.'

She left the room, headed for the bathroom. Then it was quiet.

'Here it is, Cullen.'

'Here what is?'

'The thing that's been stinking up your house like a mortuary.'

He found her standing before the bathroom door. She pointed to the jamb. There it was all right, the poor gecko inadvertently flattened by a closing door. He'd murdered it. Its skeleton and flesh had been pressed to a sallow corpse as flat as a shadow. The same thing happened to the Holy Mount toads; one minute they were croaking in the driveway and the next they'd croaked, flattened to fossils by a few tons of passing steel. He was surprised that what he'd envisioned as a large dead rat was actually this small. He'd never suspected a gecko.

'That's bad luck, Cullen,' she said, grabbing her cosmetics and leaving.

23

This end of Kapahulu was familiar turf for Cullen. A chainlink fence and a high wall of vegetation separated him from the animals, but he could discern the silhouette of two peacocks roosting high in a monkeypod; he could hear coos, gurgles, hoots, and the distinctive bark of a seal; and he could smell their enduring odors. A pigeon had shat on him once as he sat observing the mating habits of Galapagos turtles, and Alice had read more into it than if the pigeon had shat the I Ching.

He stumbled over a banyan root. Why was he walking here, in the shadows, when he could be walking under streetlights? He headed for the sidewalk and followed it to the ocean, crossing Kalakaua to the beach. A brightly lit pleasure boat had passed the ruined natatorium. A narrow jetty shot straight out toward the moon. He followed it, high silvered swells rolling shoreward on both sides of him, some nearly reaching his feet. It was almost like walking on water. The sea smelled mysterious. He stood at jetty's end, staring back at Waikiki. Its high-rise hotels twinkled silver and gold. It was another world over there, but that hardly mattered. He turned toward the moon and surveyed the horizon where a dark-edged sea met a brighter night sky. Waves rumbled toward him with a rising power, then broke with a boom on nearby rocks. That seemed an apt metaphor for his romantic illusions, dashed once again to pieces. Well, if he were going to do it, he might as well do it now. The waves seemed insistent. He went over it once more, offered himself one more chance to back out. He could simply turn around and go home. The truth, like the ocean, could be avoided. Then he decided that yes, hell, he might as well do what he'd come for.

He followed the jetty back to Kalakaua, then crossed to the hotel side of Kapahulu. He peered into a couple of chandelier-lit glass lobbies, testaments to the glitter and glamor of wealth, and was soon at Marvin's Grotto. One couldn't tell much from the entrance: black swinging doors with round portholes. A poster advertised The Penetrations. He braced himself and walked in.

It was dark inside – like a grotto. Softly carbonated light issued from numerous aquariums set in what seemed to be lava walls. Not bad. The narrow end of an elliptical bar stood before him, a few booths to its right and a larger room with an empty stage to its left. Quiet jazz came from speakers on the ceiling. He didn't recognize it. There were perhaps a dozen patrons in the whole establishment. Felicia had said it got crowded.

He took the nearest stool. Then the man he had come to see emerged from the darkness at the far end of the bar, glass and towel in hand.

'Hi. What can I do you for?'

'Hmm.' He should have thought of this beforehand.

'Baltimore Bracer, Buffalo Blizzard, Klondike Cooler? Chi Chi, Mai Tai, Pina Colada? Gloom Lifter, Singapore Sling, a Horse's Neck With a Kick? We got 'em all.'

'What's a Gloom Lifter?'

'I don't know, no one's ever ordered it. You order it and I'll look it up. I need the experience.'

'Okay. Gloom Lifter.'

'One Gloom Lifter coming up.'

Cullen felt no immediate upwelling of hatred and jealousy. What struck him most was that the bartender *looked* like a bartender: a little bit short, a little bit stocky, a little bit Irish, and damn if he didn't part his black hair more or less in the middle. As for age, he looked no younger than Cullen.

A waitress passed and smiled. Cullen smiled back. She was attired, he noted, not in a tail and ears but in a full-length silky black dress with a neckline that plunged not as far as her navel but to a point somewhere south of her breasts. He supposed that by the standards of the day it was modest, but nevertheless it aroused him. It was a dress Felicia would look great in. What did it do when she stooped to serve? Did she wear his jewelry and cologne when attending to other men?

'This is one hell of a drink,' said the bartender upon his return. 'You're gonna love it. How 'bout your friend?'

Cullen was startled to follow his mirthful eyes to the stool on his right and behold there a wizened old man in a shabby brown overcoat. Like a woolly sculpin, he had simply appeared from the shadows. But why had he sat beside Cullen?

The man drew a cigarette from his pocket – not from any visible *pack* of cigarettes, but simply from his pocket.

'Whiskey neat, please,' he said in a voice like old shoe polish.

'A man after my own heart,' said the bartender.

'Got a light?'

Cullen did indeed have a light. He'd brought his pipe for protection. In the glow of the match flame, he saw that the man's brown, deeply etched features were probably Chinese. He was not the sort one expected to find in a jazz club. His cigarette crackled, live ashes falling like miniature fireworks to the floor.

'Ahh,' said the man, exhaling.

Cullen sampled his Gloom Lifter. It tasted much as he'd imagined a Horse's Neck With a Kick might.

'Visiting?' asked the man.

'No, I live here.'

The man nodded acknowledgement while inhaling.

'Whiskey neat,' said the bartender. 'That'll be two bucks.'

Cullen wondered why the old man should have to pay on delivery. The man reached into the pocket of his overcoat. He pulled out a cigarette and placed it on the bar. Then, steadying himself with one hand, he made a shaky attempt to reach into the pocket of his baggy pants. Only when he swiveled halfway off his stool did Cullen realize he was tottering from more than old age. The bartender watched patiently.

'Just put it on my tab,' said Cullen.

This was good enough for the bartender.

'You're a prince,' said the man. 'My wallet's stuck.'

'That's all right. My pleasure.'

The man made an abrupt gesture that consisted of raising his hand and lowering his head.

This was not at all what Cullen had envisioned when he thought he might sit invisibly at the bar to hear how the waitress addressed the bartender.

'My name's Ching,' said the man minutes later.

'My landlord's named Ching.'

'There's a lot of us.'

Laughter broke out at one of the far tables. Half the clientele, Cullen noticed, were women.

'What's yours?'

'Pardon?'

'What's yours?'

'Oh. Dick. You can call me Dick.'

Quick thinking, Cullen. If you were a dog, you would've said 'Spot'.

'Pleased to meet you, Dick. You can call me Yuen.'

'You like jazz, Yuen?'

'Sure, I like any kine music. Jazz, polka, fox trot. I wen dance the rhumba with a girl in Brazil once. Or was it the samba? Maybe Argentina.'

'You were in . . . South America?'

'Oh sure. I been all over. Merchant marine. But this is home.'

'Do you know this band that's playing here tonight?'

Yuen looked at him with genuine concern.

'That's a tape.'

'Is it live or is it Memorex?' asked the bartender. 'How are you gentlemen doing? Gloom lifting?'

Before Cullen knew what was happening, he'd bought Yuen 'one nodder one' and was describing to the poor man how Galapagos turtles mate.

'The female just sits there. Someone knockin' at the back door? News to her. As is so often the case in the animal world, it's the male who does all the work. And it's dangerous. He puts his front legs on the back of her shell and slowly, slowly walks his way up until he's standing almost vertical. He's gotta slip it in there under her shell and it's really not that easy. And just when he's about to stick it in and he's standing straight as a tombstone, she spies some tasty crumb of lettuce on the edge of the mudhole and goes walking off, leaving the poor guy tottering. I've seen this with my own eyes. It's frustrating for the poor geezer. Not only is it inaccessible, but if anything goes wrong and he falls backwards, that's it. He'll die belly up, eaten alive by seagulls or something. Of course, in the zoo they just flip him back over, but imagine the embarrassment, performing in front of all those people with cameras. Frankly, just between you and me, I don't think he really enjoys it.'

Yuen was crinkling with glee, laughing quietly like crumpled foil. The way his head bobbed on a furrowed neck reminded Cullen of the very turtle he'd just described.

'That's where Chinese comes from. From turtles.'

'How's that?'

'In the old days, to tell fortunes, they threw tortoise shells in a fire. And then they'd pick them up and read the cracks in the shells. Those cracks became Chinese.'

'Ideograms.'

'Yeah.'

'I'll be.'

When Yuen went to the bathroom, the bartender wandered over and leaned conspiratorially toward Cullen.

'So, how's Tai Won On doing?'

'He's fine. Ever seen him in here before?'

'Never, but we get all kinds. The other day we had a guy going around the world on a bicycle. In Hawaii! I guess he cycles from island to island.'

Yuen returned on silent cat feet and lit another cigarette. He simply stared into his own smoke for a minute then said, 'So, you've got wahine trouble, huh?'

Cullen nearly dropped his drink. 'What makes you think that?'

'It shows. Around the eyes. It's no shame. I got woman trouble myself. The woman I love can't stand the sight of me. It's my teeth. Every time I smile it's like the Black Plague.' He smiled to illustrate his point. 'See what I mean?'

Yuen's teeth surpassed even Father Plecko's for wayward decay. Black, brown, yellow and tea-stained, his smile did indeed raise alarms.

'Maybe you should get dentures.'

'Too late for dat. A young, good-looking boy like yourself, though – you shouldn't have any woman trouble.'

Much to his amazement, Cullen proceeded to tell the whole sad story, even about the spying, stopping short, of course, of any mention of Marvin's Grotto or the fact that he was here tonight for the sole disreputable purpose of ascertaining if the bartender's name was Steve. It all came pouring out freely. No priest had heard from Cullen the sort of passionate pent-up confession he now unburdened on Yuen.

'I know what my grandfather would say,' said Yuen.

'Don't tell me your grandfather's still alive.'

'No way. He would say the pepper pot story.'

'What's that?'

'Back in Szechuan, my grandfather was on the village council. Anyhow, there was a missionary who lived in the village, a Jesuit priest named Father Wilton. He was very well liked and always very polite. A fat, quiet man. And one day Father Wilton was invited to a special New Year's dinner. The whole council was there. You like Szechuan food?'

'Sure.'

'Some ono, yeah? The first course was pepper pot soup. This was a very spicy egg soup with a ball of Szechuan peppers in the pot about like so.' With thumb and index finger, Yuen made a circle the size of a ping pong ball. 'Whoever got the pepper ball in his bowl was very lucky. The whole year gonna be one good one for him. But on the first serving nobody got it, so – everyone gotta have one nodder helping. And then the soup was all pau, but still – no one got the pepper ball.'

Yuen grinned like a disease.

'So, something was wrong. There's one pepper ball in the soup and the soup's all pau and nobody's got the pepper ball. And then someone noticed that Father Wilton was looking sort of pale. That's when the man keeled over and started rolling on the floor. I have to laugh every time I tell this story,' Yuen coughed. 'He got the pepper ball and he was too polite to spit it out! So he swallowed it! Hee hee hee wasn't supposed to do that. "I thought he looked funny," my grandmother said. The poor man died that night. Burned his insides out. So there you go, Dick.'

Cullen stared into Yuen's deep-set eyes to discern the moral of this story. He laughed.

'That's a great story, Yuen. I gotta remember that one. But

what's it got to do with women?'

'You no see? If something's gonna tear you apart inside, you gotta spit it out. You don't have to swallow it. You can just spit it out. It's no good luck if it kills you.'

'You're saying I should let this woman go?'

'I'm saying you should spit out the pepper ball.'

Cullen downed his Gloom Lifter and ordered another. The fact that the fish were illuminated while the people were not gave the bar an underwater ambience, as if they peered from the depths of a sunken vessel or, of course, a grotto. Back on land there was a lecture to prepare. He pumped Yuen for more China stories, then asked for the tab.

'Leaving now?' asked the bartender. 'The band's gonna blow any minute.'

'They any good?'

'They're great. They're from LA. You never heard of Dicky Long and the Penetrations?' he asked grinning.

'Have one nodder one,' said Yuen.

The band was surprisingly good, perhaps even great. By the end of the first set, the club had filled. Two pretty girls sat to Cullen's left, and the one with eyes like minnows kept appraising Cullen and his date with dark, darting glances. Yuen, like Cullen, was carried away by the saxophone, so much so that at one point he almost sailed off his barstool into the void. When the bartender looked at Cullen to ask if he should add one more whiskey to his tab, he shook his head *no*. He wondered where Yuen would sleep that night.

'How much do I owe you?' he asked after the third set.

'Twenty-five.'

He gave him thirty.

'Mucho mahalo. How were the Gloom Lifters?'

'They did the trick.'

'And the mickey I slipped your friend worked pretty well, too.' He was referring to Yuen, who sat sound asleep.

'Take care of him, will ya?'

'Sure.'

'By the way, what's your name?'

'Dwayne.' He held out his hand and Cullen shook it.

'I'm Dick. Are you the only bartender here?'

'Except for a useless shit named Steve.'

'Well, thanks a lot.'

'Come again.'

The phone was ringing as he unlocked the door. He raced across the room and made a drunken dive for it.

'Hello?'

'Where were you?'

'Out drinking.'

'Alone?'

'No. With an old buddy of mine.'

'I didn't know you did that sort of thing.'

'You drove me to it.'

'What sex was this old buddy?'

'Are you jealous?'

'Just answer the questions.'

'An old Chinese guy about a hundred and three.'

'I bet. Where'd you go?'

'The Zebra Club. What did you call about?'

'Do I need a reason?'

'I thought maybe you called to apologize.'

'Nope.'

'So . . .' He drummed his fingers.

'So . . .'

'Maybe you'd like to tell me about Mr Tillman?'

'You seem to know all about him already.'

He said nothing, bluffing. In his mind he was lighting a cigarette, drawing in his suspicions, exhaling smoke. He didn't have to do this.

'What do you want to know?' she asked.

'I'd like to know . . . Well, let's start with how long you've been seeing this guy.'

'I haven't been seeing this guy. I stopped seeing him when I met you. I thought you were so much more mature than him.'

'What does he do?'

'Don't your detectives tell you these things? He's a tennis instructor at the Kahala Hilton.'

'I see.'

'Any other questions?'

'Who wrote the Book of Love?'

'What?'

'Was it the Lord up above?'

'I can't find my bunny slippers. I wonder if Mom washed them.'

'Would you like to get married?'

'I suppose I will someday.'

'I don't mean someday. I mean soon, in the near future. To me.'

Like a gaseous blimp, a long, volatile silence nudged its way through the darkness. He lay down. It had seemed unreal even as he'd said it. The very air was now heavy with improbability. He had transgressed, somehow, an unspoken boundary.

'I'll think about it.'

'That's what you told Dunk It Plunkett when he asked you to the luau.'

'That's what I tell lots of guys.'

'Yeah?'

'Yeah.'

'The reason I ask is because . . . I love you.'

'You love me, but you don't trust me.'

'I don't trust my luck. I'm afraid of losing you. I can't stand this fighting all the time.'

Felicia was silent, a powerful strategy. He wondered at what age he might reach the point where his professions of love no longer sounded maudlin.

'I don't like it either,' she said.

'Can I see you tomorrow? Take you out to dinner?'

'Okay.'

'It's Steve the bartender, isn't it?' was a bullet he was itching to shoot into his foot as they dined at Matteo's the next evening. 'I'm crazy about you, I want to marry you' would have been equally masochistic given the adroitness with which she'd defused his last proposal. And his visit to Marvin's Grotto was not a viable topic of conversation either, though he was dying to tell her about Yuen. He supposed he could move Yuen to the Zebra Club, but that was dangerous as it might alert Felicia to the fact that the Zebra Club existed only in Cullen's imagination, where it had striped wallpaper but no clearly defined walls, not to mention address. It was difficult to support even a little lie, especially when one lied so badly. So he spoke little, despite two Mai Tais. He'd made the mistake of ordering Vinda D'Alhos when what he'd really wanted was Mahimahi, the same as Felicia. He always fell for exotic names.

'That looks good,' he said.

'It is. Here, try some.'

'Thanks. Want some of this?'

'No, thanks.'

If she did agree to marry him, which she wouldn't, there would be a scene in her parents' living room, he on the edge of his nerves and the tragically green couch, and they in the flanking hemlock chairs. Her father would wear whatever he wore in the yard and would wonder why he'd been summoned, and her mother would wear a print dress the color of mixed vegetables. Felicia would sit opposite him on a footstool, her hair done up in ridiculous pigtails.

'Well,' he'd say, 'we wanted to talk to you because . . .'

Both parents would lean forward to await the completion of his subordinate clause. A priest had once told him that Notre Dame said a prayer in every huddle.

'. . . because, well . . . we'd like to get married.'

Mrs Mattos would gasp and insert her hand in her mouth. A deep gurgling sound would rise from Mr Mattos.

Cullen would pause to let them calm their hearts and the spirits of their ancestors. He would look to Felicia for guidance, but she would have changed into an elfin creature who smiled artlessly and drummed her fingers on her knees.

There was no point in pursuing this really. But just as he abandoned his little daydream she said, 'You know this marriage thing you talked about yesterday?'

'Marriage thing. Yes.'

'You were serious about that?'

'Yeah.'

'Then I'm afraid I have to break your heart.'

'Why's that?'

'I can't marry anyone until I at least finish college. It's a promise I made to my parents. It's part of the deal.'

'Because they're paying for it?'

'Exactly.'

'I see. Well, I guess I can understand that. Besides, I don't think your mother would approve anyway.'

'Hell no. She calls you "the old man".'

'Yes, I think you've told me that before.'

'And I'm not sure my father would approve either.'

'Okay, you needn't belabor the point. I get the gist of what you're saying. You don't want to marry me.'

'It's not a matter of whether I want to or not. I'm too young.'

'You are.'

'Did you hear that the volcano's erupting on the Big Island?'

'What? Are you serious?'

'Sure I'm serious. It was on the news.'

'What did they say?'

'The volcano's erupting.'

'They say where?'

'On the Big Island.'

He nodded.

'You know,' he said. ' even if we don't get married, we could still have a honeymoon.'

She looked.

'What I mean is . . . we could get over there. We could see this. You know I've always wanted to see this. And if my memory serves me well, that very first day we spent together at the Kuhio, you said you'd always wanted to see this, too.'

She chewed her fish, stared over his head, and made a sort of thinking man's gesture with her hand, as if she were about to tally something.

'I know,' she said. 'But there's no way my mother would let me go with you.'

'Tell me something I don't already know. But if you go, and I go, and we just happen to stumble into each other over there . . .'

'She's not gonna let me go by myself. She's not that dumb.'

'How dumb is she?'

This was the wrong thing to say.

'No, no. Wait a minute, wait a minute. What I mean is – she'd let you go with Melanie, wouldn't she?'

Felicia considered this. 'You mean really go with Melanie. And then the three of us stay together?'

'No, of course not. We ditch Melanie. We just use her.'

'Unh unh.'

'Okay, the three of us stay together, more or less. But not completely together. She could stay outside in a tent or something.'

'It might work. Maybe.'

'Ask Melanie. She'll do it for you. Want some dessert?'

'Just coffee.'

Felicia was now toying with the candle on their table, as she always did, tilting the glass holder to redistribute the wax. She seemed to be irresistibly drawn to fire. Cullen was too, he supposed – drawn to her, drawn to the volcano – but he could easily resist the allure of a candle. Felicia couldn't. For her it was a toy thoughtfully provided by the management. He was not at all surprised when the flame went out and she squealed with embarrassment, holding her hand to her mouth as if she'd said something gauche. As if she'd extinguished the Olympic torch, the waiter promptly appeared to relight it.

'That's the second time you've done that, you know. You did it at the Windjammer, too. You're not mature enough to take to a restaurant.'

'I guess I'm a pyromaniac, huh?'

'No, you're not, you're just the opposite. A pyromaniac is fire's best friend. You're a pyrodepressive is what you are. Fire's not safe around you. You're a danger to fire.'

'Then you should carry matches.'

'I could smoke my pipe more if you like.'

'Not really.'

'So what d'ya think? Melanie owe you any favors?'

'She'd do it for me, if that's what you mean.'

'We've gotta act fast, before next term starts.'

'And before the volcano dies down.'

'Exactly. We've got a window of opportunity here. The timing's perfect. We need to seize the moment.'

'I'll see what I can do. I'm not making any promises. I'll talk to Melanie tomorrow.'

'Okay. Let me know what she says.'

24

Earl's was a jute and sisal seaborn cottage in which one felt every subtle turn of weather. Now a tentative summer breeze was lifting from Lanikai Bay, carrying with it a powerful bouquet of the sea. They had shared a joint by candlelight and had settled, like monks with armchairs, into solemn appreciation of the world's pervasive mystery. Beyond the screened lanai lay the backyard with weathered volleyball net and catamaran, the narrow beach, and the black bay which held like a serving tray the dark Mokuleeas, two small islands, often photographed, rising moundlike a half mile offshore. A fisherman's moon was slowly climbing the eastern horizon, its reflection spilling into the bay like a bucket of golden minnows. *Winter Consort* played on the tape deck.

'Did you see this morning's paper?' asked Earl.

'No.'

He left without a word, like the hotelkeeper of his ghost story, and returned momentarily with the *Advertiser*.

'Look at this.'

Cullen took the paper and felt a charge akin to *déjà vu* as he registered the scene burning before his eyes. Although it was now in black and white, not color, it seemed the same scene he'd admired in the *Nikon Annual* on that fateful day when he'd gambled on Felicia and won: a curtain of spattered fire throwing a foreground of ohia into stark relief. 'Volcano Delights Spectators' was the heading of the lead article, which detailed the activities of Mauna Ulu Crater in Volcano National Park. Each candlelit phrase aroused him: *incandescent caldera, wall of fire, lava fountains, torrents of lava, raging lava lake*. This was the spectacle he'd longed to witness ever since his arrival in the islands. There were few desires of which he was certain, but this was one. As he sat there, in Earl's overstuffed chair, a lake of molten lava was churning in Mauna Loa's newest crater, a sight available to any visitor willing to make the mile-long hike from the Chain of Craters Road. There was speculation that the eruption might eventually result in one of Hawaii's most treasured sights: a river of lava pouring over the coastal palis and eventually into the sea.

'This is perfect. Felicia told me about this yesterday. We were just making plans to visit the Big Island together.'

'Put them in motion. I'd go myself if I could get away. Do you believe in Pele?'

'Well . . .'

'Come on . . . Either you do or you don't.'

'You mean the soccer player?'

'Right. Typical mainland haole attitude. There's a famous lodge over there, on the rim of Kilauea. It's called Volcano House. You know it?'

'Yes.'

'Well, just a few weeks ago it got a new manager, mainland haole. Every manager's supposed to make an offering to Pele, when he starts the job and every year on Mother's Day. He's supposed to throw a bottle of gin into Halemaumau. This guy just laughed it off. Wouldn't do it. Said it was against his religion.'

'I am the Lord thy God. Thou shalt have no strange gods before Me.'

'Right. Just a week ago he saw a whirlwind rise out of Halemaumau and head in the direction of Mauna Ulu. The next day this eruption started. At Mauna Ulu. That night two of his waitresses get in a car accident right after work. They're taken to the National Guard Clinic up there, near the Volcano House. They call him up and he goes to the clinic to see them. For some reason he has an argument with the doctors and stalks out all huhu. Whammo! He falls right into a puka and lands on a ledge about twenty feet down. Lucky for him. He's barely conscious, but he manages to yell for help. Eventually, an attendant hears his cries and goes looking for him. Whammo! He falls into the same puka. But not as far. He calls for help and someone finally hears him. Eventually, they manage to get them both out. The attendant's okay, but the manager's in worse shape than his waitresses. He needs serious medical attention. So they have to call for an ambulance all the way from Hilo. That's about thirty miles. After a long wait, the ambulance finally arrives for the manager. What happens to the ambulance on the way back to Hilo?'

'It sees an old lady hitchhiking.'

'It's a clear night – no wind, no rain, no nothing. But what happens? Something – something – lifts the ambulance off the highway, flips it once in mid-air, and sets it back down again like nothing ever happened. This was in the paper just a couple days ago. Everyone in that ambulance swears to it. They had an interview with that manager, too. He's still in the hospital in Hilo. Says he's gonna toss a bottle of gin in Halemaumau as soon as he gets out. He admits he was an asshole.'

'Now I believe.'

'I'm gonna show you something I've never shown you before. I don't know why I've never shown you this before. Yes I do. Wait here a minute. You can flip that tape if you want.'

'You're gonna show me your ghost certificate from that haunted hotel,' Cullen yelled at his back.

'Yeah, that too. You should take Felicia there someday. Give her a taste of the real supernatural.'

Like a cloud, he had to let this pass.

Earl returned with a large envelope and a slide viewer. He placed the envelope on the rattan coffee table and handed the viewer to Cullen.

'Take a look at this.'

He saw a cloud of red smoke rising from a crater, illuminated, apparently, by lava below. Superimposed on the smoke was, one might easily imagine, the face of a woman. It was indistinct, but it was there, Polynesian features neatly juxtaposed with the billowing contours of the smoke itself.

'That's Pele you're looking at. My father took that picture when Halemaumau was erupting. He didn't see her until the picture was developed.'

'Could be a double exposure.'

'Could be, but it isn't.'

He reexamined the transparency. He had to admit that it didn't look like trickery; the face conformed to the smoke, was one with it. Those disturbing dark eyes seemed to dare the viewer to doubt them. The lips were strong, almost masculine. It was, indeed, a noble face in a cloud of smoke, the sort of visage one might attribute to a goddess, if one believed in such things.

'There's a story that goes along with that picture, sort of. You won't believe it because it was told to my father by an old Hawaiian who lived in a small house near Kapoho. He was a papaya farmer. He claims to have been driving home from Hilo in his pick-up one night and to have stopped for an old woman hitchhiking.'

'Ahh, yes.'

'So maybe you've heard this one before.'

'A variation perhaps. Go on.'

'She asked to be let out near some steam vents in the middle of nowhere. He thought that was pretty strange, so he asked her why there. "I live here," she said. "It's my home." "Here?" he said, but when she smiled he suddenly understood. He was talking to Pele. She can be any age she wants, you know.'

'Doesn't she have her own car?'

'She likes to toy with people. She's a prankster. She warned the old guy that she had some mischief planned and told him to plant ti at each corner of his house first thing in the morning. She promised to spare his house if he did.'

'And he did.'

'And he did. First thing in the morning, a stalk of ti at each corner, as instructed. Later that afternoon the earth began to tremble and a tremendous eruption broke out west of Kapoho, which is even farther from Kilauea than Hilo. There was a double fountain a quarter mile high. The lava started heading for the village. His home was right in its path. His wife wanted to run for it – she went coconuts – you know how women are – but he slapped some sense into her and told her to stay put. When the lava reached his backyard it came right toward the house. "Owwee!" cried the wife. "Shut up," said the husband. Then the lava divided miraculously into two channels. It flowed around the house and came together again on the other side. The poor wife was having fits.'

'Was this house on a hill, by any chance?'

'This house, a shack actually, was near Kapoho. The house is still there. Kapoho isn't. It was wiped right off the fucking map. You can see it with your own eyes if you want to. I have. Even without the story it's pretty incredible. That eruption lasted over a month, but the house is still standing. Of course, he lost his farm, but you can't have everything.'

'Okay, I believe you. May I have the envelope, please?'

'*Chotto matte*.' This was one of Earl's verbal seasonings, or affectations, that he had picked up in Japan. Cullen gathered that it meant 'just a moment'.

'Are you really planning to take your honeypot to the Big Island? 'Cause if you are, I might be able to get you our old cabin in Volcano. My father sold it to a friend of his, Mr Nitta, a few years ago. He doesn't usually rent it, but he might make an exception for us. He's been sick lately and probably doesn't get up there much anymore anyhow. He and his wife live in Hilo.'

'Isn't it dangerous during an eruption?'

'Naw, Volcano's safe because it's above Kilauea. Why would they build a town there if it was dangerous?'

'Pompeii was a town.'

'Naw. It's the little towns below that have to worry. By below I mean in Puna. Or Rainbow Gardens. You might feel a tremor now and then, but that's all. If there were any danger, you'd be notified. This is a small eruption. But if it breaks out and goes over the pali, call me. That's a sight I'll pay for. Then it might hit the sea and start steaming and cackling like a Hakka restaurant. Make a new black sand beach.'

'Okay, I'll toss it around. Sounds good. I want to get over there as soon as possible. Ask Mr Nitta what he wants for his cabin and I'll talk to Felicia tomorrow.'

'Her parents approve of this?'

Cullen made a vague gesture with head and hand. 'You see, the truth is she's never been anywhere. Lived here all her life and hasn't even made it to the outer islands.'

'Right, so they're happy to have you show her the world, are they?'

'We thought maybe it would be better if they didn't know.'

'Thou shalt not lie.'

'Yeah, well, you gotta lie to your parents, don't ya.'

'Honor thy father and thy mother.'

'Sure, that too. But these things aren't carved in stone or anything.'

'Thou shalt not fuck thy student.'

'Gee, you know all ten of them, huh?'

Earl smiled.

'I'm hoping her friend Melanie will help us out. Make it look like the two of them are going over to check out the Volcano. Then they could meet me in Hilo.'

'Then what do you do with Melanie?'

'Where, exactly, is this puka you were talking about?'

Earl smirked.

'See what I'm hoping is that her parents don't actually come to the airport. Then Melanie could drive Felicia to the airport, I could meet her there, and we could be on our way to one big eruption after another.'

'Is Melanie a looker?'

'Naw, she's more a . . . what d'ya call it, a sort of . . .'

'Ugly person?'

'Well, no, I wasn't going to say that. I was going to say that she has a very nice personality. I know that's a really overused, uh . . . hackneyed cliché . . .'

'Euphemism.'

'Or that. But she has special qualities. Physically though, if we're talking about the crude, physical . . . uh, male-dominated world in which a woman's worth is judged by her appearance . . . well, then I don't doubt that a prick like yourself would probably judge her as, um, somewhat, shall we say . . . fat.'

'That bad, huh? So what does she do while you guys are on the Big Island?'

'She goes underground. She likes local surfers. Likes to boogie.'

'With your luck, it will all go gloriously wrong. Melanie's body will wash up on the beach, or you guys will get your picture splashed on the front page of the paper and you won't even know it till you get back.'

'The danger of discovery only intensifies the thrill.'

'Speaking of intensifying the thrill, have you ever had a Filipino blow job?'

'Not knowingly. I've had a blow job while driving, does that count?'

'No. I think you're thinking of a blowout. That's thrilling, but it's not the same thing. No, it's like this. It's a blow job with shave ice. Got it? The object of your desire fills her mouth with shave ice – and just drives you fuckin' wild. You don't know *what* you're feeling, but it is intense. It's like Saint Augustine having a clash between passion and will; on the one hand, will's really cold and slushy, but on the otherhand, passion's firm and hot. Maybe that's too philosophical. It's fire and ice, see—'

'Yeahhh, I think I do see. It's like your cock's an overheated icebreaker. And you just gotta keep pushing through, despite the danger, 'cause you got this important load to deliver.'

'Look, it's like one of those finely tuned motel showers that's within one degree of scalding and then suddenly it goes cold because somebody somewhere flushes a toilet. You don't know whether you're comin' or goin'.'

'Coming, I should hope. And Jesus, where do you get these metaphors? A finely tuned motel shower?'

'That was a simile actually. A comparison using *like*.'

'I was using metaphor in the generic sense of the word. Like Kleenex to refer to all tissues – including Puffs, including Kleenex.'

'That's another simile.'

'No, that's an analogy.'

'And *Kleenex* isn't generic. *Tissues* is generic. Ask Felicia to give you a snow job sometime and see what metaphors you come up with. I'm sure they'll be very creative. What I'm talking about here is a nuclear meltdown at the pole, okay? Something really steamy. I highly recommend it. Five stars.'

'You know, that's something they didn't forbid.'

'They didn't even have Filipinos in those days.'

'So what flavor shave ice do you recommend?'

'I don't think you understand, Cullen. You don't administer the blow job. You receive it. The flavor's totally immaterial. It's entirely up to the lady.'

'But different flavors probably have a different feel, don't ya think?'

'Like flavored condoms? No, Cullen, I really don't think they do. Try soy sauce. Turn on that light, will ya?'

Cullen turned on the lamp beside him. Earl extinguished the candles, then opened the envelope on the table.

'This here's my ghost certificate. I'm mighty proud of this, so treat it with respect.'

'Ah, the famous ghost certificate.'

Cullen took a look.

> This is to certify that Mr Earl Ogilvie has slept in Room #4 of the Kauailani Hotel, hereafter referred to as the haunted hotel room, for five consecutive nights from May 4th, 1971 to May 8th, 1971, inclusive, and has witnessed the physical disturbances attributed to the ghost of Mrs Lenora Waddy, fatally knifed by her husband on the night of December 17, 1962, to wit: opening of closet door at or around midnight, rattling of coat hangers in said closet, and rattling of chain locks on front door – all living actions performed by Mrs Waddy in her last breathing moments in an attempt to escape the wrath of her irate husband, Solomon Waddy, who caught her *in flagrante delicto* with her lover – Richard Roland Medeiros, also fatally knifed – and who now resides in Oahu State Prison. The holder of this certificate has displayed great courage above and beyond that required of the average hotelgoer.

The certificate itself was embellished with a picture of the hotel fronted by palm trees, at the top, and at the bottom with one of those lurid drawings often found on the cover of such magazines as *Male* or *Saga*: a desperate ravishing beauty clad in lingerie fortuitously torn to expose her breasts and thighs. He thought he detected a slight resemblance to Felicia.

'Was this hotelkeeper working his way through law school or something?'

'I helped him write it.'

'You?!'

'It was my idea. I thought it might help his business. Tastefully done, don't you think? He loved it.'

'"Hereafter referred to as the haunted hotel room"?'

'And then never referred to again? Yes, I thought that was a nice touch.'

'And the drawing?'

'Pretty good for an amateur, yeah? I copied it off a men's magazine. I think she was being chased by an alligator.'

'You're a fraud, Earl.'

'Naw, I'm just an ordinary guy who keeps his wits about him. Clear that table, will ya?'

He soon unfolded a topographic map of the Big Island, a green island wearing a lei of Hawaiian place names.

'Here's Volcano. The cabin's right here. Care for a smoothie?'

'Sure.'

Earl went to the kitchen.

'Someday they're gonna discover a missing life form in here,' he shouted, chipping ice from his freezer.

Cullen loved a good map, one with few roads and dramatic contours. With a map, one could imagine the world one wanted, free of the dross and clutter of humankind – no billboards, no neon, no rusting sugar mills or bulldozed forests, no visible signs of progress, poor taste or poverty. A map was to the real world what a novel was to real life.

At the center of this map rose Mauna Kea and Mauna Loa, two majestic volcanoes from which flowed the whole island – as much today as in the formative past. This was a map like none other, its landmarks not cities and rivers but lava flows and cones, rifts and pits, cracks and craters. And on the coast – with names such as Kaloli, Mahuka and Puhi'ula anchored offshore – points and parks, bays and beaches, caves and coves. And everywhere heiaus – ancient temples – as many, it seemed, as towns. He thought to look at Kalapana, where Laura's brother had seen flying shadows, and found not one heiau but four in the immediate vicinity. Just as close was Pu'u Lapu (Haunted Hill). Interesting that the map-makers should have felt compelled to translate that. A quick scan revealed five petroglyph sites and two 'ancient paved trails' that began and ended nowhere, cut off by flows. It was impossible to visit an outer island without considering the ancients who named it, men and women born into a world where every wind and rain had a name and every rainbow a prophecy.

He found Kilauea Caldera encircled by a road he'd once driven, and next to Chain of Craters a warning in red: 'Some roads on the island are subject to closing due to volcanic activity; enquire locally of status.' Volcano, less than two miles from the caldera, had its rectilinear streets intact, but in Royal Gardens, near the sea, an ugly green blot flowed through the streets like spilled miso. Virtually all flows were dated, and some bore names. The National Park ran from Mauna Loa to the sea, where it fanned open to stretch thirty miles from Kapao'o Point to Kupapa'u. A rainforest abutted Volcano. Portuguese Springs caught his eye, and Ka Lae, southernmost point of the island and hence of the United States. A nene sanctuary, an ancient shelter, a reconstructed City of Refuge. A Buddhist temple, a 'painted' church, a heiau dated 1275. Waterfalls, sea arches, a green sand beach. He had been there but had missed so much, and had known while missing it that he must someday return. That went without saying. He'd return when the volcano was erupting, and that would somehow close a chapter in his life.

'Here you go.'

'Thanks.'

'See anything you like?

'It brings back memories.'

'That's right, you've been there. With Alice. I keep forgetting.'

'We missed so much though. It's a big island.'

'Well put. This dope came from here,' he said, placing a Zig Zag over Puna. He proceeded to roll another.

'What's this "Haunted Hill"?'

'Beats me. Never heard of that one.' He drew the joint beneath his nose like a fine cigar. 'How's Felicia doing with her ghost?'

'Are you going to light that or vacuum it?'

Earl obliged while Cullen pondered the question. No one had ever before asked him to speak on this subject.

'She claims she still experiences . . . What did you call it, the same sensation Noriko had?'

'*Kanashibari*.'

'Right. Well, it's still there; it hasn't gone away.'

'How 'bout a visit to the psychiatrist? Maybe that would help?'

'Is that what you recommended to Noriko?'

'That's what I would've recommended if she'd asked me.'

'I'm surprised to hear that from a guy who spouts more tales of the supernatural than Edgar Allen Poe. Why are Felicia's beliefs neuroses? Because she's Portuguese or because you don't like her?'

'I like her well enough. She's a good lookin' babe, I'll give you that.'

'Oh, come on. You've been down on her since Day One.'

'Was Day One the day she jumped all over me because I stabbed some Gouda with a cheese knife?'

'I wouldn't say she jumped all over you, but yes, that was Day One.'

'I just felt the whole thing was rather silly, that's all. I can't quite view the conjunction of cheese knife and cheese as sinister. I've got nothing against the Portagees though. But there's a difference between believing in something you've personally experienced and being superstitious.'

'But Felicia has personally experienced *kanashibari*.'

'Okay. That's different. But if you were experiencing it, what would you do – seek professional help or call in an exorcist?'

Cullen had no immediate answer for this. It was a question that certainly struck at the heart of the matter.

'Hey look, Cullen. Calm down. You've got me all wrong here. I've got nothing against Felicia personally. I hardly know the girl.'

'I asked her to marry me.'

'You did what? What'd she say?'

'She said no.'

'You dodged that bullet. She was doing you a favor. Marriage is a terrible thing. My parents were married. It starts out as love and sex and it ends up with some poor jerk working his balls off just to keep his wife in clothes and labor-saving appliances. I wouldn't want to see you work, Cullen. And then the kiddies come along and they need diapers and Montessori and violin lessons and they're allergic to your house and they've got to be smarter and cuter than everyone else's brats and every once in a while you have to sew a limb back on and get their teeth straightened out and before you know it you're trapped. I haven't seen an English teacher yet who could support a family.'

'Is that why you're still single, because you don't want to support a family?'

'I'm still single because I've never met a woman I loved . . . more than all the other women. You know what I mean? Women are a sort of collective organism. I don't care how nice the girl is, I don't want filet mignon every day of the week. It's that simple. Everyone appreciates a little change now and then. It's human nature. It is not normal to make love to the same woman for the rest of your life. That is aberrant behavior in my opinion. Deep in his groin, every man knows that. That's why we've got prostitutes and business trips. I'll bet not one man in a hundred is faithful, and that man jacks off with a girlie magazine. Anyway, after a year at most, I'm bored. She's still a nice girl and everything, but in the words of the great B. B. King, "The thrill is gone." It's that simple. I always thought you were the same way.'

'I can't believe what I'm hearing here. You're disgusting.'

'You know, I can't entirely disagree with you on that. Sometimes I say to myself, "Earl, you're disgusting." But then my self says, "So who gives a fuck?"'

'Oh, well that's very profound. Nothing cynical there. But you know, there's more to life than just sex.'

'Sure there is. I know that. Nothing leaps to mind offhand, but' – he glanced around the room – 'Good books! Sure, that's one thing. Culture, sports, poker, great intellectual pursuits. I was just talking about things one could do with a woman – you know, other than balancing the checkbook, painting the nursery pink . . .'

'I can't believe what a chauvinist you are.'

'And what are you, Gloria Steinem? All I'm saying is what my father always told me: "Love is blind, but marriage is an eye opener." Now this comes from a guy whose wife impaled him on his own marlin, so think about that before you make the mistake of asking her a second time. But if you're so deeply in love, go ahead and get married. I don't care. Anyhow, you want me to set you up with this cabin or not?'

'Yeah. The cabin sounds great.'

'Okay, I'll get on it first thing in the morning. Trust me. And speaking of Portagees, did you hear about the Portagee who bought his wife a wig because he heard she was getting bald at the office? Pass that joint, will ya?'

25

'Elegant,' said Cullen. He was referring to the plan. The plan that Felicia and Melanie had just outlined as they sat in his living room.

'Isn't it beautiful?' said Felicia.

'Quite.'

They had arrived unannounced around three. It had been a while since he'd seen Melanie, and though he was initially disappointed to discover her at Felicia's side, her presence being a marker for sexual abstinence, he soon warmed to her company.

The plan was simplicity itself.

'Melanie picks me up at my house. She's got two tickets in her hand and her bag's in the car. The two of us are off for a big adventure.'

'Okay.'

'She drops me off at the airport, where, once I'm sure we haven't been tailed, I meet you.'

'Okay. But what if your parents call Melanie's?'

'No one will be home,' said Melanie. 'My folks are going to San Francisco and I'll be staying with friends on the North Shore.'

'Doing what?'

'Surfing. Snorkeling. Hanging out. Don't worry 'bout me.'

'Sounds good.'

'So me and you fly to the Big Island together and spend a week at your friend's cabin. Then, Melanie flies over and we get to spend some girl time together, a couple days on our own, just the two of us.'

She paused to let him absorb this condition.

'Then,' she said, 'Melanie and me fly back together. She'll have her car at the airport. We both return with wonderful souvenirs of the Big Island. You fly back later, whenever you want.'

'Felicia's never flown in an airplane before,' said Melanie.

'You'll love it,' said Cullen. 'It's the best way to see the islands.'

What he loved was the implications. Felicia wanted to be with him, so much so that she had asked this favor of Melanie, had plotted to deceive her parents, had moved quickly and decisively to make it happen. They'd skip the wedding but have the honeymoon. And one of his dreams would come true.

'This deserves a round of drinks,' he said.

Melanie reached for her purse and began the search for a joint in the dark and wondrous realm within.

Outside his kitchen window hung orange heliconia and massive monstera leaves perforated by large ellipses through which the sun flowed benignly, perhaps even approvingly. It was simple. It was elegant.

26

Melanie delivered Felicia to the airport as promised. Both appeared with a luggage trolley, engaged in solemn conversation. Cullen appeared from behind a concrete column and exhaled. It was permissible now to believe. He and she would be alone together, would spend entire nights together, would awaken together. Their lovemaking would not be followed by parting but by tender embraces. And together they would view a live volcano erupting in fiery splendor. Cullen would take a picture of the volcano, a dramatic shot, and that would close one of life's magic circles begun that day in the Kuhio when their love had been primed by a few golden beers and a copy of the *Nikon Annual.*

The three formed a huddle and congratulated each other on the success of the mission thus far. Melanie exchanged kisses with Felicia. 'See you next week,' she said. Then she was off.

He added Felicia's luggage to his and together they queued to check in. They were like man and wife.

'Look what my mother gave me,' she said.

'What?'

'A hundred bucks.'

'Great. You can take me out to dinner.'

'Dr Kinnell! Dr Kinnell!'

Where was that coming from? At any given moment the surrounding air is a pandemonium of electromagnetic radiation and pressure waves, yet just as only that narrow band of radiation between infrared and ultraviolet stimulates the human eye, so, too, do only those waves vibrating twenty to twenty thousand times per second agitate that delicate aural membrane that—

'Hey, man! It's Killer Kinnell!'

Cullen turned his head as slowly as a tank turret toward this happy, familiar, yet not readily identifiable voice.

'Hey!' said Felicia cheerily.

It was Dhabul, grinning wildly, already upon them. He took both of Felicia's hands in his long-fingered brown ones. Hula girls danced across his red aloha shirt.

'Yo!' He turned toward Cullen, still beaming, threw an arm over Cullen's shoulder, draped his other arm around Felicia, and said, as if they were all the best of friends, 'What you guys doin' here?'

A good question. What were they doing here?

'I'm just—'

'We're flying to the Big Island,' said Felicia.

There, it was out. They were flying to the Big Island. It could hardly be denied that they were flying somewhere.

'Whoa. You and Doctor K here? You and your English teacher? Your English teacher and yourself? I think I see da light!'

Cullen smiled wanly like a man neatly mugged.

Dhabul shook his head in cheerful disbelief.

'You're sho nuff breakin' my heart, Felicia. I hope this doesn't mean it's over between us.'

She smiled. But Cullen thought he'd caught a combustible glint. He stooped to advance their luggage and came up free of Dhabul's muscular grip.

'The Big Island, huh? Hilo's on the Big Island, ain't it? That's where we're goin'! You comin' to watch us play?'

'Who ya playin'?' asked Felicia.

'Who we playin', Dunk? The Hilo Honkies, the Hilo Hookers, the Hookie Mookies?'

Duncan had appeared almost magically. But then, he always did. Dhabul let go of Felicia.

'Ah bleeve we're playin' the Hilo Warriors. Sort of a charity match.'

'Like you two,' said Dhabul. 'What flight you on?'

'505,' said Cullen, beneath whom the ground seemed to be slowly sinking. How else to account for the way Plunkett and Dhabul suddenly towered over him like gargoyles in a nightmare?

'505!' said Dhabul. 'That's our flight! You're gonna be flyin' with the Holy Mount Trojans.'

'The only team named after a condom,' said Cullen in disbelief.

Duncan leered.

Only now did Cullen become aware of his encirclement by Trojans – tall white boys, mostly, milling about in twos and threes, bags slung casually over their shoulders – and the effect was eerie, artificial, as when one stumbles into a clutch of bodysnatchers trying to converse like humans. Just then a whistle as loud as a referee's pierced the air, summoning the team as if they were dogs and breaking the peculiar trance that Cullen seemed to be falling into.

'Look,' he said to Felicia, 'we can't get on this flight. We've got to take a later one.'

'Why? Our dirty little secret's out anyway.'

'It's just gonna get worse. When we pick up our bags together at the other end and get into that car . . . Oh my God. Oh Jesus. I can't believe what's coming this way. Don't turn around.'

'What is it?'

'It's my doom.'

'Give me a hint.'

'It starts with P and it rhymes with *gecko*.'

Felicia, seemingly oblivious to the disaster about to befall them, broke into a broad smile and turned to greet the man just as he breached their luggage.

'Father Plecko!' she said, almost hugging him.

'Felicia. Cullen. I heard you were both on this flight.'

'A bit of a coincidence, really,' said Cullen. 'I'm off to see the Volcano, and apparently Felicia's meeting her parents in Hilo.'

'Oh.'

'Are you traveling with the team?'

'No, no, I'm just here to see them off.'

'Forgive me, Father, for I have sinned. Grievously, I know. I met Felicia in the rain, we had a few beers, swam nude in the sea, and before I realized the impropriety of my actions we were engaged in habitual fornication and other activities not sanctioned by the Church, but now we've decided to put an end to all that, and—'

What would Plecko say to that sort of confession were he rash enough to make it? *Let he who has not sinned cast the first stone*?

'It's quite a coincidence all of us running into each other like this,' said Cullen weakly.

'Yes, isn't it.' He suddenly twitched toward Felicia in that uncanny way he had of abruptly repositioning himself. 'And what are you going to do with your parents in Hilo?'

This seemed to unnerve her.

'Me? Oh we're just gonna see the Big Island.'

Mercifully, as the line advanced and they nudged their luggage forward, a young man came running to inform Father Plecko that he was wanted by the coach.

'I'll be off then,' he said. 'Have a nice trip.'

'Thanks.'

'Jesus,' said Cullen as soon as he was out of sight, 'that guy's as flaky as a bag of onions.'

'He didn't do anything. And I didn't appreciate that lie about my parents.'

'I'm sorry. I had to think quick. I was desperate. You could have handled it better.'

'Can I have your tickets, please?' asked the Hawaiian Air representative. They had reached the head of the queue.

'Are we taking this flight?' asked Felicia.

'I'd rather not. Do you have any seats on the next flight to Hilo?'

'Sir, there is no next flight to Hilo. Not until tomorrow morning.'

'Then I guess we're taking this flight.'

Soon they were boarding. And as their seats were in the front of the plane and the Trojans boarded last, he had the privilege of watching Felicia greet half of the team by name as they filed by in the prime of their manhood. Most failed to acknowledge him, but Jesse proved a notable exception, seeming genuinely happy to see him.

'Hi, Dr Kinnell. How ya doin'?'

'I'm fine, Jesse. How are you?'

'Jes fine, sir.'

The team filled the plane behind them like a raunchy Greek chorus lacking legroom, and Cullen imagined that every whoop, giggle, and snicker had something to do with him, the stuck-up asshole professor who had somehow managed to snatch the hottest snatch in school. He brooded, staring at his fingernails.

Felicia had a window seat. The plane was rolling. The plane was airborne. And that, for her, was new. She ticked off landmarks she had never before seen from the air – Magic Island, the Yacht Harbor, the Sheraton, the Royal Hawaiian – and there, tucked into the sea as neatly as handkerchiefs, tacked a myriad of white and striped sails, while surfers rode the waves off Waikiki and tiny tourists waded in water waist-deep – then came the zoo, giant banyans, and a swath of sunbathers sprawled like seals as far as the natatorium; the parched crater of Diamond Head opened beneath her; the immaculate lighthouse stood proudly; the solid roofs of the rich nestled in greenery; the reef peeled white foam off incoming waves; and there rose Black Point embroidered by surf, there were the palms and pools of Kahala, and only then did she think to look inland for her home, but too late, yet there was the ridge that rose to Cullen's home – and the plane dipped a wing toward the Hilton – Hi, Steve – and far behind that should be St Mary's, her high school, and then she realized that they were going to follow the coastline to her uncle's, and that that tiny white dollhouse fronted by palms was probably it – 'Look, Cullen! Uncle Bebe's!' – and this was how people's lives looked from above, like a sunny colony of like-minded creatures bound joyfully and purposefully together, like nest builders, like industrious toy cars and trucks proceeding harmoniously at a snail's pace, and before she knew it the shadow of the plane had slid past Hawaii Kai and Koko Head and the green horseshoe of Hanauma Bay was falling behind them, its snorkelers infinitesimal, and she thought to look for their cove but found instead black rocks breaking up swells like meringues, and a single yellow fishing boat motionless in the channel, then soon Molokai – a rain dog in a lone, deep valley; a turquoise sea behind the reef – and already she could see what Cullen had meant by adventure, this bold new life, and when the stewardess asked if they'd care for a cocktail she said yes, she would, let's celebrate, and Cullen said yes, he would too, most certainly, make it a double please, let's celebrate our glorious fucking luck flying with the fucking charming Holy Mount Trojans – say that ten times fast, why doncha – and let's drink with varying degrees of horror and indignation to the almost certain removal of Cullen Kinnell from the Department of English, which academically supports, as you know, the sporting extortionists of the aforementioned Trojans – and then just let the aforementioned instructor lie peacefully in a tar pit and bury him under a thick geological layer of rock. Because it had hit him – like a giant piece of space junk falling out of the sky. It had pummeled him. It had slapped him hard on both cheeks and shaken him by the collar. And it wasn't the fact that rushing toward an active volcano seemed an apt metaphor for his life now that his future lay in the hands of a smoking priest likely to bury him. It wasn't the distressing prospect of seeking gainful employment in a sadly sobering world unlikely to hire him to do something he didn't really want to do anyway – say advertising or technical writing. It wasn't his inadequacies or his poverty or his execrable luck. No, it was something much worse, something insufferable if true, and he was trying it on now as a misery to see if it fit. It was the look she had given Dhabul when he said 'I hope this doesn't mean it's over between us.' It was horrible imaginings. It was 'I fucked Felicia Mattos.' It had appeared in his favorite stall, writing on the wall, straight subject-verb-object, at a time when he thought he could blot out reality with a can of black spray paint. That had been a couple of months after the misspelled death threat. And he, like a fool, had convinced himself that this crudity represented nothing more than an imaginary conquest. But now the very fucker was perhaps sniggering, sneering, defacing Cullen's love with vulgarities. If so, it was intolerable. And yes, there was an added indignity in imagining the perpetrator was black. That added another layer of disgust and revulsion. He could see that now; he could finally admit that to himself. He was something of a racist after all. Despite his adulation of Jackie Robinson, despite his support of the Civil Rights Movement, despite voting for Dick Gregory in '68, despite his impassioned defense of 'Negroes' in arguments with his mother, despite personal friendships, he was now feeling the same repugnance that his mother must have felt when she'd said, 'But, Cullen, they want to swim at the same *beaches* that we do.'

But this was madness. He was letting his imagination run

rampant. No black ram had tupped his white ewe. The green-eyed monster was mocking him. The unthinkable remained unthinkable, which was as it should be. When he gazed at Felicia he saw a sweet child absorbed in the miracle of flight. Well, there was nothing for it really but to soak oneself in rum like a fruit and enjoy the splendid scenery. The dark clouds over Maui held not a rain dog but a whole rainbow, one of those perfect promises on air, while the sun streamed in below, turning pineapple fields to patchwork amber.

'That's Maui,' he said.

'God but it's beautiful.'

Maui brought memories. He and Alice had once been bumped from a small plane at the Kaanapali Airport. It had been a voluntary thing – a hysterical rich lady had been circling the lobby like a chihuahua with an infected urinary tract and they had agreed to speed her on her way in exchange for a free bar tab till the next flight arrived. That was before Alice had given up alcohol.

The second-floor bar had doubled as a control tower, for only from there could one see past the sugarcane to the windsock at the far end of the runway. One could also see the blue glittering channel in which whales were known to breach and backflip. They were not far from Lahaina, where Melville the harpooner had been discharged from a Nantucket whaler.

'How come every stool has a woman's name?' Alice had asked suspiciously, ever alert to potential chauvinism.

'Those are all my ex-wives,' explained the bartender cheerfully. 'All ten of 'em. You're sitting on Barbara, my first wife.'

'Are you married now?'

'Absolutely.' He proudly flipped open his wallet to a snapshot. 'This is Stella. Ain't she a beauty? She's touring South America now. She'll be back next month.'

To Cullen, who was sitting on Babs, Stella had the look of a divorcee.

'What if this one doesn't work out?' he asked.

'Not a chance,' sang the bartender. 'Stella's the love of my life. I'll tell ya a secret. It's the eleventh time that's the charm. Most men give up too soon.' He winked.

'Doesn't she get jealous of all your barstools?'

'Naw. It's the alimony that drives her crazy.'

Cullen suddenly realized that at the time, he and Alice had also been bound for the Big Island. He remembered Alice popping shrimp into his mouth while they drove the empty coastal road to Kalapana in windblown rain. He remembered dragging all the mattresses from the beds of the cabin they'd rented to form a single love nest on the floor. He remembered her making him guava pancakes for breakfast. At the time, it had seemed like love. Now this did.

27

A syrupy golden light poured into the cabin as the aircraft began its descent. Then the plane dropped into the dark shadow of the clouds crowning Mauna Kea. When it touched down at Hilo and taxied to a stop, Cullen and Felicia were the first to exit. At the bottom of the ramp stood a line of official greeters, bare-armed local girls in muumuus, each with a hibiscus in her hair and several plumeria and pikake leis draped over her arm. They smiled beyond Cullen and Felicia, readying themselves for the descent of more important personages. A photographer stood by as well. The whole tableau seemed to hold its breath until Cullen and Felicia had passed, then squeals filled the air and the photographer went into action as the first Trojans appeared whooping and whistling. Cullen was sure it was Plunkett who said, 'Hey, I'm gonna get lei'd!' He hurried Felicia to the canopied baggage-claim area, where a breeze carried the scent of recent rain and the sound of a slack-key guitar.

Bedecked with flowers and filled with high spirits drunk on the flight, the Trojans soon surrounded the luggage carousel. Duncan offered Dhabul five dollars for his lei.

'No way! This lei is here to stay.'

Cullen recalled that Dick Gregory, when a guest speaker at the university, had removed all his leis, saying that as a black he felt uncomfortable with anything around his neck. Cullen felt naked without a lei of his own, but he and Felicia were not the only flowerless visitors. There were also two local businessmen and a pair of portly tourists, none of whom had been mistaken for team members. The conveyor belt that offered up luggage was a languid clock of sorts, and though two of their bags appeared early, faithful as pups, the tardy third was the last to arrive. To Cullen's astonishment, it bore a Trojan sticker. How had they done that? He looked up to see who might be enjoying this joke, but the team was already heading for its bus.

'See you at the game, Dr K,' said Duncan, who had somehow gotten behind him.

'When is it?' asked Felicia.

'Sadday night. Come root us on.'

'We might do that,' said Cullen.

'Where you guys goin', anyway?'

To answer this question was to admit that they were going somewhere, together, which was why Cullen remained silent. Nevertheless, Felicia filled the void with 'Volcano.'

'Whatever. Don't be no stranger now, Felicia. Oh oh. Got a bus to catch. Later, Babes.'

'Bye,' said Felicia.

'What did he mean by that?' asked Cullen.

'What does he mean by half the things he says? I don't know.'

They picked up their rental car, a Toyota, which took longer than it should have. Then they found themselves on the road to the Nittas', where they were to pick up the keys to the cabin. They passed a golf course and a Japanese garden, crossed a canal brimming with fishing boats, then drove alongside an overcast bay before turning inland just before the river. Simple and wooden, quiet as its Japanese, Hilo had an appealing modesty. They passed the post office and a small park crowded with tangled banyans whose roots had been varnished by a recent rain. Passing through a row of two-story houses sheltered by monkeypods, they came to the school. Just around a corner, they found their destination: a weathered frame house fronted by ti and tiare.

'Remember now,' said Cullen as they pulled into the driveway, 'we're married.'

As they exited the car, the front door swung open and a gaunt silhouette in a cardigan appeared behind the screen. Mr Nitta greeted them at the threshold.

'Hello, hello. You must be the Kinnells. Did you have trouble?'

'No, it just took us a while to get our rental car.'

'Oh, I'm sorry. We operate on Hawaiian time here. I'm afraid it's not as efficient as Honolulu. Could you find the house easily enough? I think we gave very poor directions.'

'Not at all. Your directions were excellent.'

'I'm sorry we have such bad weather today. It's been beautiful all week.'

'Really,' said Felicia.

A frail, stooped man, Mr Nitta had gotten them as far as the hallway. He might have felt more comfortable greeting strangers in a colder, less hospitable climate where he could make a great fuss about taking their hats and coats while berating the weather as if it were his wayward child. As it were, they had nothing to remove except their shoes, which required no assistance on his part, and so his hands fluttered aimlessly and apologetically with all the nervousness that true Japanese feel in the presence of guests. Cullen had donned a constant smile to reassure the man, then realized that that's what the Japanese do, as well.

A diminutive Mrs Nitta appeared at her husband's side, her hands clasped before her as if molding mochi, and when she nodded, smiling, she all but bowed.

'We were worried about you,' she said.

It was she who guided them into the living room and got the old man to sit on the couch. It had been Mrs Nitta, not her husband, who had provided the entirely adequate directions. And it had been she who had called to reject Cullen's first offer as overly generous.

'Please excuse me for a moment,' she said, backing out of the room slowly as if they might object.

It was a room in which one heard the clocks tick, as if time were a sinking weight turning a heavy ratchet. A large emperor clock squatted on the shelf like a headstone, and a grandfather clock as big and shiny as a coffin marked time beside the couch. Why did the elderly like clocks so?

'And how are the Ogilvies?' asked Mr Nitta. 'Are they well?'

'Oh, yes. They're doing fine,' replied Cullen, assuming that if they weren't, Earl would have told him.

'And their son Earl? How is he?'

'Earl's fine. He's teaching at the University now. We're good friends.'

'Yes, I know. He's a nice boy.'

Obviously you don't know him as well as I do, Cullen wished to say.

Mr Nitta reminded Cullen of Yuen Ching. His gnarled neck seemed too long to support his skull, too insubstantially rooted in the hollow between his shoulders. His eyes peered from exaggerated shadows. Any fool could see that death was nibbling away at him. Nevertheless, a stubborn warmth shone in his smile. He suddenly frowned, however, as if something dreadful had happened. 'It's raining again,' he said mournfully.

Mrs Nitta returned with a pot of tea and asked if they'd like some.

'Yes, please,' said Cullen. 'That would be nice.'

They could hardly refuse, though something in the way Felicia had slid forward in her chair suggested she would do just that. Now she stood to help Mrs Nitta lower the lacquerware tray. Try as he might, he could not envision Felicia and him together in forty years. Would she nurse him in his dotage, clean his bedpan, wipe his spittle, wheel him from room to room? Would he administer her medicines, portion out her meals in teaspoons, bathe her with a sponge, remind her of who he was? None of this seemed likely.

He admired her legs as she sat. It was reassuring to be young, and best not to dwell on the way we shrivel into eternity.

The tea proved virtually tasteless, an infusion of lettuce. Perhaps it was some sort of contract-sealing ritual. Mr Nitta spent considerable time explaining the usage, quirks and dangers of the wood stove, gas stove, and water heater, and offered them the use of a flashlight in case they reached Volcano late. He then traced with wrinkled forefinger the crude map he had drawn, his spotted hands shaking like windblown plumbago.

Steadier than her husband, Mrs Nitta balanced a cup and saucer on her knees without a rattle. She was a mountain deer, demure yet bright-eyed. She too apologized for the rain. But Volcano, she assured them, would be lovely in any weather.

'A few years ago we saw an eruption that shot up sixteen thousand feet,' said Mr Nitta.

'Sixteen *hundred* feet.'

'Sixteen *hundred* feet. Straight up, like a geyser. You could see it from Puna. Beautiful at night.'

'Sounds fantastic,' said Cullen. 'We're just hoping to see Mauna Ulu in action.'

'Oh you will. You will.'

Mrs Nitta adjusted one drooping flower in a vase of yellow ginger.

'I'm sorry,' she said, 'but I wasn't able to clean the cabin since the last time we were there. We don't usually rent it out.'

'That's okay. We're just grateful to have it.'

'Do you need to buy food today?'

'Yes. We were planning on it.'

'Then you might want to stop at Pay-N-Save on the way up. You'll go right past it on the Belt Road. There's only two small stores in Volcano, and their prices are very high.'

'They won't be open anyhow,' said Mr Nitta, who drew a long face and suddenly began to cough quite violently, collapsing like a beach chair. Mrs Nitta set aside her tea cup and leaned forward, not quite as alarmed as Cullen and Felicia. When his cough subsided, she rose to fetch keys from the kitchen.

'Take this flashlight, please. There aren't any streetlights up there. This is for the driveway and this is for the garage.'

'Thank you.'

Hilo seemed virtually abandoned – a rainy old town, wooden and slightly warped. It was that hour of the day when the world withdraws but people live quietly on. Soon they were passing through the town's unromantic outskirts, also abandoned – a long careless row of car dealers, gas stations, warehouses, and yards of machinery, lumber, and scrap. Pay-N-Save, by contrast, buzzed with activity. Once supplied, they began the gradual ascent of Kilauea. By the time they had passed the macademia plantation, it already seemed an adventure. Among the sugarcane fields beyond Keaau, Felicia sighted the 500 feet elevation marker. They slowed to forty at Kurtistown, a ramshackle assemblage of frame houses with corrugated roofs. A Dairy Queen and an Assembly of God Church seemed equal in the rain. The nearby towns had names like 9½ Mile Camp, Iwasaki Camp, Elevenmile Homestead, names that spoke of hard labor. A sign sailed by on their right: FILIPINO CEMETERY: IN MEMORIAM.

Ti and banana plants flourished in front yards, and tall palms swayed languidly, their fronds dishevelled by wind. A wooden Antique Store cried out in blue. Then came Mountain View and the anthurium farms, red plastic hearts under glass. The last greenhouse had no sooner dwindled to a raindrop in the mirror than eucalyptus and lasiandra rushed forward to choke the highway, making their claim where man had not. This continued for miles. Higher up, waves of ferns curled to sweep over the car. Even when they had driven out of the rain, it continued to drip from each passing frond.

'Did you see that hawk on the pole?'

'No.'

They passed a gas station with a glass-bubble pump and a crooked sign reading CLOSED. 'Closed for the day or forever?' asked Felicia. One couldn't tell.

They drove again through banks of lasiandra – purple flowers, green and scarlet leaves – then traveled for miles with rain forest on their right and stunted ohia on their left, all that would grow on that particular flow. The air had grown predictably colder, the gray sky closer. Felicia spied the 3000 feet marker among wind-battered ginger. Soon the vegetation drew close again – tree ferns towering over the car, ohia strangling smaller ferns, ohia stifling ohia. There was no sound but the hum of wind and the drone of the engine. They had entered a fine, seemingly atomized mist. A sign read VOLCANO.

'This is cute,' said Felicia. 'I hope ours looks like this.'

Quaint wooden houses with white window trim – all miniature estates smothered in tree ferns and flowers – lined the highway. Most appeared vacant.

The Christmas lights strung along the berm were red and purple fuchsia. A single low-lying wooden structure fronted by a flag bore two signs: GENERAL STORE and POST OFFICE. Further on they found Okamura's Store, a landmark on Mr Nitta's map. They turned right, into a cloud.

'The Blob!' cried Felicia.

He slowed to a crawl and turned on the headlights. Tree ferns surrounded them, crowding the already narrow street to little more than a single lane. *Tribune Herald* mailboxes sometimes materialized in the fog like buoys, and beyond these they could sometimes discern the features of a lifeless cottage. The yards of such bungalows presented little evidence of formal gardening – it was achievement enough to hold back the jungle – but occasionally they held large nests of perfect blue hydrangeas. Most of the houses appeared on the right. On the left, where the cabin road should have been, stood an impenetrable wall of vegetation. They saw not a soul, not a light, nothing more than the occasional car or truck parked on gravel.

They crept forward, searching the fog for Laumilo Street. Felicia sat seemingly enchanted, her lips rounded as if to utter the smallest of exclamations. When a tree fern slapped the windshield, she jumped.

'Watch the road, will ya?'

A thin shadow became a street sign, but not Laumilo. Another sign read PAVEMENT NARROWS. Twisted ohia slid through the fog like ghost ships, the tallest hanging ragged sails. Behind one skewed tree would be less of another, beyond that a few wraithlike branches adrift in a pale sea, beyond that only the intimation of a presence . . . perhaps land, perhaps an endless expanse of uncharted water. It was a thick, viscous fog in which skeletons receded like ancestors. The red stains in this vision were lehua flowers. The ancients believed picking lehua invited rain, but in such a fog, thought Cullen, it must surely invite transformation – into a pillar of stone only vaguely resembling a man, or into that mournful sound now present in the wind. It seemed that they had traveled as far from Honolulu as possible.

'Did you catch the name of that street?' he asked.

'Dead End.'

'Seriously.'

'LAU something, but I don't think it was the one we wanted.'

He backed up cautiously, in fits and starts, his engine whining unhappily. The sign read LAUKAPU. They drove on, past dendrobiums and impatiens, past azaleas, past NO TRES-PASSING and PRIVATE PROPERTY KEEP OUT. Maile Street appeared on the left, Elepaio on the right, but these were simply roads laid out by an ambitious developer; it seemed unlikely that they contained more than a cabin or two.

ROAD NARROWS.

'How can you narrow *this* road?' he asked.

'Are you sure we're supposed to go this far?'

'I've only seen one road on the left, and it wasn't Laumilo.'

They bobbed on, the road now nothing more than a series of bumps and dips. Occasionally a cabin would pierce the fog unexpectedly, a large rock in a treacherous channel, slowly dissolving to port or starboard as they pushed forward on faith into the void, a featureless brume from which abruptly emerged three tall figures charging toward them. Cullen slammed on the brakes, the front of the car plowing through wild grass, the rear tires squealing. Then all was silent. Felicia still braced herself against the dashboard, frozen in disbelief.

Three barren ohia towered above them. They had materialized from nothing and, for a horrid moment, had appeared to grow larger, drawing themselves up like warriors poised for battle. Cullen's heart had faltered; he hadn't expected trees in the middle of the road. In their mantle of fog, these conveyed an eerie dignity, as if guardians of whatever lay beyond. But of course there was no beyond: they had come to the end of the road without finding Laumilo Street, and now the fog was darkening.

'Will you watch where you're going,' said Felicia, drawing a breath. She turned to him apprehensively. 'I don't think these directions he gave us are all that reliable. He seemed a bit . . .' she squinted her eyes and rocked her open hand back and forth.

He smiled bravely, practicing confidence, wondering if the car was now stuck, which would be all he'd need. He shifted to reverse and prayerfully pressed the accelerator. The tires spun, kicked up mud, wailed bitterly, but hit something solid and lurched back on to the road. Feeling foolish, he turned the car around and headed back in the direction from which they'd come. He didn't know if he should be worried or not. The only thing wrong with Mr Nitta, he'd felt, had been that he was dying. He thought he'd understood the directions pretty well, but if he had, Laumilo Street should have been on the forested side of the road, where prospects now seemed dim. It was cold, and the fog had become indistinguishable from rain. He was surprised to discover that he had already turned on the wipers. They retraced their route, their faith rapidly diminishing. No new hope appeared on their right. He'd have to find the cabin soon; the loss of daylight would only compound his difficulties. He'd return to the highway and start over. They had almost reached it when they passed a narrow gap so overgrown with lasiandra that he had at first mistaken it for a private drive. But backing up, he saw that it might indeed be a street. Laumilo? The street sign, if there was one, had been swallowed whole.

'Think this might be it?'

'It's worth a try.'

The car brushed against lasiandra, bravely plunging into the unknown. A road appeared magically before them. To their right stood thick underbrush and a tangle of ferns and ohia. To their left stood a large forested lot, and then a cabin. With its red cedar shingles and chained driveway, it fit Mr Nitta's description. A neighboring cabin, barely visible, showed no signs of occupancy.

Felicia turned toward Cullen hopefully. 'He said there wouldn't be any cabins on the other side of the road.'

'Right. Let's try this key.'

He left the engine idling and stepped into tall grass that soaked his trouser cuffs. A wet chain barred the cinder drive. He squatted before the padlock and inserted the key.

So this was it. Cozy, weathered, surrounded by tree ferns and sugi pines, it was everything he'd hoped for. Even the fog was a treat, one more blanket for their bed. He tossed the chain aside and drove the car into the drive.

'Let's bring the food in first.'

The fiddlehead of a single fern coiled beside the stairs, each of its fine hairs crystalline. The pine needles, too, were draped with a delicate filigree of mist, or what the brochures had called 'fog drip'. The flashlight proved unnecessary; despite the rain and the hour, the cabin seemed bathed in a final effusion of light, a scintillation of the air itself. As they unlocked the door, groceries in hand, a wooden, almost charcoal smell greeted them. They stepped into an L-shaped room and surveyed its stark furnishings: double bed, punai, two rattan chairs, folding bridge table, four shelves of books, and a large handcarved Go board squatting on the wooden floor. They put the groceries beside it. Felicia opened the curtains of the picture window to see once again the fiddlehead beside the stairs, and the pines beyond that. A narrow strip of high windows ran across the front wall, near the center of which sat the wood stove, its black chimney creaking in the wind. The hushed sound of rain drifting through the trees was then swept away by a sharp, truculent downfall.

'We made it just in time,' he said, closing the door behind them and only then remembering their luggage. It could wait.

'It's freezing in here.'

'We can warm it up,' he said. 'There's a stove.'

'That?'

'That.'

Through the high window behind the chimney they saw raindrops sliding along, then dripping from, the eaves. He swung open the clangorous lid of the wood stove. He'd make a fire later.

Together they explored the rest of their estate. The first door they opened revealed a surprisingly large bathroom. An imposing tub the color of a well-scoured elephant stood almost in the middle, the green linoleum stained brown around each of its ponderous feet. Brown stains also surrounded the base of the toilet next to the tub. Cullen thought it customary to place a toilet adjacent to a wall, but this too sat almost in mid-room. To the right of the door stood a linen closet, and in the far corner, next to the window, hung a sink and mirror.

'Where's the light switch?' she asked.

'I don't know. I guess there's just this.'

He pulled a chain which illuminated a single bulb dangling from the ceiling. A globe of light hummed in its center, surrounded by a dirty halo. From the window he could see a large wooden watertank attached to the back of the house by a gutter. A solitary brown moth clung to the top of the windowscreen. When he touched it, it fell to the sill, where it lay among flies.

'At least it's spacious,' she said.

He agreed, but its spaciousness seemed the result of some miscalculation on the builder's part. The bathroom was large enough to have served as a bedroom.

Felicia proceeded down the hall, turning on lights as she went.

He joined her in the door of a cramped, musty bedroom housing two twin beds and a dresser.

'I guess we'll sleep in the front room.'

'Yeah. It'll be warmer.'

At the end of the hall he bumped his head on the lintel of the kitchen doorway.

'Ouch!'

'Hey! Look at this!'

A shotgun hung over a closed door. She climbed a chair to reach it. Without dismounting, she aimed it at him.

'One step closer, Mister, and I'll blow you away.'

'Hey, don't fool with that. It might be loaded.'

'This is just like my daddy's.'

'Come on, put it back.'

'What's the matter? Afraid I'll shoot you?'

'Yes.'

Pouting, she turned to replace it in its cradle above the door. As she did so, he caught sight of her legs tightening beneath a rising skirt. He now took the forbidden step.

'What's in here?' she asked, stepping off the chair and opening the rickety door before her. He peered over her shoulder into the darkness of a dingy toolshed lined with shelves of cobwebbed Mason jars.

'Embryos,' he said.

She turned toward him coldly. 'That's not funny.' Apparently he had struck one of her Catholic nerves.

From the windows of the long but narrow kitchen, they could see the water tank and a dense, dripping wall of tree ferns. The rain had slackened, but here, too, raindrops queued like abacus beads.

'I'll get our stuff.'

When he returned, narrowly avoiding a second collision with the lintel, he was struck by the hollow echo of water drumming a metal sink. This was interrupted by the tinnier sound of water filling a percolator. The water here did not gush forth with the reassuring force of Honolulu water but flowed, instead, in inconsequential fits. Still, the Nittas had assured him that there had been ample rain to fill the tank.

'Where's the coffee?' she asked.

'I'll find it.'

'Can you light the stove?'

'Sure.'

They'd forgotten to buy wooden matches, but he had a book in his pocket. He tried the front burners with no success. Same with the rear. The stove was dead. Perhaps it was necessary to push in the knobs as one turned. Every appliance had its own idiosyncrasies. Then he remembered, like a fool, that he had to open the valve on the tank. Mr Nitta had told him that, and he had even written it down. Where was the tank?

'We're going to freeze in this place, Cullen.'

'I'll light the fire in a minute. Where's the butane?'

'I don't know.'

It wasn't to the left of the stove and it wasn't to the right. Could it – ?

He opened an enameled panel that in his stove would have been a drawer for pots and pans, and there it was, a large gray tank the size of a small bomb. It seemed to be properly attached. He opened the valve, heard the quiet hiss of gas, thought of Sylvia Plath. Soon he had a burner ringed with blue-orange flame.

'Here it is,' she said, speaking of coffee.

Everything in the kitchen was shabbier than he'd imagined. Years ago, someone drab had painted the cabinets green, and now they were peeling. Once they'd been blue. Before that, ecru.

He thought to plug in the refrigerator. Its yellow light revealed three Nehi bottles, several packages of saimin, and a jar of peppers growing gills. He added their groceries and a bottle of champagne. Whatever else they'd need they'd buy at Okamura's. A splattering rain was falling into something tinny outside the window.

'There's dead flies all over this place!'

True. Flies littered every windowsill and lay belly up on the floor, where a few fat live ones struggled hopelessly, incapable of flight. The cabin had not been open for weeks, maybe months. Perhaps several generations had lived and died here, frustrated by the false promise of windows. He offered this theory to Felicia while they sat drinking a murky coffee she called 'fog drip', then tended to the wood stove while she rinsed out battered pots and pans. First came a layer of crumpled newspaper, then kindling, both of which he found in a box near the stove. Mr Nitta had told him he'd find wood in the garage. He found his way by flashlight but had to fish in his pocket for yet another key. He was getting wet. When he popped open the swollen door and shone the light inside, two severed hands quietly spread their fingers. My but he was jumpy. They were stiff workman's gloves propped on the posts of the sawhorse. It seemed a sensible place to put them. He found the light switch. There was the necessary ax, and the saw, and three elegant stacks of logs, most too large for the stove. He could picture neither Mr nor Mrs Nitta doing the work he now did, fighting for purchase with the axe, then driving each adamant log against a hard stump serving as chopping block. He worked with the peculiar fear that at any moment some demented stranger would appear in the doorway and he and Felicia would find themselves entangled in a thriller. When he had splintered enough wood he gathered it, then returned to the cabin with a heavy crate and backache.

'Cullen, the stove doesn't work!'

One could easily shout from one end of the house to the other.

'What's the matter now?'

'It was going fine and then it just died. I can't relight it.'

He tried two burners without success. He checked the hose.

'It's out of gas.'

She folded her arms and sighed.

'Nice of them to leave us with an empty tank,' he said.

'Don't get all huhu. He said there were spares somewhere.'

She had put on a flannel jacket in his absence. Now she was bouncing on her toes and breathing in tight knots. 'Have you lit the fire yet?'

'Do you want me to light the fire or fix the stove?'

'Both.'

He opened the door beneath the shotgun. In the middle of the shed sat two cobwebbed tanks.

'Where's the broom?'

Finding it himself in the corner of the kitchen, he brushed off the nearer tank and lugged it to the stove. When he tried to uncouple the used tank, it wouldn't budge.

'Do you see a pair of pliers anywhere?'

'No.'

'There has to be a pair somewhere around here.'

'Why?'

'Because I need a pair. You need pliers to uncouple the butane.'

'Maybe they bring them from Hilo.'

'I doubt it.'

After a five-minute search, Cullen found some in the shed. Eventually, with bruised knuckles and low curses, he succeeded in providing them with gas.

'There's no hot water, either,' she said. 'This dinner's gonna be terrible.'

He failed to see the connection.

'I'll get to the water later. Right now, just let me light the fire before I lose all sensation in my toes.'

'Yes! Please do.'

He added the wood he had so proudly splintered, crowned it with one thick log, and lit the kindling on the third try. Through the stove's window he monitored the flames, which spread with alacrity, a miniature inferno. The fire failed, however, to provide heat to the distant kitchen, and the next time he thought to check it it had died, smothered by its own fuel.

'No sex tonight,' she said. 'I'm frigid.'

He gave her a look which meant nothing. Strangely enough, he'd scarcely considered sex all day, his only erection arising on the plane.

'This will be the first night we've ever spent together,' he said.

'Yes. Won't that be different.'

Dinner was hot, shrimps and scallops on steaming rice, but they'd forgotten to buy butter.

'Rice isn't rice without butter,' maintained Felicia.

'We'll get it tomorrow.'

She began a list.

'Add matches,' he said.

After dinner, he cleared the table and opened Earl's map of the island. Felicia produced a sheaf of brochures. When her pen rolled under the table and she retrieved it with her foot, both pen and foot came out covered with cobwebs. The cold forced both of them to don heavy sweaters, she insisting that he relinquish one of his favorites 'forever', a bulky brown turtleneck so large it hid her mouth and hands. Though she fussed about the cold, complaining she'd been misled, she seemed to actually enjoy each missing degree. Perhaps her initial complaints hadn't been as ominous as they'd sounded. She was hard to read today. They made plans to visit Kilauea the next day, saving Mauna Ulu till evening, when its colors would be more spectacular. It was difficult to believe that only a few miles away, the earth itself was erupting. There seemed enough rain to extinguish it.

Folding the map and brochures, they suddenly found themselves alone, in a cabin uncluttered with plants or knickknacks or any souvenirs of their lives. It had never occurred to him that the place would be so empty, echoing their footsteps and even their conversation. It was quiet in the country. A tree fern brushed the window. He had noted before the remarkable ability of an outer island to quickly strip a man of all the concerns he mistakes for his life, and leave him, instead, simply alone. It did the same for couples. For a moment, both seemed at a loss. Then Felicia, poking her head from the sweater, pecked him on the cheek and called him her little *pondus*, refusing, as always, to tell him what it meant. Now he was suddenly afraid she might not be happy, that the cabin might disappoint her, that rain might ruin her days, that she might wake in the morning cursing the cold of the night. He held his cheek to hers, floating tenderly upon his affection, until she withdrew saying 'Tell me a story.'

'It's been an exhausting day,' he replied.

He had never told her a story on demand, had no great repertoire of stories, had no intention of building one, and had no gift for invention, but it was a custom of hers to demand a story nonetheless. She had never been one to linger in a caress. She still bounded from bed, a minute or so after sex, on one pretext or another: to shower, to brush her hair, to model various articles of his clothing, to raid the refrigerator. Still, it had been a voyeur's delight to simply lie there and watch her provocative passage. Not that he could view her kitchen activities from the bedroom, of course, but he had once seen her stooping before the open refrigerator so that only her taut legs and buttocks showed, and the thought of all that arctic whiteness buzzing around her thighs still stirred his imagination whenever he heard her scavenging treats she'd soon cart back to the bed.

Now that there'd be no need for her to hasten home to her parents, he hoped they might lie quietly together for hours, entwined like vines in lazy embraces, but only in indulgent reveries did he believe it would ever be so. Felicia was a rare tropic fritillary; it simply was not in her nature to alight for more than a moment. Every week she had new ambitions, every day new plans, every hour new interests. The interests were impulsive, her golden spark, but the plans and ambitions were always voiced more as dreams than possibilities. Her dark eyes were cast perpetually into the future, where something was going to happen, and it was this very quality, this cloudlike detachment, that made her seem distant to some. At least, that's how Cullen had analyzed it. Nevertheless, when later that night they lay beneath an untidy mountain of warm woolen blankets, she settled into his arms with a kind of tenderness, a little-girlness, and as she slept he felt one tear of bewilderment form, but remain, in his left eye. Felicia, he felt certain, would have called it 'fog drip'.

28

In his dream it advanced as the sound of the headless army marching across lava, cinders crackling underfoot. Warriors held their heads by the neck or swung them by their topknots. All carried ornate spears sharpened to kill. From behind a rock, he studied their tattooed faces as they passed. He had the distinct impression that the countenance of each no longer bore any relation to the body, that each face no longer reflected the body's moods. Some laughed, for example, while their bodies strode sternly onward, bellies undisturbed by a single mirthful quiver. The two were autonomous, body and head. Heads talked to each other, smiled, exchanged eloquent glances, while bodies tramped on with their spears.

But even after the soldiers had gone, the sound of marching continued. It now seemed to be crossing his skull, a vast desert of bleached bone. He drew the covers over his head like a rainstorm. Like the headless army, that too passed by. But still the sound marched on, a persistent shuffling now that seemed to come from within. When he opened his eyes to darkness, he heard a rough scratching behind them. Under the pillow! He sprang from the bed and pushed the pillow to the floor. A living shadow crossed the sheets.

He switched on the bedside lamp to discover what he had feared. A fan of long brown hair lay on Felicia's pillow, and tucked in the shadow beneath it was the centipede, that Chinese dragon with poisonous claws. It was a long one, four or five inches.

He crossed the chilling floor and removed from the bookcase its largest volume. His pants lay folded on a nearby chair. He removed the belt. Feeling vulnerable in bare feet, he sat to put on his hiking boots. Returning to the bed, he stared with some dismay at the spot where the centipede had been. The word *conniptions* twitched in his mind. Felicia would have conniptions. Then she'd see him standing there naked in his boots and leave him.

Careful not to awaken her, he drew back the covers on his side of the bed. Revealing no centipede. He was reminded of an Alfred Hitchcock story in which a hysterical man claimed a black mamba had crawled into his pajamas. He shook out his pillow and put it on a chair. Then he returned to the bedside and steeled himself for the task at hand. He raised Felicia's pillow as far as he dared. Nothing scurried beneath it. He leaned over her sleeping face, over those eyelids cupping small blue shadows, but saw nothing on that side either. If he woke her and they couldn't find it, that would mean trouble. If he didn't wake her and *it* found *her*, that would mean trouble too. Big trouble. Plenty pilikia. Not to mention the fact that it would be hard to return to that bed knowing that centipedes, like humans, are drawn to body heat. Felicia wore Cullen's t-shirt and nothing else. In the Hitchcock story, they had tried drugging the snake with anesthesia.

He examined the head of the bed. The seam on his corner of the mattress, in the shadow of the headboard, looked suspiciously thick. He leaned closer. That was it, that was the centipede. Cullen was freezing. He wanted to get this over with.

He approached gingerly, looped belt in left hand, big book in right. He struck quickly, flicking the creature to the floor with the belt. It charged him without hesitation and he danced decisively backward before attacking it with one swift blow of *The Pictorial History of World War One*. It was a blow heard round the room. When he raised the book, he was surprised to discover his feisty prey still very much alive, curling now with some evil design, so he slammed it down again with more vigor. And then again, for good measure.

'What the hell are you doing?'

'I'm killing a bug . . . I think I got 'em.'

He peeked under the book. There lay the unfortunate arthropod.

'It must be a big bug.'

'It is. It's a centipede.'

She shot bolt upright. 'Oh Jesus! I hate those things.'

'It's dead now.'

'Are you sure?'

He prodded it with his belt.

'Dead as a doornail.'

'What does that mean?'

'No one's certain, but one theory is that doornail refers to—'

'Cullen!'

'What do you mean what does it mean? It's dead. Finished. Pau. No one will ever buy stock in this centipede. All vital bodily functions have ceased. It's dead as a doornail.'

'Let me see it.'

He sighed.

'Well, let me see it. This dead as a doornail centipede.'

'Honey—'

She smirked. 'You weren't killing no centipede. You were jerking off, weren't you?'

'Jesus. Let me get something to pick it up with.' He envisioned a fork.

'You chicken. If it's so dead, pick it up with your hands.'

'It's cold out here.'

She glared.

With his hands, he picked up *The Pictorial History of World War One* and placed it on a chair. The centipede appeared still dead. It was not moving. He poked it with his belt. This time it moved, as anything dead will when poked. With thumb and forefinger he pinched its midsection as delicately as possible, lifted it a centimeter, and dropped it. Nothing happened. He tried three centimeters. Same result. Then he pinched it again and held it up for her perusal. It felt alien to the touch, one of those bizarre life forms that merely share the planet.

'It's enormous!'

'Yup. It put up quite a fight.'

'Where was it?'

'On the floor.'

'On the floor.'

'On the floor.'

'And a centipede crawling on the floor woke you up just in time for you to kill it?'

'Well, yes, that's pretty much how it happened. I heard it in my sleep.'

'Throw it out the window. Those things give me the creeps.'

Crossing the arctic wasteland of the room, his boots clomping on the floorboards, he opened the window above the stairs and pitched the insensible centipede. As he did so, a blast of cold air charged in like yet another beast eager to share his bed.

'You've got your boots on?'

'You didn't expect me to slay him barefoot, did you?'

'Let me get this straight. You're sound asleep and you *hear* a centipede crossing the floor. Then you get out of this nice warm bed, put your boots on, and you get a *big* book out of the bookcase. Then you *drop* the book on the centipede.'

'Okay, it wasn't on the floor. It was under my pillow.'

'Under your pillow! Oh, Jesus. Give me your sweater.'

He did as ordered. She stepped half-naked from the bed, donned his turtleneck, pulled it to her thighs, and crossed her arms.

'Well?' she said.

'Well what?'

'Strip the bed.'

'It's cold.'

'You've got your boots on.'

Thus it was that Cullen spent the first night of their vacation undressing not his lover but his bed, unpeeling layer by layer not lingerie but linens – all in search of partisan chilopods. Heavy blankets fell to the floor. Pillows were shaken from their cases. The fitted sheet was the last to surrender.

'Check the mattress.'

He flipped the mattress to the floor.

'Now check around the bed. Check the springs. Check the molding.'

He dragged the bed from the wall. He checked the molding. He lifted the box spring and shook it. He dropped it back in place. He checked the frame.

'I declare this a vermin-free bed.'

'It better be. Because one more centipede and I'm gone. I . . . *don't . . . like* . . . centipedes.'

'Neither do I. This is part of the adventure of travel.'

'You sleep next to the wall.'

'You don't like this place, do you?'

'I don't like sharing my bed with other species.'

'That's all?'

'Well, it's not exactly a honeymoon suite, is it?'

'You don't like it.'

'I didn't say that. I just wasn't expecting it to be so . . . austere. It doesn't matter though. It'll do.'

It'll do – her very words when he had tried to dissuade her from subjecting her hair to his towel on that portentous day of unmitigated rain so many days ago.

'Maybe it will look better in the morning, with a little sunshine. Give it a chance.'

'Maybe.'

29

He awoke to the stoic smell of wool, a crisp vacant blue filling the windows, and the twitter of birds, perhaps elepaio, flitting among the pines. Felicia had turned her back to him in one of those feline readjustments meant to postpone awakening. The day had begun without them, a brisk country day with neither ambition nor direction. Nothing in its demeanor suggested volcano.

A thick chill had penetrated the cabin. He could feel it in his calves – or rather imagine it – sensing that the floor would be cold, the hall cold, that even filled with steaming water the tub would be cold at his back. He moved closer to catch the scent of her hair. It was there as always, a white bloom in darkness, faint but unmistakable. Her shoulder blade had sliced a pale shadow from the morning light. He knew her to have a barely discernible moth-brown down running the length of her spine. In a certain illumination – that of his bedside lamp, for example – it often burned in a golden line of floating lanterns. He could hear her breath, follow the subtle pitch of her shoulder moored in sleep. He could envision exactly how the light would fall the length of her body were he to remove the covers.

He touched her tentatively, ever so slowly brushing the down on her thigh in a game of modest titillation, the blankets pressing his forearm as if to restrain it. Through the window he could see a small yellow bird alight on a fern frond then depart.

He moved his hand to her belly, remembering that dark Moorish blood flowed through all Portuguese, that in Felicia was a bit of Fatima. Xelb in the Algarve. Six thousand put to the sword at Alvor.

She stretched a leg, touching his, and he pressed closer to cup a breast in his palm and to think irrelevantly of how the Portuguese had introduced the ukulele to Hawaii, of how its strings had always held a taut, salty sound like a ship too long at sea. And on the other side of that sea, sounding in her ear now as he kissed her, a wine-grained guitar, luminous as port, whose pear-shaped body no man can touch without caressing, running his hand repeatedly along its curves, returning always to the valley of its waist where the hand gains illicit momentum.

If allowed, he could have gone on like that indefinitely – half loving, half drifting – but to evoke a response from Felicia one had to be more direct. She had said so herself once, early on, discouraging lengthy foreplay in the same way she mocked maudlin romance. ('Do you know *why* I suddenly lose interest? Because when you've got me wet and ready, you just keep fingering me like a clam till I'm completely dry again!')

He rolled her nipple between thumb and forefinger and considered the possibilities. She had begun to rock gently against him, teasing him with her buttocks. The word *butt*, he recalled, included in its bases the Middle English *but* – target – and the French *abuter* – to aim. He had never, he wished to protest, stooped so low as to finger a clam.

He drew his hand across her belly, grabbed rudely at her cunt as at a caged canary, and pried her toward him. She moaned as if awakening. He massaged her gently till she moaned some more, then found a familiar wet spot he slowly widened till he could slide two fingers in and out with a sucking sound wondrously lewd. *Pudendum* came from *pudendus*, something to be ashamed of.

'Delicious,' he said, as he kissed her *Hot Soft Legs*, *Tasty Red Legs*, juicy *Li Hing Mui*.

She responded in her usual fashion as though it were all quite naughty, protesting 'no, no, noo' in childlike mock distress while pressing his head to her shame. He served her with pleasure, laboring underwater with all the happy industry of a walrus rooting for mollusks.

At some point he rose for breath and they mated. But like all beds they'd romped in, this was too small. Soon she hung over the edge – her hair fanned in disarray on the floorboards, her scalp whitening at the hairline. She liked to be plundered, to be rocked, to have her belly slapped by his with each attack. The bed, too, slapped the wall as he dirked her – now swiftly, now slowly – propping himself with his hands on the floor, more a trained seal than a walrus, always stopping short of losing control and dropping the well-balanced ball. He relished her moans of surrender, treasured the sincerity of guttural urgencies. Now he was a ship, there being no mixed metaphors in the bedroom. Violent seas tossed him, a hot wind filled his mouth, his ears, scorched the length of his neck as she lured him into wilder, more treacherous waters with piratical bites and scratches. With Felicia he felt always at the edge of a turbulent world, thrashing a long time in white water before plummeting. She lashed his legs with hers and let loose a long shuddering cry of wounded delight. He rode out this storm until it subsided, then nuzzled her hair just to smell it. He imagined plumeria, a blush of yellow on a white petal.

'I can't breathe,' she said, not quite complaining.

'My juicy crackseed,' he whispered experimentally, rolling her back on to the bed so that she lay atop him, an awkward maneuver. He slid a hand to her buttocks and toyed with her. She was wet even there.

'Don't be so naughty,' she scolded. She tongued his ear, teasing him, darting in and out like a hummingbird till he, too, shuddered with delight the length of his spine and sent his sweet sour baby seed reeling into darkness.

With one need met, one could always discover another. Had he imagined a hot bath? Then he would have to contend with the water heater. He found it in the bathroom, connected to two tanks of butane. Would they, too, be empty? Lifting them, he thought not. He turned on the valves and followed the explicit instructions dictated by Mr Nitta. But when it came time to light the pilot, he found his matches too short. He fetched the pliers from the kitchen and began again.

'Got it!' he cried exultantly. Felicia seemed unaware of the grandeur of such achievements. She was cutting his grapefruit the wrong way, the way her mother always cut it, around the circumference.

'Whoever heard of cutting a grapefruit like this?' he asked at the breakfast table. 'It defeats the whole purpose. You don't get any leverage. Look. What do I do now? It's ridiculous.'

She crossed her arms and looked at him as if he were a dog with no tricks.

'Okay, wise guy, how do *you* do it?'

'I can't illustrate with this one. You've butchered it. Give me a new one.'

With considerable drama, she placed before him an unravaged grapefruit.

'First you bisect it at the equator, like so. You've got that right. Some things are universal. Then you cut like this, see, radially from the center. It takes a bit longer, but it's well worth it. And notice that I made a little notch, here, so I know where I started?'

'Otherwise you might just keep going forever, dingbat?'

'Hey, don't take it personally. I'm sure it's just a cultural difference.'

She now spoke with crenellated stress. '*You* expect *me* to *in*dividually cut *each* and *ev*ery wedge of *your* grapefruit? Are you serious?'

'No, of course not. There's no law that says we have to have grapefruit every morning.'

'You're lolo! From now on, you cut yours and I'll cut mine. Okay?'

'Okay, okay. Look, I may not agree with your method, but I'll defend to the death your right to employ it.'

'That's it. That settles it. From now on, separate grapefruits.'

'Okay. No big deal. It's not like we're married or anything.'

'And a good thing, too. Now I see why people live together first.'

After breakfast he put the empty but nevertheless heavy butane tank in the car and drove it around the corner to Okamura's, a family-run general store with a Texaco pump in front and a greenhouse in back. Felicia preceded him inside with a list of life's necessities.

When he entered carrying the tank by its head, Mr Okamura looked at him as if he were carrying a child, and for an irrational moment Cullen was afraid he might be scolded in a foreign language.

'Bring that around to the side. Don't got no top for it?'

'What's that?'

'A screw-on thingamajiggy to carry it with. You could damage the valve that way. Here, follow me.'

Cullen followed him to the side of the store and was shown the screw-on thingamajiggy. There was so much to learn when abroad.

'You want one new tank?'

'Yes, please. How much is it?'

'You can use this to carry it to the car, but you'll have to leave it here. I need it for the empty.'

'Okay.'

He had to agree that the thingamajiggy made life easier. When finished, he dutifully returned it to Mr Okamura, paid too much without a murmur, and dug a little deeper when Felicia appeared with a basketful of sundries topped with crackseed.

'What'd you get?' he asked in the car.

'Sweet Salty Earlobes. Want some?'

'No, thanks.'

'Come on. Have a nibble.'

'Not right now.'

'Open up.'

'Hey, I'm driving! That looks obscene.'

'It is obscene. Try it. You'll like it. Thatta boy.'

'Ghhh!'

He rolled down the window to spit out an anchovy pickled in hell.

'What *is* that?'

'Li Hing Mui. Don't you like it?'

'I feel like . . . Holy shit. Look.'

Turning from Okamura's into the road they'd driven in fog, his vision had soared unexpectedly down the road and beyond, climbing effortlessly to the very heart of the island – its proud, cloudless summit. The white gleam of a miniscule observatory beckoned like a beacon.

'The mountain?'

'Mauna Kea. Yesterday we couldn't see ten feet in front of us, and now, that must be thirty miles.'

'I didn't even know it was there.'

'Neither did I.'

Mauna Loa was admittedly impressive, still young and hot-blooded, but from the air it had seemed only a mammoth mound that had swollen its way to splendor. Hence its name: *long mountain*. Despite its volcanism, it rose so gradually from the sea as to appear tame, a sleeping dog becalmed by the Pacific. In contrast, Mauna Kea, *white mountain*, leapt growling at the sky with bared teeth. One could never mistake it for the shorter mountain; it was too ferocious.

The cabin sat warm and inviting, its tree ferns arranged like kahili. A red and black bird flew out of the pines and over the roof.

When Felicia closed the refrigerator on the last of their purchases, their chores seemed completed at last. A fern pressed against the window, innumerable spores dotting its fronds. It reminded him of candy he'd had as a child, dots of sugar on paper.

'Did you see this?'

She'd purchased the *Tribune Herald*.

'Cat Eats Parrot and Talks?'

'No, Bozo. Where do you see that? This one.'

'Mauna Ulu Puzzles Scientists. Scientists at Hawaii's Volcano Observatory confessed today that they have no idea where the lava erupting at Mauna Ulu volcano is actually going. Hmm. They speculate that it's flowing underground in a westerly direction and might break out somewhere along the pali.'

Reading on, he was intrigued by a tidy possibility.

'Remember that day at the Kuhio when we were choosing our favorite photographs? Remember I chose an eruption?'

'Yeah.'

'That might have been a picture of the first rift eruption a few years ago, the one that made this volcano we're seeing tonight. I'll bet it was.'

'Maybe. Maybe this was all predestined.'

'Why not?'

'That's what I'm saying.'

She stepped to the stove and turned on a burner for coffee.

'I didn't sleep well last night,' she yawned.

'No?'

'I never sleep well in a strange place.'

'It's sleeping two in a bed, don't you think? We've never actually *slept* together in the mundane sense of the word. Not for the whole night.'

'I never sleep well in a strange place where grown men stomp around in combat boots dropping encyclopaedias on centipedes.'

'Oh. Well . . . That won't happen again.'

'I hope not.'

'You know how many legs a centipede's really got?'

'How many?'

'Eighty-eight.'

'Ohh.'

'Let's go soon. It's beautiful out.'

'Gotta have my coffee.' She stood there before the stove, arms folded, waiting. 'That sorta gives me a whole new outlook on things,' she yawned. 'Eighty-eight, huh? A person—'

She sniffed the air, her nose twitching cutely like a rabbit's, her eyes shifting with playful suspicion, and then she broke into a wild calypso, swatting some unseen insect on her back and cursing with such frenzied and incoherent vehemence that he gathered this was not just frisky fun or charades but something truly serious. Something quite serious indeed. Nevertheless, he was slow to comprehend just what, and not until she yelled 'I'm on fire!' did he realize that she was. Her hair was sizzling, crinkling into ash. He rushed to her side, struggled out of his sweater, and awkwardly smothered her in it, extinguishing not flames but a smoldering burn that had climbed the slow fuse of her tresses. It was over as quickly as it had begun.

'Are you okay?'

He could now smell what she'd smelled, a pungent black acrimony, one strand of the stench that escapes crematoriums.

Her eyes wide with disbelief, she took her tresses in hand – charred, withered strands that crumbled at a touch – let out a petulant whine, and cried.

'How bad is it in back?'

'It goes from about here to here. And these at the bottom.'

'You could have moved faster! What did you think I was yelling about?'

She stalked off to the bathroom.

How the hell was he supposed to know what she was yelling about?

He turned off the guilty burner. She had carelessly stood leaning against the stove, her long hair had naturally ignited, and a miniature brushfire had ensued. It was an open and shut case. Nevertheless, if he had only realized sooner . . . Now there was nothing for it. Her hair was her pride; there'd be no consoling her. Fantastic sex, a minor conflict over citrus, and now this. Their vacation was deteriorating rapidly.

Furthermore, like Father Plecko's cigar, the smell had resurrected a painful memory. When he'd dropped out of college for lack of funds, he'd worked as a salesman in the Menswear section of a large downtown department store. And one Saturday lunch hour, with fifteen minutes to kill, he thought he would smoke his first cigar in the mezzanine while eyeing young lovelies unfolding from the elevator like flowers from blossoming buds. The mezzanine was the hothouse of teen fashion, and he was a new man, in a new suit, adopting new poses, filling the vacancy over his head with smoky, extravagant reveries. But when it was time to return to work, the cigar, which had not been cheap, was only half smoked, so he stubbed it out in the sand-filled ashtray, popped the remainder in his breast pocket, hopped on to the elevator, and pressed the button for seven. He had chosen his elevator carefully; there were five other passengers, all pretty. When they reached the third floor, where two exited, Cullen smelled smoke. He crossed his arms and tried to nonchalantly smother his embarrassment. One girl looked at him oddly but said nothing. Though a spot was warming over his left nipple, he was determined to wait until the elevator was empty before taking action. He crossed his arms tighter while the obdurate cigar continued to smolder. One girl exited on the fourth floor after casting a curious glance. The buttons for five and six were illuminated.

'I am not burning,' he said to himself, though he was growing disagreeably warm. Some men had the strength of will to be impervious to fire. Some men could walk on burning coals. He stared straight ahead. 'I do not exist.'

The next girl exited at the fifth floor, and mercifully no one entered. It never occurred to him to bolt from the elevator; he was committed to his plan of inaction. Only one witness remained, an older, intelligent-looking girl, heading for Books & Records, who seemed the sort he might marry. But that devilish cigar turned the heat up. Cullen squirmed. It burned through his pocket to his shirt. Cullen silently cursed. The cigar cursed back. Cullen bit his lip. The cigar found an agreeable patch of virgin cotton and flared up gleefully like a branding iron. Cullen flung open his jacket, plucked out his tormentor, threw it to the floor, stomped it into oblivion, removed his jacket and angrily smothered the burning black circle that had appeared in his pocket like a stigma.

'I *thought* you were on fire,' said the girl kindly before exiting. She might have patted him on the head.

Cullen burst into shame, as if the whole world had witnessed his humiliation. He felt the total fool. He'd burned a hole through his jacket pocket and had scorched his new white shirt, all money up in flames, and his vision of himself as a maturing young man had gone up in smoke as well. When he arrived on the seventh floor at last, literally dizzy with disgrace, he almost swooned as he reeled past the one unsuspecting customer awaiting the elevator.

And that was how he felt now, flush with foolishness, red-faced among the ruins. He told himself that it was not his fault – it was Felicia who'd been foolish – but he couldn't escape the feeling that he could have responded more sensibly to rescue his damsel in distress. Now the whole trip was endangered.

He sat at the table and waited. It was quiet and bright in the kitchen. He studied it – the wooden cupboards, the refrigerator, the stove, the battered coffeepot – all plain, old, utilitarian. Two flies had died in a spider's web in the corner of the ceiling.

After a few minutes of such prosaic contemplation, he found the courage to join her in the bathroom. She sent him a sullen look through the mirror. She'd obviously been crying. She brushed out the last blackened strands and held singed remains.

'Great,' she scowled. 'Just great.'

The damage in front had been confined to the left side, where she had lost a few inches, the only scar an embarrassing asymmetry. But in the back an irregular swath had climbed much higher.

'It could have been worse,' he said. 'It's a miracle you weren't burned.'

She trimmed singed ends and cast despairing looks into the mirror.

'I'll never get this smell out. Here.'

'What?'

'Cut it even in the back.'

'Are you sure?'

'I can't go around looking like I've been run over by a lawnmower, can I?'

'It's not *that* bad. Why don't you just let it grow out again? You can wear your hair in a ponytail and no one will know the difference.'

'Ponytails are for horses. Just trim it up even and then I'll get a hairdresser to do something with it.'

'You won't find a hairdresser up here.'

'That's why you've got to cut it first. Don't make such a big deal out of it.'

'You're sure?'

'I'm sure.'

Thus it was that Cullen became an accomplice. A single cut severed a strand he could wrap around his fist. He felt he was cutting the thread of life, severing in a moment a miracle. Soon curls lay everywhere.

When he reached the front, she screamed. 'That much?!'

'That's what you wanted.'

'Not *that* short! Are you crazy? Give me the scissors. Now it will take years to grow it back the way it was!'

Surely this was an exaggeration.

'Why did you have to take your stupid sweater off? You could have just swatted it out with your hands.' She was about to cry again.

He slipped from the room without answering. This was unfair.

She spent the next hour ministering to her hair while he restlessly cleaned out the wood stove and half-heartedly surveyed the Nittas' eclectic library. When she emerged, her hair was once again symmetrical, clipped short on both sides and cleverly swept back. He suddenly felt like crying himself.

'It looks good,' he said encouragingly. 'It could be a new style.'

She smiled with that half of her face not paralyzed by indignation.

'I'll still need a trim.'

It was two o'clock when he finally coaxed her out of the cabin and into the sun with a picnic, one he had prepared personally to spare her a return to the scene of her combustion. They spread their blanket on a hill of cinders overlooking Kilauea. In the west, in one long line from summit to shore, the gentle slope of Mauna Loa served as dark horizon. Below it lay a broad, featureless tumble of old lava. A silvered flow, the newest, could be traced back to the southern wall of the crater from which it had spilled. Now a parking lot sat at the edge and tourists from around the globe spilled into the crater to view Halemaumau, the volcano within the volcano, the home of Pele. One of three tour buses was just reloading, gathering its children underwing like a mother hen. The human detail was too puny, however, and too transitory, to encroach upon the larger majesty of the elemental landscape.

'It's just a long black pit,' she declared.

'A pit three miles long. A pit that did all this.'

He swept his arm over the surreal tableau behind them, the remains of what had once been a forest. Many ohia, bleached white, still stood, their branches empty gestures addressed to a cloudless sky. Others lay, whole or broken, on a field of black pumice. Always eager to make a sculptural statement, ohia was driftwood that had never seen the sea. Here broken limbs were well displayed, white on black, with an occasional branch piercing azure.

He poured the wine, broke the bread, sliced the cheese, and ate reclining on one elbow, luxuriating in the scene before him, inhaling the wafer-crisp air and marveling at the ingenuous blue sky. As a child, he had been deprived of nature, thinking it something that flocked behind a garbage scow. The greatest prospect his parents had shown him had been from atop the Empire State Building. He had treasured their visits to the Bronx Zoo or Ebbetts Field, but he had never spotted a wild animal or spent a night in the woods with his father. In fact, until he was a teenager, he'd never seen a waterfall or stood on the edge of a canyon. And never had he seen a volcano. He imagined that Felicia had been similarly deprived and that a hike to Mauna Ulu that evening might enlarge her, but first he'd have to nurse her through her loss.

She ate with her knees drawn up, surveying the scene before her as if considering improvements.

'Where's Mauna Ulu?'

'Over there somewhere. We'll find it tonight.'

'What's that building straight across from us?'

'Volcano House.'

'And that one?'

'Volcano Observatory.'

'What do they do there?'

'Observe the volcano.'

'What's that yellow spot down there?'

'Where?'

'Right there, inside the volcano.'

'I don't know.'

'You *don't know*?'

'Don't know.'

'Hmm.'

He realized then that almost everything she surveyed had been consumed by fire and would be, for her, a reminder of charred hair. The air that was wine in his teeth would carry for her a certain burning smell. Still, she was trying to be brave about it, even when, drawing her fingers through her curls, she'd all too soon find them combing emptiness.

'Shall we investigate it?' he asked.

'What?'

'That yellow patch.'

She thought about it. Life and time would pass regardless.

They dutifully followed the path of all tourists to the rim of Halemaumau, a jagged smoking crater whose walls bled ferric red. This was the home of Pele, the crater in which the manager was to have sacrificed his gin. It was one of those great gaping wounds in the earth that the viewer easily encompasses on first glance but lingers over deferentially in an attempt to imagine more. Cullen imagined falling in. Then this new-looking woman was tugging his sleeve and dragging him on, across the chaotic floor of Kilauea itself. Were her spirits lifting? Cinders popped underfoot, boulders that had once flown through air lay where they'd fallen, and from scattered mofettes all around them rose steam that stank of Hades. Soon they were walking in a confusion of pahoehoe, every step taken on rippled stone that had once flowed as fire. She climbed a wall of whorled lava from which sprouted a single red ama'u fern. One could see that the wall had been liquid once – and horizontal – but nature had rearranged it. Here and there grew kupukupu and scraps of ohia, tenacious life staking its claim to a wasteland.

Minutes later, surmounting a hill of cinders, they came upon that curiously yellow patch that had attracted them from a distance, a single slash of vivid color among acres of gray and black. It had been easily seen from above, but was almost invisible from the floor of the crater itself. Now they realized they had discovered something the others had overlooked. Below them lay another transient landscape of torn and precipitous lava, but over this particular nether region some jocular devil had cracked a god-sized egg, pouring yellow and white over the whole frozen yet fitful heap. 'A *rotten* egg,' said Felicia, when Cullen gave voice to this metaphor. A malodorous cloud, wafted by dubious winds, hissed intermittently from a short slit with bright ochrous lips, the source of the sulfurous ash that had transformed the surrounding jumble into a forbidding wonderland.

'Look at that one,' he said. 'It looks like a petrified tsunami.'

Before them crested a high yellow wave, stilled, as in a Hokusai woodblock, until the next eruption. The whole scene suggested a tempestuous sea, which, after all, was what it once had been. A black shard sprayed with white pierced the surf like a prow. A large cinder cone, white at its summit, was Mauna Loa as the first Hawaiians had seen it, dry land in a restive sea. Cullen recognized a rare photo opportunity.

'You're not going down there?'

'I'm just gonna take a few pictures,' he replied, spurred by the thought that she considered it adventurous of him to do so.

'Well you can do what you like. I'm going to Maui.'

The winds shifted quickly, marked by the noxious cloud. The main thing was to dodge the fumes and bracket, shooting swiftly, recording the sight from all angles. He began with an overview. The shattered landscape that appeared in his viewfinder looked worthy of *Nikon Annual*, the surreal desolation of an unknown planet. As in Felicia's favorite picture of Nuba warriors, it was the contrast of ash and black that made for high drama. He needed no filter to intensify it. In that scene the wave offered itself as a focal point. Now he approached it. He began horizontally but saw that he needed to shoot it vertically, to fill the frame so that it broke over the viewer. He drew continually closer, and having exhausted the possibilities of composition, changed the angle to include the white-capped dome. These were surely his best shots ever. He then thought to capture the slit itself, the source of all this wonder. He approached cautiously and shot quickly.

'Get out of there!' she yelled, but too late. The wind had shifted. He caught an acrid breath raw as quicklime and reeled back, gasping for air, his lungs on fire. He scrambled away awkwardly, scraping his camera, losing a lens cap, wondering if there would be a greater price to pay. Never had he drawn such a painful breath; it had shot down his throat like a flame. He imagined the alien sulfur within, scorching his all too collapsible lungs. He wheezed. Once again, it seemed, success had turned to failure.

Felicia stood on higher ground. He climbed past huge silver bubbles the size of bicycle wheels, apparently formed by hot gases. As he clambered toward her, still breathing experimentally, the fragile crust beneath his feet kept collapsing like sheets of ice. Cavernous vents appeared on both sides of him, the color of iron ore at their mouths – gaping holes one could slide into and disappear forever. Why the hell had she gone this way? He now understood why none of the other tourists had ventured off the trail. They'd had common sense. He remembered Earl's story about the manager of Volcano House, though these were pukas one would never survive. The inferno itself lay beneath them. This was, after all, a volcano.

'I caught a whiff of that stuff,' he said bravely.

'I told you to get out of there.'

'You know what the mantles in a Coleman lantern look like, when you light them and they turn to ash? That's what my lungs feel like. One false move and they'll collapse. They sort of tickle.'

'I tried to tell you.'

'I need a drink.'

'Look at this.'

She handed him a long strand of volcanic glass.

'Pele's hair,' she said.

'Wow. This is a beauty. Where'd you find it?'

'Right here.'

'Well done.'

'The irony of this does not escape me,' she said wistfully.

He ran his fingers through her abbreviated glory.

'Let me take your picture holding your treasure.'

'Not looking like this.'

'You look fine.'

'No.'

'Well, this is a real find. We've got to display this when we get back.'

'It's mine!' she cried.

He handed it over and she threw it into a nearby vent.

'What did you do that for?!'

'It's bad luck to take lava from Pele. Don't you know that? No souvenirs. It's her property.'

'You're incredible.'

'Yup!'

'I thought you didn't believe in Pele.'

'I never said that. Why take chances?'

Unlike many of her superstitions, he'd heard of this one. Each year the *National Enquirer* – that purveyor of *ex post facto* predictions, extraterrestrial abductions, sightings of Hitler, bizarre tribal rites, freakish births, and Virgin Mary eggplants that weep real tears – publishes as a public service an article detailing the vindictiveness of Pele. It's unwise for a mainland haole tourist to pocket so much as a Pele's tear or a petrified strand of her hair. Perpetrators of such crimes invite a dark shadow into their lives. Accidents happen, relatives die, jobs are lost, well-watered plants wither, pampered pets lose their hair and gentle demeanor, and in general events take a turn for the worse, all because of that igneous rock on the mantle. And each year, in the wake of the article, Park Headquarters is deluged with enough packages of pilfered lava to build a new crater, many accompanied by desperately scrawled notes to Pele, Hawaiian Fire Goddess: 'Please take off the curse!'

At the moment, he felt like making such a plea himself. His curse was wedged in his lungs like a jagged chunk of a'a. Breathing deeply hurt, and if it still hurt by evening it would spoil everything.

Therefore, they returned to the cabin, poured tall drinks, carried chairs on to the lawn, and waited calmly for the dark. The sun sank below the trees long before sunset. Then small birds appeared, testing their wings and their songs. He soon found that his breathing had returned to normal – as usual, he had dramatized the damage – and it seemed to him that Felicia had come to some similar understanding regarding her hair. Still, to be on the safe side, he followed the afternoon's model, preparing dinner himself to protect her from the stove, and nudging her gently into action by example – conspicuously donning warm hiking attire, thinking aloud of good reasons for wearing thermal socks with his boots, and in general, as she put it, acting like a mountie taking a bimbo on a hike.

30

Half the night sky was obscured by cloud, but all the stars had crowded into the other.

'That's something you won't see in Honolulu,' he said.

'I didn't know there *were* this many stars.'

No sooner had she spoken than one streaked to oblivion, a white flare swiftly extinguished by darkness.

'Did you see that?' he asked.

'Another soul released from Purgatory,' said Felicia.

'Who says that?'

'My mother.'

He smiled an unseen smile.

At first they'd followed a narrow depression thick with broomsedge and ohia, but now the flashlight illuminated a path of black cinders on black rubble, with only kupukupu stubbornly filling the cracks. Large shards of the earth lay left and right like broken crockery – fractured, buckled, pitched at haphazard angles. This was a new, raw landscape, a rearrangement of the earth itself. The trail rose, dipped, detoured abruptly.

'This trail keeps you on your toes,' said Cullen.

'By stubbing them,' smirked Felicia.

It was not until they had climbed much higher that the glow of the volcano first appeared on their distant right, a soft wavering light that had painted the clouds rose amber. The silhouetted rim was a smooth, swollen horizon.

A chill wind swept over broken lava, there being nothing here to impede it. Felicia zipped her jacket and raised her collar.

For the past ten minutes two bobbing white lights had been approaching from the east – vanishing, then reappearing, suggesting a vigorous descent over rough terrain – and now a father and son appeared before them, flashlights in hand.

'How far is it?' enquired Cullen.

'About a mile. Keep on the trail. There's plenty pukas.'

Plenty pukas. That was life all right; it was riddled with them. And Cullen had known a man on Oahu, the fiancé of a friend, who had presumably fallen into one while hiking in the Koolaus less than a mile from his home. He was never seen again. But Cullen was too enthused to dwell on life's bottomless pits when the very air was a guiding hand on his shoulder. This would close a perfect circle begun that day in the Kuhio. There were paths that led to the predictable, and paths that led to the prodigious, and they had wisely chosen the latter.

When the cinder path petered out and the ground became nothing more than a petrified flow, small cairns marked the new trail. But still the trail ran more or less parallel to the volcano, not yet turning south to ascend to the summit. Soon a hill called Huluhulu rose before them. An old crater itself, it too had once painted the clouds with fire. Now it was a dark, rounded shadow rising before the stars. Then, surmounting a ridge, they saw the restive glow of what seemed a blaze at its base. This was unexpected, far from the summit of Mauna Ulu.

'Do you think . . . ?' asked Felicia.

'Think what?'

'Think it's an eruption?'

'I don't know.'

In its circuitous manner, dipping and climbing as it went, the trail was heading toward it. Could it be an entirely new eruption they were seeing, an outbreak of lava in a rift? If so, should they be eagerly approaching it? The landscape seemed to buckle with heat. Advancing nearer, they saw the same stark skeletons they'd seen that afternoon, a denuded forest of ohia, bare branches rising skyward.

'It's a forest fire!'

That was it: charred trees dwarfed by a flickering curtain of flame. But as they drew closer they saw the sight for what it really was, something far more wondrous than a fire. What they saw was not a conflagration, but an entire hillside of naked ohia silhouetted by clouds of volcanic red light. The fire, or more likely the shower of pumice, had probably been months ago, perhaps when the rift last erupted. The blaze now before them was ruddled clouds burning through dead trees.

'Pele's halo,' said Cullen.

'It doesn't pay to be a tree around here, does it?'

At last the trail turned toward Mauna Ulu, with the sky before them roiling red. What had looked like a smooth dome from a distance now seemed a ragged heap. For days he had been silently repeating the name of this volcano, rolling it about like a well-rounded stone. It was part of the anticipatory joy of travel, this incantation of place names. Now it stood before them, the cloud-borne light above it merely a dim reflection of the violence within.

The flashlights of a descending party showed the trail to be an erratic zigzag.

'I can't believe how cold it is,' said Felicia.

'It is amazing, isn't it? This wind doesn't help any.'

'Is that the roar of the wind or the roar of the volcano?'

'I think it's the volcano.'

'Are we really going to the top of this thing?'

'You're damn right we're going to the top.'

They met the descending party, a family of three, halfway up.

'It's fantastic!' shouted the father, a girl on his shoulders, and the mother smiled her assent.

If a family could do it, they could do it.

Now, without doubt, the roar they heard was not wind but a tumultuous rumbling of the earth itself, a rumbling that intensified as they climbed toward a cloud the color of a halved blood orange. They carried on, drawn by the roar and the buckling red sky. Soon they could see a small cluster of like-minded tourists huddled insignificantly at trail's end, where a viewing platform had been carved from lava. They ascended the last twenty yards, and when they reached the top walked straight to the low lava wall at the edge and peered over. And what they saw surpassed all they had ever seen, swept away all past spectacles, all displays of power and majesty, as if they'd been nothing more than garish picture postcards.

'My God,' said Felicia.

Less than a hundred feet below seethed the promised lake of molten lava, not boiling from the center like a cauldron, but churning instead from east to west, not really a lake at all but a vast underground river momentarily exposed. From one end of the crater to the other, jagged bolts of surging yellow melt cut through slag the color of dried blood, edging it in crimson. The stress lines fanned out from a single agitated source in a cavern of the eastern wall. Its roar was constant thunder, and with thunder so near, the image of lightning was unavoidable. The pattern changed with each passing minute, yet was always that of a garnet night shattered by yellow lightning.

All rose and fell in perpetual upheaval. Origin and destination unknown, the lava crashed repeatedly against a jut of the southern wall, spewing incandescent fountains of spray and clots of fire that either fell back to the lake or struck the wall and froze, cooling quickly from orange to black, from molten lava to solid rock. It was easy to see why the ancients might assume that their gods changed shape, when stone could turn to river and river to stone. Raw lava – the island was made of it, from seafloor to summit, under forest and farm, the foundation for all the works of nature and of man.

'Mauna Ulu,' shouted the attendant ranger, beginning a lecture, 'is a shield volcano. That is to say its top is a broad, gradually swelling, gently sloping dome. It measures approximately three-eighths of a mile from east to west and is more than three hundred feet high and still growing, hence its name, which is Hawaiian for "growing mountain".

'Its formation began three years ago, on May 24th, when lava erupted along a fissure between Alae Crater, to our left, and Aloi Crater, to our right. You needn't strain to see these craters because neither exists anymore. Both have been filled by lava from the various eruptions of Mauna Ulu, which has recently resumed activity after a brief dormancy.

'Early eruptions were characterized by dramatic lava fountaining, the highest reaching 1,800 feet. Overflows have buried much of Chain of Craters Road and have sometimes reached as far as the sea. At present, we don't know exactly where the lava from this eruption is flowing, but it is possible that it will someday break out further down the mountain. If it does, we may see a lava flow this year that again reaches to the sea. Last year Mauna Ulu added ninety-seven acres of new land to the island.

'Originally, Mauna Ulu was a smaller, rounded crater. It's shape today is the result of last year's collapse of several secondary pits on the side of the shield.'

'Is there any chance it could collapse again today?' asked a grinning visitor.

The ranger smiled knowingly. 'I wouldn't be standing here today if I thought there was. But,' he added mischievously, 'one never really knows.

'Last year we experienced a subsidence and cooling of this lava lake, which was quickly followed by summit eruptions in Kilauea itself. If you've visited Kilauea, or if you plan to visit, much of the pahoehoe that you'll see on the caldera floor was a result of those eruptions. Pahoehoe is the smooth or ropy lava as opposed to the rougher, more cindery a'a.

'This February, Mauna Ulu resumed activity, until the lava overflowed the shield at the east end, on your left, filling what was left of Alae Crater. A new fissure later opened above Alae, creating a lava lake that has fed many flows. Can I answer any questions?'

'How hot is it down there?' asked one man.

'We estimate the temperature to be about 1,150° Centigrade. That's about 2,100° Fahrenheit.'

This drew numerous exclamations.

'What does it look like when it's dormant?' asked Cullen.

'It looks like a bathtub with the plug pulled out, just a big gaping hole. When it subsides, the lava just drains away, lowering the floor one or two hundred feet.'

When all questions had ceased, Felicia turned again to the volcano. 'My mother would die,' she said, her face suffused with restless gold. Then, quietly, she added, 'It's wonderful.'

Cullen, who had thought never to hear such reverence in her voice, felt miraculously vindicated.

'Indeed,' he replied, struck by her loveliness in molten light. Something like a warm flood of emotion was slowly engulfing him. It was a rising awareness of what he had done – captured a woman whose beauty burned holes in darkness. Even with clipped hair, she was a floating candle, a vision, a wavering delight. She was certainly more than he deserved. He felt like professing his love, but restrained himself, wondering how he could hope to hold her when the earth itself was inconstant. He unsheathed his Pentax to capture her on film, despite her objections, then recorded the tumult below for all time.

The oddest sensation as they stood there was that of being sandwiched between extremes. As they peered into the turbulent cauldron, a searing heat drew their faces into taut paper masks that might momentarily ignite. At the same time, however, a raw polar wind whipped their backs. To avoid combustion, it was necessary at times to retreat, to turn away and cast their eyes toward the desolation of Huluhulu. But the night air blowing across this broken landscape chilled as quickly as the volcano warmed, and it soon became a comfort to return to the edge, to that vision of the inferno, and to be consumed once again by the waves of heat scorching their faces. There was simply no middle ground.

He gave her a kiss on the cheek and found it warm.

The yellow flame tapered to a point, fattened, wavered, then flared without warning. 'Ouch!' He dropped the match, kissed finger and thumb, and watched disappointedly as the flame died within an inch of kindling. He lit another. This one fell among wadded paper. A brown stain spread slowly at first, then the fire took, and soon it hissed and crackled reassuringly. He sat beside it and carefully lit his pipe. Felicia was in the bathroom.

'Ghosts, as a rule, do not move around much,' he read for the fourth time. 'They may be seen in one part of the house or another, not necessarily in the room in which they died as people, but there are no cases on record in which ghosts have traveled any kind of distance to manifest.'

These comforting words had been written by Professor Hans Holzer, an expert. Educated at Columbia, Vienna, and the London College of Applied Science, he'd taught Parapsychology for eight years at the New York Institute of Technology and had written no fewer than eighty-one books on the subject of psychic phenomena. This particular one, found between Durrell's *Justine* and Roget's *Thesaurus*, was called *Best True Ghost Stories*. It was the unlikely coupling of *true* and *ghost* that had caught his eye and drawn his thoughts, once again, to Uncle Ricardo.

And tucked inside it, marking this very page, had been an article torn from a magazine. 'In Search of Ghosts' was its title, and it was illustrated by a photograph of a luminous nightgown, perhaps with head and arms, floating above a dark staircase. Plutarch, Pliny, Socrates and Cicero were all believers, according to the author, and Dr Johnson viewed the question of ghosts as 'one of the most important that can come before the human understanding'.

Appeal to Authority, countered Cullen silently.

The article's author rated the likelihood of actually sighting a ghost at 10 percent. It was thought that poorly understood atmospheric conditions had to be 'just so'.

> One of the most consistent findings about ghostly activity is that it takes place at a lowered temperature, sometimes as much as eight or nine degrees centigrade below that of the immediate vicinity. A cold spot has been noticed in practically every haunted house, and it may be, in some way we don't yet understand, that ghosts themselves withdraw energy from the surrounding atmosphere.
>
> I have always felt that ghostly activity is linked to concentrated, perhaps obsessive, thought – another form of energy. This would explain why churches and places of learning are often sites of hauntings.

And then there was this:

> Ghosts seldom speak. They seem to exist in another dimension, unaware of observers, walking through walls that didn't exist in their lifetime. Indeed, they often follow the course of their original perambulations, often above or below the current ground or floor level.

Cullen compared this with 'Ghosts, as a rule, do not move around much.' Both assertions added something new to his arsenal of wishful thoughts regarding Uncle Ricardo, something that might free him from the necessity of ever confronting anything as dreadful as a disembodied spirit. Wasn't it true that ghosts haunt abodes rather than people? Weren't they fated, like Sisyphus, to a treadmill reenactment of some futile act, some eternal incompletion?

He recalled Earl's story about the haunted hotel room. The closet door opening each night at midnight, the coat hangers rattling, the chainlock coming undone – all testified to Lenora Waddy's reenactment of her murder. Why hadn't she chosen to haunt Oahu State Prison, where she could torment her husband instead of innocent hotel guests?

And Claire's and Ernest's ghosts had come with the house. All ghosts did; they were never noted for their travels. But most of all he recalled what Claire had said that night he had fallen in love with her. She had talked about penetrating a time barrier. He remembered her very words: 'It was like seeing into the past.' Therefore, he now reasoned hopefully, ghosts may be nothing more than the breaking down of time, a temporal malfunction, the stuck record of a human soul – or, more fanciful yet, memories harbored by a house or hotel room. This was preferable to imagining nightly murders on some invisible plane, or spirits lost forever in a Möbius maze. The gist of his thinking, the hopeful conclusion, was that Uncle Ricardo might be incapable of following Felicia from her home, that once she had left he'd remain forever a frustrated lecher passing through the walls of a modest three-bedroomed house near the freeway, a house in which he had inconveniently expired.

He failed to acknowledge that such a hope was tantamount to belief. But whether ghosts existed or not was a secondary matter; more important was that he not encounter any.

That Felicia's ghost *had* spoken, had even – by her account – lifted her on to a stool, failed to disturb him. The article had said that manifestations before a loved one were common soon after death, so in that regard her account proved faithful to form.

He studied again the article's photograph. The nightgown did seem to clothe a figure, if one allowed it. He could even imagine a hand gripping the balustrade, a tenuous connection between that world and this. Perhaps spirits were like literature, or religion, or nature: they held no power but for believers. To the unattuned, they were meaningless, even nonexistent things. He had stood on the very brink of an active volcano and had peered inside. He had witnessed power and glory. For him it had been like glimpsing a god, the source of these islands and more. For another it might be nothing more than a checkmark on an itinerary. 'Well, Gladys, this here is one of yer genuine Hawaiian volcanoes. Now let's go get us some eats.'

Where was this argument leading?

Felicia called from the bathroom.

'Just a minute,' he said.

He returned the article to the book and the book to the shelf. Only then did he ask himself who had put it there. The Nittas? Why had they bothered to keep such an article, and why keep it here instead of at home? Could the book have ever belonged to Earl? This possibility intrigued him; the library's eclecticism argued for more than one contributor.

She summoned him again and this time he obediently appeared at the bathroom door.

'Where's the deodorant?' she enquired earnestly.

'Are we using the same deodorant?'

'For now we are.'

'But then we'll smell alike.'

'So? If we get married like you want, in ten years' time we'll *look* alike. Where is it?'

This reference to marriage, as if it were a possibility, as if his introduction of the subject had not been entirely in bad taste, surprised him. He smiled, warmed by the sultry bathroom and the ludicrous picture of he and she bearing any resemblance whatsoever. What ghost, what mystery, could possibly survive the mundane?

31

By morning the weather had changed to a gauze of gray rain swathing the cabin like a dirty bandage. 'Lucky we went yesterday,' he said to no one, for Felicia, who lay buried under covers, had not yet acknowledged his presence. Cullen rose first, but not until ten. Stooping to examine himself in the bathroom mirror, he saw that the night had done little to alter his appearance.

In the kitchen, he cut his own grapefruit half and respected Felicia's. When she arrived, she sat sullenly, holding both hands around her coffee mug to draw its warmth.

'What's wrong?'

'Nothing.'

'Do you always start the day with coffee?'

'Yes. I always start the day with coffee.'

'See? I didn't even know that about you. They say it's bad for you first thing in the morning, but . . . what do guinea pigs know? It's *your* body, right?'

'Right.'

'I was just curious.'

'Yesss.'

'What's wrong?'

'I'm just not sleeping well.'

'Let's go to a movie today.'

She raised a skeptical eyebrow.

'There's one at Park Headquarters. I saw it in one of the brochures.'

'I want to get my hair done today.'

'Where?'

'Hilo.'

'That's thirty miles.'

'So?'

'You'll need an appointment.'

'This is an emergency. Will you call for me while I do the dishes?'

'Me?'

'Please?'

'Call who?'

'Look in the phonebook.'

'What do I ask for?'

'A compassionate trim.'

And damn if he didn't do as asked, braving the rain to call from a sheltered puddle outside Okamura's. He was fully prepared to call all three beauticians in Hilo alphabetically, but as it happened, he succeeded with his first attempt. The woman he talked to seemed delighted to learn that someone had been foolish enough to burn her own hair.

'It's all set for three o'clock. The Beauty Box.'

'The Beauty Box? Sounds like take-out wigs.'

'They specialize in fire damage.'

Like a cigarette tossed from a passing car, the sudden flare in her eyes surprised him. 'I'm afraid I don't find that very amusing.'

'Oh, come on now.'

She left in a huff and closed a door behind her.

Christ, the second salon in the Yellow Pages had been called Curl Up and Dye. He supposed he'd be keeping that tidbit to himself. He soon heard water running in the bath. He swept up the flies – and one long hair – and dumped them in the garbage. If she found the hair, she'd cry again. Then he stood before the bathroom door and meekly knocked.

'Who is it?'

The room was steaming.

'I can hardly see in here. Look, I'm sorry. Really I am. What can I say? You made a joke, I made a joke.'

Lathering her arms, she burned him with those eyes.

He sat on the toilet, admiring her.

'But wasn't that something last night?' he asked. 'Huh? You've got to admit that was something.'

'Yeah. It was something.'

'I'd like to go back.'

'Not in this weather.'

'No . . . Some other weather.'

'Perhaps.'

He'd never actually seen her languorously sprawled in a bathtub. At his place she'd always showered – with hurried thoroughness, as if destroying evidence.

It proved a chilly afternoon, consumed by drizzle and the dispiriting drive to Hilo, where he sat reading women's magazines while a professional cropped her hair even shorter. He disapproved, but said nothing. Afterwards, she insisted on buying a flannel nightgown, she who, by her own accounts, had always slept naked or negligéed.

'She did a good job,' he said, referring to her beautician, whose own hair had suffered a breakdown. 'It's cute.'

'Yuck. Anyone can look cute. I liked it better the way it was.'

'Well . . .'

They drove through Hilo looking for the equivalent of Zippy's Saimin Lanai. Old men in straw hats stood before an empty fish market, while across the street young men in shorts and zoris shot pool in an open arcade. Dry goods, hardware, grocer, jeweler – all shops seemed deserted. America had not yet placed its stamp on the town; they saw no McDonald's, no Pizza Hut, no K-Mart or Sears. Instead they saw K. Fujimoto's and F. Takahashi's. Cullen felt more a time traveler than a tourist. The town seemed suspended in amber. They ate seafood in a weathered diner, where locals talked story over pupus and beer, then walked along the waterfront until it rained.

Felicia wanted to see a movie at the Palace because she had never sat in a balcony, so they saw the early showing of a samurai epic. While they sat in the first row eating popcorn, a flashlight-wielding usherette scolded them for propping their feet on the railing. For Cullen, nothing like that had happened in twenty years. She was lucky Cullen was not as hot-headed as the warriors in the film; they just could not resolve their differences peacefully.

When the blood began to spurt from severed limbs, Felicia asked to leave.

The night streets glistened from a recent downpour, and a few men eyed them from the doorway of a bar. He'd experienced that before, lusty men eyeing them like predators. It never failed to make him uneasy. The car smelled fertile and damp, as when they'd first met. Compared to Honolulu, Hilo seemed an outpost precariously pitched between volcano and sea. He supposed the town had never quite forgotten the tsunami of twenty years before. When they left Hilo behind, they were in wilderness, the return drive unrelieved by a single streetlight. This made the passing flora seem to swim out of gloom, odd shapes materializing eerily like those in a diver's lamp, each with its own sensibility. The road seemed endless, the night opaque. Tree ferns reared in the high beams. And at the end of their journey sat the cabin, dark and empty, with only a bed for comfort.

32

The next morning he woke again to rain. Felicia's first broadcast to the world at large was – 'I'm not feeling well.' She couldn't quite pinpoint the problem, however, which throughout breakfast remained as ill-defined as the eggs she'd put on his plate. The view from the kitchen proved ill-defined as well; like melting wax, rain slid erratically down each pane. Perhaps she only needed a second cup of coffee.

He recalled the winter rain when they'd met in the college arcade – not drizzle or sprinkle or mizzle or mist, but an impassioned, festive deluge that had danced through the streets like a dragon, rolling its head and shaking silvered scales. But that had been city rain, a drunken dragon with many shoes on. This country rain was sober; it fell necessarily, without joy.

When it let up, he walked to Okamura's to buy her aspirin tablets, and, perhaps spurred by the etymological link, bought her an amusing tabloid as well, avoiding that claiming a poodle had combusted spontaneously in the final round of a dog show, lest she again plunge into irrepressible mourning for her hair. A 65-pound tumor had been removed from an English woman feeling poorly, a tribe of bespectacled Buddy Holly impersonators had been found in the Peruvian jungle, and in Norway a baby had been born with a wooden leg, proof at last of reincarnation. Many of the famous people mentioned in the tabloid were newly famous people he'd never heard of. He recognized Elvis, who'd grown momona, but the two lovers picking fuzzballs off the backs of each other's sweaters were new to him, as was the unfaithful wife in a bikini.

The twisted fates that filled the tabloid gave him the courage to step outside and make his fateful call.

'Hello.'

'Hello. May I—'

'Hello.'

'Yes, hello. Can you hear me?'

'Yes.'

'Is this Holy Mount College?'

'Yes.'

'May I speak to Sister Lucia, please.'

'I'm afraid Sister Lucia's not here. Perhaps I can help you?'

'Is this Father Plecko?'

'Yes.'

Then how can you possibly help me?

'Father Plecko, this is Cullen Kinnell. I'm calling from the Big Island.'

'Oh, Cullen. Yes. What are you doing over there?'

Perhaps his addled brain had failed to record their unfortunate encounter at the airport?

'I came to see Mauna Ulu erupting. It's quite a spectacle. I just—'

'What's Mauna Ulu?'

'It's a volcano on the slopes of Mauna Loa. Listen, I just wanted to talk to Sister Lucia about next term.'

'Next term. Well, I'm afraid Sister Lucia won't be here next term.'

'Oh?'

'No. She's . . . she's going to be working more closely with the Police Department.'

'Oh? Really? What will she be doing?'

'Well, I don't know actually. Something more secular I think.'

'More secular?'

'Yes. Well, you know how she's always had an interest in supporting the police force.'

'Yes.'

'Yes. Um, I don't know how to say this really. You see, Sister's decided that chee can, *she* can cherve, *serve* the Search, *serve the Church*, better – well, service God better, actually – and humanity – by going out into the world and . . .'

Such incrassation, thought Cullen, was rare in a human being.

It was usually limited to sauces thickened by cornstarch. Normally he would have taken great delight in listening to Father Plecko fish for his words with a tattered net, but this was serious – Sister Lucia, Plecko had said, was leaving – would not be there next term – and Sister Lucia was the buffer between Cullen and Father Plecko. She was the rubber on his bumper car. She was the demilitarized zone. She was the only thing that kept Father Plecko from advancing like a wall of spluttering a'a. Fortunately, after another minute of not knowing how to say it really, Father Plecko stumbled upon one possibility. 'Well, to make a long story short, it appears that she's decided to leave the Church.'

'No!'

'Yes, I'm afraid so. It comes as quite a shock.'

'I'll say. And does that mean she'll be leaving the English Department as well?'

'Oh, most certainly. Yes, she's already left.'

'*My God.*'

'Yes, I'll be chairing the department now.'

My God!

'So it's just the two of us then?'

'The two of us? No, that's the good news. I think we'll soon be joined by Lamont Skyler. Have you heard of him?'

'No, I can't say that I have.'

'Really? I'm surprised. He's published quite a few things on Shakespeare's comedies and also on Restoration Comedy – he's just spent the past year in Oxford on a Fulbright – and he's also quite a fine poet. I'm sure you'll enjoy meeting him; he's an old friend of mine. I think he'll be a great addition to the faculty.'

'Wonderful. Do you have any idea yet what I'll be teaching next term? I'd like to—'

'What he'll be teaching next term?'

'No, what *I'll* be teaching next term. I'd like to start—'

'Well, no, I haven't really worked that out yet – Sister Lucia's left things in a rather confused state. Hopefully there'll be something for you in the evening.'

'I see. So, I should call you when I get back then?'

'Yes. Yes, do that. We can talk about it then. I'm afraid I have to go now. I've got a meeting in five minutes.'

'Okay. Well thank you for talking to me. I'll call when I get back then.'

'Yes, do that. I should have things shorted out – *sorted* out – by then.'

'Good. Good. Well, I won't keep you any longer. See you then.'

'Yes. Yes. Goodbye.'

'Goodbye.'

Yes, well, there it was, straight from old flannel lips himself. *Up yours, Cullen. May the Load be with you.* '*Hopefully* there'll be something for you in the evening.' He could just see the man's smug little grin stitched into his face like a pinch pleat. Well, what the hell, he'd find *something* new, something with no morning hours and three months off each year. He could handle whatever Plecko threw him. Now that he and Felicia had so brilliantly managed to book a flight with the Holy Mount Trojans, he suspected his little secret had been announced at halftime. This was one indiscretion that would not be overlooked.

He crossed the puddled lot, reentered Okamura's, and bought Felicia a small box of chocolates. She liked sweets. But when he returned, there she sat, still in the kitchen, sad as a grouper. She eyed his gifts uncomprehendingly. So the whole day passed underwater, submerged in unfathomable torpor. Cullen lay on the bed and read books, about Hawaiian history, volcanism, the supernatural – nothing by Lamont Skyler. Felicia befriended the wood stove, drank coffee, nibbled chocolates, also read discursively. She made him chop more wood at noon, his only exercise, and he was grateful for the therapy. He'd place a thick log on the chopping block and talk to it. 'Yes, just place your head right here, Father, and let's see if we can't do something about that nagging headache you've become. That's a boy. Care for a little extreme unction?' Sometimes, in honor of Saint Peter Martyr, he'd stand him up and bisect him. The man was dry bones inside. 'Now let's see if we can't work out that schedule, shall we?' He felt good after that, less like a discarded condom, more like a prick. He was feeling strangely good despite everything. Never mind that the axe would soon fall on him.

At times the rain would cease, the birds would chirp, the ferns would drip with green extravagance. Then the rain would return to pester the window and needle the roof, confirming the wisdom of their surrender. Cullen actually enjoyed such forced idleness, while Felicia seemed to endure it. He told her nothing about his dismemberment of Father Plecko, nor did he mention that it was Plecko's corpse now burning in the stove. She wasn't in the mood for small talk. They treated her mood as a malaise and left the world that day to others.

33

Fissures rent the earth, scarlet fountains seared the sky, cinders fell in a crackling black rain. A methodical wall of a'a bulldozed a row of papayas, pahoehoe flowed over the pali, lava convulsed in the sea. Such cataclysmic violence filled the darkness. The Park Service film had captured the volcano's solemn power, the turbulent transformation of stone to fire to stone, but like the eruptions, it ended.

They stepped from the auditorium into the same cold rain that had fallen the day before and the day before that. He searched the sky for the merest suggestion of sun, but found nothing there on which to pin his hopes. A brutish cloud seemed to squat on the mountain. When they returned to the car, wet once more, Cullen realized he'd run out of ideas.

'Let's go over to Volcano House,' said Felicia.

It had never occurred to him. Though it appeared in the rear view mirror, they drove to it. It was painted the same barn red as their cabin. Lava columns supported a high wooden canopy that failed to shelter them.

Inside, the lodge buzzed cheerily with fellow refugees. A fire blazed in the lobby, where two elderly gentlemen, one a turbaned Indian, were thoughtfully engaged in a game of chess. Pele peered from the fireplace's lava mantle, her features stolid and black. She appeared in the flames of paintings as well, oils of past eruptions hung among the portraits of royalty – King Kalakaua, Queen Liliuokalani, Princess Kauilani.

Felicia made her first exclamation of the day upon sighting the gift shop. She left him standing before a display case containing a red and yellow feather cape. The Hawaiians had caught their birds of plumage with sticky breadfruit sap smeared on trees. They'd plucked from each a few colorful feathers and then released them, unharmed. This had greatly impressed Cullen, who disapproved of death even in nature. The labor that had created such a cape was incalculable.

He saw his reflection in the display case. His mistake appeared obvious, as if also mirrored there. The Park was indeed a place worthy of visitation. The weather was fickle and not his responsibility. But had they stayed here in the lodge rather than the cabin, they would have felt the same reassurance that all tourists feel in the presence of others. They would not have been lonely. They would have sat before the fireplace on cold evenings, he with his pipe, she with her crackseed, free of kitchen drudgery. They would have met interesting people in the cocktail lounge, people who'd invite them to sail to Maui or visit their Hanalei ranch. Felicia would have glowed in candlelight as she had glowed in volcanic light. She would have dined in a different dress each evening. And most importantly, her hair would have been spared its ignominy. Earl had suggested the cabin and he'd accepted it as a stroke of good fortune. The idea of cuddling in a cozy cabin had sounded romantic at the time, but now he supposed he had only been frugal. Like a feather cape, their love should be displayed, not sequestered.

He made his way to the picture window overlooking the caldera. Below him lay a mute upheaval, a dark bowl of vaporous lava so vast it left little room for anything else. A scratch of a trail traversed it, but no one hiked it. Within Kilauea nestled Halemaumau, today devoid of tourists. Plumes of steam rose from its fissured walls.

He could just discern the sulfur vent where he had scorched his lungs to take his best pictures ever. A fair trade. On the far side rose Puu Puai, a large cinnamon cinder cone, and beside it, swept by low clouds, was the spot where they had picnicked. His view was suddenly obstructed by a fan of postcards held inches from his face.

'How do you like these?'

She seemed to have one of each.

'Fine. Listen, why don't we kill some time in the cocktail lounge and then have dinner here?'

'There's nothing else to do!' she said with her broadest smile.

In the near-empty lounge, overlooking the crater, Felicia wrote her postcards, all sardonic.

Dear Mom & Dad,
It may be August where you are, but it's Winter in Volcano. Send blankets, umbrellas, and soup. On Sunday we saw Mauna Ulu erupting. It's rained ever since.
Wish you were here (instead of us).
Love,
Felicia

'You can't send that,' he protested.

'Why not?'

'They'll think you're not having a good time.'

She looked at him with arch compassion.

'I didn't tell them my hair caught fire.'

'You can't tell them that. They'll think you can't be trusted on your own. Why don't you tell them about how you and Melanie did something really fun together?'

'What would that be?'

'Tell them about how Melanie killed the centipede.'

'She crushed it with her bare feet. I really admired her for that.'

'Tell them about the volcano.'

'I did.'

'Describe it. Provide concrete details they can actually visualize.'

'Hey listen, I'm not in your Freshman English class anymore, okay? It's just a postcard.'

'You're really not enjoying this, are you?'

She stared into Kilauea. 'Sunday was nice. It was wonderful. But now that we've seen the volcano, what else is there to do?'

'Well, we could make love without having to worry about your getting home on time.'

'Ehhh, we already did that.'

'Then we could smoke in bed. Read Kahlil Gibran. Tell each other our innermost secrets. It won't rain forever.'

She absent-mindedly toyed with her hair. He missed that part destroyed by fire. The woman he'd fallen in love with had had long hair – hair that fell to her breasts, that stirred the air, that framed her face like dark smoke – and now, somehow, the fire extinguished, her lost hair seemed to have tragically slipped through his fingers. Maybe smoking in bed had not been one of his better suggestions. And he didn't like Kahlil Gibran.

'So what are you saying? You don't like it here?'

'I didn't say anything. I'm just worried. I feel like my parents are gonna find out.'

'How could they find out?'

'They could run into Melanie. I don't know. The two of us could be killed by a volcanic eruption and have our names splattered all over the papers.'

'And the worrying thing about that is that your parents would find out?'

She sighed and looked out the window, while he felt woefully insufficient. Had the thrill of the volcano subsided so soon?

By dinner they were in love again, he with his Mahimahi Almondine and she with her Alaskan Crab Legs ('I can't see how crabs get around in these things'). After two drinks in the lounge, she had insisted that he drive her back to the cabin so she could dress for the occasion. She now wore a fiery red dress he'd never seen before – it struck him as Spanish – or Portuguese – and in her hair was the vanda orchid that had been served with her cocktail. Her longer hair would have swept past the orchid, a current past an eddy. Her shorter hair seemed to break abruptly upon an unexpected shore. But what she had lost was extravagance and degree, not beauty itself. There sat nearby, for example, a voluble young vine of a man who, despite his rapt wife or lover, furtively eyed Felicia with twining glances. Long hair or short, there would always be such a man.

Felicia slowly turned the small vase of anthuriums on the table, there being no candle to extinguish, while outside, a bullying wind buffeted the windows. The weather had grown tempestuous since their return.

After dinner, a Hilo trio strummed Hawaiiana in Uncle George's Lounge. Cullen found something reassuringly Hawaiian in the band's solidity. The chunky brown hands of the ukulele player smothered his instrument as if it were only a toy, and even the bass seemed insubstantial in the clutch of its master, a robust bull whose beefy face beamed dreamily. Both had arms thick as koa and proud bellies rounded by poi and Primo. They were, in pidgin lingo, *momona*. But most momona was Auntie Leilani, the lead vocalist, a mountain in a muumuu. There had always, one could tell, been a lot of Auntie Leilani. She was the one for whom the desks at school had always been too small. Yet despite her abundance, she had that Polynesian grace – that mountain breeze, that rolling ocean – that sent her soul soaring with her soprano. She had hula hands that wove the night into smoke. She had the playful eyes of a knowing woman. Her hair in a bun wreathed by pikake, she swayed like a manatee, yet sang like a siren, often in pure Hawaiian. The music was buoyant – joyous ripples on the sea – a counterpoint to the clamorous rain at the window.

Felicia excused herself to go to the ladies' room, leaving Cullen alone with his drink. A long-haired girl dressed entirely in black – black dress, black nylons, black heels – drew Cullen's admiration as she passed, stirring within him a black desire, until he reminded himself that he now had a girl like that and need no longer sigh for the unattainable.

'Is that a good Mai Tai, Dr K?'

Why was he not surprised? He didn't flinch or flounder, failed to gasp, felt no inner twinge. It was all predestined. Ernest had warned him that Plunkett's great talent was to pop up where least expected.

'Yeah. Here, try it.'

Duncan accepted the proffered drink and took a critical sip.

'Not bad, not bad. Not as good as Marvin's Grotto, but not bad. Can I join you?'

If the mention of Marvin's Grotto had been meant to put him on red alert, it had succeeded.

'Felicia's sitting there. Sit here.'

'Thanks. We gotta talk.'

'About what?'

'About old times, when Dhabul and me was in your class. About pickin' out the prepositional phrases an' all that.'

'Listen, Duncan. I don't live to pick out prepositional phrases.

It doesn't give me any great thrill, okay? And I don't get off on flunking people. But you got nothing less than what you deserved. You were cheating, plain and simple. I notice you're still playing basketball, so it hasn't hurt you any.'

'Oh yeah, we was cheatin'. I don't deny it. No problem. No big thing. I can't bleeve you flunked us though. You're spose to give us another chance. Sister Bretagno would of. But like I say, you're a hard man, Dr K. If you was a judge, you'd be a hangin' judge. They'd call you Killer Kinnell. They call you Killer Kinnell anyway, but you know what I mean. A guy's up for jaywalkin'? Hang 'em by the neck until dead. A little old lady doesn't pick up her doggy's poo poo? Throw her in the slammer! A guy's up for sellin' porno flicks? Oh, a guy's up for sellin' porno flicks, you probly let 'em go. Everybody makes a mistake sometime, yeah? We can't always be saints.'

'I think you're trying to get more mileage out of this little thing than it's worth.'

'Mileage? I ain't even got my foot on the pedal. You're always takin' me wrong, Dr K. I admire a man stands up for what he bleeves in. Peace, not war, brother. Ain't nothin' to get huhu about. I was jes sittin' over there in the dark with my good time buddies and I suddenly got this sensation that Felicia was in the room. You know how you get that feelin' bout Felicia. So I look up, and I don't see no Felicia, but sho nuff, here you is drinkin' your Mai Tai. So here I am jes to say Hey, I know we was cheatin' and I doan begrudge you doin' what you done did. Know what I mean? Bury the hatchet. Let bygones be bygones. My English never was so good. I need one of them refresher courses. But we talk different where I come from. It wouldn't be cool to go round sayin' "The rain in Spain falls mainly on the plain". Know what I mean? You get your ass whipped talkin' that jive. You even say the word *preposition* and you be laid out flat. Especially if you try toooo . . . preposition . . . some other guy's girl. Wham! You get your modifier dangled real quick that way. Know what I mean?'

Cullen knew what he meant and said so, but Felicia had returned to the table, and Duncan had gone absolutely still, his jaw dropping and his crossed eyes almost switching sockets.

'What the hell happened to you?'

'Do I look that bad?'

'Nooo. No. You could never look bad, Felicia. But you sure look different. I still love ya though.'

'My hair caught fire.'

'Your hair caught fire? How the hell did your hair catch fire?'

She seemed, at first, unwilling or unable to answer this, and Cullen was wondering if she might cry again. He'd worked so hard to console her, and now Duncan, who shouldn't even be here – not on this island, not in this lounge – was going to undo everything.

'It's a long story,' she said. 'You play with fire, you're gonna get burned.'

'Well you sure musta been playin' with some fire.'

'What are you doing up here?' she asked.

'Seeing the sights. We're stayin' here tonight.'

'You're staying in Volcano House?'

'Yeah. But it's kinda cold.'

'I'll say. You should be staying where we're staying.'

'Where you stay?'

'In a cabin in the woods.'

'No kiddin'! The two of you are like—'

'Yeah, we are,' said Cullen. 'It's a cozy, romantic place with a bar, jacuzzi, fireplace and everything.'

'Sounds tight. Anyhow, Dr K, jes wanted to say no hard feelings for stealing my woman. You guys go in peace now and mind your P's and Q's. What's that mean anyhow, Dr K – mind your P's and Q's?'

'What's it mean? It's just the letters when you write them out. A p looks like a q. Don't mix 'em up.'

'A P don't look nothin' like a Q!'

'Sure it does. Small p, small q. One's the reverse of the other.'

'It don't mean Perverts and Queers? Like Watch out for Perverts and Queers. Mind your P's and Q's now.'

Cullen smiled. 'That, too, of course. P could stand for Plunkett. Plunkett and . . .'

'Quick break. Yeah, I like that. Or Peckers and Quim. Mind your peckers and quim now.'

'Could be that.' Cullen would not be drawn by this vulgarity. It was Duncan's favorite ruse: feign friendship, test the limits.

'Anyhow . . . anyhow . . . jes want you to know that I don't begrudge no bygones. No way. But there's one other thing you probly doan know. Somethin' I gotta fill you in on.'

'What's that?' asked Cullen, struggling to fix Duncan's disturbing eyes with his own.

'The score. You doan know the score. Do you, Dr K?'

It seemed to Cullen that he said it just the way Bob Dylan had once said, 'But you don't know what it is. Do you, Mr Jones?'

'Depends on what you mean, Duncan.'

'I mean 102 to 74. And that was goin' easy on those chumps. Like I said, it was a charity match. They said we raised over $3,000 for charity.'

'What charity is that?'

'It's for sick kids that need special operations. Livers and stuff. I doan know what they call it, but it's good. I scored forty-four points. And I cracked the backboard.'

'You're a superstar,' said Felicia.

Duncan smiled. 'You're not so bad yourself, Felicia. So you guys mind your P's and Q's, your don't's and do's an' all that. Come down to the gym some day, Dr K, an' I'll teach you how to foul without gettin' caught.'

'That's cheating.'

'Tee hee. Jes kiddin'. I gotta go see what happened to my main man.'

'So long,' said Cullen.

'Yup. Bye, guys.'

'Bye,' said Felicia.

They watched his lanky silhouette crossing the room into darkness.

'I wonder if that means the end of the death threats against me,' mused Cullen.

'Death threats?'

'Yeah, sometimes when I go to the men's room to meditate there's a message in the stall – "Dr K, your dead".'

'What makes you think Duncan would do a thing like that?'

'*You're* was misspelled. Besides, he's got the motive.'

'Which is?'

'I stole his woman. He said he loves you.'

'And you flunked him.'

'There you go.'

'Get serious, Cullen. He likes you. Besides, I could think of lots of people who could issue a death threat against you.'

'Felicia . . . did you ever . . . did you ever go out with this guy?'

'Plunkett?'

'Yeah. I mean, he was always asking you.'

'No.'

'Why did he say I was stealing his woman?'

'To put a hair up your ass.'

'He said he went to Marvin's Grotto a lot.'

'Did he?'

'Yeah, he did.'

'He used to show up about an hour before closing. He'd ask me to go dancing with him, but I never went.'

'Never?'

'Okay, once. We went to the Point After once. With Melanie.'

'You went dancing with Plunkett? When you were going out with me?'

'It was one of those times when you weren't talking to me. It was just a disco.'

'He didn't just let you go home afterwards. I know him better than that.'

'He did actually. He gave Melanie and me a ride to my car and we drove home.'

'Why don't I believe you?'

'Because you're a suspicious bastard, that's why. Okay, if you must know, I gave him a blow job in the car. The kind you like so much. It was the least I could do.'

He glared at her.

'Cullen, nothing happened. Okay?'

'He sure acts like something did.'

'Most men do. Let's get out of here before any more of my lovers turn up.'

Most of the guests had returned to their comfortable rooms, but Cullen and Felicia would have to brave the storm, which was now a howling downpour. They passed through the lobby, whose fire, they'd read, had not been extinguished since 1941.

'Let's put it out,' whispered Felicia halfheartedly.

'You do that while I get the car.'

Getting the car was an act of gallantry. Although he made a run for it, he was mugged by the torrent as soon as he left the portico.

'You're drenched,' said Felicia when he pulled up to the entrance and she slipped dryly into the passenger seat.

'No kidding.'

He pulled out into the tempest.

'What the hell's that noise?' she asked, referring not to the steel drums of rain pelting the roof but to what he thought he'd heard when driving the few yards to the portico, something anarchic and metallic, a horrid cacophony coming from the rear of the car, where, as all VW owners know, one finds the all-important engine.

It sounded like the engine had thrown a rod, whatever that meant – it was something like throwing a fit, he assumed – or the transmission had packed it in or was about to – something was going around and around, something was loose, perhaps growing looser, it was bad, it was major, it was something he couldn't fix if his life depended upon it, and the timing was excruciatingly inopportune, to say the least. There was no way he was going back to Volcano House, not with the Holy Mount Trojans in residence. Besides, they had only a short way to go, the oil light hadn't come on, and the car was still running, though with the wind bullying it it was impossible to tell whether it was running well or not. Furthermore, come to think of it, it wasn't a VW and it wasn't his car, which meant he wouldn't have to endure a mechanic telling him that he needed a new rear polysegon and it would cost him a thousand smackaroos, unless, of course, he wanted to get a rebuilt one and put it in himself, which is what I would do if I were you.

'Shouldn't we stop? Did we run over something?'

'I'm not stopping in this.'

It was raining, raining, raining, and the wind was battering the car with a series of jabs and powerful right hooks. He had no idea what he might do if the car broke down on the darkened road. There was no shoulder to cry or pull off on, just a fern-infested gully. It was necessary that the car keep running, that it carry them to safety in a secure insular bubble sealed from wind, rain, and unpleasantries. A thrown rod, a defunct transmission, a frozen polysegon – these were unacceptable options, so Cullen drove on.

Just get us back to the cabin, he prayed. Get us back to the cabin and I'll give you a lube job. Get us back to the cabin and we can both break down together. Get us back to the cabin and I'll go to sleep, safe and warm in the covers, and deal with this in the morning, if at all.

Flailed by the same wind that lashed the tree ferns, the Toyota bucked and lurched through a darkness its beams barely penetrated. It was no better than Cullen's VW in high winds. He drove in the middle of the highway, equidistant from disaster and oblivion.

'We're gonna be blown off the planet,' she said.

'We should've left earlier.'

The wipers had grown hysterical, unable, like Cullen, to cope. He imagined what it would be like if an invisible force other than wind playfully flipped the car for effect. That would give them something to talk about. But no such force materialized, nor invisibilized, and the trusty Toyota soon juddered back to Volcano, where they rode out the storm in bed, the cabin groaning like a trawler in a gale.

34

Something was different. A different smell, a different sound, a different quality of light. Something. It was brighter, perhaps warmer. The sun was shining! He opened his eyes to confirm this impression. Not only was the sun shining, but the wind had died and small birds had been resurrected. What would they do with such a gift? Take a walk? Return to Mauna Ulu? Take a picnic up the Strip Road? He couldn't quite focus on the surfeit of possibilities. Then he remembered that the car was ailing and that he'd have to call Cut Rate Rent-a-Car to do something about it. He supposed he should at least go through the motions of inspecting it before calling. Getting a replacement vehicle would probably consume the whole day.

Still, as he opened the door to birdsong, he couldn't help but feel grateful. Nothing in the prior night's weather had led him to expect such an accommodating morning. The wind had blown the stormclouds out to sea.

He stepped to the back of the car, for that had been the source of the clanking, and as he did so, the scales fell from his eyes. On the driveway lay the source of last night's grief – three tin cans that had been tied to the bumper. And there on the bumper itself – ineradicable, unassailable, perhaps even eternal – were two shiny new Trojan stickers. He didn't know whether to laugh or cry. He'd tell Felicia and let her decide.

When she showed signs of awakening, he hummed a Cat Stevens song while preparing an inspired omelette. He soon heard water running in the bathroom. She appeared in the doorway on schedule, scowled in his general direction, then shuffled like a zombie to the table.

'Morning, love. I've made us an omelette.'
'Hrrmb.'
'Want some juice?'
'Kuff.'
'Pardon?'
'Kuffy.'
'Kuffy?'
'Coffee!'
'Coffee! You would *like* some coffee, please. Is that it?'
'Yesss.'
'You're not much of a morning person, are you?'
'Nope.'
He brewed some coffee for the wax figure at the table.
'I found out what was wrong with the car.'
'Yeah? What?'
'It seems to have three tin cans tied to the rear bumper. I guess it's supposed to be like we just got married.'
'I wonder who would do something like that.'
'I wonder.'
'Jesus! What is this?'
'Kuffy.'

His coffee depressed her all day. She seemed withdrawn, even tense, and nothing he did could change that. In the bird park she studied the ground. In Volcano House, where they lunched, she failed to construct imaginary lives for fellow diners or to steal a single morsel from his plate. The smile she offered the waitress was as thin as egg soup. Lilikoi chiffon pie she let pass by, though she had pointed praise for the coffee. And on the Strip Road, when he stopped to examine a massive flow, she claimed she had seen enough lava, both hot and cold, to last a lifetime. No, she did not want to hike to Mauna Ulu that evening, but he could go if he wanted.

That evening she prepared a curry – a muddled, khaki goo in which shrimp shriveled dispiritedly – and served it over rice. He suggested they open the champagne.
'What's to celebrate?'
'Our first time alone together. Our secret love nest.'

She brought him the bottle in silence, dragging it by the neck. Even in short hair and shapeless sweater, she had the wild, sultry look of an Italian film star. It was the espresso eyes that aroused him.

He uncorked the bottle at arm's length, expecting the plastic stopper to ricochet off the ceiling. It never escaped his hand. Having no champagne glasses, they drank from mugs.

'To us,' he said.

'To us.'

Rather than clink, the mugs clanked.

'You look a bit tired,' he said. 'Why don't we go to bed early tonight.'

'That's what I'm afraid of.'

'What does that mean?'

She poked her curry.

'I should have bought some chutney.'

'What does that mean?'

'It means . . .' She looked angrily toward the shotgun. 'You know that I have these dreams, these . . . experiences, when I feel paralyzed, like something's . . . holding me down and I can't move, I can't wake up . . .'

'Yes.'

'Well . . . it's getting worse. Much worse. I've had that feeling twice since we've been here. The night we hiked to Mauna Ulu, and last night. I feel like some demon's trying to possess me. I used to think I could handle this, but now I'm not so sure. I'm scared. I'm afraid to go to sleep anymore. You think I'm crazy, don't you? That's what you've always thought.'

'Would I be with you if I thought you were crazy? I don't know what to think. This is what's been bugging you all this time? I thought it was your hair, or the rain, or something I did in my sleep. Why the hell didn't you tell me?'

'I don't know. I didn't want to ruin things. There's nothing you can do about it.'

'Maybe, maybe not. Maybe I can wake you up when I see you're in trouble. I just haven't seen it. I wasn't even aware . . . You didn't tell me. Just tell me one thing now.'

'What?'

He stared into her downcast eyes. To look there, one might imagine that all the emptiness in the world had found its way into the kitchen. It had been in a kitchen, too, that Claire had complained about *her* ghost. How sweetly she had embraced him that night, he with a knife in his hand, she in her dress of orchids.

'Is it Uncle Ricardo?'

She drew her collar to her throat. She had a broad repertoire of such poses, theatrical gestures that came to her as naturally as waves to the ocean.

'Is that what you think?'

'I'm just asking what you think.'

'I don't know. Sometimes I think it's a nightmare. Sometimes I feel like I'm haunted. I've thought of Uncle Ricardo. He was a real womanizer. He had a real lust for life. They say ghosts are the ones that just can't let go. But somehow I can't think of Uncle Ricardo as being like Uncle Frank.'

'Uncle Frank?'

'Aunt Maria's husband.'

'Aunt Maria being the one Ricardo shafted?'

'Right. Well after Uncle Ricardo, she married Uncle Frank.'

'Okay. So what about him?'

'Promise that this is just between you and me?'

'Oh shit.'

'Promise?'

'I promise.'

She held out her right hand with the little finger extended.

'Pinky promise,' she insisted.

This seemed absurd but he complied, wrapping his pinky around hers in a miniature handshake he considered nonbinding. He knew what was coming.

'Uncle Frank is my dirty uncle. Aunt Maria married him when I was in the seventh grade. He was okay at first, but one night he and Aunt Maria and I were in the back seat together. I don't know where we were going – I think we were coming back from a family gathering. I'm almost sure of it because he smelled of bacalhau and wine and he and Dad were laughing like hyenas and Mom kept telling Dad to watch where he was going. Mom and Dad and Dana were in the front seat. Unfortunately, Aunt Maria was sound asleep, snoring. That woman snores like a drunken sailor. That was one of the things they were laughing about. Anyhow, it was dark in the back seat and Uncle Frank did something naughty.'

'What did he do?'

'I don't want to go into detail, all right? Use your imagination. He put his hand under my dress and started playing caterpillar.'

'Right in the same car with your father and mother?'

'Right. And all the time carrying on a normal conversation.'

'Why didn't you tell your father?'

'I don't know. I was confused. I didn't know what to do. And he was acting like it was just good fun.'

'That son of a bitch.'

'Don't get all worked up, okay? I knew I shouldn't have told you. Now you're gonna make a scene someday, aren't you.'

'The guy's a pervert.'

'All men are perverts, Cullen. Some just hide it better than others. Besides, that was a long time ago. He's much better now. He's still sort of kissy-touchy, and I still think of him as my dirty uncle, but I'm not afraid of him anymore. I can handle him. He just had a little too much to drink that night.'

'Your Aunt Maria really knows how to pick 'em.'

'Anyhow, I'd like to think that Uncle Ricardo wasn't like that.'

'From what I've heard, I wouldn't count on it.'

She held her cup with both hands, thought deeply, raised her eyes.

'I wish Melanie was here.'

'Why?'

'I just always feel more secure when Melanie's around. And the sooner she gets here, the sooner I can get home to Mommy and Daddy.'

'Thanks.'

'It's not you, Cullen. It's this place. It depresses me.'

'So what will you do tonight?'

'What can I do? I've got to go to sleep. Everyone's got to sleep. You can't just avoid it. You can put it off as long as possible, maybe a few days, get all edgy and irritable and start to panic, and then fall asleep a nervous wreck with no control, or you can try to stay calm and go to sleep as always, telling yourself that this night's gonna be just a normal night, with no complications – when you want to wake up you can wake up. But either way, sooner or later, you've got to go to sleep and deal with it. I've always tried the second approach. But it's not working so well anymore.

'When I was a kid I used to have this terrible nightmare. I'd be alone in my bedroom and suddenly I'd see my . . . I'd see a monster. A monster would jump out of a dark corner and start chasing me. I woke up every night in a fright. Then one night I learned how to control my dreams. It was easy, really. I just decided that when I turned a corner or opened a door, I'd see what I wanted to see, not what my dreams wanted me to see. It worked like a charm. I need to learn how to take control like that again.'

'How can I help you tonight? Would I know it was happening if I saw it?'

'I don't know. If you even suspect, please – wake me up.'

'One more question.'

'What?'

'What was your uncle doing at your house the day he died?'

She glanced so decisively at the door – as if someone had just entered – that he turned to see what she saw. Nothing. When he turned again, he saw that she had drawn a napkin to her face. As with her burning hair, he was slow to realize. He hadn't expected it, and he didn't know what to do for it. For the longest time, she simply wept. He left the room and returned with a pack of tissues.

'Thank you.'

She wiped each eye, then spoke to the table.

'He was all bloody. It was—'

That seemed to be all she could manage. Yet somehow he knew without knowing.

'Yes?'

'It was horrible. It was the most horrible moment in my life. He woke me up with his cries. He was covered with it, lying there on our living room rug. He was stabbed in Waikiki, but he drove all the way to our house. Aunt Maria was staying with us because he beat her so bad. When I came into the living room, he was spitting blood, and I thought every breath would be his last. There was a gash in his chest, right here, where the blood kept spurting out. If he'd gone straight to the hospital . . . they might have saved him.

Aunt Maria was in hysterics. She didn't know what to do. It was Dana who called an ambulance. We were both just kids. I didn't know what he was talking about. He tried to hold me, but Aunt Maria tore me away. She shrieked at him in Portuguese. Mom and Dad came home – they'd been out. They saw me covered with blood and freaked out. He was talking crazy, with blood trickling out of his mouth. I couldn't understand. Dad blamed Aunt Maria. Mom screamed for him to call a priest. He died in Mom's arms. She almost never left the house after that. She changed completely.'

'Why would he ask for you? You were just a kid.'

'He wanted to say goodbye. He wanted to hold somebody. But it wasn't just me. It was Aunt Maria, too, but she was afraid to go near him.'

'Why?'

'The blood, I guess. That woman can't stand the sight of blood.'

He simply sat there, trying to absorb it all.

'Why did you tell me he died of a heart attack?'

'That seemed close enough. I would have told you the truth someday. It's family, and you're not family.' She blew her nose. 'It's crazy the things my family went through. Working like slaves, sleeping on sticks. Sixty hours a week for next to nothing.'

'Your parents?'

'No, not my parents. Their grandparents. From Madeira. My father can tell you some stories though. He worked like a dog to get where he is today. So did Uncle Bebe. Dana and I are the first ones in our family to go to a real college, the first ones to be free of all that. And people still call us Portagees. Even you. Should I drag out my crazy dead uncle?'

'Who stabbed him?'

'Some jealous husband. Did I mention that he was stark naked? I'd never seen a naked man before and here was one bleeding all over the carpet like it was a religious ceremony or something. I think that bothered Aunt Maria more than anything else. She covered him up with a sheet.'

'Stark naked?' For Cullen, something clicked, like the hammer of a gun held to the temple. 'Did this jealous husband stab him in a hotel room?'

'Yes. You know the whole sordid story, thanks to your friend Earl. He stabbed his wife to death too. A week before Christmas. I remember we had a treeeee . . .'

This last sentence was swept away by a surge of tears. He sat it out, then wiped the mascara from her cheek. This was considerably more than he'd bargained for.

'Felicia . . .'

'What?'

'Are you telling me . . . that you sat through that whole story that Earl told, knowing it was your uncle he was talking about, and you never said anything?'

'I'd heard it before.'

He leaned back and bit his lip. 'I don't know if I can take all this in. I mean . . . you know, I'm from New York. We don't have ghosts in New York. We've just got dead people. Lots of them.'

'Oh goddamn you and your ghosts! Do you think my whole life depends on whether you believe in ghosts or not? I don't give a damn. I'm talking about my uncle. He was flesh-and-blood . . .'

Mostly blood, thought Cullen, who was wounded by this outburst.

'But that story you told me about seeing him after he died – was that true?'

'Yes. And I should never have told you.'

'Why not?'

'Because you treat me like I'm some kind of fool. And you blame everything on Uncle Ricardo. But you don't believe in ghosts. So why Uncle Ricardo? I don't understand.'

'If you were being haunted – and you must consider that a possibility, whether I do or not – wouldn't he be a natural candidate? A man who can't let go?'

'I don't know. I don't know what to believe anymore. I think I'm being punished for my sins.'

'What sins?'

'Whatever sins I've committed.'

He closed his eyes and pinched the bridge of his nose.

'I think I need help,' she said.

'What kind of help?'

'I don't know. What kind of help is there? None of this makes any sense to me. All I know is that I felt safer at home. I've lived in a very little world, you know.'

'Maybe you *could* get help. Maybe a psychiatrist could help.'

'It's all in my mind?'

'I'm not saying that. Maybe, maybe not. I'm just saying a psychiatrist might know how to cope with it. Other women have had it, too. Maybe there's a cure.'

'The nightmare I used to have wasn't about a monster. It was about the last time I saw Uncle Ricardo. I'd dream that I was about to get on my stool, and then, just like it actually happened, someone would lift me on to it instead. I'd turn to see Uncle Ricardo. But this time he wasn't smiling. This time he was crying and covered in blood. And he was reaching out to me. That's the nightmare I had to take control of. And now I need to take control again and get my life back to normal. Until I can do that, nothing's going to be quite right with me.'

Resting his chin in one hand and slowly drumming his fingers on the table, he considered all she had told him, though not with the same scrutiny as in the years that followed.

'I agree,' he said quietly, compassionately engaging her eyes.

35

He had meant to awaken himself in the night, to watch over her like a guardian angel, but when next he opened his eyes the room was bruised by the half-light of early dawn. He turned toward Felicia. She wasn't there.

He listened for footsteps, or the creak of a floorboard, or the groan of a water tap, or any reassurance of her presence. She was sitting quietly on the toilet. She was drinking coffee in the kitchen. He listened for the slightest clink or rustle. When he heard none, he propped himself warily on one elbow, still half-asleep, reluctant to consider possibilities.

There, at his knees, lay her head. He sat up abruptly, alarmed. One arm hung lifelessly off the bed, and in the dawn light that seemed to be all there was of her, head and arm, two fragments of the mysterious woman she'd become. Blankets hid the remainder. If they rose and fell, it was imperceptible.

Now, rising to his knees, he saw that she had apparently slid halfway off the mattress without awakening. Dismayed, he studied her face, leaning closer in the feeble light. He saw nothing there to suggest fear or discomfort. He saw only a blank template of the face he loved, devoid of not only torment, but also of its customary pride and innuendo. Despite her contortions she seemed at peace, breathing without perturbation. How long had she lain like this?

'I can't believe this,' he said aloud, hoping to awaken her. She slept on soundly. Perhaps he should simply leave her as she was?

He bent to kiss her on the cheek. This startled her – her eyes snapped open to roll like a cow's at slaughter, then closed as suddenly. It was that momentary vision that alarmed him. A shutter had opened on her nightmare, betraying an inner turmoil he would never have divined from her face.

He lifted her back to the bed and shook her softly by the shoulders. He had never enjoyed awakening another human being. He shook her harder.

'Whaat?'

'Are you okay?'

She shrugged him off angrily and turned away.

The clock read 8.20. Not dawn at all. So why was the room . . . ? He saw, then, what had tampered with the light. She wouldn't like this. Fog darkened every window, a huge drab blindfold tied tightly round the cabin. A visit to the bathroom and kitchen confirmed this impression. Even the birds had fallen silent, hooded like falcons by fog.

Well, he wouldn't let it depress him. Perhaps he even liked it, this sense of being adrift, or stalled in a steamboat on the Congo. He returned to the bed and lay awake, luxuriating in an accumulation of private ironies: that this fog bank was his romantic adventure; that Uncle Ricardo, if he existed, had not only escaped the three-bedroom house near the freeway, but had managed somehow to accompany them, like invisible luggage; that Uncle Ricardo was Richard Roland Medeiros, the ill-fated lover in Earl's bogus certificate, a coincidence too eerie to ponder; that even though Cullen's own middle name was Richard, a name he'd hacked down to R in high school and had buried alive in college, he hadn't recognized it in such a thin disguise; that the story of Uncle Ricardo's death had more or less vindicated Earl and all he had claimed regarding the haunted hotel room, yet how could one believe a thing so preposterous? He wondered what he'd find if he himself visited that room in Waikiki, and he wondered why he hadn't.

He donned warm clothes, both turtleneck and sweater, and prepared breakfast, though he had hoped that she might do the honors this morning. Not until she'd had her first cup of coffee did he broach the subject of nocturnal posture.

'You know how I found you this morning?'

She eyed him with sudden intensity.

'How?'

'You were sprawled halfway off the bed like a ragdoll. Your legs were completely off the mattress, but you were sound asleep. Even when I lifted you back on to the bed, you didn't wake up.'

'Last night was horrible. Horrible! I *couldn't* wake up. I felt like I was suffocating.'

'But when I woke you up, you got mad at me.'

'I don't remember. When was that?'

'This morning, when I lugged you back on to the bed.'

'I'm talking about last night. This place gives me the creeps. Look at that,' she said, pointing to the fog at the window. 'Is it supposed to do that?'

'Do what?'

'Surround us. Press its nose right up against the window like that.'

'As I recall, you had this problem long before we came here. You've had it for years.'

'Not like this, I haven't. Not anything like this. Three nights in one week? There's something spooky about this place. There aren't any *people* around here.'

'That was the idea.'

'That was *your* idea. Maybe not such a good one. I have a bad feeling about this place. I feel threatened here. I know you think I'm just a superstitious Portagee. I know you don't believe in such things. But I feel it. I feel it right here in my gut.'

'Melanie will be here tomorrow.'

'Thank God. Tonight's the last night I'll spend in this place.'

'There's nothing wrong with this house.'

But here he was lying. The truth was that he, too, had found the cabin disturbing, a lonely place inhabited by inexplicable creaking sounds that seemed to reside in the attic. At night, when the wind blew, every window struggled against it. And there was something disquieting about Volcano itself with its unwelcome fogs and interminable dusks. There was only dusk, never a sunset proper. Above the trees, the sky would be lit by a luminous mist from which the light would be slowly leached for hours. No extravagant gesture of turquoise and pink, no smoky clouds laced with dying light, no night stars emerging peacefully at twilight; only an imperceptible fading of light, and the vanishing silhouettes of tree ferns. At dusk the light in the cabin was never quite right; it had the sickly cast of old newspaper clippings. As the night edged closer, one saw nothing in the darkening mist, only heard, as a kind of prelude, the distant gunning of big engines not so much breaking the silence as beating against it. The same two motorcycles performed the same rite nightly. But the roads led nowhere: it was thirty miles to Hilo, almost a hundred to Captain Cook.

And there was the cold, for which he was ill prepared. It girdled his chest, stippled his arms, chilled him at the knees where his pants had worn thin.

And now the fog at the windows made him suddenly aware of what had been subtly depressing him ever since their arrival. It was so obvious. Why hadn't he noticed it before? The house had been made for the Japanese! What an odd discovery. It was its ownership by the Ogilvies that had blinded him to the obvious. When he shaved, or merely verified his reflection, he had to stoop to the mirror. To avoid bumping his head he had to stoop, also, at the kitchen lintel. And to see the sky above the trees, when a sky was there to see, he had to stoop when looking out the windows. Even the trees seemed too close, especially those forming a high, unbroken wall on the opposite side of the road. The impenetrable fog and the proportions of the cabin had, without his quite realizing it, made him claustrophobic. There was, furthermore, a slight warp in certain windows that created a stifling distortion. Felicia had discovered this defect and had pointed it out to him as a novelty. By focusing on a tree and slightly rocking one's eyes, one created a rippling effect, as if viewing the world from underwater. It hadn't fazed him at first, this imperfect glass, but now it seemed to constrain him. Often, as now, he'd felt the need to escape; but outside, the fog pressed too close as well, like a drunken relative sharing some pathetic funereal confidence. Like Felicia's sleep.

She sat with her head buried in her hands, the perfect symbol of hopelessness. He still hadn't swallowed such sudden despair.

'Can we please drive out of this fog?' she asked.

'Good idea. Where to?'

'The beach.'

Without complaint, he chauffeured her thirty miles down the mountain to Punaluu. He should have done it before. They escaped the fog near the park boundary. With luck, they wouldn't return till early evening, by which time, perhaps, sunshine and warmth would have dispelled her forebodings.

His time alone with her was almost over, and though they'd seen the volcano as planned, all in all he rated the trip a disaster, a verdict underscored by the fact that they'd made love only once. First there had been the fiasco of encountering Plecko and the ubiquitous Trojans, a mishap that had probably cost him his job. Then there had been the passion-quenching misfortune of her hair catching fire just because she had warmed it over a gas burner. Now there was her ghost, or nightmare, whatever one chose to call it. He didn't understand how leaving the cabin could save her from Uncle Ricardo, and he was furious to think that the very violation he'd been preparing to counter had transpired right by his side in the night. Some of his rage showed on his face when he met the eyes of a bearded swimmer staring openly at Felicia as if she were on display. The swimmer went into his backstroke while they walked the nearly abandoned black sands until Felicia found a suitable place to lie and do nothing.

When his rage subsided, he knew he would entertain different thoughts. Uncle Ricardo would again become an improbability, would dissolve to nothing as ghosts often do, and Felicia's supernatural ordeal would enter the light as just another run-of-the-mill psychogenic disorder. Perhaps, like the Japanese, science would have a name for it. He tried that on for size.

Endless visits to the psychiatrist, an expensive, bespectacled goat with poorly repressed erection eager to drag the dark lake of her past while purfling his notepad with men's-room graffiti. He'd show her pictures and tell her to utter the first word that popped to mind. He'd snatch a phrase or, worse yet, slip of the tongue, and pin it to the table for careful analysis. He'd tell her to lie on the couch, close her eyes, and relax. He'd prod the body of a dream until it cried *ouch.* He'd ask about father, mother, dirty uncles, and maybe even Cullen. And when it was all over, when the final sands had sifted through the final hourglass, when all the layered petals of the psyche had been dutifully peeled away like Claire's echoing lettuce, what would he find there? What would her bogeyman look like naked in the light?

He surveyed the curt horizon. The incredible thing about the ocean was that it just kept going, clear and blue, the opposite of life. All the murky things stayed on the bottom.

Some Midwesterners saved all their lives just to wiggle their toes in the great Pacific and lie happily like beached squid, pale and misshapen but rapidly reddening; but the woman beside him, in a black bikini that shrank from her buttocks, lay as tense as a cocked trap. He lay supine, closed his eyes, and did what he always did at the beach – grew groggy while watching strands of impurities glissade across his cornea. When they reached the end of their tether, he effortlessly jerked them back again.

Later he opened *Justine*. He had not read long before encountering his thought for the day: 'There is no pain compared to that of loving a woman who makes her body accessible to one and yet is incapable of delivering her true self – because she does not know where to find it.' Did every book in the Nittas' library contain for him some message? How clearly that focused his anguish, how easily his bitterness rose like bile. Her body was accessible, true – had been, at least, until she'd set herself on fire – yet what had sex become but a blind thrashing, a finely honed resentment. Gratifying, yes – like well-plotted revenge. Dirty words whispered in an ear, vulgarities rushing to orgasm. Cock, cunt, ass, tongue, desires grappling in animal heat. And he was so caught up in it that he had an erection even then, lying beside her, appraising her darkening body – bronze against black – thinking crudely, 'I'm the one who fucks her', imagining the envy of other men, the men who stared openly everywhere. And despite his claim to her, he recognized, too, that he had been somehow emasculated by the fear of losing her. And Uncle Ricardo, who once again seemed real, had become more than a lascivious ghost; he was now a knowing leer, an affront, a provocative slap in the face. He closed the book. It was dark poetry unsuitable for sunlight.

Someone down the beach had tuned a radio to pop. He had never understood how music could travel through a blue sky soundlessly, then emerge from a little toy box to say 'Ooh, Baby', but he accepted it as magic. Such music promised a simple happiness he'd never found in life, but he accepted that as well – that it existed for others, that it could be found. He gave himself to the beat of what he recognized as a Frampton song muffled by sand and lay there roasting, basted in oil. They'd come a long way from Volcano.

Later, when Felicia seemed asleep and he could no longer endure the heat, he waded into the water to sidestroke languidly, absorbing the solitude of bay and mountain. The sand formed a black crescent on which surf played its fugitive fugue. Above the beach rose a ravel of green, a few clumps of palms sketching the breeze. And to the right rose the cloud-capped volcano. This was indeed paradise. And if you couldn't make it here, you couldn't make it anywhere.

On the long drive back to the cabin, the noxious gas of her discontent silently filled the car. The fog had lifted, but not her spirits. Once in Volcano, she insisted that he stop at Okamura's so she could phone Melanie on Oahu.

'I didn't think you had her number.'

'I've got her friend's number. I've gotta phone Mom, too.'

Okamura's appeared busy – two rental cars and a jeep were parked before the lanai, and a farmer stood beside the Texaco pump pumping Regular into a battered pick-up loaded with papayas. Felicia slipped into the phone booth while Cullen entered the store.

Wisps of mist slid furtively across the highway.

Entering Okamura's, he sensed immediately that the store was in the grip of something electric. Amid the overpriced groceries, toiletries, sundries and hardware, fragments of animated conversation collided noisily in mid-air. Intrigued, he edged toward the register.

'One year it wipe out da whole town – Kapoho. One big a'a flow movin' like one centipede, you know.'

'Well, it's nothing like that this year, but it's always quite a show.'

'Oh yeah. Dat Pele one unpredictable wahine. Me, I got my whole house protected by ti leaves.'

'What's going on?' asked Cullen.

'You no hear? Da lava makin' one beeline for da sea, dat's what.' This was delivered by the farmer, a dark, affable, grimily tee-shirted man who made a straight-arrow gesture with his right hand tracked by beady eyes now glowing with the vacant intensity of a mongoose subjected to taxidermy.

An elderly tourist stocking up on film tried to explain it to him.

'The lava flowing through Mauna Ulu has emerged above Holei Pali. At this very moment it's flowing over the cliff. In a couple days, it should reach the sea. We're going to drive down to Kalapana tonight and see how close we can get. The hell with hotels! How often will you get a chance like this?'

'You'll get plenty close,' said Mr Okamura. 'I've seen it before – a waterfall of lava hundreds of feet high. See it at night; it's better than Niagara Falls. Anything else?'

'I don't know. What am I forgetting?'

'Me, dear,' said the tourist's wife, depositing a basketful of groceries on the counter. 'We've still got to eat. What about that Chain of Craters Road? Can we take that down?'

'No way!' laughed the farmer. 'Closed for years.'

'That's right,' said Mr Okamura, ringing up her purchase. 'Covered by lava. You'll have to go the long way, through Keaau and Pahoa. It'll be worth it though. I wish I could get away myself. How 'bout a flashlight and batteries? Need those?'

Cullen caught the contagion. This was the sort of spectacle one hoped to witness when visiting the Big Island. Many kamaainas who had lived on Oahu all their lives had never seen an actual flow. Felicia, for example. Every flight *from* Honolulu would be booked solid for the duration of the fireworks. And here they fortuitously were, in the right place at the right time. A simple drive and they'd be there, watching lava pour from the night like fire from obsidian – adventurers, eyewitnesses. He strode past the saimin and dashinomoto to look in the final cramped aisle for something that might qualify as dinner. When he returned to the checkout counter, he was surprised to see Felicia descending the stairs.

Back in the car, his curiosity was piqued by the small package on her lap. He didn't ask.

'How'd that go then?'

'Fine. She'll be here tomorrow morning, as planned.'

'And your parents?'

'They're fine. They got my postcard.'

'Did you hear that the lava's flowing over the pali?'

'Yes.'

'I know you and Melanie have girl stuff planned, but this is a once-in-a-lifetime opportunity. Wouldn't you like to see it before we go?'

'I promised her we'd have time alone.'

'Where you guys going? Think you'll go see it together?'

'We'll probably just stay in Hilo.'

'Then let's drive down the coast tonight. We can see the lava flowing over the cliff and be back here by morning. If you really hate this cabin we could sleep in the car.'

'No way. I've got to pack my stuff and clean up the place. That's what I should've been doing today. I'm really not feeling well. I've got cramps.'

'Okay, if that's how it is, you go to bed and relax. *I'll* clean up while you're gone.'

The plan was that she and Melanie would have two days together, then return on the morning of the third day so that Melanie could spend some time in Volcano, presumably to view the eruption. Felicia wanted to treat her to dinner at Volcano House. On the next day she and Melanie would fly back to Honolulu. He'd follow in a day or two.

They'd already arrived at the cabin, which seemed, with a few birds flitting among its eaves, innocent of any wrongdoing. Upon unlocking the door and entering, he was surprised to hear it shut behind him with Felicia still outside. He heard something hit the door with a sharp crack, and then heard the blow again. He reopened it warily, perplexed. There burned Felicia, luminous with intensity, and firmly embedded in the muntin, neck-high, shone one blade of a small pair of scissors.

'What the hell did you do that for?'

'To ward off the *bicho-papao*.'

'Oh. Does he live around here?'

She brushed past him into the cabin.

'Okay, what's the *beecho papow*?'

'The Bogeyman.'

'The Bogeyman. And what about the Nittas' door?'

'It can still be a door.'

'Those scissors wouldn't ward off the Sunday paper!'

'Size doesn't matter.'

He remained astonished. This was simply beyond his comprehension. A perfectly good door had been impaled by a pair of scissors. How would he explain *that* to the Nittas, he wondered, realizing as he did so that he'd probably never have to. Worse, there was something about the scissors that held the appeal of a pert poetic image, one dissociated from any easy meaning. The door was weathered; she had found its weakness. He admired her for that. A part of him was secretly pleased by the drama of it. But why did he adore a madwoman?

36

That night he sat by the wood stove, smoking his pipe, worrying, while Felicia bathed in the ashen tub filled almost to the brim. The thought of the scissors in the door struck a nerve again. He worried that the Nittas might come in the morning, perhaps on a mission of mercy, but then he supposed that they wouldn't. They were old. And Mr Nitta was frail as shoji.

He worried about Mrs Nitta, soon to face her final days alone. It seemed unjust that one should die without the touch of the other.

He worried that there were some things in life – *many* things in life – too painful to endure.

He worried about Felicia.

But mostly he worried about his inability to ascertain just what, exactly, worried him.

For some time he had been aware of a quiet yet persistent rustling – like that of moths at screened windows – but only now did he acknowledge it as rain. When had that begun? How could one possibly say, for the fog that had come with the sunset had been a stillborn rain as well. Such transformations were subtle. Now the rustling grew to a loud, rattling clatter. He decided again, as rain dripped from the eaves, that they hung too low.

When Felicia appeared, clad in a towel, she seemed, at first, a disturbingly different woman. But of course – he should be used to it by now – her wet hair no longer reached her shoulders. This meant she could no longer fling it dramatically, like a whip snapped in air, before fixing him with her sensual glare.

Instead, she toweled it dry, then donned her new flannel nightgown. No sooner had she put it on than she took it off again.

'Why are you wearing your nightgown inside out?' he asked, adopting a condescending, paternal air that his pipe somehow encouraged.

'To ward off the *bicho-papao*.'

'Did you do this sort of stuff at home?'

'No.'

'Then why are you doing it now?'

'Because I'm scared. I'm sorry. Goodnight, Cullen.'

'Goodnight.'

No kiss? They seemed to be reaping all the rewards of marriage without having actually performed the act. He turned out the light and sat listening – to the percolation of rain, to the crackling of fire. A cast iron darkness contained the glow of the stove. A cold finger seemed to probe his sternum.

Uncle Ricardo, he thought. *Uncle Ricardo*. The name itself was an ugly pulp, the moist ball of fuzz mice cough up on the kitchen floor. Repeated silently time and again, it had assumed the venom of a curse. *Uncle Ricardo*, the cavalier uncle who, after ten years abroad, had returned to widow his wife and haunt his niece. Who, when the house had been blessed, had merely wandered off till the blessing had grown thin. Who, as licentious dead as alive, had quietly watched his favorite niece grow from child to woman. When she'd stood naked before her mirror, he had floated within it, as much a voyeur as the man next door. When she'd touched herself with the hands of another, he had guided her. And when she began to dwell for indolent hours upon her visions of certain young men, when she no longer believed sleeping naked in moonlight deforms the body, the man who had terrified her as a child pressed his ghostly body to her new one, forcing his entry into private sleep. Like an eel in dark water, something evil had entered her dreams.

Was that a fair summation? It all seemed a bit theatrical. Like ghosts, these morbid thoughts rose only at night. He strove to convince himself that he believed none of this. But to deny Uncle Ricardo would be to deny Felicia as well. He could tolerate an occasional superstition – that made her Portuguese, invested her with ethnicity – but inventing ghosts, or ghostly experiences, was too close to madness. Yet what about Earl? What about Claire and

Ernest? What about Socrates, Pliny, and Johnson? Had they invented their ghosts? Who in these islands was a true nonbeliever? Who dared to openly scoff? He moved in reasonably intelligent circles, yet whenever the subject of ghosts arose, eyes ignited with unmistakable glee as even the most reserved found a story to tell, some creepy little tale of private horripilation.

This had been confirmed most recently at a party hosted by Claire and Ernest, when Wayne Takemoto, a young lawyer Ernest had once described as 'tightlipped as an opihi', claimed that as a teenager he had awakened on the night of his best friend's funeral to discover an apparition of golden light hovering just inches above him. According to Wayne, it had been the soul of his friend seeking a new home. Was that what ghosts sought from the living then – a bodily abode?

His pipe had gone out. Rain pelted the roof and gurgled through the gutters. It would be filling the large stilted tank behind the cabin, perhaps to overflowing. Dark rain. Ripe black fruit with thin, bitter skin. Occasionally a forsaken sound winged its way from the forest and swept over the roof. It had to be raining everywhere. At the summit of Mauna Loa. In the restless cauldron of Mauna Ulu. In Kilauea. Along Holei Pali, where lava now tumbled to the desert below. Even in the desert itself, where the river of lava now flowed. Even on the ocean, superfluous as tears. Everywhere rain. Tonight, in truth, he was glad to be staying in the cabin. He could drive to Puna tomorrow, after Melanie picked up Felicia.

A shifting wind tugged at the house on all sides, testing it like canvas. Among the flaps and rattles sounded the duller blows of tree ferns slapped against the windows. He imagined the wind crushed lehua as well, those frail red puffs that emerged like beacons from fog. But such frailty, he knew, was deceptive. The plants bearing such flowers were tenacious, and, like Pele, could transmute to serve their purpose. Ohia in Volcano stood thirty feet tall, but on the inhospitable heights of Mauna Loa, ohia was the obstinate shrub at one's feet. In the nearby rain forest, ohia took seed in the downy hapu of a tree fern, then strangled its host methodically until all that bore witness to the fern was a vacancy among the assassin's aerial roots. He had learned all this from a

Park Service brochure. The brochure described sights he still wished to see. They hadn't, for example—

An abrupt gust slammed the windows, rattling his nerves with equal ferocity. A short shrill whistle piped in the chimney. Cloaked in a chill, as if the wind had blown straight through him, he drew his arms to his chest and sat quietly for minutes, slowly regaining composure.

He sat there worrying about the next day and those queued beyond it till the last. He had just fished a dead guppy from its bowl when he heard the familiar sounds of his father at the door. He saw him standing in the doorway, Windsor knot already loosened, and he remembered how his impulse to rush toward him had been choked by that sudden perplexity in his face, as if he'd recalled something undone at the office. And then his father had swiftly drawn his briefcase to his chest and collapsed, on the wilted floral carpet that the landlord had promised to replace. He had never seen his father on his knees with such prayer in his eyes. Cullen held a meaningless guppy in a tiny green net. When his father looked at him almost apologetically and fell to his side, he screamed for his mother. She came running from the kitchen, stood awestruck for one moment, then ran to her fallen husband, calling his name in disbelief. And then, unable to drive, she'd attacked the phonebook in a frenzy, tearing its pages, determined to wrench from it the number it withheld. When she finally managed to call for an ambulance, Cullen thought to hear its siren instantaneously – reckless and urgent – but the neighborhood had curtained itself with unnatural silence. Sunlight streamed in the windows. His father lay curled on the carpet, trembling, his lips turning purple. Cullen had always loved him. He knelt before him and placed a hand on his shoulder.

'The ambulance is on its way, Dad.'

His mother gently removed his father's tie, as if that might be the source of his agony.

'Oh, Jack, Jack. What can I do?'

Jack had grimaced, taken the hand of each of them, and stuttered what Cullen had always believed was 'I love you.' And then, Cullen felt, he'd died, though those who arrived via ambulance claimed otherwise. And so mother and son were not spared the violence of attempted resuscitation nor the agony of renewed but futile hope. Cullen remembered praying; his father was much too important to die. At the hospital, his father was promptly declared dead, the victim of a massive coronary. Cullen found himself staring at a cart of dinner trays while he cried. He was confused about this, for he also remembered crying in his mother's arms.

He had been older than Felicia at the time, he had been spared the horror of blood, but it *had been* his father, half of all his world. And not once, in all the years since, had the world repaid him for that loss. Nor had he ever experienced the slightest wisp of his father the spirit, though more than once he'd tried to summon him, not with spiritualism but with longing. Instead, he'd experienced a profound and convincing absence, a void in his soul that could not be filled by prayer or meditation. Death was an end, as much for a man as for a guppy. It was final and absolute. Every putrid corpse hammered home the truth of this, every sustaining murder in nature spoke of an underlying ruthlessness, yet still we wove visions of immortality out of nothing more than denial.

He closed his eyes, drifting for a long time in fog-shrouded ohia, tree ferns, the volcano, the cabin itself. Scraps of the week's events floated within. He tried to capture and arrange them, but found it futile, like molding the sand of a sentence into a fortress when falling asleep while reading.

Felicia's last words – 'Goodnight, Cullen' – now marched headless across an expanse of barren lava. A dark rift opened silently before him, he heard a tinkling as of crystal in a tremor, then a faint subterranean rumbling rose to the surface like a heartbeat, a gout of black. The volcano erupted in rain, an orange fountain spewing blue cinders, glass hair, molten droplets descending as polished tears. The heat threatened to erase his features; the cold pressed knowingly upon his shoulders.

He awoke to discover the room illuminated by a single bedside lamp. It was a spartan, heartless room, a room in which one slept without living. Not a single picture adorned its pale blue walls. He happened to be looking at the door before him when it swung open with a woeful creak. He confused it with the door of the shed and thought it might open upon the void in which souls float, without thought or sensation, like embryos in formaldehyde. But he saw now that the shadowy room beyond was merely a closet, empty but for its hangers. No, there was something else as well, something attached to the back wall. He strained to discern what it was. A golden crescent. A doorknob. He had never before noticed this door within. A rumbling of sorts – the muffled sound of a bed banging the wall? – came from the other side. He closed his book and listened. Then he rose and walked to the closet. He stood in its doorway and listened. He heard nothing now, and wondered if he'd really heard something before. He parted the hangers and stood before the door. Then he opened it.

There stood Ricardo, knife in hand. Felicia lay bloodied on the bed, her astonished eyes straining to see who had entered. Ricardo handed him the knife.

'Here. Give me a hand with the body.'

'The body?'

'Get the feet.'

'But she's still alive.'

'No she's not. They always do that when they're dead. Come on. I'm not supposed to lift things.'

Her astonished look had softened to one approaching acceptance, even beatitude. Then that look congealed, fixed for eternity. When Cullen escaped it, Ricardo was gone.

It was then that he noticed the water at his thigh. It had filled the room and his own as well, and it had made of Felicia a sort of flowerless Ophelia, fanning her long hair and framing her pear-shaped face. To wake up, he knew, he'd have to return to the bed. In the dark channel of the closet, the water reached his waist. His passage chimed the hangers – an eerie, inconsequential jangling of wire and nerves. In his room he saw that the water at his chest was black with blood. It rose to his chin, which he raised defiantly. When it reached his lips, he stood on his toes. When it passed his lips, he clutched wildly at the air above as if mere desperation might produce from nothing a branch or hand or single substantial fixture he might grasp. But it was the absence of these that closed his eyes, anointed his forehead, pushed him firmly downward.

And then he knew he was drowning in darkness deeper than the sea, the conspiratorial depths below a dream. Numbness spread through fingers and toes, arms and legs, with the stealth of a stain in a rain-soaked wall. It was the weight of the horror that gagged him. He grew frantic for breath – real, waking breath – and thrashed from the depths toward the too distant surface of his sleep. And when he could no longer resist and all he'd resisted burst in, he found himself gasping, awake in the dark, a solid black slab larger than a tombstone. Thinking he had cried out, he strained to catch the echo of that cry. But the only sounds were those of tattering rain, thumping heart, and heavy breathing. He sat alone, a clot in darkness, uncertain of where he'd awakened. Then the island, the volcano, the ohia and tree ferns all loomed as one like some proud liner sounding its dolorous horn, its one black note, as it materialized whole from fog. The cabin reaffirmed itself and sat, as before, on the flank of a live volcano. Slowly the ocean swam in to frame the island and his life. Everything was out there as it had been, his world restored.

Nevertheless, when he sought to gather the disparate parts of his body into a meaningful whole that might grasp the arms of the chair and rise, he found it an impossible task. He could not move. Something was wrong. He'd had some goal in his dream that remained unaccomplished. He had awakened too soon, a patient who drifts from anesthesia to see his own clamped organs reflected in the surgeon's light. But here, of course, there was no light.

He tried to raise his right arm. It was dead from the elbow, useless wax. He tried the left. The same. His legs hung like seedpods from a tree, two unresponsive appendages.

Determined to rise, he willed repossession of his body, which seemed not so much leaden as dumb and disconnected. But it was all to no avail; sleep had bound him to the chair in some anteroom of wakefulness. He sat insensible, waiting for sleep to recede – as it always had, as he knew it must – while in lieu of sensation, mounting terror coursed through his nerves. Then two dreadful questions bobbed to the surface. Was this what Felicia had described? Was this Uncle Ricardo?

He tried to calm himself with an objective assessment. He was paralyzed, it was true. One might justifiably say he was bound hand and foot. He was certainly afraid, afraid that all he had taken for granted might not be restored that he might take it for granted again. It was harrowing to think that his very faculties had been denied him. But for all his dread, he sensed no ghostly presence, no oppressive 'thing' holding him down. It was rather an absence of self. Some essential part was missing, had yet to return from his nightmare. He had done nothing more than we all do in sleep – had stilled his body and trustingly departed it, another spirit stepping outside of its house – but this time the door had swung shut behind him.

From a corner of the room came the sound of Felicia rearranging herself. To extract a cry from his throat he would first have to fill his honeycombed tongue with a word, with the thick molasses of a single sound. He summoned his strength to do so. But what he produced was a moan that fell so far short of what he'd intended, that was so pathetically furred and tragic, it frightened even him. He hoped she hadn't heard.

He tried again to raise his right arm. Again he failed. Approaching despair, he tried the left. This time it responded, but with the remoteness of a mechanical limb. Slowly, deliberately, beating back panic with reason, he maneuvered left toward right. He might have been laboring underwater, such was the difficulty of this simple task. He lowered his hand to his forearm and waited, having accomplished little. He was too terrified of failure to test his powers further. His right arm seemed alien, a brittle limb that might dissever at the elbow.

And so he sat, petrified. The island was full of nonbelievers that Pele had turned to stone. They stood naked now on dreary terrain, often mistaken for tree molds.

The zealous rain swarmed busily over the roof, crabs scuttling over boulders. The wind piped fitfully in the chimney. And what could he see – the glow of the fire, orange and black logs burning like lava? No. The fire had died. He saw a vague shape swaying at the window, presumably a tree fern and not a hungry ghost. He saw that the blackness before him was irregular, had depth, was indeed the blackness of the cabin at night, not plush but stark. The bed was a deep shadow darker than floor or wall. He would simply be patient. He'd outlast it. It was only a matter of time. As if to mock him, a fat fly buzzed noisily nearby. If it landed on his arm, perhaps he'd feel it. His volition fell like virga, trailing wisps of rain that vanished short of earth. He tried to imagine warm rain falling through the roof and into his porous body. He tried to will it. He urgently envisioned such a rain. He listened carefully to the crinkling on the roof.

When, later, the first hot, prickly drops trickled into his cells, he wished to weep consonant tears. Sensation seeped slowly into deep recesses, crept through his limbs with the stealth of lava. It would take a while. Reservoirs of warmth were gradually filling within him. Soon numb limbs tingled and chimes of sensation tinkled throughout. He had only to wait, bitterly bemused by the thought that sensation was 'returning'. From where? Was there absolutely nothing in this world a man could simply accept as a given? Not even his body? Of course not – foolish of him to have thought so. Consider the alarms sounded by his heart. Consider the siren sounded by his father's. Consider the millions each day weighing the doctor's diagnosis, or the many more deprived of even that. Think of the embalmer extracting one's innards and fleshing out a strangely grave smile. *There* was a man who would know the truth about lifelines.

Soon he was able to reclaim each arm with the other, alternately flexing and massaging them, kneading them like clay. The rest of the body soon followed. He was back. Only then did he realize how very cold the night had become. Who would've imagined such cold in Hawaii? Years in the tropics had thinned his blood. He checked the stove to be certain the fire had died. It had.

He gingerly rose to test his legs. He could stand. But a headache swam in with his senses, and the disquiet in his stomach soured to acid green. It was true, he knew, that he had worried himself into such a state, but it was a very real nausea that drove him shuffling to the bathroom, where he waved his hand in the dark, searching for the light chain. Finding it, he was dizzied by the sight of his shadow swaying before him. He had to steady himself at the edge of the toilet to contain his vertigo, but the light swayed on. A fly seemed to buzz inside it. He closed his eyes. That proved no cure for the swift, bilious nausea swirling within. Nevertheless, after several minutes, he had still not vomited. When he grew convinced that he would not, he merely sat on the toilet, waiting for his various ailments to subside. His feet were cold on the linoleum. He could see, through his flesh, a vivid network of blue-green veins. A draft seemed to blow through the wall. But to feel its chill was better than to feel nothing at all or to be lost in a labyrinth of dreams, waking from one to another. Perhaps Felicia had been right about the cabin. They could have, perhaps should have, stayed elsewhere that night.

He was puzzled by his peculiar loss of sensation. His arms had never 'fallen asleep' before. It had always been his feet, usually in theaters, and he had never dreaded the experience. It hadn't bothered him at all that his foot had turned into a numb, pachydermal lump that might better serve as an umbrella stand. On the contrary, he'd always relished the tingling recovery, the million silver minnows swimming in the thaw. He had never once feared the condition might be permanent. He'd had more faith than that. All his life, sleep had never betrayed him. Even now, he'd be willing to trust it again, to call his paralysis a minor anomaly, one of those rare disjunctions of body and soul – what Alice would have blithely classed as a premature awakening from an out-of-body experience. He would trust it, place himself in its care. As Felicia had said, what choice did one have? But this time he would lower himself as if into a casket, cautiously, aware of the danger that some prankster might seal it. Even if his experience had not been Felicia's, it had nevertheless provided him with a distressing taste of her terror. From now on, he'd be more attentive. He would listen and would help, not simply humor her with an amused, skeptical smile.

He rose slowly and carried himself across the room as if he were a goblet that might spill. The buzzing fly was an annoyance; it seemed to have some thwarted purpose in life, some goal residing in the light bulb.

He felt fragile, jaundiced. A thorough perusal of the medicine cabinet revealed no aspirin, though he had bought some the day before. Felicia had used it; perhaps she'd packed it. As he swung shut the mirrored door, he caught, once again, a vivid glimpse of his vertigo. And another man's face. He spun around to confront the unthinkable. He confronted, instead, Felicia's bathrobe hanging on a hook. How many times now had this happened? How many times had he been startled by a stranger, a stranger who soon resolved himself into carelessly draped clothing or curtains stirred by a sudden breeze? The spin had dizzied him even more, depriving him of the will to rearrange the robe so it might less resemble a visage. Perhaps he was ill.

The face was familiar though, enough to resurrect an image from his dream: the same man wearing a sleeveless undershirt that exposed his tattoos, ornate bruises of which Cullen remembered nothing. Uncle Ricardo. He had been trying to hand Cullen something, as if they were friends or accomplices. What was it?

At the picture window, the wind noisily lashed the tree ferns. On some unaccountable impulse, he opened the door to check the scissors. When he did, admitting a howl, he deeply regretted what he had done. It was impossible. It defied all logic. They were gone.

Who would brave such a rain to remove such a thing? Who in this remote, sodden, half-abandoned village . . . ? It simply made no sense. They had to have fallen, dislodged by the wind. He stooped to the landing, seeking a shape. He saw nothing, only that it was slatted, leaving open the half-inch of possibility that they had fallen through a crack. That seemed the only plausible explanation, but he was not about to test its validity. Not in this weather. That could wait until morning, when Felicia would accuse him of having removed them. In a way, this neatly solved the problem of her vandalism. She would see for herself that the wind and not he had dislodged them.

Half-expecting some ghoul to materialize in the gloom, he shut the door and locked it. That was it – her final closing of the door had shaken them loose.

He shuffled back toward the bed and was still in a kind of stupor when he realized that the muffled moans he was hearing were not the wind but Felicia. A needle-pointed chill shot up his spine, raised the hair on his neck, prickled his arms and legs. Fear was just as books described it.

He moved furtively to the middle of the room. When his vision came to him through darkness, he saw Felicia writhing on the mattress, half uncovered, her hands seemingly pinned beside her head.

Everything he had thought about ghosts, everything he had heard, all his readings and imaginings, had failed to prepare him for this moment. His hands were clenched fists, but he stood frozen, the cold air paring him to the bone. 'They bring a musty chill into the room,' Earl had said. *Or drive it into your heart like a steel blade*, he thought.

With each pelvic thrust, Felicia moaned louder and sank back into the bed as if driven. Was it possible that he could ever have slept through such an attack? He thought of how Ricardo had died, stabbed in the very act. Was this his eternal incompletion? Was he here again, riding his niece? Could his grip on life and its ardors be *that* tenacious? Solomon Waddy had had a real knife and real flesh in which to plunge it. Cullen had nothing; his fists had shrunk to knotted nerves.

Another long moan rose from the bed, a deep moan easily mistaken for passion. He remembered Alice's happy description of having been ravished by a spirit. The mere thought made such an assault intolerable. It was somewhere in the depths of his outrage that he found at last his resolve.

He slowly crossed the room to her side. He saw no ghost, no incubus, no preternatural emanation – only Felicia struggling. But sweeping the air above her with one timid hand, he encountered . . . nothing. Had he really expected more? He passed his hand again through thin air. No clammy flesh, no presence, no hostility. Nothing reached out to grab him. Nothing horrified. There *was* no Uncle Ricardo. Not for him.

'Felicia.'

He'd spoken too softly. She moaned and writhed.

'Felicia!'

It was no use; she was trapped beneath her nightmare. If that's what it was. He knelt on the bed and touched her cheek. A hand came flying through the darkness to rake him across the face. He felt its immediate sting, the sharp furrows of blood. He reached for her wrist but she resisted, delivering a brutal knee to his groin.

'Jesus!'

He then found all the strength he needed. Tears welling in his eyes, he locked his legs around hers, pinned one shoulder to the mattress, and slapped her brusquely across the face.

Her eyes snapped open like a doll's, eerily fixed on his. The room was cold again, the only moan a widowed sound rising in the wind. He smelled, acutely, fresh flannel and churlish wool.

'It's all right. It's all right. You were only dreaming.'

This failed to erase the terror from her face. She had the look of one doubly alarmed to discover an intruder wearing no mask but a face one knows. And after a while, kneeling there with his legs locked around hers, seeing his reflection in her horror, even he knew what she was thinking.

37

When he awoke, he was alone. On the other side of the room, Felicia, already dressed, neatly folded her ghost-repellent nightgown and placed it in her overnight case. Not once did she glance in his direction as he lay observing her, and just as he said 'Hey,' a car pulled up noisily on the gravel driveway. Her eyes fixed on his.

'Melanie's here,' she said. A car door slammed. By the time he'd pulled on his boxer shorts, Melanie was already at the door. He could hear the flutter of their greetings before lowered voices retreated conspiratorially down the long hall. He finished dressing, brushed his teeth, and shuffled toward the kitchen, where the two of them sat drinking coffee.

'Hi, Melanie,' he yawned.

'Hi.'

'Did you find this place easy enough?'

'Yeah, Felicia gave good directions.'

'Nice, isn't it?'

'Nice location.'

'How was the North Shore?'

'Awesome.'

'We're off,' said Felicia decisively, rising to her feet. 'We'll be back Wednesday morning.'

'Do you know where you're going?' he asked.

'We'll be checking out Hilo. Maybe go to Akaka Falls.'

'Know where you're staying?'

'We'll find a place.'

Melanie rose slowly, draining her coffee. Both seemed strangely subdued.

He followed them down the hall and out to the car. It was

Melanie who carried Felicia's bag.

'Bye, love,' he said. 'Have a good time.'

'Bye.' She kissed him on the cheek.

He waved half-heartedly as they pulled out the drive, leaving him stranded in the rarefied air of the mountain and the sunshine of a glorious morning.

'That was quick,' he said. He felt sick. It was unfortunate timing, to be sure. He and she had much to discuss, confusions to clarify, emotions to elucidate, but when she returned it would be with Melanie, and then the two of them would be off for Honolulu, leaving him stranded once more in Volcano, and when he returned it would be sadly alone, a rehearsal for the time when Felicia would leave him and Plecko would fire him and life would start inexorably anew.

When she'd awakened the night before, wide-eyed beneath him, it had seemed a defining moment. There he was, holding her down, filling the role of her goblin. She might have screamed; her terror seemed real enough. But when he'd released her, she'd gone off to the bathroom, and when she'd returned, she'd rolled wordlessly away from him as if in her sleep. Loose ends. Painful uncertainties. His love for her was a weakness.

He climbed the stairs, admired a russet fiddlehead shimmering in the sunlight, saw the gash in the front door, and remembered. Odd that Felicia hadn't said anything. He descended again, dropping to his hands and knees at the base of the tree fern. It was dark and dank under the landing, but the scissors lay there in the dirt, just as rational analysis had predicted. If only he could approach every problem as efficiently. He stretched out an arm and retrieved them.

Back in the cabin he sat on the edge of the bed, faced with the perennial problem that had plagued him throughout life: what to do next. Before he knew it he was lying down, not *laying* down as his students did. This was one of the many ways in which he was hopelessly different from others. He *lay* down for most of the day, rising once to take a meal at Volcano House and once to stare at the innumerable stars that had been herded together in too little darkness. One star made a break for it and was extinguished well before infinity.

The next day he drove to the Park Headquarters to enquire about Mauna Ulu. The rangers confirmed that lava was pouring over the pali, but said they had no idea when or if it would reach the sea. He considered making the drive to Puna, but the truth was that he felt enervated by something more viral than the absence of Felicia. Perhaps he'd feel better the next day when she and Melanie returned, and then the three of them could make the excursion together.

Nevertheless, despite his feverish listlessness, that night he again made the pilgrimage to Mauna Ulu. His ascent was slow and fitful. He paused often to sit and survey the play of volcanic light on low clouds and mounds of cinders. He felt almost religious, as if he carried an offering to a mercurial deity. He supposed it was simple awe and admiration. It was not difficult to see why the Hawaiians had created Pele as a repository for such feelings.

When he reached the rim and crossed to the edge of the viewing platform, less crowded now than before, the volcano still raged below in molten glory, the lava still crashed relentlessly against crater walls, and sulfurous bolts of lightning still slashed the ragged red crust caked with slag. Again the heat drew his face into a taut paper mask. Again the volcano defied all attempts to encompass it. Again it looked remarkable in his viewfinder.

'Excuse me. Could you do me a favor and take a picture of me and my boy?'

'Sure,' said Cullen. The request had come from a local man with a child of perhaps seven. The man handed him his camera.

'See if you can get a shot of the volcano in the background.'

'No problem.'

The inferno cast his subjects in a wavering crimson light. Cullen, bracketing as always, took three shots to be on the safe side. He loved the boy's gap-toothed smile.

'Thanks, yeah?'

'My pleasure. I hope they come out.'

'You visiting from the States?'

This always amused Cullen as Hawaii was, presumably, one of the States.

'No. I live in Honolulu.'

'Oh yeah? Where?'

'Kaimuki.'

'We live in St Louis Heights.'

'Small world.'

'I lived in the islands all my life and this is the first time I've ever seen the volcano. I really wanted Roberto to see it. He's old enough now to remember this for the rest of his life.'

'I know I will,' said Cullen.

The man smiled. 'Paul Pereira,' he said, extending a hand.

'Cullen Kinnell,' said Cullen, taking it.

Later, Paul shared his flashlight with Cullen as they walked back to the car park together, then he offered to buy him a drink at Volcano House, where he and his son were staying.

'I'll settle for a soda,' said Cullen. 'I'm not feeling one hundred percent.'

In Uncle John's Lounge, the boy put his head in his father's lap.

'Looks like we wore him out,' said Cullen.

'He's had a long day. We just flew in this morning.'

'What do you do in Honolulu?'

'I work for Brent Cummings Engineering. I'm a designer. And you?'

'I teach English at Holy Mount.'

'Oh yeah? Did you come over for the game? They got a good team this year, yeah?'

'Yeah, I flew over with them. Plunkett and Dhabul were my students.'

'Not!'

'Yeah, I flunked 'em.'

'No way. You mean those guys aren't good students?'

'Those guys are good basketball players. That's what we hired 'em for. Good students? Naw. I gotta correct their graffiti in the men's room. I got a special pen I carry around just for that purpose.'

Paul chuckled.

'Are you gonna take Roberto down to Puna to watch the flow?'

'Might do. We Portagees have been known to do stupid things before.'

'Ahh,' said Cullen, 'you're Portuguese. That's good. Can I ask you something?'

'What's that?'

'Well, my girlfriend's Portuguese, too.'

'What's the name?'

'Mattos.'

'Oh yeah. Lots of those.'

'Anyway, she's always calling me this one thing but she won't tell me what it means. It might be a bit risqué, I don't know. I can't find it in any dictionary.'

'What's she call ya?'

'Well, does this mean anything in Portuguese? *Pondus*?'

'*Pão doce*. Sure. It means *sweetbread*. She's calling you *sweetbread*.'

He wrote it out for Cullen.

'That's how you spell it? No wonder I couldn't find it.'

'Yeah. Sweetbread. That's what it means all right.'

'Why wouldn't she just tell me that?'

'Hey, women. They're mysterious creatures, yeah? I guess she wanted you to find out for yourself.'

'I guess. *Sweetbread*, huh? That's not so bad. I've been called worse than that.'

'Sure, that's a nice thing to call somebody. I think she's probably sweet on you. Anyhows, I gotta get this boy to bed. He's fallin' asleep on me.'

'Well, thanks for the drink.'

They shook hands and Cullen drove back to the cabin, which he found foreboding now that he was alone. It was cold and spartan, as always. He wondered how Felicia and Melanie had spent their two days. Chilled, he curled up in bed beneath a surfeit of covers, smelling her pillow to drink in her scent. She was still there, still a presence. It was odd how one came to invest so much of oneself in another, how one depended on the other's touch, the other's approval, how one carried around the image of the other in the mind's eye, reconstructing her again and again, imagining what she might say, might do. It was painful as well. He doubted that she shared such vulnerability. He loved her more.

He read a bit of Kawabata's *A Thousand Cranes*, another love story, then fell asleep in unwelcoming darkness. It was a fitful sleep. All night long his dreams awakened him, tossing him about until dawn like a stone passed among menehunes. It was typical of him to spend a restless night before even a minor event, and Felicia's eagerly awaited return was anything but minor. They'd said they'd be back in the morning, so he awoke at 9.30, made breakfast, and waited.

38

It was well past noon when he heard a car pull into the gravel drive. They would, he was sure, be cheerful about their tardiness, making him the odd one out. They would point out, reasonably, that they couldn't phone as there was no phone. Whatever their excuse, however feeble their explanation, he would have to accept it and do so graciously. He would act disgruntled though, make her apologize for her thoughtlessness. The cup of tea in his hand would help him feign nonchalance, help him maintain his dignity.

But as he stepped out of the house and on to the lawn, he saw that Melanie, still sitting in the driver's seat, was alone. Something within him seized up. Rather than perplex himself with possibilities, he would leave his mind blank, receptive to whatever unfortunate truth, or lie, was about to present itself.

Melanie slid out of the car, graceless as always, her eyes fixing his from a distance.

'Where's Felicia?' he asked.

'She's still in Hilo. We need to talk.'

Seeing the look upon his face, she quickly added, 'She's okay. There's nothing to worry about. Can we just sit down?'

He gestured toward the house, then followed her up the stairs. So if Felicia was alive and well, if no harm had befallen her, the endangered one must be Cullen. That was the meaning of Melanie's solemnity: she bore bad news, news that would weigh on his heart forever.

She took a chair beside the wood-burning stove.

'What is it?' he asked.

'Felicia's in the hospital. In Hilo.'

'Why? What happened?'

'She wants to see you.'

'Of course. But what happened? Is she hurt?'

Melanie couldn't quite meet his eyes. She would try, but the weight of her gaze kept drawing it toward the floor.

'Things didn't go exactly as we planned.'

'What do you mean?'

She shrugged. 'I mean we haven't been completely honest with you.'

'We?'

'It's really Felicia you should talk to.'

'Melanie, is she sick, is she injured, what the hell is it? Did you guys have an accident?'

'No, she's not sick. She's gonna be fine.'

'Then why is she in the hospital? Will you just tell me that?'

'I'm trying to tell you. It's just that it's a bit complicated.'

'And it's not anything I'm going to like, is it?'

'No. No, you're not gonna like it. See, I came over here for just one thing – to help Felicia. She wanted me to be with her when she went to the hospital. She had an appointment there. She had it all arranged.'

'She . . .'

'She was pregnant.'

'She was pregnant.'

'Yeah.'

'And she's not pregnant now, is she?'

'No. She had an abortion. The plan was no one was supposed to know about it. We'd go off for a couple days, we'd come back, and her parents would never be the wiser.'

'And neither would I, right?'

'You know how her parents are. She just couldn't tell them. She was afraid to even have it done in the same city. So she made arrangements here. There were complications, though. She started hemorrhaging. So they had to keep her there.'

'But now she's okay.'

'She's fine. She's in good hands.'

There are tears that begin as a burning wave behind the eyes. He held his face in one hand and heard Melanie leave the room. He'd known this feeling before, when his father had died. He was leaking a vital substance that gives one volition, meaning, even character, and the world had sprung a leak as well and was rapidly deflating.

He heard her footsteps approaching down the long wooden hall.

'If you'll just follow me, I'll take you to her.'

As in a dream, he followed. There was still a green ocean of tree ferns and lasiandra. There was still a mountain of lava tumbling to a distant blue sea. There were still tall palms and macademia nut plantations. But none of these could quite assert its reality. He followed her for almost thirty miles, and in that time the closest he could come to formulating a thought was to wonder if he had any right to believe in his paternity, if paternity was the right word for fathering a child unborn. He followed her through the outskirts of Hilo to the hospital parking lot. She pulled over and he pulled alongside, rolling down his window. Hers was controlled electronically.

'Just pull in here,' she said. 'She's on the second floor, ward two. I'm gonna get something to eat. Tell her I'll be back around six.'

'Okay. Thanks for coming to get me.'

There was a parking place into which he pulled. There was a glass door he opened. There was an echoing corridor down which he walked. There was a gift shop fronted by flowers. He stood before it, trying to remember something basic. He found himself inside searching for something soft, something with no hard edges at all. There were many stuffed animals for newborns – all cute and cuddly, all fresh and plump, with ribbons of pink or blue and eyes that could not be swallowed. A visitor to the maternity ward would be spoiled for choice. But none seemed appropriate consolation for one who had – what was the favored euphemism these days – terminated a pregnancy? Emptied the womb?

He bought a white bear with a quizzical expression. The saleslady smiled and said, 'I'm sure this will make someone very happy.' He removed the blue ribbon and her smile faded altogether.

There was an elevator. There was a sign. There was a nurse in pale green sitting behind a desk.

'Can I help you?'

'I'm here to see Felicia Mattos.'

'Felicia Mattos,' she said, looking at a chart. 'And you are?'

'Cullen Kinnell.'

'Just a minute, please.'

When she returned, she was smiling reassuringly. 'That'll be the second door on your right. Down there.'

'Is she alone?'

'Yes, she has a private room.'

There was an open door, a blank television, a white curtain barely stirred by a breeze. There was the foot of a bed. She was propped at an angle, half sitting.

Her eyes settled upon him like a blanket of light. Free of mascara, they seemed remarkably childlike. She neither smiled nor frowned. She seemed pure, transcendent, almost virginal.

He handed her the bear, feeling, as he did so, that either it, or he, was woefully inadequate.

'Thank you,' she said, neither dismissing it nor drawing it to her.

'Can I sit down?'

'Of course.'

There was a chair. There was a moment of silence as he hunched forward, arms on knees, fingers entwined. There was a pattern of diamonds in the blue carpet, each surrounding an ill-defined flower. That's what he would stare at. That's what he'd remember. There was always something meaningless one fixed on, something insignificant one turned in one's mind or one's hand. Years later he'd imagine that he might have said or done something different, but difference was not really an option. He felt as if someone had knocked the wind out of him.

'Well?' she asked.

'Well what?'

'What are you thinking?'

He thought hard about this. It seemed too petty to tell her what he was thinking. He hadn't made any of the tough choices. She'd made them all herself.

'I don't know. I suppose I'm feeling a bit used, a bit lied to.'

She smiled weakly, whatever that was supposed to mean.

'Are you all right? Melanie said there were complications.'

'I'm okay. I was hemorrhaging something awful, but the doctors were right there. They took good care of me.'

He, of course, hadn't been right there, and couldn't have taken good care of her if he had. When all was said and done it was the professionals one turned to. They patched things up, made things right again. In his view, doctors were deities who performed miracles beyond understanding. They, and nurses, were among the most admirable of human beings. Beside them, he felt unworthy, even cowardly. Cullen had an aversion to blood. If the world had been peopled only by Cullens – that is, by men and women of Cullen's persuasion – doctors might apply tourniquets to stanch unfortunate outpourings of this vital bodily fluid, but no wounds would be sewn, no foreign objects removed. Cuts would be bandaged and painkillers freely dispensed, but anyone screaming in agony would be promptly euthanized. There would certainly be no such things as heart bypasses, artificial limbs, or transplants. Surgery would have never been invented. No part of the body would ever be opened, no flesh drawn back, no vein or artery clamped. The inner sanctum would remain sacred and taboo. Internal anatomy would be synonymous with eternal mystery. And not even the most free-thinking, adventurous Cullen would devise a means of surgically removing a developing fetus from the womb. Such things would be unthinkable in Cullen World. Such advances could only be found in the real world.

'When can you go home?'

'Tomorrow. Melanie's arranged it all. We called my folks. It's all set.'

She saw the question in his eyes.

'No, I didn't tell them. And I'm not going to tell them. They're never going to know. Not ever. Okay?'

He met her eyes, looked away, nodded. 'Okay.'

She turned to lay her cheek on the pillow.

'I'm just wondering why you found it necessary to lie to me in the first place,' he said. 'I mean this whole thing, this little romantic getaway, it was just a ruse, wasn't it? You must have had this planned before I even mentioned the Volcano. Your whole purpose in coming here was just to . . .' He put his head down, ran his fingers through his hair. 'I didn't even figure into it, did I? I was just a convenience.'

'Not exactly.'

'In what way not exactly?'

'I wanted to be with you as well. I just didn't want to tell you.'

'All the way down here I've been asking myself why you lied to me. I mean if you were pregnant, why wouldn't you tell me about it? And there's really only one answer to that question, isn't there?'

'What's that?'

He looked at his hands. Even this took strength.

'I guess there are two answers really. Either you're not sure who the father is, or you are sure . . . and it's not me.'

Her eyes hardened.

'I'll tell you what I think. I think all this time we've been together you've been seeing this Steve guy as well. I think you figured you'd try it out with him just to . . .' He breathed deeply. One had to remember to breathe at such times. He shook his head vigorously, rattling the pain like red dice. His eyes burned. He rubbed them with his fingers and spoke without opening them. 'This hurts too much. It's too painful. And the sad thing is that I really love you.'

'Don't say that.'

'Why not?'

'Because it isn't true.'

'But it is,' he said, opening his eyes to affirm it.

'It isn't,' she insisted. 'I had the strangest sensation the other night, when you woke me up. I was dreaming that I was being held down – like always – but when I woke up, I *was* being held down. By you. What was eerie was that you were such a perfect fit, as if it had been you all along, even before I knew you. I felt that you were the weight, that you were the hands . . . As if all my dreams had been nothing but premonitions. It was a horrifying moment, like waking up underwater.'

'I could tell. And I wanted to talk to you about it. But that doesn't mean—'

'But I also felt . . . I felt like I had awakened for the first time. And it was all so simple, really. It was so utterly simple. You don't love me. You possess me. That's why you wanted to get married, to make it official, so you can dangle me before your friends like a little trinket.'

'And how about Steve? Does he love you?'

She glared at him. And that, he felt, was as good as a confession. The question made sense to her. Steve was present tense. He had been with them every time they'd made love. It was him she'd run to whenever they'd quarreled.

'It was your baby,' she said. 'If I didn't tell you about it it's because I know how you feel about it. You think it's murder. You made that perfectly clear. The way I see it, I did your conscience a favor. You haven't had to wrestle with it the way I have.'

He sighed. 'I don't want to argue with you about this. That's not what I'm here for. I had a strange experience myself the other night. I fell asleep in the chair beside the stove, and when I woke up, I couldn't budge. I couldn't move a muscle, not even to cry out. It was one of the most horrifying experiences of my life. It was the same sort of thing you described. It made me—' Suddenly something swam through his consciousness, a glimmer of something larger, a vision of Felicia supine, staring at him from an odd angle. He struggled to hold it, to connect it, and then the closet door swung open.

'It made you what?'

'What made me what?'

'The experience you had the other night!'

'I don't know. It made me feel sympathetic, that's all. It made me think about what you've really been going through.'

'Maybe my nightmare sits on your chest now.'

'Don't say that. Please. Don't even think it.'

'I'm really tired.'

'You want me to go?'

'No.'

A nurse smiled at him as he trudged down the corridor. Rather than cheer him, this merely puzzled him. His stomach was feeling sour. He entered the empty men's room and, while standing at the urinal, rested his head on his forearm. 'Hope I die before I get old' read the sole graffito. *Christ*, he thought. Washing his hands, he encountered the mirror. There he was again, good old Cullen, dismayed by his own reflection. He looked more dissolute than disillusioned. The eyes seemed bleary, and though he stood stock still, his reflection seemed to waver. There were already streaks of gray in his unmanageable black hair, penumbral shadows beneath his eyes, and the first signs of erosion in two shallow wrinkles running from nose to mouth. He stared at himself intently, with anguished hostility. In class, sometimes, a word might dissolve before his gaze, reneging on its agreement to hold meaning. Certain conjugations might plod ponderously across the board like the footprints of a brontosaurus. Swim / swam / swum. Lie / lay / lain. Bear / bore / borne. Slay / slew / slain. Such verb forms might, at unguarded moments, take on for him the same unreality that they possessed for many of his students. But it needn't be the descendant of an Old English verb; any word, stared at too closely – the most friendly and familiar – could stubbornly cease to function as a symbol and become alien instead, mere arbitrariness.

That's how his reflection struck him now – as dubious, tenuous, inappropriate. At fifty, said Orwell, one has the face one deserves. He supposed that meant one has gained a face reflecting one's character. He wouldn't, therefore, expect to find strength accreting in the mirror like some wondrous pearl, but he thought he might justifiably expect some warmth or sensitivity, some of the light that falls to earth through high branches. In his eyes should be at least the twinkle of the sun seen through a tree fern, something denied the dullard or common criminal. But his eyes lacked luster. And the nose, the tragic nose – not chiseled, just duly appended – at fifty it would be his grandfather's nose, pocked with pores, crisscrossed with a network of purple vessels. And the weak chin was a disappointment as well. There should have been a foothold there, a broad ledge to reassure children. He felt that the scintillations within each wave that had ever washed over him, each moonrise, each sunset, the glow of the volcano – all these should have somehow ennobled his features. Jasmine should bloom in each eye, and plumeria just under the skin, revealing a bounteous kindness within.

His face – the more fixedly he stared, the more tragic and inadequate it grew. When words lost meaning, it was best to erase them before they undermined the language.

Other people – he passed several on his way back to the parking lot. Each seemed a cipher, a meaning that failed to materialize. There were too many to care about, so what was one less? At least he could wash his hands of this whole affair. She had never given him a choice. And surely if he was honest with himself he'd have to admit that given a choice, he would've arrived at the same decision. One less person, one more ghost.

He drove slowly into the main street, turning right because it was easier. Love should have sufficed. Why *did* everything he touch turn to ashes? He remembered now that it was she who, over dinner, had introduced the subject of the volcano. Had that been planned as well? Was he simply one of the most gullible men who had ever walked on the planet?

Only after he'd reached the heart of Hilo did he realize he'd been driving aimlessly. He turned left to work his way back to Volcano and there it was, in bold black letters, almost obscene in its timeliness: CURL UP AND DYE. *Yes*, he thought aloud. *Yes, yes, yes. Curl up like a salted slug and die.* The salon seemed dark and empty. *Curl up in the fetal position . . . The physician will be here shortly.*

Dilatation and curettage. That had a nice ring to it.

Dilemma. Students were always getting that wrong, thinking it synonymous with *problem.* No, good word, *dilemma.* Between a rock and a hard place. You could bang your head on either one. With a good dilemma, a truly superb dilemma, you could take a Black & Decker drill to your head and still not reach a solution.

He hit the accelerator and headed toward Puna.

The darkness had grown around him like an enveloping dome, the night sky slowly affirming itself as the stars came out of hiding. In the blue afternoon the falling lava had seemed little more than a distant waterfall, but now it was a torrent of fierce orange cascading down the pali, a bright sword plunged into the base of the mountain. One could also now see the soft orange glow of Mauna Ulu itself, high above and to the left of the cascade. The lava that fell in the distance had crossed black miles of frozen whorls and ripples, had flooded the cracked troughs and broken waves of older flows, and had now overrun the Chain of Craters

Road to crawl sluggishly toward the ocean like some ancient, venerable tortoise driven by instinct. Sixty feet to his left, a single ohia stood on an island in a stream of clotted fire, an island gradually succumbing to the entreaties of molten lava. And on both banks of that stream, wild grass, easily ignited, crackled in fits as her hair had.

Cullen felt certain he had taken some excellent photographs. He had almost exhausted his film, but was saving his last roll for the grand finale. He couldn't understand why so few people – less than thirty, mostly local – had made the same drive as he, to stand, now, in rapt admiration of this relentless march to the sea. He felt Hawaiian, a witness to the source of creation.

'Shit,' said a large Hawaiian next to him, so gently he seemed to spread the word on toast.

'What?'

'Look.'

He followed his eyes. The old lava on which they stood had been riddled by the vagaries of the last flow, and now, looking down, he saw trickles of new lava filling the recesses beneath their very feet. Should the lava collapse . . .

'Shit,' agreed Cullen.

'I never did learn how to walk on fire,' said the Hawaiian.

Together they retreated to safety, then walked to the edge of the cliff. The surf churned fifty feet below. Cullen stood, hands in pockets, squinting into the brisk breeze blowing off the Pacific.

He glanced back toward the wavering light of the volcano, effectively checking the fear that a silent wall of lava might be fatefully approaching. The calm demeanor of the others reassured him. The smoldering pachyderm before him, shapeless and sluggish, was the central flow, a wrinkled river of pahoehoe that might reach the sea in minutes. The lava's cooling crust snapped crisply as it fractured, and veins of scarlet broke through black to surge forward boldly, until they themselves cooled and darkened. The flow advanced in such spurts, the bright melt sloughing off its outer skin to promptly form a new one. Small fires erupted where it brushed scrub ohia, grasses twinkled and died, and a single sapling burst noisily into white incandescence, drawing exclamations from all.

Like a falling star, the young tree burned out before them.

'Know why it did that?' asked the Hawaiian.

'Why?'

'It's so hot that its gases exploded.'

'Amazing.' Cullen had been expecting to hear something less prosaic – a local superstition, perhaps, or another good story about Pele.

'There's petroglyphs over there.'

'Where?'

'A couple hundred yards over that way. Wanna see?'

He had gestured in the direction of the lava.

Cullen hesitated, not wanting to miss the magic moment.

'Hell yes. I've never seen petroglyphs.'

He followed in the wake of the big man, who had a flashlight. They seemed to be walking in a line that pointed straight toward the lava descending the pali.

'It's somewhere around here,' said the Hawaiian. 'I haven't been here in a couple years.' He shone his flashlight over the broken landscape, revealing only lava and grass. He surveyed the desolation slowly.

'There it is,' he said.

Cullen followed him.

'Jesus. Look at that.'

The man hadn't lied. On the mauka side of a large slab of rock marched an unruly procession of stick figures carved into the stone. There were also irregular shapes, series of dots, and circles with various protrusions. But mostly there were crude symbols of men who had passed this way hundreds of years before.

'Is that a canoe?' asked Cullen, pointing to a possibility.

'Might be.'

'What does it all say?'

'It says "I was here!"' laughed the man.

'You think the lava's gonna cover this?'

'No way. I been comin' here all my life and the lava nevah touch it.'

'Maybe it's protected by Pele.'

'That's right.'

Cullen stooped to take some pictures with a flash, then rose gingerly, cradling his camera as if it were the sole repository of human knowledge.

'Those pictures there,' said the Hawaiian, lowering his voice respectfully, 'the ones you just took – they say "We went halfway around the island, but had to turn back. We couldn't go any further." They had enemies, you know. Other tribes. They couldn't just go wherever they wanted.'

He stood to his full height and proudly surveyed the scene before him, the river of lava pulsing toward the sea, cooling to stone in the vanguard, then being surmounted by a new wave of pahoehoe, while minor fountains of fire marked the river's course.

'There's no place like this on earth,' he said, as if they were on another planet.

'That's for sure,' said Cullen.

'It should marry the ocean any minute now.'

'Have you seen it before?'

'Once. And my father saw it a couple times. You visiting?'

'Sort of. I live in Honolulu. What's your name?'

'Call me Taro. All my friends call me Taro.'

'I'm Cullen.'

Taro made a shaka sign, his arm muscles gleaming as if oiled by molten light.

Together they retraced their steps to the viewpoint overlooking the ocean. So there Cullen stood, at the edge of a cliff, on a burning island, above a hot spot in the planet. All along the coast, the patient sea had carved ragged arches and cliffs from volcanic headlands. Below him the surf crashed noisily, impeded by a landmass.

Someone startlingly close raised a cry. He looked up to see a momona woman in a floral dress bouncing gleefully along the clifftop like a flea. Beyond her a slag and scarlet stream had reached the end of its terrestrial journey. It paused, massing like molasses into a small mound, then an orange stream erupted from its base and poured decisively over the cliff and into the ocean, where it hissed and crackled, flashing to steam, bursting once more into rock, the stuff of black sand beaches. A roiling white cloud rose before them, obscuring the frenzied collision of two irresistible forces. Waves continued to crash, lava to flow. The island would grow larger.

Cullen shot his last pictures.

'I was here,' he said.

He'd seen it, even documented it. Fire and water.

The calmly scintillating sea lay beyond, untouched by this minor cataclysm.

'It's Primo time,' said Taro. 'Want a beer?'

'Sure,' said Cullen.

But first he had an irrepressible urge to throw something of substance into the ocean. He stooped to a chunk of jagged a'a, hefted it once, then hurled it skyward. It rose toward the heavens, lost heart, dropped abruptly, vanished in the darkness, fell into the sea, and was now one of many tumbled by the surf.

He supposed he could accept that.